Pulling the Goalie

CEDAR RAPIDS RACOONS

LASAIRIONA MCMASTER

DRAMA LLAMA PUBLISHING

Dedication

For Tracie,
I never knew I needed a big sister until I met you.
This book was a royal pain in my ass, just like you every
morning at 6am, rain, wind, or shine.
Thanks for believing in me so much I had no choice but to believe
in myself.

Content Warning

This book contains certain subjects that some readers may be sensitive to, including but not limited to: substance abuse (alcohol and drugs) and PTSD.

There are also MF/male-female, MM/male-male, and MMF/male-male-female sexual relation scenes throughout this book.

As with any book that contains content warnings, please be cautious when undertaking this story and take care of your mental health.

Pulling the Goalie

ARES

(Prologue)

"Gooood morning, Cedar Rapids! This is Marshall Bryant, and you're listening to Rock 108. Summer's almost over, which means we're on the slippery slope into the new college hockey season, and Coach Bales is putting together an interesting roster of Raccoons over at the University of Cedar Rapids. Speaking of the Trash Pandas, I lured one of them onto the show. You know I like to have interesting guests on the show from time to time, so joining us this morning for a quick Q&A is rookie UCR goaltender, Ares de la Peña. No stranger to the limelight, the youngest of four siblings, Ares already has twin older brothers on the team and is suiting up to play between the pipes in the fall. Thanks for joining us today, Ares."

I shift in my seat. No one can see me since I'm in my apartment, on an online call with Marshall, but nervous energy still courses through me. "Thanks for having me, Marshall."

I hate interviews. Interviewers always go for the jugular,

and I always know *exactly* what they're going to ask. They know I'm a recovering addict, a stripper, and they want aaaaall the juicy gossip.

When did you first realize you were an addict?
How did you get into drugs and alcohol so young?
Are you cured?
What were your drugs of choice?
Did you really break that guy's orbital socket with your foot?
What does your family think of the fact you're a stripper?
What made you give up drugs and go clean?
How often do you dance at the strip club?
What was rehab like?
Why are you so blasé about the fact you're an addict?

It got to the point where I made a list of answers ahead of time, and I just read them off like a damn robot. If Oprah were to call me up right now, I'd have a first-class performance ready to go.

Lots of people don't believe I'm a recovering addict because, at only eighteen years old, I'm pretty young. But I've been an addict since I was fourteen years old. It began with alcohol and weed, then escalated to Percocet, Vicodin, and eventually cocaine, *perico*. I might have been young when I first used, but I was also rich, and learned quickly that money really can buy just about anything. Including silence.

I always thought the only one being harmed by my addiction was me, but I hurt other people, too. Even I got tired of hearing people make excuses for me. Even so, it wasn't a fear of ending up in jail or the morgue that stopped me, but a fear of not playing the game.

It takes an average of seventeen attempts for someone to find sobriety, and someone dies from an opioid overdose every twenty minutes in the United States. So, I was never optimistic that rehab would save me, or even help me. As far as I was concerned, I was beyond help, but, at the behest of Mamá,

Papá's money bought me access to the best treatment programs available. And when I got out, Alcoholics Anonymous, Narcotics Anonymous and Reddit's *Redditors in Recovery* forum got me through. AlAnon—a support group for the families and friends of alcoholics, especially those of members of Alcoholics Anonymous showed me the impact my actions had on those around me.

Ultimately, though, it was hockey that saved me. It's all I've ever wanted to do since I was old enough to walk and the thought I might never be able to play again by my own doing? It was too much.

Did I play while high? Sure, I did. And for a while I was even convinced I could do it forever. Full of false confidence, I thought I was the best hockey player to ever skate on ice. But the more I moved away from prescription meds to coke, the more things unraveled.

My heart rate spiked and stayed there any time I was on the ice. I was out of breath all the fucking time, and my feet wouldn't work as quickly as my brain.

Shuddering at the recollection, I clear my throat, ready for the onslaught from Mr. Marshall over in Hiawatha. Since this one's my first interview as a Raccoon, I imagine there'll be something in there about committing to my team and to the game and to my sobriety.

"First question, Ares. What feels better on your thighs? Goalie pads or dollar bills?"

I can't help the snort that bursts out of me. "Nothing comes close to the soft flutter of Benjamins against the skin, Marshall."

"That's what I thought. So tell me, which one of the de la Peña brothers have scored the most?"

Ha. I like this guy already. Maybe this interview won't be so bad after all.

Eloise

Ugh. What. An. Arrogant. Butthead.

CHAPTER 1
Eloise

I hate sports.

And I'm not saying that because my dad's back in town and dragged me, damn near kicking and screaming, to the University of Cedar Rapids Raccoons hockey game tonight, though that might be a contributing factor. I'd rather be studying for finals.

It's cold. I'm cold. All the way to my size seven feet. Can your bone marrow be cold? As a nursing student I should probably know the answer to that question, but I'm only a freshman. Maybe you learn that particular answer in your sophomore year.

Whether or not it's possible, it's happened. Maybe I'm the first ever person to have cold bone marrow, but I'm cold all the way through. I'm going to get frostbite on my fingers and nose.

I tug my coat higher on my neck, and the person sitting next to me glances over. Then stares. At least if my nose turned purple or black, people would have a reason to stare at my face other than the jagged scars.

Through a soul-deep shiver, I turn my face away and fluff

my pink bangs to cover them. Pain stabs into my chest, stealing my breath for a moment and making it nearly impossible to swallow past the lump in my throat.

I can't cry at a hockey game. From the looks of the swinging fists on the ice, there's no crying in hockey. Plus, if I let myself cry, my tears will freeze my eyes shut. And that's inconvenient.

Huh. It's tempting though, considering how much I hate this experience.

Maybe if they played on a beach, where it's warm and sunny and people could bring me fruity drinks with umbrellas in them while the athletes do their...sportsball thing, it would be better. I blow out a heavy breath and tuck my hands in my lap for warmth.

The fight escalates. Other players are literally dragged in by their shirts. One guy has his opponent in a headlock; another is gripping someone's shirt so tightly that any time the trapped player tries to move he wobbles on his skates.

The only player not involved is the goal guy...goalie? Netminder? Keeper of the gate?

Whoever he is, he's off to the side of the mob by himself despite the fact that the melee has broken out right in his space. If that was me, I'd be yelling "Get off my lawn." He stands, face impassive, focused, leaning on the top part of his stick as he takes it all in. Is he bored, too?

The crowd is screaming around me, cheering the gladiators on in their battle. But the goalie stares on.

I wouldn't be so calm if a fight broke out at my front door, but he seems so chill. What's it like to be calm in the face of chaos? Or, you know, at all.

Dad covers my hand with his, stopping me from twisting the hem of my shirt between my fingers. My stomach's churning. What if someone gets hurt?

Perhaps the goalie feels the same way I do. Not to call him

a coward—I mean, ultimately, he's crazy enough to put himself in front of a really fast flying...thing that people keep smacking toward his face—but right now, he's all the way off by himself.

My heart ticks up as one player's helmet tumbles to the ice a split second before he lands on his ass. Instead of moving to help, the goalie shuffles a little farther away.

I can't see his face through his mask-helmet-thing, but his fuck-off vibes are pretty clear. He is not partaking in anyone's bullshit. And he looks as though he might want to sweep them all the hell away from his goal with that broad stick of his.

I could be projecting, but he seems to be a loner, like me. Always on the edge of the action, but never participating. I'm not brave enough to step forward, but perhaps this guy is just uninterested.

Dad gently pulls my hand from my face, where I've been twisting the stud in my nose.

"This is part of the game, Ellie-Rae." He pats my thigh in a bid to calm my anxiety. "They're all going to be fine."

When the game resumes, five players get sent to the time-out area, and yet their benches don't look any emptier. The announcer starts listing off the reasons everyone's been sent to the naughty step as the referee drops the disc between two players.

I can't remember what the disc thing is called, but the players are now chasing it around the ice like labradoodles scampering after a tennis ball.

Something changes, because all of a sudden, the athletes that were on the bench with the other players a minute ago are throwing themselves over the barrier and gliding over the ice. Why the hell don't they use the door like a normal person?

Okay, so less labradoodle, more elegant, athletic, brick walls on skates. In my periphery, the light over the goal blinks on and everyone is on their feet screaming.

I missed another one. There have now been five goals scored in this game, and I've missed all of them. Every last one.

It's all too fucking fast.

The people around me start throwing their ball caps and hats onto the ice. Why would they do that? Hats are freakin' expensive. I bought Dad a Hawkeye's baseball cap for his last birthday, and it cost me thirty bucks.

If he threw that thing onto the ice, I'd be pretty pissed.

Where do all the hats go? Can you get them back? Who picks them up? Are the people picking them up hired specifically for that job? Hat picker-upper? I'd love to read the listing for that job. "Must be able to walk out on the ice without falling on their face and pick up a bazillion hats."

"He scored a hat trick," Dad says. "That means hats on the ice. You have two weeks to claim them back."

With fewer than five minutes left in the game, I can't stop glancing at the goaltender. He tripped that guy standing in front of him up with his stick. Can he do that? I mean, if someone was in my space, and I had a big-ass stick like that, I'd wanna smack him with it too. But how come he wasn't sent to the glass box of shame?

The player from the other team is kind of asking to get beaten with a stick. He's back in front of the UCR goal, and he's all up in the goalie's business. My guy is very clearly unhappy about it. I take my eyes off the net for like a second to check if the referees are watching this guy pissing off the goalie, but a blur of movement draws my attention back. The goalie has clearly taken things into his own hands. Quite literally. He's swinging his fists at the opposing player's face.

Man, they got undressed quickly. One minute they had helmets and gloves and the next, bam, fists in faces. An actual fight? But... What if they hurt each other?

I'm not sure who's winning in this battle of the punches, but the scowl on our goaltender's face says that he's mad. Big freakin' mad. Those huge pad things covering his legs are getting in the way of him kicking that guy's ass, and he's mad about that too.

But he's still standing, and that's pretty impressive. His hair is dark brown, or black, I can't tell because it might be wet, and he has a strong jawline covered with a smattering of stubble.

The visiting player lands a punch, and the goalie grins despite the trickle of blood down the side of his face. It's a dangerous grin, intense, full of assurance, and it sort of dazzles in all the wrong ways like a lion grinning at an antelope right before he chows down on it for lunch.

The goalie bursts into action, and before I can blink the other guy is on his ass on the ice. My muscles are so tense they're sore, and my stomach is clenched so hard it might squeeze dinner back up. This is...barbaric.

Holy crap.

I rub my chest, trying to encourage more oxygen into my lungs. This is intense.

Dad's gripped, his attention firmly pinned on the action. The referees intervene, and one of the guys on the goalie's team hands him his weird looking gloves and stick.

Once the drama is over, the final few minutes tick down without incident. At the last buzzer, the crowd erupts. Final score six to zero in favor of UCR, and the team is loving on the goaltender pretty hard. I mean, he did keep all the disc things out of the net so I can see why they're so happy about it.

They all line up to either tap his pads, glove-bump him, hug him, or pat his helmet like they're trying to ruffle his hair through the plastic. When the other goalie from the Raccoons' side gets to the guy at the net, they jump into this chest-bump and hug combo that has my heart warming.

After all the seriousness of the game—the intensity, the

bloodshed— this wholesome, bromance display of joy and open love is quite a shift. I'm totally here for it though. They're like one big family hugging the heck out of each other right out on the ice for everyone to see.

Emotion wells in my chest, and I blink back tears. The yearning in my entire being for a squad like the one on the ice is almost overwhelming. My dad is the best, but there's only one of him, and the goalie has like a dozen dudes piling love on him.

Dad claps and whoops next to me. "What'd you think, kiddo?"

That nickname always makes me feel like I'm eight rather than eighteen. But I don't hate it. "Some of those guys need to go away and think about what they've done."

His shoulders shake, but I can't hear his laughter over the still-roaring crowd. My ears might explode from the noise ringing around the arena.

"Would you come again?" he yells. "They play again next week and I'm in town for it."

I'd rather pull my fingernails out one by one with a pair of pliers, then pour vinegar into my nail beds. But my long-distance trucker dad is around so little these days, and our relationship so strained since Mom died, that I gotta take what I can get, because otherwise, it's just me, alone, and that's even worse than going to a hockey game.

CHAPTER 2
Ares

Everything hurts and I'm dying.

I'm regretting my life choices right now. After our game last night, I went to the club and danced for a few hours before I swung by the hockey house.

At the time, I thought I had some excess energy to burn off, hence the dancing, but now that I've hauled my ass out of bed to go to class, my muscles are telling me otherwise.

Like I said, I have regrets.

I laid in an ice bath until my feet turned blue and my dick shriveled up so much it thought it was a turtle and tried to climb into my balls. My knees click, and my hips have a bone-deep ache in them. It was worth it for the game win, though.

Halfway to campus, inspiration strikes. Fuck sexuality studies. I'm getting a mani-pedi. I drop a text to my number one girl over at Get Nailed and pull a u-turn.

I dunno why more dudes don't get mani-pedis. There's literally nothing more relaxing than sinking into that massage chair and having someone rub your hands and feet for an hour. Okay, there's one thing more relaxing than having her rub my hands and feet, but Get Nailed ain't that kinda place.

And I don't like Alaïa that way. I don't think she bats for my team, either, but that's none of my business.

What *is* my business is how good she is with her hands. After an hour with her, my hands feel super smooth for days and smell good enough to eat.

The bell chimes over the door as I walk inside. Alaïa waits at the counter with a huge smile. "How's my favorite hockey player?" Her eyes narrow. "You're limping, Goal Stopper. I guess last night's shut out came at a cost. Third goal?"

Grunting, I don't need to answer her. She saw the game; she knows how it went down.

She's not only the best nail technician in Cedar Rapids— she's a bigger hockey fan than anyone else I know.

"You got overzealous and stretched farther than you needed to, didn'tcha?"

Part of me wonders what her history is. Did she play? Does she play? But every time I try to dig, she pivots and changes the subject. She analyzes my game as though she's lived it.

"Rookie goalie eager to please?"

I level her with a bored stare. Shifting my weight because I hate how well she can see right through my bullshit. And trust me, I come with a lot of bullshit.

"There's someone in your usual chair, you wanna wait or sit somewhere else?"

I'm a stereotypical, temperamental goalie, and if I don't appease the gods of superstition and do all my shit the same way, they'll punish me between the pipes.

Rationally speaking, that's obviously not true. But I know what I like, and I don't tend to stray from my routines. Unless I'm blowing off school for a mani-pedi just 'cause.

A chick with pink hair covering most of her face is sitting in my favorite chair. She's not chatting to Candice, the woman filing her toenails, and her nose is buried in a textbook that covers most of her thighs. Who the hell brings school with them to a nail parlor?

No one who knows me would call me an empathetic person. My ability to read other people's feelings isn't exactly on point. Unless, of course, I'm pressed up against a rock-hard cock or my fingers are buried deep in a soaking wet pussy. Then, it's pretty obvious.

But this chick's discomfort is emanating from her like ripples from a pebble tossed into water. She doesn't look up from her book, and though I can't even see her face, I also can't stop staring. When I finally tear my eyes from her, Alaïa has an arched eyebrow and smirk waiting for me.

I roll my eyes and take one of the chairs facing the tiny little elf girl. I'm not sure her feet would even touch the ground if the basin wasn't attached to the massage chair.

Alaïa gets to work on my feet first, so I pull out my phone and hit up the socials to see what's being said about the game last night. I've worked hard to get where I am, but the weight of my father's name on my shoulders means I have to keep working hard to stay there.

Plenty of people assume I've made the team because my older brothers are already players, and because Papá Dearest contributes money to the university every year. They're not entirely wrong. I fucked up a lot before I figured my shit out.

Okay, fine. I had no choice but to figure my shit out. Papá threatened to pull all financial support after my last soiree got busted by the cops. Thankfully his PR team was able to keep it out of the news, and the record is sealed so it's not likely to impact my future. But, he said enough was enough. Fix your shit, or you're out.

I dunno, some days even I believe he is the only reason I got a slot on the team. But others, I tell that voice of doubt to shut the fuck up and sit down. I've got wicked skills, and I busted my ass to get back on the path to hockey glory.

Alaïa works on my digits while I pretend to scroll, sneaking glances so I don't look like a creeper. Alaïa makes small talk, but my attention is on the girl with the pink hair who stays quiet. The elf doesn't lift her gaze, not once. She finishes her mani-pedi in silence, pays Candace with a quiet "thank you," and leaves without so much as looking up from her pretty pink toenails.

The quiet ones don't usually catch my eye, and I'm definitely not enchanted by the smart ones. Quiet and smart aren't terms I'm synonymous with. But something about that girl has me thinking about her long after I pay Alaïa for making my hands silky smooth.

I could have gone to class, but I didn't. I also didn't go to the gym. And if I went to my family's restaurant, Guac 'n Roll, Abuelita would twist my ear and haul my ass back onto campus. She's surprisingly strong for a three-hundred-year-old woman.

Okay, she's not quite three hundred, but since she doesn't look anywhere near her age, nor does she ever admit to what that might be. I'm pretty sure she has magical powers. Which means she *could* be three hundred. I wouldn't be at all surprised.

I'd love to say I'm not bougie, but tell that to the grande iced brown sugar oat milk chai latte I'm sippin' on. I give zero apologies for being extra. I mean, sure, my money isn't my own, but I donate a healthy portion of Papá's money to charities near and dear to my heart. And being the youngest son of a billionaire isn't always easy. So, I guess on some level I feel like I'm entitled to treat myself to overpriced drinks from Starbucks on his dime.

A huge slug of chai goes down the wrong way, making me cough and slosh my drink all over my arm. Should have gone to Bitches Brew. Taryn's oat milk chai latte is way better.

Ugh. I cough again. Oat milk's probably leaking out of my nose hole right now.

The back of my throat burns, my eyes are watering, and I'm mumbling a string of semi-coherent swear words. I *hate* this bougie coffee after all and dump it into the trash.

What a fucking waste. I hate wasting shit. Even if it is on Papá's dollar.

"Uh... hi?" A young kid with a backwards ball cap sticks out his hand.

As much as I love fans of the game, now really isn't the best time. My hand is covered in sweet, sticky coffee, I have snot running down my face, and my lungs still aren't convinced that I'm trying to pump oxygen into them as opposed to brown sugar and oat milk.

Something is familiar about this guy, though I can't put my finger on what. Maybe he's a regular, someone who hangs out after games or around campus. Has he asked for my autograph before? Who knows? Sure as shit not me. Regardless, he should probably know when it looks to be a good time versus when it isn't.

I glare at him, hoping the fuck-off vibes will be strong enough to dissuade him from hanging around and trying to talk to me.

Instead, he produces a napkin from his jacket pocket. It doesn't look as though he's snotted into it or anything, but at the same time, how do I know it's not covered in chloroform? I'm glad we're standing in public right now.

I'm not a small dude, and God knows swinging my fists is my skill—it kinda comes with the hockey territory—but some seriously intense vibes are radiating off this kid. I wouldn't put it past him to be able to take me wherever he wants me to go. I'm praying it's not his cold and dank basement.

An awkward laugh escapes me. I've clearly been watching way too many true crime dramas with Raffi.

The kid—who can't be more than sixteen—stares at me like I've sprouted a second head. Or he's waiting for me to return his greeting. But too long has passed since he said hello and now it would be awkward as fuck to actually say "hi" back. Except now it's even more awkward that we're both standing here staring at each other while goopy, cold liquid drips from between my fingers.

"You're Ares de la Peña, right?"

I nod and finally take the out-stretched napkin from him. Desperation to not be sticky trumps chloroform potential. Plus, kidnappers don't generally hand their drug-soaked rags to their kidnap-ees, right?

What is it about this kid that's throwing me so off my axis?

"Thanks." While I wipe my hand clean, my dude shifts his weight from one foot to the other. "Shouldn't you be in school?"

"Shouldn't you?" he shoots back. Something about the firm set of his jaw that tickles at the back of my gray matter. Who the hell is this guy?

I toss the napkin into the trash on top of the remnants of my drink and arch a brow at the kid. His fuck-you attitude is similar to the one I held a couple years ago. Does he like liquor too?

"I'm Thiago."

He already knows I'm Ares, so I can't really say anything in reply. I nod again. "Something I can help you with? Are you a fan? Would you like an autograph?"

The kid snorts like it's the funniest thing he's ever been asked. "Thanks, but I'm good."

The hairs on the back of my neck rise, and there's a sinking feeling in my stomach that I don't quite understand, threatening to bring up the few mouthfuls of chai latte I chugged before choking.

"Was there something...?" It's not like I carry much cash

with me. But other than my car, and my watch, I don't tend to outwardly show that I'm wealthy.

Who the fuck am I kidding?

That's a bald-faced lie. Every article of clothing on my body comes with a designer label and an accompanying extortionate price tag. My twin brothers are the understated sons of a billionaire. Athena, our sister and the oldest of the pack, has class and an appetite for nice things, but she doesn't quite flaunt it like I do. Except for her car.

I'm a walking ad for brands. Okay, so I happen to have a penchant for the finer things, and it's about to come back and bite me in the ass any second.

Does this kid have a gun? Is it even legal to carry in Iowa? Does it matter? If I'm being robbed in broad daylight by a dude in a ball cap, does he really care about gun laws?

In an instant, the confident kid regresses to a child in front of my eyes. His shoulders sag and his face pales. His eyes turn hopeful. My stomach clenches, waiting for the hit.

"I'm your brother."

I'm your brother.

Thiago's words echo around my head on repeat as I lock my thigh around the cool metal pole.

"Back again?" My boss, Ryker Hartmann, calls out from behind the quiet bar. It's still early. Some regulars are dotted around, but they aren't interested in me.

The technical term is male exotic dancer, but I prefer stripper. It sounds more badass, less refined, less suitable for a de la Peña. I also prefer when the bar is quiet, so I have space to try new things out on stage or the pole. That way if I fall on my ass, or my head, a limited number of people get to laugh at me.

Dancing is every bit as serious to me as hockey, but they

feed into different wells. I grip the pole with both hands, one above my head and one below, and lift my legs above my head into the air, planting one foot below the knee of the other and stay there. I hold position until my muscles burn and beads of sweat trickle down my face.

Do I use this place as an escape from my life? Almost always.

I don't need the money—though if I did, let me tell you, there's a pretty penny in exotic dancing if you take it seriously and put the work in. But I live for the freedom, the expression, the creativity.

Finally shaking too hard to maintain my grip on the pole, I dismount and make my way to the bar. I'm not concerned about bare feet on the floor—this isn't that kind of place.

When Protocol Cedar Rapids opened a few months ago, I wasn't sure what to expect. Former Minnesota Snow Pirate, Austin Morgan, one of *the* billionaire Morgans, helped his best friend grow his business into Iowa from Minnesota.

There is a BDSM club that lives in the basement downstairs, a bar next door, and this club. I'd love to say it's some skeevy strip joint, but it's the cleanest and most upmarket dance establishment I've ever seen—which doesn't say much considering I'm only eighteen. But, then again, I've seen my fair share of skeevy even in my short life.

It's top level. Everything from the equipment and the staff to the clientele. It's not the place you go to for glory holes and a baggie of coke.

I slide onto the barstool with a grunt. I'm not on the schedule to dance tonight, so I jerk my chin at the fridge behind Ryker.

"Nice try, kid. But we both know you're not twenty-one."

"Old enough to take my clothes off for money but not to consume alcohol in a bar." I accept the root beer and take a long pull from the cold glass bottle. "There's something fucked up about that." Also about the fact that I spent most of the past two years of my life either high or drunk, but I keep that to myself, too.

"Wanna talk about it?" Ryker nods toward the stage.

Nope. No, sir, I do not. I shake my head in response, but a million words hurtle around the inside of my brain.

I come to Protocol to throw myself around on stage or wrap myself around the pole so I don't have to talk or think. And I sure as shit don't want to talk about the fact a stranger stopped me in the street earlier and told me he was my brother.

Nor do I want to talk about the tiny voice, way in the back of my brain, screaming that I should believe him.

In retrospect, I didn't exactly handle things well. I kinda blew my stack. I told the kid to take a long walk off a short pier and to leave me the fuck alone. Then I got in my car and left a few hundred bucks of rubber on the road as I tore away, tires squealing, like someone was chasing me.

It's not an unheard-of thing. Wealthy men from the Dominican Republic having affairs, illegitimate children, other lives entirely. But I refuse to accept that my father, my childhood hero, has stepped out on Mamá.

I can't. I just... can't.

And yet, the boy is familiar— his features, his mannerisms. I shake my head and attempt to drown my thoughts with root beer. It's not enough, though. The dancing barely took the edge off the fizzing energy coursing through my veins, and I wish this was *exactly* the kind of establishment with glory holes and baggies of *perico*.

Hell, I'd settle for a hit from a joint at this point. Something. Anything.

But I can't.

When I got clean, I made a choice. A choice to be an athlete. Then when I made the decision to come to UCR to play hockey it was at the expense of my former life as a playboy.

I can't remember much of my years between the ages of fifteen and seventeen, and that was the point. The more Papá worked, the more I partied in a bid to claw at his attention, and the more he and Mamá fought over getting me "in line."

The bubbly root beer sours in my throat. I haven't craved a hit in months, maybe even a year, but it's here, tugging at my entire being, tempting, teasing. I should hit up a meeting. How long has it been?

People find it strange how you can know at eighteen years old that you're an addict or an alcoholic, but I can guarantee I knew.

I know every fucking day.

I have the ninety-day rehab under my belt to prove it. Times two. Because the first one didn't really stick. The only thing I wanted more than getting high was to play hockey.

And the love of my father, but I think that ship has sailed.

I couldn't keep getting high and play and keep my family. As much as I sometimes feel like I'm Mamá's favorite, even her patience had a limit, and she was fast approaching it.

My stomach gurgles again, and I drop my forehead to the bar with a groan.

The boss man chuckles. "Woman trouble?"

I wish. Or even man trouble. I'd take any form of relationship woes over this. What the fuck even is this? Between the addiction clawing under my skin and my brain going a mile a minute about the potential half-brother out in the wild... And what the fuck am I supposed to do with it? Sit on it and hope it goes away? Tell my siblings?

Fuck.

I rake my hands through my hair. I can't tell Athena this. She idolizes Papá. She's desperate to take over the business when he eventually keels over and dies. But if this came out—indiscretion, scandal—she'd burn it all to the ground.

And Mamá. My heart pinches. Does she know? Doesn't the wife always know?

Maybe I'll hand Athena the matches and watch it all burn.

CHAPTER 3

Eloise

The school term has started, which means virgin strawberry and basil daiquiris at my favorite Mexican restaurant, Guac 'n Roll, while I read over my notes from class.

I've never minded spending time alone.

I get stared at when I eat out by myself, especially for dinner, and since I rarely let anyone see the scars on my face, I figure it must be because I'm alone. I've always felt sorry for people who stare at me with pity for sitting by myself. I've known people who can't be by themselves for any length of time, and to me that's sad—not the being by yourself part, but the being unable to be by yourself

I might be on my second plate of sweet patatas bravas, and I already put in an order for the halloumi al pastor tacos. I want to sink into the tapas-style menu and devour everything the server places on the bar in front of me.

I've never met a potato I didn't like. My eyes roll back in my head at the explosion of spicy flavor on my tongue. I can die happy now that the last things I've eaten are Guac 'n Roll's crispy potatoes.

The volume in the restaurant picks up by a few bazillion decibels and I rub the bridge of my nose. Ugh. It's getting a little too loud in here.

A crowd of people that I'm almost sure is a sports team of some kind hangs out at the table behind me. They don't strike me as football players, but it's my first semester of my first year, so what the hell do I know? I don't recognize either of the girls sitting with them, but again, that means nothing. I generally keep to myself.

It's not that I don't want to make friends, but I'm not really sure how to. The accident that took Mom from me happened when I was sixteen. I missed so much of school that everyone decided it would be best for me to repeat the year.

Which was fine, I needed the time to catch up, but it meant that all my friends moved on without me. I tried to stay in touch, but when they went off to college, and I stayed in high school, it was hard.

So, here I am, a eighteen-year-old freshman with limited social skills and who knows very few people in her year. When someone introduces themselves to me, it doesn't take long to get from "Oh, hey I love your fantastic pink hair," to being the girl with the dead mom and the fucked up face who doesn't *really* belong in this year.

It would help if I moved onto campus instead of staying at home. But with Dad gone all the time, it's the perfect, quiet, well-stocked place to hunker down and absorb all the details that fly over my head during classes.

Am I overreacting in thinking that I'm already falling behind only a few weeks into the semester? Perhaps. I mean, it's early days, and I'm already settled into a great routine at college. From what I can tell, most of the other freshmen are either scrambling to find their feet or partying.

I didn't think a nursing degree would be easy by any means, but heavens to Betsy, it's already a lot.

A *lot.*

I slide my second sweet potato graveyard across to the guy behind the bar, except it's not really a bar. Behind the counter is the kitchen. I've already vowed to sit somewhere else next time I come in because the staff have been a distraction. It's enthralling, watching them plate up such vibrant and amazing dishes. Competent knife skills are hot, who knew?

Not to mention, I love watching people. Especially the little old grandma in the corner pressing flour tortillas between her palms. She looks like she's a hundred years old and has seen things. The sparkle in her eye and her wicked grin suggests she's not one to be messed with.

The guy behind the counter exchanges my empty plate for a taco stand and a huge dish of the green sauce I practically drank with my potatoes. He gives me a knowing smile, like he's aware he's converted another patron to be addicted to the secret sauce.

If I'm not careful, I'm going to spend my entire savings in this place. My hand drifts to my hair, tugging it to hide the deep ridges and rough skin of the scar covering my left cheek. This scar, the accident, and Mom's death are the only reasons I have savings of any kind to speak of.

She made good money as a surgeon, but she and Dad didn't have the best financial situation. And I'm not naive enough to think I'd be able to afford to comfortably go to college if it wasn't for the fact we got awarded money from the courts for the accident. I almost snort. It doesn't feel like getting hit by a drunk driver was an *accident.*

In the grand scheme of things, I'd much rather hand the money back to the judge and get Mom back in return. But no matter how hard I pray every night before bed, that doesn't seem to be an option.

So, I guess I'll take my "free" ride at college and work my ass off to make her proud. Even if she's not here to see it. I hope she's watching over me with a smile on her face, but I'm not God's biggest fan right now either, so I'm not quite sure where I stand on the afterlife anymore.

I'm already on my second taco, shoveling halloumi in my face like it might dull the ragged feelings poking out inside my chest. My arm pulses in time to my heartbeat. I've been to so many therapists, PTs, surgeons, and no one can tell me why there's still pain in my arm sometimes other than the fact they all think it's in my head.

After three surgeries on my arm alone, I'm on a first name basis with most of my medical team—not the doctors though, 'cause, well, they're *doctors*. And *doctors* seem to like reminding everyone at every turn that they went to school for a million years and know better than everyone else. Is arrogance a specific class they take at some point during college?

I swallow down a mouthful of squeaky cheese with another gulp of this delicious daiquiri. I don't hate surgeons. Heck, I wanted to be one, like Mom. But with my injuries I wasn't sure I would regain enough movement or control over my arm to be able to operate, and with the fall out of the accident... my grades weren't where they needed to be for med school.

I can't say I settled for nursing, even though it sometimes feels that way. All that time spent in the hospital surrounded by nurses, I developed a deep and unwavering respect for them, and my dreams changed. The nurses who got me through the worst of times... they're my heroes.

Mom wouldn't be at all upset that I'm not following her footsteps to the letter, but sometimes it feels like another way I've let her down.

My hand strays from the bumps on my cheek to my chest. It could be heartburn from eating too many spicy potatoes or heartache from missing my mom. But either way, I'm verging on crying into my last remaining taco and that really would be kinda embarrassing. Eating alone, studying in a restaurant—I can live with both of those things. But crying into my virgin drink?

Oof. That's certainly not a good visual for my first semester in college. Especially 'cause my glass doesn't say it's virgin, so I'll look like a pathetic freshman crying into her drink.

I push all those thoughts and memories aside, leaving my last taco for a minute to let all the other food I've eaten settle in my stomach while I work through this knot in my chest, and take another drink. I'm about ready to go back to my books when my right side warms.

"Do you have the time?"

I answer, but so does the guy behind the counter. And now I want the ground to swallow me whole.

Tears in my tacos is one thing, but speaking to a stranger who wasn't even talking to me... eek. I'll never recover from this moment playing out in front of me.

The server gives me a small smile, and the guy to my right, who asked for the time, is staring at me. I know he is. Maybe it's my pink hair. Maybe it's the fact I inserted myself into his life when he asked someone else for the time, or perhaps he wants my last taco. I dunno. But either way the weight of his gaze is pressing on my skin, giving me no choice but to look up at him from under the pink curtains of my hair.

"Sorry. I thought you were asking me." I swallow, not meeting his eyes, unsure of why I'm even apologizing for attempting to be helpful.

The smile tugging at his lips only serves to amplify my embarrassment, so I double down. "Have you tried the sweet patatas bravas? They're..." I blow a chef's kiss. A stupid frickin' chef's kiss... And a wave of kill-me-now heat engulfs my entire being.

Stop talking. Just, stop. Don't let any more words come

out of your mouth. Ask for a to-go box and get the heck away from these guys and this awkward situation.

"Have I tried the sweet patatas bravas?" He places an elbow on the bar and leans forward like he's trying to peer around my hair and look into my eyes, or at my face.

Instinct kicks in, and I reach for the left side of my hair, making sure my scar isn't visible. He crooks a brow, like I'm mildly unhinged, and he might be right.

He stares at me for a long beat as though he's waiting for something. Since I'm not meeting his eyes, I can't see what he's thinking, and I'm afraid if I look, he's going to either laugh at me or make me say something to further my mortification, so I go back to reading my notes.

After an even longer beat, he hits the counter and points at the chef in the kitchen. "I'd *love* to try the sweet patatas bravas. Recommended by the resident nerd."

It takes every ounce of strength not to reach into the bag at my feet and smack him with one of my textbooks. His voice drips with sarcasm and judgment. Is he intimidated by women, intelligence, or is he just an asshole? He could be a combination of all three.

He moves away from me, and I can take a complete breath again, but hints of his cologne linger in the air. I'd be lying if I said I wasn't tempted to lean into the space where he stood just to breathe it in a little deeper. He smells good enough to eat even though I have a full stomach.

I try to ignore his presence, but something about him has the air around me feeling charged, alive, so I track his movements in the kitchen.

He's not wearing a uniform, so I don't think he works here. Or at least, he's not on shift, but he clearly knows everyone. He's giving fist bumps or high-fives to everyone except for the little old grandmother. He stoops down and plants a kiss on her cheek. She grips him by both cheeks and levels him with a hard stare, saying something too low for me to eavesdrop.

He tips his head, but he's grinning at her, and I can't help but wonder how the cocky shit who made a throwaway crappy comment about me is the same guy being adorable with a woman who—from the striking family resemblance—has to be his grandmother. They have the same facial structure, the same chin, the same nose, and the same twinkle in very similarly set eyes. Her hair might be grey, but it also has the same thick wave to it as his. If they're not related, I'll eat my hat.

Not right now, though, because I can't even finish eating my last taco. Turns out there *is* such a thing as eating too many potatoes. So I ask for a box, pay my bill, pack up all my things, and use the restroom before I make my way outside.

It's cool, but not cold. Fall is my favorite season. Late September in Iowa when all the trees turn pretty colors, and I get to wear oversized sweaters and curl up under blankets with hot drinks like apple cider—but we don't have to dig our cars out from under five feet of snow. I shudder, knowing that winter is coming, and that shoveling snow is most definitely in my near future.

As I'm walking to my car, grunts and pleasured moans drift from an alley to my left. Sex noises. Surely not.

Someone moans, pleading for more.

Yup. Definitely sex noises. Dangit.

I have to walk past the damn thing to get to my car. Another grunt and a low male voice demands "Harder." Taking a step forward I try not to look. Wrapping my arms around myself, I make myself small, and hurry past. But curiosity burns like a beacon low in my stomach, and I can't help myself.

Two guys are going at it pretty... uh... enthusiastically

against the side of Guac 'n Roll. Right when I feel like I've seen enough, more than enough, more than any outsider should witness of such an intimate act, I recognize the guy from inside the restaurant. The one who called me a nerd, the one who kissed his grandma—he's the one doing the uh... giving.

Holy... cannoli.

He's got one hand curled into the guy's hair, seizing it in a tight fist. He tilts his lover's head back and drags his tongue down the side of his face. His other hand grips the guy's hip as he bucks his pelvis in strong steady thrusting movements.

I can't look away. Goosebumps sweep my skin, and I am embarrassingly turned on. My chest heaves with the effort of each breath while every part of me aches to touch myself.

This is definitely a first. I've never watched porn. I've never read gay romance. But I might have been missing out this whole time. These two going at it is hot in ways I can't define. My feet refuse to take me to my car, and I definitely can't look away.

The guy from the restaurant turns his head toward me, and I gasp as our eyes meet. My stomach sinks, but he grins. A wicked, dirty, knowing smile that has me wishing for the second time in under an hour for the ground to open up and take me to the depths of anywhere but here.

"Wanna join in?" He tongues his top lip. "I'm sure Séb here wouldn't mind you sucking him off while I fuck him."

The other guy doesn't seem as brash, he looks like he's not quite sure whether he's down for that or not, but he's also enjoying himself so much that I don't think he cares.

"If that's not your jam, he could fuck you while I fuck him." Restaurant guy shrugs like he's discussing the weather, and not a deeply personal, physical act, while standing with his penis inside another human being.

Does this man have no shame? Clearly not. But he's just so... on display.

I mean, I'm not a virgin. Not that it would be weird if I was. I'm eighteen, school has barely started, and let's face it, I'm a small-town girl who has lived a relatively sheltered life. But I'm definitely not used to someone so... so...

"What? Don't nerds fuck too?"

My body flares with another wave of heat, and a teenie tiny, itty bitty little part of me is tempted to join in solely to prove him wrong. At least that's what I tell myself. It's not at all because it looks so dang hot that I want to experience what they're clearly both enjoying.

But logic and reason win out, and I manage to take a step back.

He's moving his hips, and the guy he's having sex with has dropped his head forward against the brick wall of the building. Apparently, he doesn't mind that I'm watching them both either. I suppose that's the risk you take when you have sex in a public place, right?

Restaurant guy wags his finger at me. "Don't look at me like your panties aren't wet right now."

I should reply, I know how to speak, but I can't find words. He's having a conversation with himself, but it doesn't seem to bother him.

Something must register on my face under the streetlights' glow because his grin widens. "Yeaaaah. They totally are, aren't they?" He licks his lips again, and I'm a gazelle being stared down by a lion who hasn't eaten in days.

He's probably getting off on my anxiety and discomfort with the situation. He probably took a guess that parts of my body are totally into what I'm seeing right now as confusion seeps through my pores and into my veins.

"I bet you wear cotton boy shorts, don't you? Pretty pink

panties with a growing wet patch from watching me and my boy here."

I squeeze my thighs together like that might stop whatever signals I'm giving that this is hot as hell. I always thought I was plain Jane, and the realization that watching gay men having sex turns me on isn't something I'm equipped to deal with right here on the sidewalk. Especially when one of the afore-mentioned gay men seems to have an obsession with my underwear and is smirking at me like he knows how wet I am right now.

Is he bi? One of them must be, right? Why would he taunt me like this if one of them didn't like women?

Or is he messing with me? I'm pretty gullible and easy to mess with...

I need to leave. Now.

I resist the urge to fan myself, or to jump in my car, crash into the fire hydrant, and stand under the gushing water to cool down. But only just. It's a really strong freakin' urge.

Restaurant guy finally turns his attention back to his lover and it's a behemoth effort to get my feet moving toward my car.

What the heck just happened? And who the heck does that? Takes a time out from having sex to engage a passerby. Granted, I kind of asked for it when I got stuck in place and couldn't leave. I crack the window of my car, pressing my ear against the glass.

My heart's racing, my fingers are stroking the inside of my thigh, and the temptation to bring myself to orgasm right here in the driver's seat is almost overwhelming.

Muted whooping and cheering come through the window. Restaurant guy must have climaxed. Every inch of my skin prickles.

After a deep, steadying breath, I pull my car away from the sidewalk. It's time to drive home like a responsible adult.

There's no reason I need to keep picturing strong fingers and smooth skin and tight thighs.

As soon as I get home, I'm digging out my one and only vibrator from under the bed and taking care of this pulsing ache between my thighs.

CHAPTER 4
Ares

I'm so glad my cat and pig get along.

It makes my life so much easier. I mean, my black cat, Puck, is a superior being and rarely lowers himself to be around me unless he wants to, or rather needs to, so I shouldn't be surprised that Puck ignores Bacon, too.

Though, I expect to come home one day and find Bacon slices all over my living room. If Puck was an outdoor cat, I'd bet he'd be a murderer. One of those cats who leaves birds and mice in various states of aliveness for his human. So, bringing another live being into the apartment possibly wasn't the smartest move, but it seems to be working out okay.

I mean, Bacon isn't giving Puck pony rides around the room or anything, but Puck is tolerating the new addition to the fam.

Also, who knew potbellied pigs gave such good snuggles? Bacon is always down for cuddle time, and I am totally here for it.

I give him one last scratch behind his ears, shoot a warning look at Puck, who gives me that lazy "are you still here?" look in return, and leave the apartment. When I hit the ground floor, an aging doorman tips his hat to me. I swear to God the man is called Alfred, which both makes me laugh and feel like I'm secretly a superhero.

I guess I have the potential to be a real-life superhero, right? Daddy's money, troubled past, devilish looks... All I'd need is a hot spandex costume to parade around in when I'm out fighting crime and kicking bad guys in the nuts by night. Not to mention, Ares is a far cooler name than Bruce.

"Early start today, Mr. de la Peña." As though sensing I'm in trouble, Alfred raises his eyebrows, and his thick and bushy mustache lifts as well. No amount of me telling him to call me Ares makes him actually call me Ares. It's a respect thing, but Señor de la Peña is my father, not me. And every time someone calls me "mister," it's another papercut, another reminder that I'm a disgrace to the de la Peña name.

Why can't you be more like your siblings?

Why, indeed? And do my siblings include Thiago? The temptation to hire someone to dig into my father's affairs is strong. But I'm not sure I'm prepared for what skeletons we'll discover once the closet is cracked open.

"Yes, sir. Coach wants to talk to me." I offer him what I hope is a cool smile, but my insides are anything but cool.

"This early in the season?"

He's echoing my thoughts. The season has barely started, and I'm already being called into the coach's office. The look on Alfred's face confirms what I already suspect: it can't be for any good reason.

Alfred's mouth falls into a thin line before he wishes me luck and holds the door open for me. I've lived here for months now, owned the place since my eighteenth birthday when Papá turned over the keys.

My siblings got theirs when they turned seventeen. I guess Papá dearest didn't trust me not to sell it to feed my habit. In truth, that's probably a fair assessment. There was a time I would have done—and often did—anything for a hit. And some days I think about selling it to stick it to him, to cut the de la Peña umbilical cord and figure shit out all by my big-boy self. Without the family bank roll.

And then I remember that I'm a bougie fucker and like having money.

I grab two coffees at Bitches Brew—not that I'll be able to butter Coach Bales up with coffee, but it can't hurt my case, right?

By the time I get to the rink, I'm already done with my drink. So now it looks like I've brought an apple to the teacher's desk, rather than bringing a coffee so he wasn't left out. *Perfecto.*

He's sitting at his desk, brows pulled together, forehead furrowed as he stares at his computer screen. He doesn't bat an eyelid as I slide his coffee toward him. I dunno what he's staring at so hard, a vein's pulsing in his temple. Hopefully it's not the roster, or my grade sheet, or my high school report cards, or—Jesus fucking Christ it's Solitaire. He's concentrating so hard he might pop a vein on Solitaire.

I can't even.

"Are you going to stand watching me, or are you going to take a goddamn seat?"

I guess we're done with pleasantries. I drop onto the chair in front of him and shelve every ounce of bravado within me.

I know the drill. Be polite, head down, don't make too much eye contact, don't avoid eye contact, be respectful, firm, but not too firm. I've been told how to address people in power since I was knee high to a grasshopper.

Most of all, don't fidget.

Papá hates when I fidget. I don't think he gets how hard it is not to. I'm tempted to sit on my hands so I don't spin the ring on my thumb. My leg twitches, aching to bounce and jitter while I wait.

After what feels like an artificially long pause, Coach Bales clicks something on his screen, and I'm convinced I might be seeing his version of a smile. It's scary. I guess he outsmarted the Solitaire computer and won his game. Good man, Bales. Gold star for you.

A picture hangs on the wall over his shoulder of this year's coaching staff: Bales, head coach; McCarthy, assistant coach; Chabot, goaltending coach. Their faces look serious, lips flat, devoid of joy. No twinkles in the eyes, no roguish charm or grins. They're the guys who are going to get the job done. No fucking around.

When I glance back at Coach, his eyes are trained on me. "Are we going to have trouble this year with you, kid?"

Probably.

I'm so tempted to blurt it out. Not because I'm being a smartass, but because it's the truth. My name and trouble are often synonymous. And it's not always my fault either.

"No, sir. No trouble."

Another long pause. This must be what interrogation feels like, and he's employing some kind of technique to make me break.

Other than getting a pig, I haven't done anything wrong, so I focus on slowing my breathing and trying to make my racing heart slow down.

Okay, so none of my teammates currently know that we have a pig for a mascot yet. But my plan is to keep him in the apartment for a while until I know he's a good fit, to get to know the guys first. And when the time is right, I'll spring my pig on them.

I always wanted a pet pig, and now that I'm a grown-ass man, I can have one.

"I've heard the rumors, seen the stories online. I have your record from your last school." He steeples his hands together on the table as he leans toward me. "I won't have any shenanigans on my team."

Shenanigans? Who is this guy? Uncle Buck?

Also, I happen to be a master shenanigator.

The more he stares at me, the more that might be exactly what he's talking about. I swallow. Okay, so I like to party. And I have more than my share of bad luck.

But I want to play hockey. I *need* to play hockey. I want this gig more than I wanted the damn pig. And I really wanted the damn pig.

"Christmas."

I fucking love Christmas. But I don't imagine he's asking for my Santa list right now.

"You have until Christmas. Consider this a trial period." He levels me with a glare. "At which point, I'll decide whether you're a good fit for this team, this school, or not."

He placed a hell of a lot of emphasis on the "I'll decide" part of that sentence. He's probably alluding to Papá de la Dollar Fund contributing to the university every year by *anonymous* donation.

I almost snort. Alonso de la Peña never does anything anonymously. If he doesn't get the credit, how will the whole world know what a benevolent, generous, and down to earth man he is?

Okay, now I might puke. And I realize I haven't actually answered Coach Bales.

"Yes, sir."

"In case I'm being unclear, let me lay it out for you."

Here it comes.

"I don't care who your father is, how much money he donates to the school, or what *pressure* he might put us under. If you don't keep your nose clean, your grades where they need to be, and bust your ass between those pipes, you're out. Are we clear?"

"Yes, sir." Crystal clear.

My stomach tightens. While I don't like to think I got this slot solely because of who my father is, I've spent my life so far comfortable in the knowledge that he is most definitely a safety net. If something goes awry, a well-placed phone call or a quietly written check could smooth things over.

Even when I hate my family name, even if I want to be painstakingly independent and not at all connected to Alonso, he's always there like a bad smell, and Mamá always convinces him to bail me out.

From the hard glint in Coach Bales's eye, he'd sooner burn the team to the ground than let Papá exert any influence over him.

Part of me respects the fuck out of that. I hope he can stay as resolved as he wants to. Alonso doesn't take no for an answer.

But the other part, well, that part needs a fucking drink.

Instead, when I'm finally dismissed from Coach's office, I hit up the gym. I'm up early. Too early. I may as well put the extra time to good use.

But forty minutes into my training, the bad mood still hasn't shifted. I'm already on Coach's shit list.

To be fair, I'm not sure he has anything *but* a shit list, but it would have been nice to have at least started at the bottom and worked my way to the top over time instead of sliding right in at number one.

I bet I'm the only player on his team that he had a sit-down with today. Or gave an ultimatum to.

Be a good boy, or you're out.

So much fucking pressure.

Even rock bottom sounds pretty tempting about now, and I'll enjoy the ride on the way down, so I'm about thirty seconds away from picking up my phone and calling my dealer. My beloved snow never gave me an ultimatum.

Shaking it off, I do another set of weighted squats before the "Imperial March" from *Star Wars* blasts out of my phone. Papá's calling, and he doesn't like to be kept waiting.

"Sí, Papá?" I've barely spoken the words before he launches into conversation. As with almost all of his conversations, it's one sided.

As he's telling me that he's asked Coach Bales to provide weekly reports to him about my entire life, I let my gaze wander around the gym. If I was a morning person, I could get used to this. It's peaceful, and I don't have to wait for any of the machines to become free.

Granted, my boys aren't here to keep me entertained through the muscle burn, but I admit, sometimes I prefer the quiet.

Papá is still ranting in my ear as my eyes land on the pink haired pixie from the restaurant. My dick twitches, reminding me of an alternative outlet to hitting up my dealer for an 8-ball or two. She seems to be everywhere.

I have to admit, despite the nerd thing she has going on, I'm disappointed she didn't join Séb and me in the alley the other night. I run my tongue along my teeth as I take her in. I don't know what it is about clever girls, but they always see right through my cocky bullshit and dismiss me right out of the gate.

Because of the pretty boy I am, I'm not deemed intelligent enough for the smart folk, so I tend to keep my distance. This girl is probably like them, too bright for little old me. But there's something about her.

Her gait on the treadmill is flawless. Her ass and tits jiggle and bounce with each step. Her pink hair is tied up out of her face for a change so I can take in her high cheekbone, her sharp jaw, and the scars she seems to always be covering up by hiding behind her hair.

Is that why she hits the gym so early? So she can run

without hiding her face behind sweaty hair? I don't get what the big deal is. She's fucking stunning. Maybe that's why people stare at her: not because of her scars, but because her beauty renders them speechless. She's caught my attention damn near every time I've seen her. A part of me is drawn to her.

And I don't just mean my dick.

"Are you listening to me, boy?" Papá's Spanish breaks through my creeper behavior. I've never watched a woman at the gym before, but her rhythmic steps pounding on the treadmill keeps my attention and somehow eases the tension that has been holding my neck hostage for the past couple hours.

"Sí, Papá. Lo sé." Good grades. No trouble. No drugs. Yadda, yadda. I shouldn't imbibe at all; I try not to. But I do still have the occasional beer. I know my limits and what I can handle, and as long as I stay away from the hard stuff, I can convince myself it's not an issue.

On days like today, when Coach and Papá are both riding my ass, it's so very tempting to hit up a bar as soon as it opens. They say money can't buy happiness, but it sure as hell can buy fake IDs, booze and blow, and sometimes that's the same thing.

I rub the back of my neck, reciting the serenity prayer over and over while Papá yammers in my ear. Falling off the wagon would give both him and Coach even more ammo to hound me. And I'm nothing if not stubborn. Some days I swear it's my obstinance alone that keeps me on the fucking wagon.

Instead, I nod. Except, he can't see me, so I provide Papá with the answers he wants to hear. *Yes, sir, no, sir, three bags fucking full, sir*, to get him the fuck off the phone so I can move on with my day.

The pixie enigma is running on the treadmill. Perhaps I

need to run, too. Maybe I need to find my big boy panties and talk to the woman who keeps captivating me solely by existing.

Right as I'm about to step onto the treadmill two down from hers, she hits the button to stop her belt from running. Dammit, I missed my window.

I give her an easy grin, but she tugs her hair tie free, shakes her hair loose around her face, and looks straight through me as though I don't exist.

Huh. Maybe she already thinks I'm not good enough for her.

She's not wrong. But I want her. Her perfectly pouty lips, the curve of her ass as it's hugged by the bright leggings she's wearing, the playful color of her hair... everything about her says she's down for a good time.

So why is she looking at me like she wants to bury me alive?

CHAPTER 5
Eloise

"Hola." The guy from the taco place grins at me. If this place wasn't already lit up by harsh fluorescent lights, his smile would do the trick. It could power the whole city. But I fell once before for a guy with a pretty smile, and I might only be eighteen, but I'm not a complete idiot.

Ignoring him, I sweep my towel from the floor at my feet, patting down the beads of sweat trickling down my face. The temptation to keep going with my cardio is fierce. I hate what comes next. My physical therapist told me I need to work on building the strength in my muscles, and that means pain. No one believes me when I tell them I have a pain in my arm, they think it's all in my head. But it's there, and it hurts like fire charging from my neck to my fingertips.

If the pain isn't real, then why do I need to work on strengthening my arm?

"It's rude not to say hi back when someone says hi to you."

I glance over my shoulder quickly, just to double check he's talking to me. Jutting my chin at him, I smirk. "Oh. My apologies. I didn't realize I was in the presence of the rude police."

His lips twitch, grin widening. Dangit. Should have ignored him. He's caught the scent of my sarcasm now, and instead of leaving me alone, he wants to play. His eyes dance with trouble as he steps toward me, arm outstretched like he thinks he's going to touch me.

Does his arrogance know no bounds? He thinks he can, what? Just waltz up to women in the gym and touch their faces? Nice try, hot shot, but that's not what's going to happen right now.

I smack his hand away as it skims my hair. Not today, Satan.

His mouth drops as if he's going to speak, but the door behind him opens with a long, shrill screech. A younger kid with shaggy black hair pokes his head into the room. When the taco place guy makes eye contact with him, the kid pales, and Mr. Smooth seems to mercifully forget I exist and follows him out into the hallway. Was that his brother? First the grandmother in the restaurant and now the younger boy, the likeness is undeniable. I guess these people have strong genes.

My fingers glide across my hair where his fingers almost touched, and a teenie, tiny, miniscule, almost imperceptible voice in the back of my head whispers that I should have let him.

That thought slithers over my skin with a shiver as I tuck it out of the way. I do not want him touching me...

Right?

I swallow, hard, realization clogging my throat.

My face burns. My body tingles.

Nope. I refuse to have a crush on the exhibitionist.

I. Refuse.

I'm skipping weights today. My arm hurts, and that's enough of an excuse for me to give it a miss. I'm not a masochist. Grabbing my water bottle, I make my way out the door. Mr. Not-So-Smooth is kicking the stuffing out of the wall. I don't know whether to laugh or call for help.

His eyes are lit with fire, his hair falls into his eyes, and his jaw is clenched so tightly I'm pretty sure that crunching sound is his teeth.

Taking a step toward him, I hesitate. I don't think he'd hurt me, but I'm also not sure he's in his right mind. I'm more afraid he'll do himself damage than injure me.

"Hey?" I don't know why it's a question.

He either ignores me or didn't hear me. I take another step as he spins on his toes and paces a few feet away from the wall. I send up a quick prayer for his toes because we kind of need those and swinging his feet at the concrete walls of the gym doesn't feel like a great plan for an athlete.

"Are you okay?" As I touch his arm, I ready myself for the explosive reaction I expect. But instead, he stills, meeting my gaze with tortured eyes.

"Are you okay? Can I call someone?"

He holds my stare. I lean toward him ever so slightly like he's reeling me in with those eyes.

"Can I help?"

He reaches out again, fingers heading straight for my hair. I flap at his fingers with my own. He chuckles, but it's hollow and echoes around the concrete walls.

"Guys like me are beyond help. You know that." His sad smile splinters something in my chest, but he winks like it's our little secret. My breath is stolen by his vulnerability. No trace of arrogance or cockiness stands in front of me. Just a boy with pain etched in his stunning features.

As quick as it came, it leaves, and Mr. Casanova is back, winning smile in place, hair slicked back. But something tugs at me for the rest of the day. The guy from the taco place might be a little broken, just like me.

CHAPTER 6
Eloise

It's not the library, but Bitches Brew is my second favorite place to study. It has the right amount of ambient noise, it's the right temperature, and they make the best fully loaded hot chocolate I've ever had.

One of these unsuspecting students is destined to be my new best friend. If I can work up the lady balls to go talk to any of them.

I didn't think I'd get to October and not have found my people, or even a person. I'm not greedy, just one would do, but here we are. With Dad out of town so much, I admit I'm lonely as hell, and I'm not sure how to fix it. The only person who could tell me what I'm doing wrong and how to make it better is Mom. I miss her more and more.

I always thought the older you got, the less you needed your parents, but I'm living proof that sometimes it isn't so. I want my Mom.

It's not that college kids are mean. People in my classes are nice enough to me. They smile, say hey, but that's where it starts and ends. I don't know how to take that to the next level, to turn it into something meaningful.

Is it me? It has to be me, right? Quieter than most of them, a little odd and stand-offish. My pink hair essentially makes me a walking juxtaposition. I'm not shy—I can talk to people. I just can't set down this ball of anxiety pressing on my chest for long enough to actually approach someone.

Never had that one best friend, you know? Always on the fringes of a few friendship circles but couldn't ever figure out how to break into something more. Totally thought that when I got to college, I'd find another awkward, mildly anxious introvert to adopt me and become friends with.

If it's so hard for me to make friends, it stands to reason that it'd take time for my quirky alter-ego to find me too, right? Okay, I've got to reevaluate my expectations. Whoever is going to adopt me has to be at least an ambivert, or slightly extroverted, because two introverts would happily sit side by side and never make eye contact or talk with each other. I need to find an extrovert to adopt me.

Where's the sign-up sheet for that on the cork boards around the school?

With a sigh, I pull out my notes from my chem class. As much as I appreciate having a "lighter" workload my first year, I can't wait to sink my teeth into all the good "helping people" stuff waiting for me in my second and third years.

The chair across from me squeaks as it's pulled back from the table. Looking up, the bright green eyes of someone I don't recognize meet mine, and my anxiety dials up to an eleven. Oh, God. She's sitting. Doesn't she realize she doesn't know me?

Her face lights up with a warm smile as she sits, and she blows at the red hair that falls over her face. She's a natural red but not orangey ginger, or even copper; it's darker, richer, and shiny. Really freakin' shiny. Her hair falls in long waves that probably reach halfway down her back.

I barely resist the urge to tug on my own hair. Before the

accident I had long hair too, but it's easier to hide my scars if it hangs above my shoulders. I have hair envy over everyone with longer locks than me.

She's looking right at me, so she must know she's at the wrong table, and yet, she hasn't moved. It's my own personal nightmare playing out right in front of me. How is she staying so calm? I have secondhand embarrassment *for* her. Like my stomach is churning, and my palms are starting to sweat.

Is she going to sit here awkwardly for a few minutes before getting up and going to the table she was *supposed* to sit at?

"Hi, I'm Victoria." Instead of fleeing, she sticks out her hand across the books spread over the table. "Or Tori. I've seen you come in here almost every day that I do, and I figure since we're both here a lot, and we're both studying alone, we may as well study alone together, right?" Her smile is hopeful, and for a fraction of a second, a flicker of vulnerability passes as quickly as it came.

For an almost imperceptible beat, I'm jealous of this woman all the way to my core. Not only for her glorious auburn hair that I've been lusting over, but for being able to talk to a stranger in the middle of a coffee shop.

Then, the relief that someone has actually struck up a conversation with me hits, and my muscles relax a little.

Her warm smile is still in place, and her hand remains extended as she eyes me patiently. "If you'd rather I take myself back to a table by myself, I can do that too." She glances over her shoulder like she's checking that her table is available.

I cautiously accept her hand and shake. "I'm Eloise."

Her face was lit up before, but once I introduce myself, her smile grows, and I swear to God, warmth spills out of her entire being. "Let me guess, introvert, right?"

I nod. Was I muttering out loud about my introverted self needing to be adopted by an extrovert? Or is she really that good?

"How'd you guess?"

She nods back with an airy giggle. "I thought so. Don't worry, I'm not some weird energy vampire or anything, and I'm not going to talk and talk and talk at you when you're trying to study—ugh, isn't that so annoying? But I wanted to say hi and get the ball rolling by telling you I'm your new best friend."

What the heck is happening right now? Did I sign up to an adopt-an-introvert program in a fever dream? Or did this chick literally read my mind and decide to take the opportunity to present herself to me?

She starts pulling books out of her Army-green book bag and taking up the little space I've left on her side of the table. Her smile stays in place, and even though I don't know anything about this woman other than her name, that she's a student, and the fact she's very obviously the most outgoing person I've ever met, it doesn't feel awkward.

I mean, announcing herself as my new best friend is a bit presumptuous, but no other candidates have made themselves known at this point in time, so she could be right.

I'm still staring at her by the time she crams a pen between her teeth and gnaws on the end as she flicks through a notebook. I'm curious about her. I want to ask her questions and figure out why the heck she chose to plop herself down at my table. But she's jumped straight into studying and is giving me space like she said she would, and I'd never interrupt someone when they're working, so I turn my attention back to chemistry.

After about twenty minutes she picks up my mug and examines the contents. "You're empty. You want a drink or something?" She hooks her thumb over her shoulder. "I'm going to get something. Full disclosure: possibly more than one something. Spoiler alert: *definitely* more than one something. Have you tried their hot chocolate? It's orgasmic."

Yeah, okay. She might have been right about the new best friend thing. "I love their hot chocolate. I've already had one though, I should switch to tea."

She purses her lips and leans toward me. "You only live once. Have the second hot chocolate if you want it." She pats her tummy. "This chunky girl doesn't judge."

I can't help but smile. Something genuine emanates from her, something easy, something that leads me to feel as though I've known her for more than the last twenty-five minutes.

I really do want more hot chocolate. Heck, if they offered a gallon sized mug of the stuff I'm still not sure it'd be enough for me. I roll my lips between my teeth and nod like I'm doing something I shouldn't. "Okay. I'll take another."

"Something you're going to learn pretty quickly about me, Eloise, is that I'm an enabler." She drops her voice. "So, if you ever need to be talked into something, I'm your gal." She grabs her wallet from her bag and heads up to the counter to order before I can offer her money for my drink.

She pauses, pivots back to me, and her brow creases. "No allergies, right? If I get something with nuts in it, I won't find myself having to dig through your bag for an epi pen or anything?"

I shake my head. "No allergies."

She gives a firm nod and resumes her voyage for whipped cream and mini marshmallows sprayed with pink glitter. Are all brand new best friends quite as mother hen-y and considerate? Having nothing to compare it to, I don't have an answer, but it was definitely nice of her to ask.

The bell over the door of the café chimes as the door opens and a blast of cold air sweeps through the warm space. A loud group of guys make their way inside, and I roll my eyes. My peace and quiet is on the line, and I really don't want to move from this little corner of heaven.

One of them pulls a chair out from the table they've

chosen and spins it so it's backward before he slides onto it. His movements are graceful, dancer-like, even if he looks like an idiot sitting backward on a chair with a backward ball cap on his head and a lazy grin on his—oh, no.

That grin was attached to a wink that night in the alley. That grin was attached to twinkling chocolate brown eyes filled with promises of mischief and nasty, nasty sex at the gym.

That is a dangerous grin, and I need to look away.

Please, God, don't let him see me. Please, God, don't let him see me.

I don't know who the guys are, but they all look kinda buff. I wouldn't be surprised if they're all jocks.

I'm trying to peel my eyes away from him, but something about that grin is utterly magnetizing.

"Why are we staring at Ares de la Peña like he hung the moon?" My new friend Victoria places two super-full mugs of hot chocolate onto the table before taking her seat.

Ares.

It's an unusual name, and it most definitely suits him. Even as a new freshman, I've heard of the de la Peñas. There's a bench on campus that's sponsored by their father, and he donates a ton of money to the school every year.

"Don't think I can't see you behind that shield of pink hair. I know exactly who you're staring at." Her voice is low, tinged with amusement, and when I look over at her, understanding flashes in her eyes. No judgment, no mocking, no expectation. Huh.

I'm not talking about it, about him. Not with a stranger, not on our first get together. Not even our first get together, but our very first encounter. We aren't there yet. Oversharing isn't my thing. But something about how she's looking at me tells me I don't have to. It's like she already knows.

She cradles her mug between both hands and drags her

tongue through the whipped cream. "I can see it." Her gaze flicks to the way-too-loud table of rambunctious boys drawing attention from almost everyone in the coffee shop. "You'd be cute together."

I fight the urge to recoil, but I'm not sure my body got the memo. "I couldn't ever be with him." I temper my brewing snort to a derisive laugh.

She sips on her drink, sliding back in her chair. "But you want to be."

His fingers clenched in the other guy's hair, their hips slapping together.

My face burns. I thought I'd be past it by now, but I'd be lying if I said I didn't dream the replay every single night since. And sometimes mornings too.

I risk another glance over at him, and my new friend's smirk grows.

Do I want to be with him?

Perhaps before I knew who he was. But he's a de la Peña. It's UCR's worst kept secret that those kids are largely only here because their parents are rich. I meet her eyes again.

"He's the youngest." She takes another casual sip, as though she's discussing something she watched on TV last night. "The bad boy."

My stomach flips, and every cell in my body struggles with the idea that I might be attracted to a "bad boy."

Before the accident, I had been a straight-A student my whole life. I never skipped a day of school, never flunked a test, and always turned my homework in on time. Ares wasn't wrong when he called me a nerd. It was *how* he said it that bothered me. With contempt, like he's allergic to books or something.

I widen my eyes at Victoria to suggest right now really isn't the time. She nods, reading the subtext and taking another slurp of her drink, getting a little sparkly whipped cream on her nose. I can't risk him hearing us talking about him, or worse, actually seeing me. He'd probably ignore me in front of all his cool guy friends, but on the off chance he might talk to me, I keep my head down.

Instead of turning my attention back to my books, I pull out my phone and type Ares's name into the search browser. Holy cannoli, there's a lot of stuff on here about him.

With everything I have I fight looking at him while I scroll. He's our hockey team's new goaltender, which means he's probably the one I kept watching the night I went to the game with Dad. That also explains the graceful movements. Man, thinking back, I want to fan myself. That boy is... bendy.

The more I scroll, the more stories I find about crazy parties, sex, drugs, and a rock-and-roll lifestyle that is likely bankrolled by Daddy Moneybags.

Tori wasn't kidding—he's the ultimate bad boy. A shiver dances up my spine, and I don't think it's revulsion.

According to the internet, he's majoring in gender, women, and sexuality studies with a social justice minor. And that surprises the hell out of me.

It seems to contradict his disdain for smart girls. Why would he put himself in that situation? I figured he'd be studying something easy, something he wouldn't have to work hard at. Something jocks study so they can spend their time playing sportsball. Yet here he is, studying something profound and important. Something that speaks to my feminist heart and makes me want to get to know him better.

"I can see your screen."

I snap my phone against my chest, my cheeks now sizzling. I don't know why I'm so curious about this guy, but his entire life is on the internet, impossible not to get sucked into. It's like reading a soap opera script.

"You should totally shoot your shot with him."

This time I can't help but snort, dropping my phone on

my lap so I can throw my hands over my face at the awful sound that escapes from me. "But he's gay."

She shakes her head. "I can see why you'd think that, but click the photos tab. You'll see him with both men and women. He's bi."

She sure knows a lot about him. I take another look at her. Has she been with him? Does she want to be with him? Have some of her friends been with him? Shit. Is she related to him? Ohhhh crap.

She wags her finger. "Don't look at me like that. I have a kid at home. I don't want any part of your nasty boy. I mean, he's a fantasy come to life. Athlete who moonlights as a stripper. Bad boy who takes gender studies. He's a walking contradiction."

Wait. A... stripper?

I'm not sure if I want to see what pictures of him live in the photos tab, but after that declaration, my mouth has gone bone dry. It's bad enough that he's what my dad would call a ruffian. Add in the stripper thing, and Dad would lock me in the basement if he ever got wind of me so much as even talking to that boy.

He's bad news.

Trouble.

No good.

And no amount of adorable cheek dimples, Colgate smile, or chocolate brown eyes can distract from the fact he's not the boy for me.

My thumb hovers over the photos tab as I sip on my now lukewarm hot chocolate. I can look, right? Once I see him with a myriad of lovers, I can put the final nail in the "heck no" coffin and not give him another iota of space in my brain.

Except the first three photos are of him in various stages of undress, and instead of a dry mouth, I'm drooling.

The first picture is him upside down on a stripper pole.

He's still wearing that stupid backward ball cap, clinging to the pole with his thighs, and beaming at the camera. Oh... my... those thighs.

I've seen videos on social media of guys crushing watermelons with their thighs, but always wondered if they were legit. Sitting here, staring at Ares de la Peña's thighs, 100% convinced he could crush... anything... with those thighs.

I've never seen such muscle definition in someone's legs before. I also can't bring myself to look away. They're so... sculpted.

I manage to pull my gaze away from the thighs for long enough to scroll down the other pages in the web browser's photo library. There are a lot. He very clearly loves having his picture taken and being the center of attention.

He doesn't seem to have a specific type, other than perfect, flawless, and breathtakingly beautiful.

I close the browser, lock my phone, and put it face down on the table before silently drinking the rest of my hot chocolate. Victoria doesn't say anything for a long time either, but her attention flits between her notebook and my face.

My body springs to life every time his melodic voice meets my ears, and I'm growing more and more frustrated with myself. When I heard him speaking Spanish at the gym, I almost needed an ice bath, but my lady parts have decided that they don't care what comes out of his mouth. It all sounds delicious. In fact, the filthier the better.

Ugh. Is this what Adam and Eve felt like? The lure of the forbidden fruit?

I'm starting to think this guy is a siren, and he's working his merman voodoo on my vagina. Tori is smirking at me again, like she's inside my brain listening to the thoughts ricocheting around.

"No." I cross my arms. His siren voodoo can go bother

someone else's vagina. It's not like he's short of willing volunteers.

Victoria rolls her lips. "If you say so." In her defense, she's clearly trying hard to keep her amusement under wraps.

We go back to studying. For how long, I have no idea, but the jock ruckus has died down when we both come up for air. I risk a glance over at their vacated table, not expecting to find chocolate brown eyes staring right back at me.

My heart stops in my chest, and for a split second I contemplate hiding. He gives me a wink, spins the chair around so it's facing the right way, and leaves. A not-so-small part of me wants to follow him.

CHAPTER 7
Ares

It's our third game of the season. We're playing the Indianapolis Storm, and I'm still on the goddamn motherfucking bench. Under normal circumstances, the incumbent goaltender would be the starter, not a freshman. Except both our goaltenders moved on over the summer, leaving nothing *but* freshman goalies.

Coach seems to be flexing his big dick muscle. I'm not quite sure what message he's trying to send other than he's not above benching our starting netminder because he feels like it. How am I supposed to prove myself, to earn my place between the pipes by Christmas if he doesn't ever let me play?

Asshole.

My blood simmers, hot under my skin, and I'm tempted to stand up, stomp my feet, and throw the team's sticks all over the ice in protest.

The urge to punch something, to work this out of my system, is strong, and there's no bright haired beauty to talk me out of breaking my foot this time. Even thinking of her brings relief to my tense muscles. She smelled like bubblegum at the gym, an achievement for someone with sweat seeping through her clothes.

Something about the way she handled me nestled deep in my chest. She wasn't afraid of me, at least not until I tried to touch her face anyway. But the empathy, the care, the gentleness with which she approached me... that was... something.

Parker makes another big save out on the ice, and my stomach drops. Not even thoughts of the colorful, calm elf can ease this burning in my veins.

I'll definitely need to hit the club on my way home. Ugh. I can't even put on my hot as hell suit and sit in the stands yelling abuse at my teammates as a healthy scratch. I've got to stay suited and booted on the bench, in case my backup fucks up and I'm tagged in.

Not that I'd ever yell abuse at my teammates. At least not when fans can hear.

For tonight, I'm the backup.

I'm not good at playing second fiddle to anyone. In fact, I bust my balls every time I step out onto the ice to ensure that doesn't fucking happen.

And yet... an impostor's between my pipes.

Okay. He's not an impostor, but it feels like he is. Maybe it's me that's the impostor. Perhaps Coach saw something during practice that he doesn't like—other than my "bad attitude"—he could be regretting signing me.

My stomach tightens, but I force out a chuckle then flex my jaw. No way. I'm good, better than good. And yet, the bench feels pretty warm under my ass right now.

It's the middle of the second, and we're up by a goal. I should know everyone's name by now, but I don't. I've got the people who help defend my net down so I can yell at them if they fuck up, but I'm hazy on the forwards. What I *do* know is that there isn't another de la Peña on the ice right now.

Thankfully, the smart people who created hockey made us

all put our names on our shirts for ease of identification while traveling at high speed. So, when someone in a Raccoon's jersey steps on the puck and falls on his face, I can clearly see that it's left winger Tate Myers. That'll make it easier to rib him about it later.

Stepping on a puck is the most embarrassing thing that can happen on the ice. Actually, it's not the stepping on the puck that brings the humiliation—it's the unstoppable, crazy awkward way that you immediately fall down that's embarrassing.

It removes all control. Not falling is near impossible. So, when Myers's face meets the ice, a mixture of laughter from the stands and wincing with mutters of concern from both benches fills the air. For those of us who haven't face-planted in a similar way ourselves, we know it could happen to any of us at any time.

Still funny as fuck, though.

Myers gets up on his skates, dusts himself off, and shakes his head like he's cussing himself out. It's funny how we all blame ourselves for shit that we literally have no control of. Yet, we behave as though we should. Myself included.

My brothers both step out onto the ice. Brothers. Does Thiago play hockey? I shake my head, but the thought doesn't dislodge.

Having watched the twins play since they started at UCR, Coach rarely sends them out together at the minute unless they're needed to send a message to someone, and this game has been pretty tame so far. Is Coach shaking things up across the board for shits and giggles?

Wishful thinking. They play so well together as a pair. Artemis has Apollo's back at all times, and it's as though they sense where the other is on the ice. It can be a thing of beauty to watch, but when they're having an off night, it can look pretty ridiculous.

While I'm distracted by my brothers on the ice, the ref drops the puck in my periphery. Could I convince Apollo and Artemis to switch their jerseys on the ice for April Fools' Day? That would be funny as fuck. Okay, so they'd need to get matching haircuts too, but it'd be worth it to prank Coach. And everyone else on the ice.

I bet half the guys can barely tell them apart as it is. If it wasn't for the scar on Artemis's upper lip from his cleft palate surgery, I would struggle to know who's who most days.

They used to switch places all the time when they were kids. Drove Athena and me mad. But drove Papá up the wall even more.

I've seen a meme on one of the socials where two players were sitting on the bench, one's shirt said French and the other said Fries. It's cute, but twin-switch would be a riot. Now that I think about it, the Sedin twins are reported to have switched jerseys for fun back in their day. It's not like it never happens. It would be funny as hell.

I shouldn't have time right now to stroll down memory lane to the days of twin-switch. I should be focused on keeping the biscuit the hell out of my basket. Not a euphemism.

You know what really sucks? Watching the fucking game you were born to play from the sidelines. We're about to start the third, and as exciting as the game is, it's nothing compared to experiencing it, living it, breathing it.

I'm trying to keep my shit together, but occasional growls are escaping me. I'm big fucking mad. We're one up as the puck hits the ice at the start of the third period. Our goalie, Hayes Parker, isn't bad—in fact, he's pretty damn good. He'd be a great starting netminder if the coaching staff hadn't procured a hot-shot-rookie who's gathering fucking dust on the bench.

An outskater for the Storm lines up the shot, and a train

wreck unfolds on the ice. Fellow Raccoon, Scott Raine's face meets what has to be a 90mph slap shot and he goes down in a spray of blood and howling.

He's not on the ice for long before help makes its way out to him, but blood gushes from the wound on his face, turning the ice around him into a scene from a fucking horror film.

It takes them a few minutes to get him on his feet and the crowd erupts into cheers and applause. The silence around the rink is always touching when a player gets injured. It's as though no one dares to breathe until the injured player has been proclaimed okay.

It doesn't matter whether the player is loved or loathed, whether they play for the home team or the away team, the reaction from every crowd is the same. One of our own is down.

It looks like it hit below his bottom lip, and no matter what damage the puck has caused, Raine will be back on the ice for training tomorrow. Apollo lost a tooth during a game when he was in high school. He skated to the bench, spat it out, and went out and scored two goals and three assists like the badass he is.

I contemplate singing out loud, or swinging my legs back and forth on the bench until someone notices me. This sucks. Like really sucks. It sucks so hard I want to scream.

Not even letting my thoughts drive to the delicious pink haired pixie from the salon can calm the raging fire in my belly. What is she up to? I don't get the impression she's a sports loving kinda girl, but I can't fight the need to scan the crowd. Maybe she's watching my ass on the bench.

The game ends and our backup maintains his shut out, which is a mixed bag of feelings for me. On one hand we won, so yay, but on the other, Parker faced some tough saves, and he did pretty damn good even if it hurts for me to admit it.

I don't need Coach realizing that he's the better netminder

and keeping me on the bench indefinitely. The benefit of us both being freshmen is that we both have to prove ourselves to earn and keep the top slot. I guess I don't have to be replaced, they just don't have to keep me.

Fuck. The thought alone curdles my stomach. I'd lose my mind.

Raine's back in the locker room by the time we make it off the ice. He lost two teeth, needed twenty-three stitches to repair the damage to his face, and as suspected, he plans to take to the ice tomorrow for practice. Like I said, badass. He's mostly pissed that he missed the end of the game.

I can relate, man. I can relate.

I've never let myself be second best at anything. Which is why I had to quit using. It gave me the confidence to think I was on top of my game, while dragging me into the depths of obscurity.

And as my team celebrates another goaltender's win, it washes over me. Feels a lot like failure.

And de la Peñas don't do failure.

As expected, Papá has tried to call a number of times. He's left three voicemails, each picking up speed and intensity, like a tropical storm becoming a hurricane. He's watched the game, he saw me on the bench instead of between the pipes, and yet he's pissed at me for not being at his beck and call to pick up the goddamn phone when he called.

What the fuck does he expect me to do? Say, "Oh, I'm sorry, Coach, but I need to go take a call from my daddy?"

I snort. Right. Like that would go down well.

I'm already on Papá's shit list, so I ignore the flashing screen, tuck the phone into my bag and head home to work on teaching Bacon how to play goalie between the pipes. He's getting better at it. For the first while he kinda stood staring at the puck as it sailed toward him. Last night he sniffed it. It's progress.

They say potbellied pigs are super smart, smarter than dogs, so I have no doubts that our team mascot is going to take over the world someday. But for now, we're starting with progressing from sniffing pucks, to stopping them.

I want to tell the guys about it, but I'm irrationally shaken by the fact I'm riding the pine. What if Coach wants to replace me?

No point in telling the guys I got a mascot for a team that may not even be mine for long.

I've gone off the doomsday cliff. I'm full of worst-case scenarios. My mood is as sour as my stomach, but I can't help it. Hockey is my life. I can't lose it. And not only because the headache from Papá would be insufferable either.

I don't take the guys up on the invite to go to The Den. Instead, my bad mood and I head home to play with my pig. And for once, that's not even a euphemism.

CHAPTER 8
Eloise

Ares's hot breath tickles my cheek as his splayed hand glides over my stomach, passing my belly button. Lower. Lower. I suck in a breath. Lower. Arching my back, I whimper. He nips at my ear, the bite of pain barely registering through the desperate aching need raging through my body.

My thighs are slick with my arousal. It's embarrassing how soaking I am right now. His fingers slide into my pussy without resistance. Slick, squelching, dripping. But his light touch is not enough. I spread my legs for him. He ignores the movement, so I pull them wider. He ignores that too, lazily swiping the pads of his fingers through my wet folds. I'm panting, needy, trembling with desire.

His teeth graze the side of my jaw before nibbling along its line, and I tilt my head to the side, granting him access to my throat. He sucks the skin where my neck and shoulder meet into his mouth and hums.

Lightning dances over my body as he breathes on me. His breath skims the fine hairs on my skin. The way we're lying, I can't move one arm to nudge his hand where I need it to be. And my other arm isn't responding to commands either. It's hanging limply at my side, like my body is resigned to submit to him.

I whine, moaning, pleading, begging with him to give me what I want, what I need. When the pad of his thumb brushes my clit, every part of my body lights up like someone flicked the switch on a Christmas tree at Rockefeller Center. My entire being hums to life right down to my core.

His trail of kisses slips down to my peaked nipple. He's sucking so hard he has to have left a path of hickeys from my neck to my breasts, but I don't care. He can mark me everywhere as long as he doesn't stop touching me.

His tongue swirls around my nipple in time with his fingers on my clit. Every now and then he pauses, sinks his teeth into my skin while I beg him not to stop, plead with him to keep going, or he listens to my ragged breaths and moans.

He's whipping me into a frenzy. I'm hurtling toward the promised orgasm. But his movements are languid, slow, in his own time. Like he controls my every breath, and my body will do whatever he wants it to.

He's not wrong.

His rock-hard dick is pressed against me, and every time he moves, the cold metal from his piercings add to my sensory overload. I fist the sheets, bucking my hips against his hand when he stops dead and drags his fingers back up my body leaving a slick trail of my arousal in his wake.

Sucking his fingers into his mouth, he moans. "My pussy is so fucking wet for me." He says it with such warmth, such wonder, such heated desire that I almost come undone.

His pussy. It clenches like it's sentient, enjoying his declaration, his possession, his desire.

His hand finds its way to the apex of my thighs, and his

fingers slip back into a rhythm of circling my clit while he sucks on my breasts.

"Who do you belong to, *mi putica sucia*?"

I'd love to say that if he called me his dirty little slut in English, I'd slap him. But I love his filthy mouth. Even if I said I didn't, the growing puddle of wetness under my ass on the sheets would call my bluff.

"*Cuéntame.*"

"*Soy tuya*. I-i'm yours, Ares. B-body and s-s-soul. P-please, don't stop."

My head is anchored into my pillow, my back is arched, my nipple caught between his teeth as I buck my hips, riding his hand, chasing my release.

"S-so close."

A low rumble vibrates through my nipple, sending shivers over my skin. He loves it when I tell him I'm close, when I tell him I'm hot for him, when I check my anxiety and shyness at the door and let loose in bed with him. What he loves most is when I tell him what I want him to do to me.

"That's my girl."

His.

My insides start to tremor and flex as much as my extremities, eyes rolling back in my head. My grip on the sheets tightens as his tongue flicks in rhythmic strokes against my hard nipple between his teeth.

It's coming. The crest of the wave I'm chasing is so close I can almost taste the release. A little further, and I'll get to where I need to be.

"Come for me, *chiqui*." His voice is so smooth, vibrating against my skin as he speaks. I suck in a breath, ready to give him what we both need, ready to fall apart on his fingers.

"Eloise?"

Eyes snapping open at the sound of my name as my

bedroom door hits the wall, my hand is in my pajama pants, body hot and flushed, and heart racing faster than it has any business doing.

Oh my... that was... a... dream? My heart free falls to the floor.

My chest rises and falls with heavy breaths.

Why is Tori standing in my doorway?

"Ah. My bad. You were making... noises. I thought something was wrong. This..." She waves a hand. "Definitely not something wrong."

She winks. I groan.

How does she know? She can't see my hands under the blankets. I jerk my head up to look down at my covered body, and she bursts out laughing.

"Oh, I don't need to see where your hands are to know exactly what you're doing. Your face is flushed, you have sex hair, and like I said, the noises. I misinterpreted the noises."

My mouth falls open. Okay, we've been friends for a couple weeks, and sure, she stayed over last night because it got too late for her to drive home when we got sucked into studying, but this? I'm never going to be able to look her in the eye again.

Sucked. Oh, good grief, I'll never be able to use that word again without thinking about Ares de la Peña sucking on my skin.

Tori is still staring at me. Cripes. I need a new best friend, and I *just* got this one.

She grins and shakes her head. "It's all good. No judgment here. But we will need to get you laid because, girl, you need to fuck that boy all the way out of your system."

Heart still racing, I open my mouth, but she holds up her hand. "Don't even. Don't you dare try to convince me you don't know what I'm talking about. I heard exactly who you were dreaming about. Plus, we talked about his pierced peen last night..."

We did no such thing. *She* told me the gossip she overheard in the girl's bathrooms about the de la Penis.

She winks again before turning to leave. "I was thinking of having some hot chocolate for breakfast since you seem to have a collection of packets from Bitches Brew on the table. I didn't realize you had, like, a real hot chocolate problem. Again, no judgment."

When I pull myself together and follow her out into the kitchen, my face is on fire. She's standing over the pile of hot chocolate packets grinning. "Do we need an intervention?"

"I don't think so." This is where I tell her that I have...a stalker? Admirer? It's a fine line. That someone's leaving me packets of my favorite drink at places I frequent around campus.

"What? What's with that face?" She points her finger at me, face pinched, head tilted. She definitely has the mama instinct that knows when something is up.

I drag in a breath then heave out a sigh. "Someone is leaving them for me."

"Someone is leaving you hot chocolate packets?"

Yeah, I know. It totally sounds ridiculous. But I nod anyway.

She folds her arms. "I need more information."

"On my regular treadmill at the gym, under my windshield wiper, even at my favorite table in the library."

She snorts. "I'm going to ignore the fact you have a favorite treadmill at the gym. Clearly that boy needs to fuck you all the way out of his system, too."

"Who? Ares?" Was he the first guy that came to mind because I was dreaming about his fingers inside me? "It can't be him."

Her brows jump. "Why not?"

It's my turn to snort. "He'd have to know where the library is."

We both collapse into giggles. Being friends with Tori has reminded me what it's like to throw caution to the wind and belly laugh so hard that milk comes out your nose.

"Okay. Fair point, well made. That doesn't give any clue as to who we think it might be." She levels me with her Mom Stare. I've seen her give it to her son, Wyatt, a couple times, though it doesn't seem to have the same bone chilling effect on him as it does on me. "Are you holding out on me, bestie?" She wags her finger.

I'm not sure how her little boy doesn't spend his life terrified of her. She's a force.

"I have no idea. I've been chatting to a guy in chem class a little, but it's not like that." I shrug. "It's not."

Her lips curve into a smile as she shakes the baggie of hot chocolate at me. "Someone's into you. This is adorable. Master level observation. They clearly know you have a hot chocolate obsession. Oh!" She tosses it onto the table with the others. "Could it be Taryn? She's served you damn near daily for weeks now."

I arch a brow. "You think the bright, vibrant, extrovert barista has a thing for... me?" I hold up a finger to buy me some time as another wave of laughter rolls through my body. My whole being shakes with amusement as she watches, lips pursed.

"Opposites attract, El. I've seen it happen. There are movies and shit. And try to deflect all you want, *someone* is leaving you baggies of powder around campus." She offers me another grin. "Most students have a coke dealer; you have a cocoa dealer." Cracking up at her own joke, she needs a minute to regain her composure.

"That... or..." Her eyes widen. "Oh my god! Are you stealing gifts meant for someone else?"

Am I? Oh boy. It can't be possible, right?

My stomach sinks, as cold dread unfurls in my limbs. The first one was definitely for me. It was. It literally had my name on it. But the idea that it was a mistake still triggers my anxiety.

I pick up the sachet with my name on it, tracing my fingers over the ink. I silently talk myself through the mist of anxiety with logic and reason. Namely the fact that if they weren't for me, they wouldn't have been where I was. Every single time.

Whoever it was wouldn't have put it under my wiper blade if they didn't intend for me to have it.

"Yeah. They're definitely for you. Your name's on that one."

I jab the cocoa pouch at her. "Is it you? You know all about my habit. Heck, you even help fund it."

She nods. "I do. But it's not me. I promise. You've seen my handwriting. That's definitely guy writing—it's so... messy." She cringes. "Plus, I'd totally take credit if it was. I admit, I was going to get you the twelve pack for Christmas, but now I need to re-think my gift because someone's beaten me to it."

She looks genuinely butt hurt that someone stole her gift idea which warms something inside my chest while simultaneously reminding me that I need to start working on my own list for Christmas. It doesn't have many people on it: Dad, Victoria, and Wyatt. But I agonize over the right gift for everyone, so it's going to take a while.

Perhaps not for Hurricane Wyatt. He broke his favorite Hulk action figure a couple days ago while slamming him with the kitchen cabinet door. Who knew such an action would lead to such a consequence?

Well, turns out, his Mom did. But he didn't listen. He totally knew better, as I'm told three-year-olds do. Or at least he believed that Hulk would survive being slammed between two pieces of wood repeatedly. His little threenager heart shattered in front of my eyes, and mine shattered right along with him. I've already told Tori I'm getting him a replacement.

Victoria's hands slapping together jolt me out of my mind's wanderings. "I love a mystery. It's so romantic."

For someone whose ex ghosted her the second the two lines appeared on the stick, she is a hopeless romantic. She never let her experience with Wyatt's sperm donor impact her desire to find true love. Or at least her belief that it exists.

"You don't think it's... creepy?" I grab the milk out of the fridge. Now that she's suggested hot chocolate for breakfast, it's all I can think about. And it's not like I'm lacking in supplies.

"I think it's adorable. And I'm burning up inside with curiosity about who it could be. You're sure it's not Ares?"

At my raised eyebrows, she nods. "You're right. This is way too... sentimental, for that playboy."

At the mere mention of his name, talking about him, thinking about him, my body flares, nerve endings springing to life as details from my dream jump into my mind.

"Uh huh." She hands me one mug. "You're thinking about him. Probably that dirty dream I woke you up from. I feel bad for being a cock block. Or I guess an O-block." She passes the second cup to me with a grin. "Should we talk about his peen some more so you get more dirty dreams tonight while I'm not here?"

My insides fold in on themselves. I can't even manage a fake laugh. I'm too busy being consumed from the inside out by mortification. I can't believe she walked in on me doing... that.

Asleep Eloise has a lot to answer for.

Tori has opened the pantry and is rifling through the basket of marshmallow options. "You know, I hear it's not all that big."

I cough, eyes bulging.

When she's found what she's looking for in the pantry, she comes back into the kitchen. She gives me a bag of mini mallows before turning to the fridge and adding "mini mallows" to my magnetic whiteboard grocery list.

She waves the marker at me. "And I also hear he knows exactly what to do with it."

When I come skipping out of bio later that day, I stall out a few feet away from my vehicle. Another packet of chocolate is pinched between the window and the wiper blade.

I turn a slow circle, looking around in all directions for anyone I might know. I mean, I've been in class for hours, so it could have been anyone, at any time, but my instincts make me check all the same.

The only person I recognize is Ares. He's standing a little bit away, saying goodbye to some of his big, burly man friends. I reach over to grab the chocolate and get the heck away before I have to make eye contact with him again. I might die of embarrassment on the spot.

I don't even know if my dream was in any way accurate, but that doesn't matter. My body thinks it was, and my body knows he's close. It's already gotten about ten degrees hotter. My cheeks are hot. I stupidly sneak another glance at him.

He's locked on to my position and walking my way.

Dangit.

His eyes hold me captive as I will my body to keep moving, to get in the car and leave. But I still as he approaches.

"That from your boyfriend?" He jerks his chin to the cocoa in my hand.

I glance down at the packet, then back to him. No trace of the vulnerability I saw at the gym. He seems so... confident...

all the time. From experience, I know it gets exhausting holding your anxiety inside all the time.

And who does this guy think he is, anyway? Isn't that a personal question? What makes him think I want to talk to him about intimate details of my life?

Someone says hi to him as they walk past us, and Ares jerks his chin again. That arrogant head-tip-hello thing that guys do. I want to be icked out by his cockiness, but my gaze catches on the stubble on his chin, and I want to drag my teeth over it.

Yeah, I'm screwed. Would he notice if I started fanning my girl parts? He's paying such close attention to me that he'd notice.

His eyes search my face as though the answer to his question might be written there. I shake my head.

If someone were to take my temperature right now, I'd likely register a fever. My body is scorched all over, and the longer I stand in his presence, the more my skin sizzles. I need to get myself out of his space. The closer I am to this man, the more likely I am to combust.

"Do you have a boyfriend?" His eyebrow arches, his chocolate eyes twinkling as though he's contemplating saying something else.

What was he going to say? That if I have a boyfriend, it doesn't matter? That if I have a boyfriend, he could join us? I try to fight the shiver skating up my spine, but it makes me twitch involuntarily.

Oooooh, rats. I've gone and done it now. The temptation to scrunch my eyes shut until he disappears is so overwhelming. My heart is stammering along in my chest, and I'm sweating through the brown paper packet in my hand.

I shake my head again.

He hooks his knuckle under my chin. My hair falls away from my face as he tips my head. My breath catches somewhere in my throat on a strangled gasp as I'm forced to look him directly in the eye. Exposed. Vulnerable.

Ugly.

He's touching me. He's touching my face. My actual face. Swallowing down the panic, I don't smack him away this time.

My stomach tightens, and the urge to recoil is strong. No one touches my face. I barely even touch my face. If he goes near my cheek, I may cry right here in the middle of the street. Or vomit on him. That'd be one way to get rid of him, I suppose.

His other hand reaches for my hair. I dunno if he's going to stroke it, or move it but I flinch so hard, the packet of hot chocolate I was clutching tightly only a second ago falls to the ground.

He pauses, like he's reconsidering touching my hair. Is that because I winced? Or because he doesn't want to touch me?

"Cat got your tongue?"

I don't know if he didn't hear the cocoa hit the ground, or if he doesn't care, but he grazes his thumb over my bottom lip. It's hard to keep my body from arching into him.

Torn. My face is laid bare in front of him, burning under his appraising stare. It feels like fire ants crawling over my scar. But he's not visibly disgusted, he's not recoiling in horror, he's not looking at me with pity in his eyes.

Ugh. I want him to graze other parts of me, too, but I don't want to want it. I also want him to say dirty, dirty things with his tongue. And I don't want to want that either.

The contradiction is tying me in knots, and despite my shallow breaths and my on-fire face, he doesn't let me go. He holds my chin, tilting my head enough that I can fall into his bottomless stare.

His eyes glance down to my mouth, then back to my eyes. His tongue sneaks out to dampen his lips. Is his tongue pierced too? If Tori is right about his pierced manhood, he could have other piercings, too.

I urge my voice to come out so I'm not stuck here, standing mute, staring into the enchanting eyes of the man I dreamt of pressed up against me last night. "I..." My voice is crusty, like I haven't had a drink for weeks. I clear my throat and try again. "I don't know who they're from."

He leans closer, his breath tickling my skin like in my dream. The way he angles my head makes my hair fall back on one side. Thankfully, it's my good side. His eyes rake along my jaw as though he's contemplating nibbling on it, and I'll be damned if I don't quietly pray to God that he does just that, willing my dream to come to life right here in the street.

"Secret admirer?" He cocks his head to the side, humor dancing in his eyes. "Interesting." He looks down at where our skin is connected. Does he feel anything at the touch? I can't tell from his face, but my chin definitely knows he's there, and when he pulls back his hand, I ache to lean forward so he touches me again.

What in the world is wrong with me? This man must be a wizard, because as anxious as I can be sometimes, I've never been so boy-struck that I stand nodding at someone without the ability to speak.

Maybe I'm stunned by his confidence. That has to be what it is.

"We have back-to-back games home tonight and away tomorrow, but we're having a party at the hockey house the night after. You want to flush out your secret admirer by being my date?"

I fight the urge to roll my eyes. Of course the only possible way to identify who is leaving me gifts is to tap into some caveman jealousy by being seen with someone else. Do boys beat on their bare chests and grunt at themselves in the mirror when they're alone?

I can't tell if he's serious. I also can't tell if he actually wants me to be his date or if he's offering it to me as some kind of charity gesture.

I know he doesn't know me, but he really, *really* doesn't know me if he thinks I'd be down for a childish act to try to make someone else jealous.

His eyes skim my face again, as though scanning my every thought racing through my mind, and his grin grows wider. "How about an exchange? A trade? I'll take you to our party, and you can do something for me."

H-e-double-hockey-sticks, no!

I've read books about Fae. If I make a bargain with him, it means he'll eat my soul or something else equally dramatic.

And I'm absolutely not thinking about him eating something else right now. Nope.

"Thanks, but I'm good." I untangle myself from his web of charm and allure and suck in a breath of fresh air. Except it's not fresh air, it's Ares. I get a full shot of *eau de Ares* right into my nostrils, and I want to turn around and sniff him.

Forcing myself into the car, I don't look at him again as I drive off. I leave the mischievous man with the magnetism of a siren and the chiseled jaw of a marble god statue in my rearview.

The audacity of that demigod. Oh hey, let me solve all the world's problems with my delicious manliness. Swagger, swagger.

Like the hockey house party is the center of the entire universe. I bet he thinks everyone with a brain cell wants to be at his dumb kegger. While in reality, anyone with half a brain cell would likely rather be anywhere else.

Ugh.

I don't fight the eye roll this time. Nor do I let myself relive how delicious he actually is.

My last boyfriend was as boring as watching paint dry,

even for me—I'm not exactly an exciting, life on the edge kind of girl. But I certainly don't date arrogant, cocky, douche nozzles who think their penis is the be all and end all of civilization.

But I also can't lie that the idea of going on a date with him is ringing every bell in my head, my heart, and my lady bits.

This is bad. This is very, very bad.

CHAPTER 9
Ares

The weirdest pre-game meal I've ever seen is Raffi's big-ass bowl of cheese. He's no Phil Kessel, but it's like he thinks if he eats enough cheese, he might be. I'm glad I spend the game between the pipes. I can't imagine the stench he leaves in his wake when he's out on the ice.

Maybe that's his tactic, gas our opponents with his ass.

A kid behind me has been chirping for the whole fucking game. He's dressed in a Kalamazoo shirt with what looks to be a Burger King crown on his head. Kid's got balls. Coming to a Raccoons' game dressed in our opponent's colors and yelling at the home team's goalie. He gives no fucks, and I kinda love it.

It's fueled my fire. Since Coach has let me off the bench I've stood on my head for each and every game. We play Kalamazoo again tomorrow in Michigan, and they're a tough team to beat in their home barn.

I'm going to give this kid behind me my stick when the game is over. Sure, he's with the visiting team, but kids with such a passion for hockey should be encouraged. And I need a new stick anyway.

The clock counts down, and the final buzzer sounds. I pull out the silver Sharpie I've had tucked in my pants and scrawl a message on the blade of the stick.

Good chirps! Take it easy on me next time.

Then I sign my name.

"Hey, kid!"

The kid's eyes widen, and he hides behind the big dude he's standing next to. Brother? Father? Either way the kid's lost his confidence now that the game is over, and I'm addressing him directly.

I pull off my mask, leaving it on top of my net before gesturing for him and his accomplice to follow me to a part of the plexi that isn't covered by protective netting.

I reach my stick up over the boards and drop it into the older guy's hands. He hands it to the mouthy little guy who looks at it, looks at me, and his face breaks into a wide smile before he flips me off and takes off running up the stairs.

I can't help but laugh. He reminds me of me at his age. I turn to see Hayes skating toward me, shaking his head. He launches himself at me for our post-game hug. "Den?"

"Damn straight. I need a burger after that game."

"Kid kept chirping at ya, eh?"

I nod. "Little shit flipped me off after I gave him my stick, too."

He laughs. "I saw. It'll be up on an online auction before dawn."

He grabs me in a side hug, patting my shoulder pads as we skate off the ice. It's another solid win in the bag, but it somehow feels hollow. It's not that the Kings didn't test us as a team—they did. I have the sweat dripping from my ball sack to prove it.

I just... I dunno what it is. I scan the dispersing crowd for a flash of brightly colored hair, but I come up empty. My stomach sinks a little, and I don't quite understand it.

When we get to The Den, I order a burger and an alcohol-free beer 'cause I know they'll serve me liquor, and if I let myself drink, I'll end up sliding into a dark space tonight. It's an odd moment of clarity, and right now I'm in control of myself, but I could easily not be. Not to mention, if they served me liquor, they'd lose their license.

The Den is above reproach—it was never one of my haunts when I was wasted. They have an extensive alcohol-free range too, which makes it easier for the younger players on the team to hang out.

I continue my search for Eloise like somehow my desire to see her will make her appear. I haven't seen the pink haired pixie since before last weekend's double header against Duluth—we split those games, losing at home and winning at the Dragon's barn—but I thought I had her within reach.

I was sure she'd want to come to the hockey party. Almost every time I see her, she's by herself. Who wouldn't want to go to a party full of cool people and make some friends? I thought I was being nice by asking her to go.

Guess not.

From the look on her face, I asked her to excise a lobe of her liver and hand it over so I could gnaw on it right in front of her.

I fucked up. I dunno how, or what I did, but she wasn't thrilled. Or so her glare said, anyway.

I can't help it. My brain goes weird when I see her. She makes me nervous. I'm not used to nervous.

Suave, charming, charismatic... that's usually where I hang out.

It's her intelligence. I Googled her. I know, I know, pathetic, needy, and yes, fine, somewhat obsessive and stalker-ish, but I was curious, and she has a Google presence.

I wasn't wrong—the girl is smart. Very smart. Too fucking

smart for the likes of me, and yet like a moth to a flame I'm drawn to her.

I want her.

From the flush of her cheeks, and the hitch in her breath when I stood next to her, I thought she wanted me too. But I'm starting to think that was an instinctive reaction to the fact I had my hand on her face.

When I say she's smart, I'm not exaggerating. She wasn't *just* a nerd in high school, she was captain of the nerds. She was president of her high school academic decathlon team, a science Olympiad, whatever the hell that is, captain of the chess club, model UN, Spanish club... the list seems endless.

There are any number of photos of her smiling with various academic awards. She looks different in the photos. Her hair isn't pink, for one. Instead, her hair is waist length, coffee colored, and wavy. In one, it's short and bright blue.

A sparkle's in her eyes in the pictures that she doesn't seem to have anymore, and I bet that's connected to the news article I found about the accident that scarred her face.

The article said she lost her mom, but from the picture, her mom looked young enough to be her big sister. That moment took the spark from Eloise's eyes. The moment that changed her entire life.

She probably dyes her hair pink to distract people from the grooves on her cheek, too. Classic misdirect. I've done it, too. Hell, I've lived it.

Her injuries made it onto the internet too. A plastic surgeon published a paper on the work he did to reconstruct her face. In truth, I can't figure out how he did it. Her face was so damaged, and he did a really good job of rebuilding it, like an artist. She's still every bit as gorgeous as she was before.

I could easily use Dad's connections at the local precinct to pull details on the accident, but that's most definitely a step too far. Even my obsessive personality knows that. It's tempting though.

Except, I want *her* to tell me. I want her to open up to me and share those details with me herself. But I can't crack her shell. Hell, I can't even get her to tell me what the weather's like outside. Huh. I doubt I could get her to pee on me if I was on fire.

I can't say golden showers are my kink, but if it made her talk to me, I'd let her pee on me.

It could be anxiety, my wealth, or probably more likely, my arrogance, but something about me makes her clam up whenever I get anywhere near her. It took all I had not to grab her pretty pink head and kiss her where she stood last week. And this week, I've spent my time searching her out to leave her little gifts that make her smile. But tonight, she's not around. I can't see her, I can't feel her, and I'm disappointed.

She's avoiding me, that's probably my pride and vanity talking. People say they're my biggest flaws. I have bigger ones, like being a fuckboy jackass, but I'm feeling... things... about this girl I don't even know, that I shouldn't be experiencing.

Things I haven't felt in a while.

Things I really have no desire to feel.

Casual hookups and booty calls are my thing. One-and-done is the way to go.

Except now, all of a sudden, they're not.. If they were, I wouldn't be trying to get her to see me. I mean *really* see me. I wouldn't be planting little packets of fancy hot chocolate everywhere she goes, just so I can see her smile. Even if only for a second.

Familiar beady eyes meet mine across the bar. One of my old cocaine dealers stares me down, head tipped in an all too comfortable suggestion. My mouth dries, heart pounds. I'm not spiraling, I'm not in a mental health crisis, and all things considered I'd say I'm doing pretty fucking well. But the allure of the adrenaline shot and euphoria from even one hit of the white powder claws at me.

I give him an almost imperceptible shake of my head. Whatever he's selling, I'm not buying.

Cabrón won't back down, though. He pushes back from his chair, adjusts his pants, and heads my way, weaving through my teammates to get to me. He shoulders me, hand outstretched. I'm sure a white bag is nestled in the hand he's trying to brush against mine, but I'm not interested.

Temptation tickles my nerves as I force breaths in and out of my body. I don't need it, I don't want it, and I have no intention of starting a fight with this guy. He has connections I'd rather not piss off by starting shit.

Another shake of my head seems to dissuade him from persisting. "You know where to find me."

He leaves, but the invitation doesn't leave with him. The lure, the pull, the addiction. The last sips of my non-alcoholic beer don't hit the spot anymore, and my jittery leg suggests I need to get the fuck out of here before I do something I'll regret.

Going out tonight has not improved my mood any. I don't want to go dancing either, so I abandon my half-eaten burger, make my excuses, and decide to walk home to my pig. Maybe the cool October air will blow the cobwebs from my gray matter and kick my sour mood in the balls. I'm not naive enough to think it'll do anything from this all body itch I can't scratch.

Spotting lights down the block I didn't expect, I detour toward Bitches Brew. They must have extended their opening times, and I'm not at all mad about it. In fact, I might even get myself a delicious hot chocolate while I'm picking up a couple packets for my favorite pink-haired sprite.

The goddess herself comes walking out of the café, alone,

eyes fixed on the ground in front of her feet and crashes right into me.

Her head snaps up on a gasp. If I wasn't already simmering mad at her for being reckless and walking to her car alone this late, it would be adorable.

Our eyes meet. I reach out and brush her hair back from her face and her arms tremble, clutching books against her chest. She doesn't even have her keys out of her backpack, ready to unlock her car. *¿Qué coño?*

A group of guys comes out of the coffee shop behind her, and I snarl at them like a feral animal. Grabbing her by the elbow, I guide her out of their way, and we're silent as they pass.

My chest heaves. I have no idea why I'm feeling so protective, so possessive of someone who isn't mine, other than the fact it's late at night, and the idea of anyone laying hands on her against her will makes me homicidal.

I know how common it is for women to be assaulted. There's a reason—other than the fact it pisses Papá off for *his* son to be studying gender studies—that my major and minor are what they are. Our cousin was brutally raped when I was twelve. They never caught the guy.

Mom's complacency about not pursuing the rapist bedded under my skin. I asked her why she didn't want justice for Camila, and her haunted expression as she recounted the statistics for prosecuting rape will stay with me forever.

I haven't told anyone other than my sister, Athena, but even if I make it to the NHL, I want to be an advocate for survivors of sexual assault when I graduate. If I graduate. I want to fight for people who have had the worst crimes in the world committed against them. People who have had their "no" disrespected and been touched without their consent, people who believe fighting for their own justice isn't worth it.

I might be a player, an asshole, and hell yes, I love to fuck and be fucked, but no means fucking no.

The twins don't know, not because I think they'll laugh or anything, but because I'm not sure I can maintain the grades I need to graduate. Apollo tried to talk me into an easier minor when I signed up for college, but I was determined. As much as I love him, that fucker will definitely stick me with an "I told you so," if I fuck it up. Best to keep my plans to myself until I know for sure whether I'm capable of achieving them.

Too many guys take advantage of drunk girls, and I haven't yet met a single woman who has either not been assaulted herself, or doesn't know someone who has. It's fucking sickening.

I'm irrationally upended right now. She should be fine walking to her car. She's not mine to feel this way about, and yet...

She stares up at me from behind her pink curtains. Her hair dye has faded, but her lips are vibrant, glossy, and calling to me.

Her brow is wrinkled, but she doesn't seem mad, only confused. I take a step toward her, and she shuffles back two. I stop my advance, not wanting to crowd her or make her feel trapped. Her back meets the exposed brick of the coffee shop, and a little puff of air escapes her.

"You shouldn't be out here alone late at night." I'm still staring at her lips, so when her tongue slips out and glides between them, I almost jizz my fucking pants.

What the hell is wrong with me?

Screw that. What the hell is so different about this girl that makes me want her so fucking badly?

Am I really such a goner for kindness and compassion? I've seen her since I lost my shit at the gym over Thiago showing up again, but she hasn't shown me pity. She hasn't pressed me to talk to her or tell her what happened, and she doesn't seem to be afraid after witnessing my fight with the wall.

She emanates strength. She's strong in ways I wish I could be, and her softness, her gentleness... I want her more intensely than anyone else I've ever been with.

I realize I'm crowding her. Out alone late at night, she's probably now afraid of me, the caveman, basically thumping his chest at the other guys who came out of the building. Except when I take half a step back, I could swear she leans forward.

"I can take care of myself, Ares."

Fuck. Something about the way my name rolls off her tongue wakes me up in all the right places.

"You don't have to." You could let me. The last part goes unsaid, but my meaning is clear.

Her face softens, and she tilts her head like she wasn't prepared for what came tumbling out of my mouth. I wasn't either. I don't do this kind of emotional... whatever the fuck is happening with this girl.

Instead of letting the silence hang between us, instead of answering the unasked questions lingering in her eyes, I slide my hand along her jaw and brush my thumb across her cheek bone.

It's an asshole move.

She's uncomfortable with her scars, and I'm touching her without her explicit consent, but I need her to know. I need to show her that her scars don't bother me. We all have them, some outside on our skin, some inside. Scars remind us that we've lived, taken chances, endured, *felt*. Anyone who isn't scarred, isn't living, they're just existing.

She sucks in a slow, trembling breath as her eyes flicker closed.

I can't kiss her without her permission, and I can't see her eyes to get even a clue as to what she might be thinking, so I lean into her, waiting. I need her to say something, anything: stop, go, *what the fuck, Ares?* I'll take any of it.

I feel like an idiot standing caressing her face, but instead of tense muscles and her glaring up at me, she's tipped her head back ever so slightly. It's probably because I'm not holding the scarred side of her face, but a not-small part of me hopes she's relaxing because it's me holding her.

Her breathing has evened out, her tits sweep up and down my chest with every slow breath she takes, but her heartbeat flutters and races in her neck under my hand.

She's like a duck on a lake—cool, calm, the picture of composure. But below the surface, her little feet are paddling frantically to keep her afloat.

"I want to kiss you, Eloise."

Her eyes spring open, and her lips part enough to draw my attention back to them. Is her lipstick long-lasting? Or would I end up with hot pink smudges on my dick?

I can't help my wandering thoughts. I tried to ignore it, but I've wanted this woman from the moment I saw her in my fucking manicure chair, and every time I see her, the want grows.

So does my dick.

"Why?" Her eyes have hardened, her lips are set in a thin line. Her chin tilt means something else now. Mistrust, cynicism, suspicion.

What does she mean, why? Why is she mistrustful now but acted like she wanted me to kiss her before I actually said it? Why does anyone want to kiss anyone? Because they're attracted to them. What am I missing?

Maybe I'm not missing anything, maybe she's been hurt before, maybe she's just thinking about my reputation, who the fuck knows?

One thing's for sure, though. I want nothing more than to press her into the wall so the bricks leave an imprint on her skin while I kiss her senseless. But if that's not what she wants, I need to give her room to feel comfortable enough to say no. Creating a little more space between us, I keep my hand cupping her face, and decide to go with the truth.

"I think you're beautiful, Eloise."

Her breath hitches at my words, and she leans into me, exerting pressure on my hand. Her jaw quivers, and her eyelids flutter as though she's struggling to hold back the tears welling in her eyes in the dim light.

"Now I know you're lying."

It's not that this woman doesn't want me to kiss her, but she thinks she's somehow unworthy, and that's a crock of shit I won't tolerate.

Instead of dropping my hand and walking away, I cup the other side of her face too. She cringes and tries to flinch away from my touch. My thumb grazes over the bumps of scar tissue on her cheek as her tears trickle down her face.

"Look at me, Eloise."

She shakes her head, making more tears course down her cheeks.

"Open your eyes, *tesoro*."

At that, her eyes open. If I wasn't paying attention, I'd miss the flicker of a smile that ghosts across her face.

Something about the way she's staring at me unfurls the knot in my chest. I don't give nicknames to people I don't know well. I don't let them in. But this woman, this beautiful woman crying into my hands... she's already somehow worked her way behind my main line of defense.

"I've wanted to kiss you from the first time I saw you, Eloise. You're beautiful. You're smart as hell, and that scares the shit out of me. And I really don't know how to talk to you."

Wow. I've never been so open and vulnerable in my entire existence. And I'm not sure I like it.

Usually I use my charm, my smile, my family name to get the things I want in life, but right now... I dunno. That wouldn't work, for one. And for two, this girl is different, and she deserves something more than my usual spiel.

It's out now, and I can't take it back. Instead of feeling better at having told her the truth, I want to slip back behind my fuck boy mask and pull my veil of confidence back over me.

I can't read the expression on her face. And it occurs to me that I've been standing here cupping her face for what could be an uncomfortably long time for her. Especially considering the tears and all.

I move my hand, but don't let go yet. Sweeping back her hair, I plant a chaste kiss on the scarred side of her face. Her body is tense and doesn't relax any as I slide my cheek against hers so I can whisper in her ear.

"I want to kiss you, *tesoro*. More than I think you realize. But I don't want to make you any more uncomfortable than I already have. So, I'm going to let you go about your business. But I'll kiss you when you ask me to."

I realize how cocky that sounds, and for once, it's not what I meant, so I hurry to correct myself. "If you ask me to."

Her face moves against mine, and I know without looking that she's smiling. I feel exposed, self-conscious, and I'm not sure I like the curiosity lingering in her gaze when I pull my head away from hers and meet her eyes.

I'm not generally above using the means available to me to get what I want. But for once, this isn't a story I'm spinning. It's not a means to an end; it's not my usual bullshit, and a piece of me wishes I'd gone with my everyday asshole persona. Papá always says vulnerability is dangerous, and that's a hard narrative to shake. Eloise makes me vulnerable, exposed, and unprotected. It's a sensation that's tempting to lean into, and I don't like *that*, and the potential loss of control that comes along with it, not one little bit.

CHAPTER 10
Eloise

I want him to kiss me. I want him to kiss me so badly that I've had to put my books down so I don't drop them. I ball my hands by my sides to stop myself from gripping his shirt in my fists and not letting him leave until he does.

I don't get why he wants to. Is this a cruel joke to him? Was he dared to kiss me by one of his jock friends?

I... maybe?

I just....

I don't know.

From the vulnerability painted across his beautiful features right now as he stares at me under the amber glow of the streetlight, all I see is truth. Maybe it's all I want to see, but I can't find a single glimmer of asshattery or bravado on his face.

I don't know what to do with that. It would be easier for me to accept if it was a dare or wager—that he was sent to kiss the girl with the scarred face.

But the way he's looking at me, the way his thumb caressed the gnarled skin on my cheek, none of this feels fake.

He searches my face, his eyes flickering back and forth as

he looks me over, and then he takes another step back. I want to cry out, I want to object, protest, make him come back, but I'm not sure how. I respect the heck out of him for being so protective of my space, of my feelings, for needing my consent.

But the voice in the back of my head says he can't possibly want to kiss me.

My high school boyfriend, my first and only, messed me up. We weren't together all that long. He was older, and I thought he cared. But he only wanted a hole to put it in. Any time we spent together was alone and almost always for sex. Any time we slept together, it was with him behind me. At first, he told me it was his preference, but after a while I figured out that he didn't want to look at my scars.

So deeply ashamed that I hadn't realized what he was doing sooner, I let him take what he needed from me. Too embarrassed to voice my feelings out loud. I stopped answering his calls shortly after I realized what was happening, and it wasn't long after that he stopped calling at all.

Looking back, I can see how desperate I was for someone, anyone to touch me, to make me feel like I wasn't a monster, to make me feel anything but the sadness I was encased in. So tangled up in grief and self-loathing, it blinded me from the truth of the relationship.

I almost snort. Relationship. He never took me out anywhere where anyone could see me, either. Restaurants with low lighting every now and then, the movie theater sometimes, but for the most part we hung out at his parents' place and never when anyone else was home.

He was ashamed of me.

Ares de la Peña lives his life in the light.

I live in the shadows.

Nothing good could ever come from him kissing me.

And yet... my entire body is screaming at me not to let him leave. He's staring at me like he's waiting for me to say something, anything. He scrubs the back of his neck awkwardly, like he's faced with a puzzle he can't figure out before nodding. "Okay. I, uh. Okay."

I almost laugh at his response. It's probably a rare instance for him to be faced with a girl who doesn't immediately throw her panties at him and spread her legs. He looks completely flummoxed. It's kind of adorable.

I mean, I get it. He is... well... he's the most delicious specimen of a man I've ever seen.

But the raw vulnerability on his face, in his voice... this can't be a joke, right?

"Ares?" I don't know what else to say. I don't seem to have words beyond choking out his name, but it's enough.

His head jerks up, and he moves back into my space. My traitorous body responds, heaving out a sigh as his warmth steps toward me.

He cants his head. *"¿Sí?"*

I refuse to come undone at him speaking to me in Spanish. I mean, why is Spanish so dreamy? Ugh. What is it about a man who can speak another language that makes me tremble inside?

He's staring at my lips like he wants to take a bite out of me.

The worst part is, I want him to.

I suck in an unsteady breath. *"Bésame."*

It's only one word, and it's whispered on an exhale, but the smile that lights up his face has me wishing I'd said it sooner. He's beautiful when he smiles. I mean, when he really smiles.

He's not ugly when he flashes his playboy grin, but this... this smile... it takes my breath away.

He doesn't say another word as he steps deeper into the space between us. My back grinds up against the edges of the rough bricks on the wall behind me again. I'll have scrapes and bruises tomorrow, but I don't care. I guess it'll be proof that this did happen. Because I'm going to wake up and think it was all a dream.

I gulp. It's almost comical, but I can't help it.

Ares de la Peña is going to kiss me, and I'm going to do my level best to shut up my inner monologue and let myself enjoy it. I'm not going to be another notch on his bedpost, or another conquest for him to leave in his wake, but I will let myself kiss him.

Because tomorrow he's going to wake up and realize that I'm not a great kisser, I'm not beautiful, or whatever bet he's made with his friends will be over.

And yet, as he pins me to the wall with his body and slants his mouth over mine, I feel anything but cheap, like a priceless Ming vase, or a rare bottle of Champagne. His hands skim up my sides, bracing me against the wall as his lips brush against mine.

He's tender, yet firm. Not demanding or aggressive. My mouth opens to him on a sigh, and his tongue brushes against mine. I moan, which makes him press harder into me.

That's his penis pushing against my thigh. I'd love to say I'm too evolved to care that he's hard, but I'm not. It's the single hottest thing I've ever experienced. I made Ares de la Peña get a hard-on. It's a powerful awareness.

His tongue explores my mouth as he kisses me with a passion I've only ever dreamed of. His thumbs have found their way under my sweater, but they're staying at my waist, brushing back and forth over the skin above my hips as he kisses me. His gentle caresses scorch my skin.

It's like he's opened all the windows on the first day of spring. He smells like shower gel and tastes like mint. My fingers have taken on a mind of their own and claw at his shirt. He presses against me, pinning me to the wall without using his hands. His leg finds its way between mine, and I'm doing my level best not to dry hump him right here in the street.

The kiss shifts, we've gone from kissing, to needing. I want him to consume me, to possess me, to light me on fire from the inside. He fists my hair, and I pant, whimpering into his mouth as he owns every inch of me against the coffee shop.

Somewhere in the distance a wolf whistle pierces the air as Ares's fingertips curl into my waist like he's fighting the urge to do more, to want more, to take more.

A horn honks a few blocks away, but it's the snarky "Get a room," some girl quips on her way out of the coffee shop that cuts through my horny stupor.

I ignore every single tingling nerve ending in my body, brace my hands on his shoulders, and push. At least, I think I do. Granted, I'm not sure if I'm trying to convince him or myself that we should stop, but to his credit (and my surprising disappointment), he pulls away. Our lips make a smacking sound as we separate, and we both stare at each other, panting shaky, ragged breaths making little puffs of steam in the cold air.

My brain doesn't want to reengage. I can't find words or move. I don't know how to talk or even exist right now. It's like I've needed that kiss for a lifetime. Now that I've had it, all I want is another.

Holy moly! That was... life changing.

I blink, because it seems to be the only thing I can do right now, and my mind scrambles to catch up. I kissed Ares de la Peña. In the street. My fingers drift to my swollen lips, and I pray that my "kiss proof" lipstick isn't smeared across my face.

I probably look like I've been dragged through a hedge backwards. I'm torn between not caring and caring way too much.

I preferred it when he was an untouchable playboy to me.

Now he's human. And he's staring at me like that was just the appetizer.

My phone rings in my backpack, and we both stare at it. Most people under the age of thirty-five don't use their ringer, but Dad worries. It's a little thing I do so I don't miss his calls, something that brings him a little peace of mind.

Oops. We're still staring. Is my brain this foggy because Ares is standing so close to me? Or is it possible for someone to literally kiss the intelligence out of you?

I'm starting to wonder.

My phone doesn't stop ringing. Its shrill noise cuts through the night air. I bet if I hadn't been kissed until my body burned, I'd be pretty cold right now. Maybe that's why I can't feel my toes, and it actually had nothing to do with Ares.

"Answer your phone, *tesoro*." His voice is gravely, like he just woke up, and it sends a ripple of desire through me. I want to grab his belt and tug him to me. I want to kiss him all over again.

I rummage in my bag without breaking eye contact, but I can't find my stupid cell, so I tear my eyes away from Ares and hope he's still standing there when I find it.

Dad's name and picture light up the screen, and my insides deflate. I need to go. I need to call Dad. I need to go back to my Cinderella life after having the kiss of a lifetime with as close to a real life—albeit playboy—prince I'm ever going to get.

"I better take this."

He looks down at the phone in my hand, nods, and takes a step back. "*A po' 'ta bien*."

He watches me, silent, as I pull my keys from my bag and start to walk to my car. What else can I do? Awkwardly wait for Dad to finish checking in so we can, what? Talk about whatever that heck was?

"Wait."

I stop dead in my tracks and risk a glance behind me over my shoulder. Yup. Still there. Still Ares de la Peña.

"Can I get your number?"

Ares has glitter on his lips. I did that. It's from my hot chocolate. I kissed glitter onto Ares de la Peña's mouth. My heart spasms again.

Dad's first call ended, and he's calling back. It's only a matter of time before he gives up and calls the police— wouldn't be the first time. I don't have long to let my mind yell that it's a bad idea to make myself more accessible to this man.

I pick up the call from Dad, tuck the phone between my chin and shoulder and say hi, and type out my number onto Ares's screen. When he pockets his phone, he picks up my hand and plants the sexiest, swooniest, most panty-melting kiss on the back of my hand before ushering me toward my car.

How does he know which car is mine?

That's a thought for another time because Dad isn't thrilled at being kept waiting.

I listen to the scolding for not answering right away for a second before starting the car and pulling away from the curb. Dad's talking, but I'm not really sure what he's saying. My fingers sweep back and forth across my lips.

"Eloise? Eloise?"

I blink and glance down at my phone, the line is still active.

"Yeah, Daddy?"

"Don't 'yeah, Daddy?' me. You're not paying attention. To me or the road."

My spine stiffens, and I glance in the rearview. It's dark, so I can't tell who is behind me, but I'd bet my socks it's Dad.

"You're following me?"

I turn onto I-380 and check my speed. This stretch of road

is notorious for speeding tickets, and right now I don't want to give Dad anything else to complain about.

"I got home, and you weren't there. I figured you'd be studying, not necking some asshole kid at the side of a coffee shop like a cheap tramp."

Shame coats my body like glue. If I didn't have to keep both hands on the steering wheel, I'd hide my face with them. I can't believe he saw that. My dad. Oh. My. Goodness. This... this is so embarrassing.

I want to change direction and drive somewhere, anywhere else.

"I used the 'find my friend' thing you taught me to use, and I was going to surprise you with a hot chocolate. Turns out, it was me who got the surprise."

My entire body cringes. This is painful. I feel like I'm twelve years old, and I can't fight the tears as they course down my face. For the first time in I can't remember how long, I felt alive, and now he's taking that from me, turning it into something cheap, something wrong. I know wrong. My ex was wrong. This... this doesn't feel at all like that.

Someone other than me touched my face, my gnarled, ugly, broken face, and breathed life into my gnarled, ugly, broken heart.

"Daddy, I—"

"I'm going to be having words with your aunt Maureen. She told me she'd spoken to you last week about getting out more, going and doing *normal* things. She didn't mean this, Eloise."

How the hell does he know what she meant? Ugh. That was unkind, and I stop the words from coming out of my mouth, but they coat my tongue with a bitter taste.

I talk to Aunt Maureen—Mom's sister—once a month, and it's always the same message. Don't let the accident ruin your life. Go and be a normal kid. Your mom would want you to live, not exist.

I talk to Dad every night, even if it's a sixty second check up on how the day went and to let him know I'm home safe and sound. Even though he spends a lot of time on the road, and we don't see much of each other anymore, he always worries about me.

I can't say I blame him. He almost lost both his wife and his daughter in a major car accident. That's left a lasting impact on all of us. Knowing he's out on the road every day twists me up inside, so hearing his voice before I lie down every night is usually a comfort to me, too.

But not tonight.

Tonight, it's like nails on a chalkboard. I drive home listening to the lecture, knowing I'll get it all over again when we get back to the house. My tears stop, but my mental running commentary doesn't. I keep thinking of things I want to say back to him, but I never will.

Never. It's not that I'm afraid he'll hurt me or anything— it's not worth the argument. Any time we disagree, he shouts loudest until I can't fight anymore, and I give up.

I always back down. Every single time. And hours later, I think of all the things I should have said to him, but I never bring it back up. I never re-start the argument, because we'd go around and around in circles all over again, and I don't have the heckin' energy. Even if I'm right.

And sometimes I am. I have to be. I can't always be wrong, even if he is my dad.

"Eloise." His stern voice pulls me out of my internal monologue once more.

It's on the tip of my tongue to snap at him. To tell him to leave me the heck alone. But I don't. I bite my bottom lip and shelve it, like I always do.

The fight deflates out of me as I pull into the driveway. "Yeah, Dad?"

"We'll talk about this inside."

I'd love to say we won't. I'd love to tell him to go screw himself. But at the end of the day, he's really all I have left in this world. Mom's death changed both of us. It made him harder, colder, angrier, and if I thought my parents were over-protective before Mom died, boy, did I learn how much more my dad was on his own.

Technically, I'm a grown adult. But I don't think Dad will ever consider me that way. To him, I'm the little girl who needs Band-Aids for grazes on her knees, who wears My Little Pony shirts, and who can't make a decision over anything.

To him, I'm the girl who needs her parents to do everything for her, including protecting her from herself.

Sometimes I wish I could find the words to tell him how much I resent it. But for as smart as I am, my years of instruction at school are of no use to me when he starts yelling. My words vanish, and I shut down. I want the argument to be over, so I stay quiet and let him rant his way through whatever he needs to say.

I make my way inside and head for my bedroom.

"We aren't finished here, young lady."

Except, I am. "I'm tired, Dad. Can we talk about this in the morning, please?"

Letting him know that he can yell at me some more the next day usually works, and I hold my breath as I reach out for my bedroom door handle. Please, please tell me he's going to let me sleep.

After a longer pause than I'd like, telling me he's pretty darn ticked off, a resigned sigh falls between us. "Fine. In the morning."

Ha! I fist pump internally. Joke's on him. I'm going to get up before the birds and be gone before he's even awake. I can't ever escape a confrontation with him, but I can make it easier to stomach. Staring into his disappointed eyes, consternation painted across his face, as his booming voice reverberates around the house, it's essentially my idea of hell.

At least over the phone I can turn the volume down, and I don't have to look at his sad eyes.

I strip and contemplate falling into bed butt-naked. But with Dad home, I don't want to risk things getting even more awkward between us. God knows I'll need a drink or something during the night and bump into him.

I put on an oversized graphic tee and some pj pants I left hanging over the chair at the foot of the bed and snuggle under my blankets. My phone chimes from across the room. I roll my eyes and turn over.

I don't need it.

I don't.

Except, what if it's Ares. What if our kiss is still making his lips tingle?

I throw back the covers with a dramatic sigh. It's probably a goodnight message from Dad to remind me he loves me. He sometimes seems to forget about that when he's hassling me about things, but texts me after the fact like he's trying to remind both of us.

I should probably reassure him that I haven't climbed out the window and run away, leaving my phone in my bedroom for him to track. I'd love to say that hasn't happened, either, but before Mom died, I ran away from home twice. Both times I was intent on going to live with Aunt Maureen, both times my parents found me at the end of the road trying to figure out which way I needed to go to get to Illinois.

Geography has never been my strong suit.

The phone vibrates again as I pick it up. The first message was from an unknown number that makes my heart race. If I could pull it out of my chest, wag my finger at it and give it a stern talking to, I would.

The new text is from Dad. As expected, it's telling me he loves me and wishing me goodnight. I reply, telling him I love him, too. Because despite all his misdirected anger, and his overprotectiveness, I really do.

I climb back into bed and hover my thumb over the other new message. I knew in my gut it was from Ares before I even picked up the phone, but seeing him calling me his treasure in Spanish on the screen makes me blush all over.

I shove my phone under the blankets.

His.

My stomach flips, and my heart flutters like the wings of a hummingbird flap against my ribcage. I need to stop this freight train right now. I'm trying to convince myself that it's not Ares, specifically. It's the fact that someone, anyone, is paying any romantic attention to me.

All I've wanted, for the longest time, is for someone to look at me and see me, to *really* see me, not the scars on my face, not my trauma, but me. He kissed me like I was a regular girl, and a seed of hope bloomed to life inside my soul. My world stopped turning.

Maybe I'm not broken beyond love after all.

Maybe there is someone out there who could be with me despite my injuries and twisted skin. My entire being aches to have someone's arms wrapped around me.

My phone buzzes on my chest. I sniff, my face wet from tears. I risk looking at my screen— it's Ares again. I will myself to ignore it, to tuck the phone under my pillow, but the lure of the delicious Dominican is too strong. Curiosity burns my insides. I need to know what he's saying to me.

My screen is blurry; the tears won't stop. Blinking seems to make it all worse, so I let them fall. I turn into my pillow and cry until my throat is raw and my chest aches. This isn't new. My pillow is intimately acquainted with the taste of my tears.

I don't know how long I've cried by the time I purge my system, but my pillow is so wet I need to flip it over.

It's probably too late to reply to Ares, but I open his messages. The first one asks me to let him know I got home okay, and I melt. My lip quivers, my eyes well, and my fragile heart threatens to crack right down the middle.

The second one asks if I got the first one, and if I regretted letting him kiss me. His vulnerability strikes in my chest. From everything I've read about him and seen with my own two eyes, I bet he doesn't expose this piece of himself very often.

So why me? I don't understand it, but I like it.

Eloise: I'm sorry if this wakes you. I'm home safe and sound.

I pause. I don't want to lie to him, but the thought of telling him the truth feels even worse.

Eloise: I was talking to my dad.

I cringe when I hit send. I hate lying. I suck at it and have a terrible poker face.

Ares: You can wake me any time. Regrets?

My heart swells. Is he this charming and charismatic with everyone? He has to be. I've seen the girls swoon and giggle when he's near. He knows the effect he has on women. This has to be part of his performance.

And yet, I can't stop my heart from doing a little jig.

My only regret is that we stopped kissing. I touch my lips again, reliving the moment for just a beat.

Eloise: No regrets.

Ares: *Buenas noches, tesoro*. I look forward to doing it again some time.

CHAPTER 11
Ares

Looking forward to doing it again some time. Ay, dios mio. ¡Allantoso!

If I wasn't stretching in front of my home bench on the ice, I'd face palm myself. Hell, when I stand up, I might face palm myself anyway. With my fucking stick.

What the hell is wrong with me?

Some time? *Some time?* What about right now? What about tomorrow? What about a solid fucking date that isn't some vague, murky event in the future?

I let out a groan, hoping my teammates think it's 'cause I overstretched my groin or something and they don't come anywhere near me to check on my balls.

A bunch of suits appear in my periphery. It's unusual for scouts to appear at a practice, but not completely unheard of if they want to get a look at someone in particular. I'm trying to pay attention to the warm up drill Coach has the guys doing. The goalie coach is late and might not make it. According to Coach, he has the shits. So for now, my backup and I are warming up our muscles and waiting to be told what to do. I fucking hate waiting.

I'm a do-er, not a watcher.

The uncomfortable feeling only grows when a familiar voice lifts above the din of the suits over my shoulder. It's Papá. *Anda al carajo.*

My blood chills in my veins. He never pops by for a visit. The fact that he's here can only mean trouble, undoubtedly for me.

I have no idea what the fuck I've done to warrant him showing up at practice.

It's always me. It's never Apollo, or Artemis, or our beloved sister Athena.

It's always, *always* me.

So... what did I do this time?

The guys he's with don't look like cops. If they are, they're the best dressed cops I've ever seen. So, I guess I'm not under arrest for anything. Or if I am, I'll at least be going to a fancy prison.

I try to adjust my position so I can see if I know the people he's with or filter out the noise on the ice to hear what they're talking about. Neither works. I guess I'll have to put my best skate forward during practice and hope they aren't here to somehow have me pulled off the team. That's way worse than prison.

As I make my way to my crease, the urge to look back over my shoulder is strong. Who did he bring with him? It's not like Alonso de la Peña to simply show off his sons' hockey talent. I don't even know if he actually likes the game.

I think the only reason we were ever allowed to play hockey in the beginning was because Mamá fought for us. But once we started getting good, I mean really good, he kept tabs on us because it makes him look good to have successful children, even if it was in sports.

I think any of us three could make it to the professional

leagues. Scouts are already starting to pay attention to us on the ice, and I've heard whispers.

My brothers are as good as any NHL players you could name off the top of your head and then some. And that's not easy to say. I'd much rather be the standout kid in the family. But when it comes to hockey, as much as I'm loath to admit it, my brothers might be better than me. Maybe.

Though I'll never say that out loud.

Despite my resolve to keep my head in the game, I'm preoccupied throughout practice.

The suits distract me as they observe our every move on the ice.

And I'm still distracted by Eloise. I jerked off in the shower this morning to the memory of last night's epic kiss at the coffee shop, but it wasn't enough.

And for some reason, I'm distracted by thoughts of Thiago and his claims that he's related to us. I can't seem to shake the gut-sinking dread that he might be telling the truth. Does he play hockey too? What's he like? What's he interested in? What's his mom like? Does Mom know her?

Part of me wants to skate right up to the bench and demand answers from Papá, and the other part of me wants to forget I ever heard the words come out of the kid's mouth. Not my circus, not my monkeys. Except it kind of is.

It's like I'm carrying around a grenade with the pin pulled. Like I have this one piece of information that has the potential to detonate at the core of our family and blow us into a million pieces.

Usually when I have a problem I can't solve, I go talk to Abuelita. There's rarely an issue she can't solve with a mug of spicy hot chocolate and her trusty flip flop. But with this… it's pretty sensitive.

Though, I'd literally give my entire trust fund to watch Abuelita go after Papá with her shoe.

Someone shoots the puck my direction. I've been working on learning my teammate's names. If I was paying closer attention, I'd know who sent me the puck, and that alone makes me want to grind my teeth and punch myself in the fucking face. I'm slower to react than usual, too, but with a little burst of speed I'm able to deflect the puck and pass it to Artemis, who is collecting the pucks around the net.

Or at least that's what it looks like.

"Don't let him throw you off your game."

"Who?" I aim for causal, nonchalant, like I don't give a flying fuck that our father is standing behind the boards evaluating every fucking breath we take out here, but I clearly miss the mark.

"Right." Artemis slides a puck back and forth with the blade of his stick as he inches toward me.

"*'toy bien.*" I sweep a puck across the ice to Raffi, then shoot another to Justin. I'm not fine, but I need to be.

"You've got this." A man of few words, Artemis smacks my shoulder, and something in the contact makes the knots of anxiety that are holding my body hostage unravel a little.

For the rest of the practice, I tune out the noise. Eloise, Thiago, Alonso, the suits—they all get shoved out of my brain. I focus all of my energy into stopping the puck from getting into the net, at all costs.

By the end of the session, my legs are burning, my eyes sting from the sweat streaming down my face, and I stink.

Papá beckons the twins over to the bench with a jerk of his head and makes introductions to the guys in dark suits. Are they investors? Scouts? Dudes he works with who happen to like hockey? I have no idea, and I hate that curiosity is burning in my stomach.

It burns even more that he hasn't called me over, too. I'm fighting the urge to skate over and insert myself in the conversation. I don't want to give him any more ammunition against me. But it's hard as fuck to resist.

I linger for a beat before I realize yeah, he's really not going to invite me to join them, so I give up waiting to get tagged in with the big boys and head to the locker room. I left it all out on the ice. Once I pulled my shit together, I put my entire existence into that practice, and I bet he never even fucking noticed.

I don't know why I ever think he's going to change. And yet, I keep waiting around for his table scraps of affection.

Once I'm out of my gear and showered, I don't hang around, stopping at the store to buy Bacon some more celery and apples—he broke into my stash overnight and ate the lot. I've never known anyone to love celery the way that damn pig does.

I'm about to check out when a flash of pink hair passing the entrance draws my attention. I've had a stressful morning; the universe definitely owes me some good luck right now.

Throwing money at the cashier, I grab my bag of vegetables, and haul ass out onto the street. She can't have gotten far. I spy her up ahead, but unless she has magic hair and it grew a *lot* overnight, it's not my girl, my *tesoro*.

It's clearly a bright pink sign from the universe that I was an idiot last night when I didn't ask Eloise out again. I pull out my phone.

Ares: *Buenos días, preciosa*. I was wondering if you'd like to get hot chocolate later.

Ares: I mean, with me.

Puta madre. I'm like a bumbling idiot. And I'm doing my level best to resist the urge to send her a third message. I tuck the phone into my ass pocket and head to the apartment. Halfway there, my butt vibrates.

It's been so long since I've gotten laid that it feels kinda nice. Sure, Séb wasn't forever ago, but it's never been this long. I don't do droughts. At least I didn't before *her*.

It's not a reply from Eloise, but rather my brother telling me that the suits at the rink were family business, not hockey. The weight pressing on my chest eases, enough to suck in a full breath. Thank God it's not hockey. If he'd cut me out of both the family business and hockey career opportunities... well, I'm not going to think about that.

Grinds my gears that he's keeping me out of the business, though. He claims I'm too hot headed, too brash, too unreliable and irresponsible to be put in charge of anything to do with the family name.

I used to want to be Papá when I grew up. I followed him around, wearing his thousand-dollar shoes, getting underfoot. But the older I got, the more I realized that he had already selected my older brothers to replace him at the top of the de la Peña food chain. And it didn't matter how well I did in school, on the ice, or by any other metric, the only things he'd ever notice me for were the bad things.

So that's what I did.

Athena, on the other hand, well, she either didn't get the memo that because she wasn't born with a dick, daddy dearest isn't going to give her the company, or she doesn't give a fuck. She conducts herself as though she's going to inherit the world and run it in her five-inch Louboutins.

I didn't always have this level of self-awareness. In fact, I drowned my daddy issues in liquor and coke for a while. And any time I got those negative feelings about myself and lack of self-worth, there were only too many beautiful people ready to purge my brain of them by sucking them out of my dick.

But now that I'm clean, well, hindsight is twenty-twenty. I don't want to be Papá anymore, but that doesn't mean some days that I wouldn't like for him to at least acknowledge my existence. Even if he is an asshole.

I shoot off a reply to Apollo. Blasé, and I-don't-give-a-fuck. And I'm trying really hard not to. Give a fuck, I mean. Can't deny the sting in my chest though. I'm sure I felt my teammates' eyes on me when Papá called the twins to the bench.

I know what they were thinking: why aren't you being called over too, Ares?

No one said it. No one needed to.

I'm a block away from my place when my phone buzzes again. My stomach sinks a little more. Still not Eloise.

Sure, a part of me is smarting. Fine, a big part—mostly my fucking pride. I'm not used to this, and I can't say I like it.

I should probably view it as a lesson in humility, and I'm one hundred percent behind setting and enforcing boundaries. If the girl wants nothing to do with me, I'll accept that. But it'll sting like fuck.

Not because I think everyone should want me. I want her to want me. And I thought she did.

Apollo's text tells me to stop pouting and go stroke my pig. I can't tell if he means Bacon, or if he's using it as a euphemism for getting off. Either way, my dick agrees that it's been too long and a date with my right hand feels like just what the doctor ordered.

As I approach the building entrance, Alfred already has it open, waiting for me, when my phone buzzes again. I damn near groan. It's not cool when the most action you're getting comes from a piece of technology in your ass pocket. It's not even like my phone is designed for sexual pleasure either.

Eloise: Thanks, but I don't think that's such a good idea.

My heart does a swoopy thing, and I might be having a heart attack. That's what this is, right?

I stutter to a stop on the sidewalk, about six feet away from Alfred.

Damn.

For so long, I've been the one to do the rejecting. Have people felt this weird chest thing when I said no? That's not fucking cool. This feeling sucks ass.

I'm torn, caught between respecting her 'no' and not actually believing it. I'm not willing to give up. That kiss was mind blowing, life altering, and I know she felt it too. At least I think she did. She had to. It couldn't have been one way.

I glance at the time. She could be any number of places, including the comfort of her own bed since it's pretty early, but I don't know where she lives on campus, and I don't know anyone who knows her either.

I guess there's no harm in checking Bitches Brew. If she's not there, I can grab one of their festive bougie drinks and pretend I went for the caffeine.

I toss Alfred a salute. "I forgot I have something to do."

He points to the bag of vegetables in my hand. "Would you like for me to take that?"

Right. Good point. I reach the bag out to him.

"I don't mean to overstep, but you might want to take the car or grab a coat." He shivers. "It's not warm."

He's got a point. And taking the car can make it look like I stopped at the coffee shop en route to somewhere else. It would track.

This is ridiculous. Creating an elaborate backstory for going to get coffee. Dios mío. This girl has me twisted up in knots.

That odd flapping sensation remains in the pit of my stomach as I park outside the café. Maybe I'm coming down with something, the same thing the Raccoons goalie coach has. I sure as shit hope not because I don't have time to get sick.

Inside Bitches Brew, no Eloise. The only pink-haired

woman in sight is Taryn, and she's not the pink-haired woman I need.

I do another scan of the cafe, hoping Eloise will appear, from the bathroom, or, no sé, out from under a table she was hiding beneath for some reason. No such luck.

"She's not here," a smug voice says. I realize the owner is standing way too close to me.

I take a step away from the redhead, Eloise's friend, and jerk my chin. "Who?"

She folds her arms, narrowing her gaze at me like she can see right through my bullshit. "I was going to help you, but instead, since you don't know who I'm talking about... well, now I'm going to drink my caffeine and enjoy the three minutes of stillness I get before my mom brings my hurricane of a kid back to me." She plops down onto a seat, swoops up her oversized mug of steaming liquid, and inhales its scent.

I want to ignore her. I want to be indignant and cocky and carry on like I don't know who she's talking about, but I recognize her. I've seen her with Eloise. I can't remember where, or when, but I know I have, and she knows who exactly it is I'm looking for.

Taryn catches my eye from behind the counter. "Usual?"

I nod, suddenly not caring about any of the bougie festive drinks they might have and lean over to the redhead. "If I was looking for someone. Where might I find them?" I offer her a smile—it can't hurt my cause, right?

She wags a finger at me. "Oh hell no, Mr. Hotshot. You can take that charm and feed it to the geese."

The geese have flown south for the winter, but I remain quiet. Hell, I don't blame them. If I could fly south and escape Iowa for the winter without getting kicked out of school, I'd be with the gaggle.

I open my mouth, but she holds up a hand. "No bullshit."

I can respect that. "I'm Ares."

She snorts like it's the most hilarious thing in the world that I think she doesn't know who I am. But not in a good way, and I don't like it.

"And I was wondering if you could help me find Eloise, please."

Her arms are folded, but she's glancing at her coffee cup like she wishes she had a huge straw so she could scowl at me with her arms crossed *and* get her caffeine hit at the same time.

"For what purpose?" Her eyes narrow further. She's glaring at me through slits now, but the full force of her fuck-off vibes are now concentrated on me.

Taryn calls my name, and I hold up a finger. Being real, humble, goes against everything everyone expects from me.

"I want to spend some more time with her."

I'm the fun loving de la Peña. The no strings, no rules, all party kinda guy. So, I don't miss when her eyebrows flicker when I come right out and level her with the truth.

She stares at me in weighted silence for at least five seconds, maybe longer, before she points her index finger at my face. "I don't care who your dad is, or how much of an untouchable big shot you are. If you hurt my girl, I will make sure they never find your body."

I believe her.

I'm also glad my *tesoro* has such a strong friend in her corner. Everyone should have at least one friend able to hide the bodies. There's nothing better than having someone willing to do manual labor to help keep you out of prison.

I'm lucky enough that my hockey brothers are bound by our mutual love of the game and the fact we're a team. I'm hoping by the time I graduate we'll be bound by something even stronger than blood, that my teammates will actually like me. It'll take some time for me to crack into their tight knit group—especially because my brothers have already been here a while. Everyone's loyal to them and eyeing me as the mildly unhinged guy who kinda looks like the twins, but who came home with a potbellied freakin' pig.

They're not wrong. And thankfully they were all cool about the pig.

"She's at the library."

That's it? That's all she's giving me? The campus library isn't small. Many floors, many, many desks, and far too many places for me to go looking for Eloise. She could be long gone by the time I found where she was studying.

I found her once before, but that was pure chance. What are the odds of her being at that same table again?

The redhead's face twitches. She's getting a kick out of fucking with me. I don't blame her. She has the upper hand, and usually that's my spot. Being on the receiving end once again, isn't fun for me.

There should be a lesson in humility or something in here, but I want to get to my girl. My chest is tight, my skin feels like a billion insects are crawling under it. I want to see the pink-haired pixie and make her mine.

Or, I dunno, at least ask her to be mine, or something.

I'll figure that part out when I get there.

I huff out a heavy breath. "Do you happen to have any... more specific... information on her whereabouts?"

It's her turn to huff. She folds her arms, and her face shifts. I'm pretty sure any good grace I had with this woman has dissipated. I've lost her. "I was going to say that it's no fun if I do all the work for you." She waves a hand. "But you're eating into my alone time and right now I want rid of you."

My stomach flickers. A pathetic beat of excitement flares that I'm trying not to read into, but I already want to see Eloise more than I've ever wanted to see another human being in my entire life.

I'm like a golden retriever and my owner's been away on

vacation. I wanna chase my tail in circles, and sure, I might pee myself when I see her, but that's beside the point.

This is fucking ridiculous.

Maybe I've built her up in my head to be something more than she is because we've barely even talked, but it's unlikely. No one has ever had an impact on me like this.

I'm vaguely aware that the redhead has said something, so I blink myself out of my momentary stupor and cant my head. She's looking at me like I'm lacking somehow. And for the first time in my life, I'm afraid I might actually be lacking. I don't like that either.

"Third floor, near a window; she likes being able to look outside."

I splutter my thanks, grab my coffee, and jog out the door, her laughter chasing me the entire way. It's like all my Christmases have come at once, and I'm only going to talk to the woman.

An alarm bell tinkles in the back of my head. What if she doesn't want to talk to me? What if she doesn't want me to kiss her again? What if it wasn't as life altering for her as it was for me?

I rub at my sternum with a balled fist. I'm not sure if it's the too-hot coffee burning its way down my chest or the idea that this beautiful, smart woman might want fuck all to do with me that's making me feel queasy.

Tempting a parking ticket, I double park outside the library. The SUV is going to need a detail because that coffee didn't stay in the cup on my way across campus.

I take the stairs three at a time, like I'm a hero in a romance movie pursuing the love of his life. I'm aware of how cheesy it all is as it runs through my head, but I don't care. I'm crushing hard on this girl, and I need to know if she felt anything when we kissed.

I squash down the idea that she might reject me, because

my gut says she felt it too.

When I pull open the door to the third floor, the smell of books smacks me square in the face. It's kinda gross. Ew. Musty old book smell is not my kink. Two steps inside, the reality of the situation crashes over me.

I'm looking for a woman I have an epic crush on. In the library. The space alone intimidates the fuck out of me. I can barely spell library. But I'm willing to do wacky things to get this girl's attention.

This is a mistake. I shouldn't have come here. I'm not smart enough to even *be* in the freakin' library, let alone date someone who spends a high proportion of her time here. I command my feet to stop, and my shoes squeak on the floor as my body comes to a halt.

I need to turn around and leave. Except, sitting right to my left next to the window, is Eloise. She hasn't seen me yet.

My heart's tripping over itself racing so hard in my chest, and while I'd love to blame it on the three flights of stairs... well, I'm an athlete. I can handle a few flights of stairs.

I open my mouth to say something at the same time my feet turn so I'm full-on facing her. One more quarter turn, and I'll be pointing toward the stairwell, but I can't convince myself to finish the job and flee.

She puts down her highlighter and looks up, her eyes sparkling between those pink curtains hanging over her face. There's recognition in her gaze, but nothing that says either "get the fuck away from me, that kiss was awful," or "Come kiss me again, you tasty brute." Or whatever the fuck smart girls think.

She tips her head like she's not sure whether I'm lost, need help finding a book, or if I'm being chased by a dragon. And I suck in a breath. She's seen me now, so I can't leave. There's only one thing left for me to do. I walk toward her and pull out the seat facing her.

CHAPTER 12
Eloise

I should have known he would have reacted poorly to rejection. But I never thought he'd hunt me down to the library, and just... sit. It wasn't even a rejection—I said no, thanks. Polite and everything. I guess he's not used to people saying no to him.

He spun the chair so it was backward before he plopped down on it, and now he's leaning on the back with his arms crossed. He looks so gosh darn kissable.

The bill of his ball cap is even facing backward. It wouldn't hit me in the face if I ignored the fact that everyone is staring at me and grabbed Ares by his shirt to lay one on him.

He smells clean, his hair is floppy. It's early, so maybe he had hockey training. He's far more alert and awake than I feel.

I wish he'd say something, but right now his intense chocolate brown eyes are drilling into me. The fact that I wish another part of him was drilling into me reminds me of how long it's been since I've been intimate with someone. What's he like in bed? Would he be a selfish lover?

The more I stare back at him, the quieter Dad's angry

voice from our argument gets. Leopards can't change their spots, but Ares looks so unlike a leopard right now that I have to admit, he's kind of tempting.

I wouldn't go so far as to say he looks "boy next door" but he certainly doesn't look like the "Devil spawn" Dad claims he is.

He opens his mouth to say something, but I point to the silence signs, then around the library. People are whispering, probably due to the fact that Ares de la Peña is sitting across the table from me, staring at me like he wants my clothes to disappear. I could totally make that happen.

I resist the urge to tug at my collar. Barely. It's like my body is reacting to his stare and suddenly wants to get naked right here in the library.

He ignores my warning, and the silence signs, and opens his mouth again. "Why won't you get hot chocolate with me?"

I can't tell him that the main reason I can't go hang out with him is because my daddy said so. I mean, I'm a grown adult with my own free will. It's a little high school to blame your parents for not being allowed to do something when you're in college.

It's not like Dad will even find out anyway, right? The likelihood of lightning striking twice in the same spot is unlikely, but knowing my luck, Dad would happen upon us once again.

I lean across the table so I don't have to raise my voice. "Why do you want me to get hot chocolate with you?"

He leans over the back of the chair, and his breath tickles my face. "I liked how your glittery cream tasted on my lips." He grins, and I'm pretty sure I just came in my panties.

My face heats. Did he really say that? Did I really react to that? I try to force an eye roll, but I'm not sure my eyes moved from staring at his lips.

"You don't need me to go with you to get glittery whipped cream, Ares." I don't mean to hiss his name, but my voice echoes around the space resulting in two people shushing me. My face heats even more.

"I want *your* cream on my face, Eloise." He inches closer, we're almost nose to nose. His voice isn't a hushed whisper anymore, and the guy behind me heard that Ares wants my cream on his face. "Why won't you come have hot chocolate with me?"

I don't have a good answer. And his eyes have hypnotized me, so I don't have any reciprocal questions to distract him with either.

He brushes his nose along my cheekbone, the ugly one, and I suck in a sharp breath as he travels toward my ear. "You can't tell me you don't like hot chocolate, *tesoro*. I know you do."

He's right, my body composition is approximately seventy-three percent hot chocolate.

"I need to study." I palm the desk, not moving back from Ares, and swipe my highlighter off the table before jabbing it on my book for emphasis. He's not looking anywhere but at me, so he doesn't see it, and we both know there's no way I can concentrate on my work when he's right in front of me.

"What do you do for fun?" he whispers, pulling back to brush his nose against mine.

I don't have an answer to that one either. I used to play my cello, but I stopped after Mom... I run at the gym, but that's for fitness, not really for fun, especially since the accident. I've got precisely one friend, and other than watching reruns of *Modern Family* together, all we tend to do is study.

Any answer I give to him will sound pathetic to the party boy with a million friends.

"What's your favorite food?"

I move away and purse my lips, which draws his attention to my mouth. His focus makes me feel exposed.

I hold up one finger. "One hour."

His lips twitch. *"¿Una hora?"*

"Let me study for one hour, and I'll answer your questions."

"All of them?"

That's definitely a trap. His brow arches, and his smile is lazy. I'm doing my level best not to remember what it felt like to have his lips on mine, but my lady garden is demanding a rematch while my nipples press against my bra.

Five questions doesn't sound so scary, so I hold up my hand. "Five questions."

"Una hora. Cinco preguntas." He tips back his head like he's sampling a fine wine and it's saturating his tongue. *"Sí.* I can do that."

He leans back again, and part of me wants to reach over his chair and yank him toward me. I drop the highlighter and tuck my hands under my thighs. If I don't, I'm not sure what I'll end up doing.

Is he going to sit and stare at me for a whole hour? Surely not.

He holds my gaze for a beat before he nods and pushes to his feet. He tucks my hair behind my ear, blazing a trail across my cheekbone with his touch, and holds up a finger. *"Una hora, tesoro."*

With that, he turns and leaves, so much swagger in his stride it's a wonder the building doesn't sway with each step he takes.

What in the name of all that's holy was that?

I contemplate leaving the library and standing him up, being gone when he arrives back in an hour, but something about that idea sours in my stomach. Ugh. I *want* to see him. I *want* to explore whatever this is. I want to believe in it and trust it. Ares has never made me feel like I'm a charity project or a science experiment gone wrong.

My scars don't seem to repulse him, nor does this feel like

morbid curiosity on his part. And it's not like he needs to use me for sex—he has a horde of people lining up for that particular activity.

I'm not an idiot. He's a player both on and off the ice and probably has a new lover each day of the week. But something warm is growing in my chest at the idea that he wants to spend some of his time with me despite all that.

Studying isn't going to happen now—my brain is mush. I can't go home and change my clothes because he'll know I changed them for him. And I don't want to flee. So, I grab my phone and text the one person who'll know what to do.

Eloise: SOS.

Victoria: He found you then.

My jaw drops open on a gasp, and I'm not really sure how to answer that.

Eloise: I'm going to need more information.

Victoria: Casanova came to Bitches Brew looking for you.

Eloise: So you... what? Pinged me on friend-finder and gave him my coordinates?

Victoria: That made me laugh. You know technology and I don't get along. No. I told him you were in the library (lucky guess). He seemed like he really wanted to spend time with you.

Eloise: And you just... sent him to me?

Victoria: After I threatened to feed his pee-pee to sharks if he hurt you, sure.

That makes me snort, which draws a few more shhhh sounds from those around me. This isn't like me at all. I'm not a noisy library goer. I respect the rules and reverence of the building, and I take my studies very seriously.

That said, I have to admit there's a lightness, a giddy flurry in my chest at this whole situation. A handsome guy went looking for me, and my best friend threatened to injure his person if he hurt me. That's nice, kind of big. I never really had that "my friend likes you" thing in high school, and I certainly don't get ditzy over guys.

But this one. He's... different.

It's not necessarily a good different either. I'm not one to go for bad boys, but this one's a motorcycle and some leathers away from being a typical bad boy romance hero. There's definitely a thrill that comes from having his attention, and I sort of hate the way that feels. It's icky.

And I *definitely* don't want him to kiss me again.

My stomach clenches. Fine. That's a bald-faced lie. I do. I want him to kiss me again, and again and part of me wouldn't care if he splayed me out on this table right here in the library and did... things to me. Even with the shushers watching.

Welp. Now my body is on fire. It's hot all over, and everyone around me might know what I'm thinking about. To be fair, they're probably all thinking about bedding Ares de la Peña too.

Victoria: You still there?

Victoria: Are you doing naughty things with the naughty boy?

Victoria: Get it girl. Ride that stallion.

I groan into my palm.

Eloise: I'm not getting anything. He's coming back in an hour so we can chat.

Victoria: Chat? Is that like, code? For you sitting on his face?

Wow. She really went there. And now it's front and center in my mind. My already hot body climbs another couple degrees. My last boyfriend hated going down on girls...or maybe it was only me he had a problem with. Either way, I haven't had someone's tongue down there in longer than I care to remember.

I've only had one guy ever eat me out, my buttface ex. And

it was kinda... sloppy. I'm not sure he really knew how to find a clitoris either. And Lord knows he never tried any of my suggestions or seemed to want to fix the error of his ways. Those were... frustrating times.

And even the thought of Ares's tongue... there... well, now I *definitely* can't concentrate on whatever it was I was doing before he got here.

Victoria: Thinking about it now, aren't you?

I hate that she knows me so well. I also hate that my clit is pulsing. I don't know Morse code, but I think my clit is beating out an SOS right now. Never in my entire life have I contemplated running to the bathroom at school to take the edge off, but right now it sounds blissful, necessary even.

Victoria: Eloise Downing! Are you...? Where are your hands, young lady? You're in the library!

Eloise: I love it when you get all exclamation point-y on me.

I'm deflecting, from this warm buzz in my chest, from the heat scorching my panties, from Dad's voice in the back of my mind cautioning me against even talking to Ares, but I can't help it.

Victoria: Nice try, Ellie-Rae. Tell me what's going on. Is he sitting watching you "study"? That's so fucking hot.

Eloise: Thankfully not. I can barely get my head straight with him not staring at me. He's coming back in an hour, and I told him he can ask me five questions.

Victoria: That's it? No blow jobs in the biographies section? No sex in statistics? No fingering in French?

Victoria: I think I'm done.

I'm struggling not to laugh. Two girls walk past shooting daggers in my direction as they leave. I'm not sure if it's because I'm suddenly the rowdy girl in the library, or because

Ares took notice of me, but either way, I don't like the new attention.

My hand drifts to my face, making sure my hair is hanging over my scar, my heart rate skips up a notch or two, and my palms start to sweat. I don't like to be noticed, I don't like to be looked at, and I certainly don't want everyone to see hotshot Ares hanging out with the deformed girl.

It has to be a joke. There's no universe in which someone who looks... well, quite frankly, like *that*, could ever willingly want to even hang out with someone like me. No matter how real it feels, he has to have an ulterior motive. Maybe he wants something from me. Maybe it's some stupid twisted bet. Maybe I'll find my lady balls and come right out and ask him.

Oof. The thought alone gives me palpitations.

Maybe not.

I'm twisting my shirt in shaking hands when my phone lights up again.

Victoria: Get out of your head.

I don't know how she got to know me quite so fast, or so well, but she's spot on, every single time.

Victoria: There's nothing I know more than bullshitting hockey players. Baby-daddy was the bullshittiest of them all. And that boy doesn't give me bullshit vibes. I have an excellent bullshit detector.

Victoria: Did I say bullshit enough in that last message?

Victoria: Bullshit.

I smile again at the messages as they appear on my screen. My heartrate's starting to slow, and my hands are no longer trembling like someone asked me to diffuse a bomb.

Victoria: You don't have to go anywhere with him, or do anything you're not comfortable with. You don't even need to leave the library. Relax.

I roll my eyes. We both know that telling someone to relax

has a poor success rate. My leg jitters under the table. What kind of questions will he want to ask me? Will he even come back? Not leaving the library sounds like a good plan. This is my safe space, it's quiet, and it has books. What's not to love?

I stare at the pages of my book. There's no point. Nothing will sink into my brain. In hindsight, I should have talked to him first and then studied, but it's not that easy to figure things out in the moment, especially when he's *right there* and he's *staring*.

Not least of all because I wanted to spin him around in his chair and mount him where he sat. I don't even know who I am right now. Getting lost in my own thoughts, tormenting myself, anxiety warring with hope. I don't know why I want him to like me, to want me, but I do. It's certainly not for street cred. I couldn't care less about being with the popular kids.

"You look flushed, Eloise. Are you okay?" His voice is right next to me. I jump as his words kiss my skin, sending shivers through my body.

He sweeps my hair behind my ear, the gesture becoming familiar, and places the back of his hand onto my forehead. "You don't have a fever."

His eyes skim my face. "Are you okay?" The crease between his brows is adorable. He's close enough that I can see the wrinkles on his forehead and at the edges of his eyes as he stares at me with delicious chocolate brown concern.

I need to sigh, to let out a swoony ginormous freakin' sigh at how cute this all is, but I swallow it down. I'm also resisting the urge to fan myself or blurt out that I'm hyper-aroused because I've spent the last hour thinking about his face buried in my girl bits.

I shift in my seat, and the movement isn't lost on him because the corner of his mouth twitches. "Are you okay, *tesoro*?"

Someone shushes us yet again, and Ares glares around me, probably at whoever did it. We can't talk here. Panic at the thought of being kicked out of the library, or worse, banned from using the space entirely, takes over. I sweep my stuff into my book bag, stand, and grab Ares's hand, and pull him away from the seating area.

Instead of leading us out the door and out of the building, or even into the stairwell to talk, this bright spark has managed to take us into the stacks. It's quieter back here, and the deeper we get into the aisles of books, the fewer people we pass.

I won't lie—I'm trying to avoid Ares's amused gaze, and the occasional strange glances from students at me hauling him away from the desks burn my skin, but I don't stop until we're at the farthest corner from everyone.

I drop my bag to the floor. My heart's threatening to burst out of my throat, it's speeding so fast. Screw my sweaty palms, screw my racing thoughts, and screw that delicious man and his delicious smile and his delicious Spanish... mouth... tongue... dammit, words.

I suck in a steadying breath, level him with my hardest glare, and fold my arms in a fruitless bid to protect myself from his charm. It's time to find out what the heck this guy is playing at.

CHAPTER 13
Eloise

"What exactly is it that you want from me?"

If he gives me a smug grin, or says something sarcastic right now I might... I... I dunno, maybe I'll stand on his toe. Hard.

I've never raised my hand to another human being in all my life... so far. I'm not beyond starting if this guy doesn't give me some answers and put my confused body parts at ease about whatever this is.

He sucks in a breath. I'm not sure if he's taking a deep breath or if he's smelling me, but considering how hard it has been for me not to bury my nose in his hair, or neck and just... sniiiiiff... I'm hoping he's fighting a familiar urge.

The idea of his discomfort is suddenly something I want to grab onto and encourage. I want him to be as caught up in knots as I am.

He takes a step toward me, and his charged gaze flickers to my lips. "I thought you were letting *me* ask the questions."

I did too, but I guess things change when someone lights up your lady garden like it's Christmas or something, and you can't find the freakin' off switch.

I narrow my glare even further. I might suffer from sometimes crippling anxiety, but that doesn't make me a pushover.

"You want to know what I want from you? *Realmente?*"

My mouth is dry. I've made a few mistakes in the last couple of minutes. In my panic not to get kicked out of the library or leave the space and go somewhere else with Ares, I've isolated both of us in a dark, quiet part of the building. I've also asked a quite sexually charged question, and from the way his teeth are holding the right side of his bottom lip hostage as his eyebrow rises, he's already a step ahead.

I manage a curt nod, needing answers. I can't wander around campus with some sparkly distraction of a crush on a guy whose intentions I'm unsure of. I need to know what he's playing at.

He takes another step toward me. I scooch back into something hard. It doesn't feel like a shelving unit and there's no sound of books tipping over, but at this point I don't really care what it is.

He licks his lips before skimming the pad of this thumb across mine. "I want your every thought, every hope and dream, every fear, every kiss, every everything."

"But why?" My voice is barely a whisper, squeaking out around the tension banded around my chest.

His thumb ghosts my jaw, and I tip my head back, leaning against the wall behind me on a sigh. I don't understand.

"I want to know you, Eloise. I want to know every single thing there is to know about you, and I want to teach you things about yourself that you don't even know yet."

My brain is short circuiting. My body is aching for his touch.

"But why?" Maybe he didn't hear me the first time. I can't find any other words in my mind. I'm staring at his lips because I'm not sure I'm ready for whatever is waiting for me in his gaze.

"You fascinate me."

My eyes close. I'm fighting the urge to jam my fingers into my ears and sing "la la la la la" over and over so I don't have to listen to whatever else he has to say.

"You're beautiful."

My head twitches, shaking "no" at his words. His warm hand cups my neck and his thumb rests along the length of my jaw as he presses me into the wall. He glides his nose across my cheekbone and into my hair.

"Look at me." His words are gravelly in my ear.

When I don't open my eyes and he doesn't move, he flexes his hand, squeezing enough to make me wonder how far he'd go. I'm not afraid, I'm not disgusted, and I'm definitely feeling something about the fact he has his hand on my throat, but it certainly isn't anything bad.

My eyes spring open at the realization, meeting his brown depths. "You don't get to tell me what I do and don't find beautiful, *tesoro*."

His dick is hard against my side, and when he's finished speaking, he drops his hand from my face. I want it back. I've never had someone's hand around my throat, and while I don't think choking is something I'd enjoy per se, I liked having the warm weight on my neck like that. It's on the tip of my tongue to tell him as much, too.

"I want everything from you, Eloise."

My body sags against the wall. I want to close my eyes again, but his heated stare holds me captive. If I don't look away soon, I might combust.

He inclines back, his eyes not freeing me from their grasp. "From the pink creeping up your neck and staining your cheeks, the way your chest is heaving with breaths, and how your body leans into me... I'd say you want some things from me too, *cariño*."

He leans toward me again and my chin tilts before I can stop it. "Do you want me to touch you, *tesoro?*"

"Yes." I squeak, and if he wasn't *right there,* I'd smack my hands over my mouth. I can't believe I said that. I can't believe I just... came out and told him that I wanted him with such ease like that.

He smiles, but it's not cocky, or knowing. It's not his playboy charm. This seems warm, genuine, like he's glad I admitted that I want him to touch me because it's something he wants too. Can I dare to hope?

"Where do you want me to touch you, Eloise?"

The way he says my name is legitimately swoon-worthy. The answer bubbles at the back of my throat, threatening to burst out if I don't roll my lips together to stop them. I can't let them out, they can't escape. I can't say those things out loud.

My body's hot. I'm probably sweating in the most unsexy ways imaginable, but I can't bring myself to peel my body from between his body and the wall to move. I jerk my head from side to side.

His hand glides up my side before his thumb teases my lips from between my teeth.

"Tell me what you need from me. I'm only too willing to give it to you, but you need to ask."

I can't fight it. The pulsing between my legs, how every breath heightens the sensation of the fabric of my clothes against my skin, and how hot my entire body is with him standing so close.

"Everywhere." The relief when I say the word out loud, even whispered, forces my shoulders to relax.

But he doesn't move closer. He doesn't touch me *anywhere*.

I frown, forcing myself to focus on his eyes and ignore my demanding body. My stomach swoops. Was that what his goal was? To get me worked up, to admit that I wanted him, and then leave me like... this?

"Be specific." His demand snaps me out of my thought spiral as his words register.

Oh, no. No, no, no, no, no. He wants me to tell him exactly what I want him to do to me? I can't. My eyes widen, my pulse thrashes. He's staring at me expectantly. I suppose I get it. He's probably never suffered from anxiety in his entire life, and the idea of being open about his desires isn't alien to him.

For me, it sits somewhere up with walking around downtown Cedar Rapids with no clothes on.

I bet he wouldn't mind wandering around naked. I bet he'd be all swagger about it too, dick swinging in the breeze. Though I suppose if I looked like that, I wouldn't mind so much either.

His hand rests on my hip, and I try to ease it lower, but he doesn't let up.

"Do you want me to touch you?" He tilts his head. I don't feel like I'm being toyed with, like I'm his prey, or like it's some sinister game. Even though it's clear as the nose on my face, he needs me to say what I want. And I want more than anything to give him what he needs. Mostly so he'll touch my freakin' clit.

I nod.

"Now?"

I nod again. I'm trying not to think about the fact I'm standing in the library and could be happened upon at any time by anyone. But part of me can't help but remember the thrill of watching Ares and the guy he was with in the alley next to Guac n'Roll.

That was some epic spank bank material, and while I've never considered the fact that I might enjoy the risk of being caught, it's not bothering me right now. Something to circle back to, perhaps.

Though that might be down to the fact that my clit is screaming so loudly it's drowning out all other intelligent thought.

"Where?"

I squeeze my eyes shut so I don't have to look at him. "Between my legs."

His fingers skim the inside of my thigh, and I shuffle my feet apart, hungry, desperate, needy, and so very, very wet.

"Here?" He brushes his knuckle along the length of the crotch seam of my pants.

I'm panting, gasping, and he's barely touched me, but I have no time to linger on my desperation. I need more.

"Y-yes."

"You want me to touch your pussy, Eloise?"

Holy moly. How does he make my name sound so dirty? Fuck.

I don't drop the F-bomb often, but I don't think any of the other words I know can come close to this pulsing ache that rages between my legs, to how consumed by hunger I am. I have never in my life been as horny as I am right here in this library.

"Five questions."

"Huh?"

"*Cinco preguntas.* Then, I'll touch you anywhere you want me to." His smile is teasing now, his eyes sparkling. And I want to rip his grin from his face, or scream, or stamp my feet preferably on his toes, but he presses his rock-hard dick into my thigh with a groan. This must be some kind of wicked foreplay.

I'll play his game. Five questions.

If he wants the PIN to my bank account, he can take it.

If he wants Mom's recipe for potato salad, I know it by

heart though my hands may be trembling too much to actually write it down.

"Okay." I arch my back, tilting my hips, but he doesn't move his hand that's now on my waist.

He dots kisses along one side of my jaw, while stroking my scars with his thumb. "What's your favorite color?"

M-m-my what? Color? He can't be serious, right? Surely, he meant sexual position? Sex toy? Piece of lingerie. Something as dirty.

He doesn't look up at me, but he must sense my surprise somehow. "I told you, I want to know it all. Every detail."

"Moss green." Like Mom's eyes.

One of his hands still sits weighty on my hip, and I find myself leaning into the rhythmic strokes of his hand on my scars. I've spent every second of my life since the accident, since the surgeries that followed, hiding that piece of myself from everyone, making sure it never saw the light of day.

Yet here's this beautiful man stroking the ugliest part of me, the gnarly reminder of the darkest moments of my life, in the middle of the library, and I relish the contact. I'm leaning into it, drawing comfort from it. I don't feel ugly, like a freak, or some disgusting weirdo—his soft touch makes me feel treasured, peaceful even.

And I'm really not sure what to think about that. I can't imagine a life that doesn't have anxiety around my scars, but I'm daring to think it might be possible someday.

He wedges his knee between my thighs. I don't know how long I can fight the urge to rub my pussy—aggressively—against his leg.

Four to go. His kisses move down the column of my neck, slowly and with purpose, sending shivers of desire skating across my skin that echo between my legs.

"What's your favorite food?"

"Potato salad."

"Hmmm." He hums against my skin as he drags his tongue lower. When he sucks on the spot where my neck meets my shoulder, I shiver.

Huh. Ares de la Peña seems to be unlocking a long list of firsts for me. I've never been sensitive there, or maybe I've never been with someone who paid much attention to the fact that my neck might be a fun place to spend some time. It definitely feels like a fun place. Especially when he sucks again at the delicate skin on my neck.

"Interesting." His word is a purr against my skin before he nips with his teeth. It doesn't hurt. In fact, it's a nice counterpoint to the ache that's searing through my body on repeat.

When he bites a little harder, it's my turn to purr, though it doesn't sound nearly as sexy as Ares's noises. I might get off on those alone.

Three questions. Three answers to give and... Jeez. Am I really going to let him touch my clit?

Color me surprised that I'm acting out of character, but I think I just might. I don't think I have a choice. I can either let him touch me, or I can touch myself while he watches. Either way, I'm not sure it's possible for me to leave this library without coming. I can barely stand right now, let alone walk. And I said goodbye to my higher brain function a little while ago.

Right now, I don't care if he's a hot shot jock. I don't care if he's the baddest of bad boys. I don't care what anyone says about him. Right now, I'm not ignoring my growing crush, I'm not ignoring the fact that I'm tangled up in his orbit, or that it's exactly where I want to be.

Does this connection run deeper than a feral, innate attraction? I don't know. And a piece of me is afraid I'll have to find out once we take things further than a scorching kiss at the side of the coffee shop. Do we even have anything in common?

I'm not letting myself overthink this. I'm not letting my inner demons tell me I don't deserve this, that it can't be real, or that he's going to regret it.

I'm powered by need alone.

And right now, I need Ares de la Peña's hand down my fucking pants.

CHAPTER 14
Ares

Why the fucking fuck did I tell Eloise that we'd do five questions *before* I sank my fingers into her pussy?

I'm such a fucking idiot. My dick is so hard it hurts. My hand is twitching, ready, aching to slip between her folds. I bet she's wet for me. Her pulse flutters at the base of her neck, and I *know* her pussy is soaking wet and ready for me.

I know why I said what I said, why I wanted to wait, to do our five questions before I laid a finger on her. To make her feel more at ease with me, to help her understand that this isn't only a physical attraction for me. That I want to know her, really, truly know her before I do anything physical to her, or with her.

I wanted her to think about it all before she gives me consent to touch her. *Something* about her is different. We've barely spoken to each other. Beyond a Google search, we know very little about each other, but I want her to be mine. And I want her to know that while I might struggle with being monogamous, I'll be willing to give it a shot, for her. It's fucking senseless.

It was all a great and noble idea at the time, but right now? Right now, my dick wants to pierce a hole through my pants and embed itself in her. It's not even fussy about which hole. That said, I can't see Eloise being a butt-stuff kinda girl. I'm happy to be wrong about that, though.

For my third question, I asked her what her perfume is, because I want to buy it and spray my bed with it so I can smell her while I sleep. She said it's *Lovely* by Sarah Jessica Parker. *Sex in the City* isn't my jam; Mamá freakin' loves it though. But I could smell this perfume every damn day and never get tired of it. Thank you, Carrie Bradshaw.

Question four is going to make her recoil, it's going to make her uncomfortable, so I brace my body against hers, not to keep her in place, but in an attempt to offer her some form of comfort, sort of like a weighted blanket. Except standing and with a raging hard-on.

I don't stop stroking the scars on her face. She didn't pull away from me this time when I first touched them. She didn't gasp, cry out, or flinch away like she has in the past. That's progress. She also seems to be leaning into my touch on her scars, but that might only be in my head.

"Why do you dye your hair pink?" I suck her delicate skin into my mouth, grazing it with my teeth. "Why do you cover your scars, *tesoro*?" I kiss across the front of her throat and back up the other side of her face to where my digit brushes back and forth across her cheek. I want her to trust me. Hell, I *need* her to trust me, and I don't even really know why.

I want to know all her secrets.

I want to know every demon she has so I can help her slay them.

"That's two questions."

I growl against her skin, and she sighs.

"You know why." Her voice is tight, strained, and full of

pain. Tears well beneath her tightly closed lids, making her eyelashes glisten. "They're so ugly, Ares."

That sad whisper is gut-wrenching, and the dragon in my chest rears its head, ready to scorch the earth for her. Who made her feel anything less than the force she is?

"I'm not lying when I say you're beautiful." I brush her hair back from her face so I can kiss her scars. Her tense body relaxes again, just a little, enough to make me kiss her face again, and again, over and over until she softens completely.

"Don't hide who you are, *tesoro*. Not from me, not from anyone. Take up space like the badass you are."

That makes her giggle, her body shaking against mine, and I want to abandon five questions and rip her fucking clothes off. But number five is important.

"Why is that funny?" I skate my teeth along her jaw, down her neck and back to the other side of her face. I draw my free hand back up to her cheek and resume stroking her scars. At this point I'm no longer sure if it's for her benefit or my own.

"That's not my fifth question, I'm curious."

"You don't know anything about me. How do you know that I shouldn't hide?" Her voice is laced with humor, but an undercurrent of lust carries her words on rasping breaths. "And I'm certainly not a badass."

I grunt against her neck. "I've read enough about you to know that you're an impressive woman, Eloise."

"We're circling back to talk about your stalkery tendencies."

I can't help but smile at how her breath comes in pants, how her chest rises and falls, and how she's arching her body into mine.

"Like you haven't Googled me, too."

She looks away.

I grin again. "What's the matter, *tesoro*? Embarrassed that you looked me up? Or impatient for question five?"

She sinks onto my thigh, wedged between her legs, and brushes her crotch on my leg with a nod.

"Question five: will you go out with me?"

Both her brows and body shoot up, her eyes flit across my face like she's searching for the catch.

"If I say no..." She casts her eyes down toward where my hand still rests on her hip.

"If you say no, I'll still make you come with my fingers. If that's what you want."

She nibbles on her lip, and I want it to be mine between her teeth. Her nod is so slight I almost miss it. "Yes."

"Yes, what?" I need her to be specific. I need her express consent, her agreement, just... her.

"Yes, I'll go on a date with you."

"I didn't say go on a date with me, *tesoro*. I said go out with me. Plural dates. More than one. Date me."

She snorts in my face. An honest to God snort before her mouth drops open and her eyes widen. I curve a brow in question, but I don't ask it aloud.

"You don't do relationships."

"You're right, I don't. But I want one with you."

The admission hangs between us, something in the air shifting, the anticipation is heavier than my confession. This is a pivotal moment between us, and I barely risk snatching a breath in case it upsets the fragile balance and startles her like a deer in the woods.

"You... want... me..."

"To be my girlfriend, *sì*."

She tips her head to one side, eyes narrowing in an assessing way that's fast becoming one of my favorite things about her. "We don't know anything about each other."

"That's the point of dating. We know enough about each other to start a relationship. We'll learn the rest as we go."

She falls silent again. My chest tightens. How will I hold it together if she rejects me? I want to spend time with her, take her out and introduce her to my pig. And my cock, which is still straining against my pants.

The silence grows right in parallel with my fear. I prepare myself to step out of her space and respect her "no," but it never comes.

"Okay."

"*Mi novia*."

She nods.

Girlfriend.

I've never had a girlfriend before. I thought it'd feel different, restrictive, maybe it's too early to tell, but the weight pressing on my chest isn't so heavy right now. But just because she's my girlfriend doesn't mean, well, it doesn't mean shit. She might have lost her desire when the conversation took a detour down reality lane.

"Ares?" She reaches her hand to cup my face, holding my gaze in hers. "Can you make me come now, please?"

Any remaining tension melts in my chest as I back her into the wall, pressing her hard against the cool stone behind her. We kiss, our tongues and teeth dueling in a dance neither of us know the steps to. She presses against my forearm again, urging it lower, and when I move it toward her crotch she sighs into my mouth.

I'm a pretty selfless lover. Don't get me wrong, I love to get mine. But generally speaking, I'm a giver. And never have I wanted to pleasure someone more than this beautiful woman whimpering in my arms.

I skim the band of her pants with my hand, and she mewls. When I do it a second time, her noise takes on a note of frustration, and by the third pass across her waist she's all but growling at me.

I've never heard a pixie growl before, but it's every bit as adorable and hot as I might have imagined.

"Ares." My name escapes her on an aggravated groan between kisses as her nails sink into my forearm. The bite of pain spurs me on. I want this woman to be completely twisted up over me, as bent out of shape as I am over her. Having her practically pleading for my fingers gives me a heady rush.

I move my hand into her pants. My eyes roll back in my head as my fingers walk lower, lower, gliding through her soft hair. The closer I get to her pussy, the hotter she is. She's soaking, her lips coated with her arousal, and I don't need to sink my fingers between them to feel how slick she is for me.

I bite my tongue to suppress a groan. This isn't about me. As much as I'm aching to blow my load in the stacks, this is about her. I want her to come for me. I want her body to tense, then release everything she has to give. For me.

I dip my finger inside her, then two, and she clenches around me, flexing her walls. She's so smooth, and hot, and so fucking wet. I'm totally here for it. I curl my fingers so I can graze her g-spot, she responds by pushing her hips toward me. I press the soft place inside her, and she grips my bicep with a strength I shouldn't be surprised she has.

Her head tips back, leaning against the wall and exposing her throat to me. She's gonna be so pissed when she sees the streak of bruises blooming under her skin, but that's a future Ares's problem.

Right now, I need to make this woman come. I slide my fingers out of her, and she whimpers again. She might not be comfortable voicing her desires, but her noises, her body's responses, they're telling me everything I need to know.

I circle her clit with my middle finger, and her entire body sags. Relief? Pleasure? Whatever it is, it makes me want to keep going. I had planned on edging her until she was clinging to the ledge of the cliff with both hands, screaming at me to let her have her release, but in the moment, I need to make her come for me.

I pick up speed with my circles around her clit, increasing pressure with each sweep. While I dot kisses on her neck, my free hand strokes one of her nipples through her shirt.

My hand is soaked with her juices, and I fucking love it. She's moaning and whispering my name between sharp breaths as I glide my fingers faster and faster over her clit. Her orgasm takes us both by surprise. She jolts back, bumping her head on the wall with a shriek that she tries to silence by burying her head in my shoulder and holding me tightly against her while her body jerks and shudders.

I've never felt so satisfied before. Knowing she's coming apart on my fingers gives me a rush I usually only experience when I'm on the ice dodging discs of solid rubber traveling at my face at high speeds.

She bucks her hips away from my fingers but the tremors continue to make her body shake. I find my way back to her now-swollen clit and pick up speed again. She's shaking her head against my chest, so I pause.

"You want me to stop?"

She nods, then shakes her head, then nods. Her mouth falls open, but nothing comes out. I'm not sure even she knows what she wants.

I move to take my hand out, to stop until she figures out whether she wants more or not, but she clasps my arm with both her hands.

"Don't stop. I just..." When she looks up at me, her insecurity and doubt swim in her eyes. And fuck that shit. "I'm so loud." Her voice is barely above a whisper as her head lolls back onto my chest. "So wet... so... embarrassing." She dropped her voice again, probably thinking I couldn't hear the end of her sentence. But I did, and again, to that I say: Fuck. That. Shit.

I'm going to make her scream, right here in the fucking library. I'm going to make her burst into a million tiny pieces of pleasure, then hold her until the wave passes and she makes her way back together again.

I've known her for only a short window of time, and I'm already tired of her making herself small and trying to blend in with mundane irrelevance.

There's a reason other than her scars that her hair is pink, a reason she stood and watched me fuck Séb in an alley, a reason she hauled me deep into the bowels of the library instead of out onto the street where I couldn't touch her.

Eloise Downing wasn't born to be insignificant. If I have to remind her of that every day for the rest of her life, I will. She was born to shine like a star, without remorse or apology.

And as she comes on my fingers for a second time on a wail she barely contains by smashing her face into my chest, I'm resolved to help her break whatever self-imposed shackles she wears and help her light up the sky. Every damn day.

She's trying to bite me through my sweater as she soaks my hand. Her cum trickles down my fingers, and while part of me wants to go for a hat trick, she's barely able to stand up as it is. She's leaning against the wall, sliding a little as she braces her hands on me. Her face is flushed, cheeks pink, her eyes bright, and her hair is roughed up enough to look like she's been up to no good, but not enough to uncover her face.

As much as I don't think she should hide her scars from anyone, I'm not going to force her to do things she's uncomfortable with. I won't let her hide from me, not one single little piece of herself, but if she needs to keep her face hidden from the rest of the world, then I'll stand right in front of her, keeping her shielded, until she's ready to step into the sun.

CHAPTER 15
Eloise

I'm not sure what I'm more stunned at, the fact Ares sucked my... my... *moisture* off his fingers right in front of me in the library, or the fact that I'm dating Ares de la Peña. Like officially dating. Like boyfriend, girlfriend, dating.

I'm in a relationship with Ares de la Peña.

After the... *moisture* incident, he led me out to his car and took me for pie in a quaint little place called GTFO. It's very sneakily hidden in the back of a laundromat on the far side of campus, and it might be my new favorite place on the face of the earth.

The little library section in the corner needs some love, and they could do with an influx of new board games because some of the ones on the shelves are... well loved.

We aren't staying, simply waiting for our order to be ready so we can take it to go. But overall, I'm totally digging the vibe here. There are no empty seats in the tiny, secret cafe. Why doesn't Brian the burly Irish pie guy scale up his business? Or, I dunno, at least publicize the fact a pie shop is this close to campus so he could bring more people in and maybe open another location. Wouldn't that be cool? Maybe he'd open up in the back of a gas station or something next.

The smells are driving me crazy. I'm pretty sure Ares has heard my stomach gurgle and grumble about having to wait for the pies that smell so darn delicious—even over the noise of the patrons enjoying their food.

He keeps glancing over at me, like he's afraid I'm either a figment of his imagination, or like I might bolt through the door leading into the laundry machines. The reality is, I'm wondering if I can go cozy up to some of the people enjoying delicious pie, share theirs, and then give them some of ours when we get it. Sometimes, I'm a simple creature.

I still can't believe I've never heard of this place before. I risk a furtive glance over at Ares, and he's staring at me, a small, intimate smile tugging on the edges of his mouth.

I guess we're doing this. We're officially a couple. We've skipped right over the first date part and we're now... boyfriend and girlfriend. So instead of diving into an awkward first date, we're diving into an awkward relationship. This doesn't feel smart.

I swallow, hard. Dad isn't going to like this, which means I'll have to keep it from him, and that thought makes it even worse.

I don't keep things from my dad, not really. I mean, I keep my bone-deep sadness about Mom to myself—and my therapist—and the fact that I feel like a twisted monster because of my face. But I generally share things about my life with him when we have dinner. Big and small things alike. We talk about things, he tells me about his latest trip on the road, and I tell him about my life.

And this... I drag my eyes from Ares's toes all the way up to his perfectly coiffed hair... this is most certainly a big thing.

I guess we're not technically skipping over the first date part, we're doing it in reverse.

I can't say I thought that this rich guy hotshot's idea of a first date would be a tiny hole-in-the-wall pie shop called Get the Fork Out. He mentioned something about going to meet his pig, and I'm honestly not sure if that's a euphemism for his penis, or if he really has a pet pig he wants to introduce me to.

It could go either way.

Though if this guy, this... *boyfriend* of mine—oh holy cannoli, Ares de la Peña is my boyfriend. My stomach's in knots as another shiver passes through my entire body. This has to be a dream, right? Or a really, really, *really* mean joke?

Oof. I don't know if I'm ever going to get used to the idea that he's my boyfriend. Anyway, if *he* thinks he's going to take me back to his place and show me any part of his naked self on the first date, he has another think coming.

My brain stalls out on the idea of Ares naked. Now that I'm his girlfriend... that's part of the whole package. I'm going to see Ares de la Peña all-the-way naked.

I'd been so stuck on the fact that his perfectly manicured fingers had been inside me, had made me come in the library, that I hadn't really thought beyond that. My skin is clammy, hot, and my panties are drenched from our *encounter* in the library.

"Is this Persephone?" The tall, dark, and brooding Irishman addresses Ares, but his face is blank.

I offer a smile. "I'd like to think I'm more Aphrodite than Persephone."

Brian tips his head. "Touché."

I'm entirely convinced that Brian knows exactly what Ares de la Peña did to me in the library because he keeps giving me a look while we wait.

That look. The "girl, you've totally been finger-banged in the library" look.

Speaking of finger-banging in the library, I pull out my phone. I have to tell Tori. I shoot off a text that says "Fingered in French" thinking I'm hilarious and instantly regretting it the moment I press *send*. Though it's creepy that Tori commented on the French section in her messages and that's where I ended up making out with Ares. Is that where everyone goes to do... *things* in the library?

That's not a thought I want to let fester, so I clutch the phone to my chest as Brian hands over our food. Ares hands him... ho—ooooohmigosh Ares is giving him two hundred-dollar bills. For four slices of pie? How upmarket is this place?

Brian doesn't flinch or argue. He offers Ares a fist bump and tucks the money into the cash drawer.

The prices are next to the specials on the menu board. Price per slice, price per pie. Nowhere on the board does it say anything about fifty-dollar slices of pie. Does he bake gold into the crust? Or maybe Ares is paying him for something other than pie.

Oh, no. Is he back on drugs? Is *that* the reason he wants me to be his girlfriend? Am I some kind of good girl cover he can hide behind and pretend to be dating while he goes off the rails?

My eyes are hanging out of my head right now, but I can't stop staring. Not only is Ares de la Peña my boyfriend, but it momentarily slipped my mind—I'm going to go ahead and chalk it up to being absolutely blinded by lust for the past couple of hours—that he is also the son of a billionaire.

My bad-boy boyfriend is rich. And possibly addicted to pie as well as alcohol and—according to the search engines —cocaine.

If you'd asked me this morning whether I'd be saying that specific combination of words together any time soon, I'd have laughed in your face.

A giggle bubbles up into my throat as Ares takes my hand to guide me back through the laundromat and out to his SUV.

I'm never showing him my house, or any of my clothes.

Okay, he has to see my clothes, but as I slide into this freak-ishly shiny beast of a vehicle, I'm reminded of my very humble upbringing, compared to his... not at all humble anything.

It's flashy inside the car, too. It's almost as shiny as the exterior with lots of bells and whistles, and the more I stare at everything in Ares's world, the more I feel like this was a huge, giant, gar-freakin-gantuan mistake.

I can't date him. I can't be his girlfriend. I can't fit into his world of... peopling and riches.

I shiver. The idea of going to one of his hockey parties chills the blood in my veins. I'm not a party girl, and he's all parties all the time. I don't even like Champagne. Ew.

This will never... ever, never in a billion years, work. We need to call it off before it has a chance to fall apart.

Looking up and out the windshield I realize we haven't yet left the parking lot of GTFO. When I turn to face Ares, he's staring at me, concern marring his beautiful features.

"What's wrong?" I ask.

He reaches over and tugs my hand away from my shirt and cups it with both of his. "You tell me, *tesoro*. You're twisting the hem of your shirt like it owes you money and muttering under your breath like Lady Macbeth."

I raise my brows, and his face turns pink. "She's the 'out damn spot' one, right?" He's adorable when he's vulnerable, unsure of himself.

"She is."

It's damned spot, not damn, but I'm not correcting him out loud. His shoulders release as though finding out he wasn't wrong was a big deal.

"You want to tell me what thoughts are racing through that head of yours, *mi cariño*?"

Clamping my mouth shut, I shake my head. Nope. I do not. The idea of letting him hear the level of anxiety that's rattling around in my mind... yeah, no. That's definitely a hard no.

He slides a knuckle under my chin and turns my head so I can face him. "*Habla conmigo.*"

I try to inhale a deep breath, but it snags in my chest. My shoulders are tight, and my palms are sticky. He's probably groaning internally at having picked up my hand at all. This isn't going to work. We should part ways and call it a day.

Wait, we should each take our pie and part ways, because there's no way on Earth I'm smelling these smells and not tasting the goods.

Tori would love to share some pie, especially if it comes with a side of tea about the happenings in the stacks. If she knew about that pie place and didn't tell me, I'm going to have to advertise for a new best friend.

He's still staring at me, patiently waiting in silence, pointing those kissable lips right at me. I want to kiss him until he forgets that he asked me something, but I can't. That would only be delaying the inevitable.

"This isn't going to work, Ares."

His frown deepens, but he stays quiet.

I sigh, pulling my clammy hand from his and placing it onto my lap.

Boundaries. Space. Defenses. Protection.

"You're... well, you, and I'm... not."

It all sounded great in the library when it was the two of us, and I was beyond desperate to have his hand in my pants, caught up in the lust. But in the cold light of day, it's ridiculous.

"And who am I, exactly?"

"You're the rich, hockey playing son of a rich man. You drive flashy cars, party hard, and do... *stuff* with people in alleys and libraries." I sound like an idiot as soon as the words are out of my mouth, but he's kind enough not to laugh in my face.

He purses his lips. "And that means we can't be together because...?"

"I hate parties, I drive an old car, I come from a family that doesn't have much money and certainly doesn't have any social standing... heck, I don't even know the rules of hockey."

"You forgot stripper." His lips twitch like he's trying not to laugh at my list of reasons we can't be together, and my brain short circuits again. Stripper.

"St-stripper. Right. My mistake. You're the rich, hockey playing, *stripper* son of a rich man." I've seen him half naked in my search engine. The ink across the top part of his chest, under his collar bone and wrapped around his bicep. I've seen his abs. Those abs should be illegal.

He has the audacity to chuckle. *Chuckle*! The nerve.

"Care to let me in on the joke?"

"It's funny that you're intimidated by my money, by my family, by my reputation. And I'm over on this side of the car intimidated by your intelligence, afraid to say something that'll make you laugh at me for being stupid, feeling that no amount of money in the bank would make me good enough to be with you."

I shake my head, like that might help focus my thoughts. What the heck?

"No amount of money can buy intelligence, *tesoro*. Not to mention, I have a past, a dark and shameful past. I know you read about it online, but that's only what was reported, what my father's PR people couldn't keep under wraps." He drops his gaze to the center console.

"I've done things, and I don't mean stripping, or being promiscuous, or loving sex and fucking people in public. I did things while I was high and drunk because I could. Because I knew that my name would protect me from consequences."

The air in the car has grown tense, heavy. "I don't care about who you *were*, Ares. I care about who you *are*."

"Like you said, you don't know who I am." He has me there. I did say that.

"You're the kind of person who pays two hundred dollars for four pieces of pie. I don't know why, but I know that's a terribly kind thing for you to do."

His head tips up so I can see into his sad eyes again. "Brian's having issues with some conglomerate trying to buy his building to put up a high rise. He refuses to move, he refuses to buy bigger premises, to grow his business. He likes things as they are. So, I pay a little extra for my pie."

I snort. "A little."

He shrugs like it's no big deal, but to me, and likely to Brian, it's a pretty big deal. "He only takes money that I make from my side hustle. I don't take a salary, but I do collect my tips and use those to pay for pie. It's a principle thing for him."

I can't help but laugh. That totally tracks from the little I know about the Irishman in the hidden pie shop. I was also right—it's a sweet gesture from Ares that warms my chest.

"Why do you study gender and social justice?"

His eyebrows twitch. "No one's really asked me that before. Simple answer is that it pisses my father off. He wants his male children to study male things and be manly men to represent the family." He shrugs casually, but a muscle feathers in his jaw, sadness painted in his eyes and the downturned edges of his mouth.

"What's the not so simple answer?"

His eyes narrow, gaze concentrating on my face before he sighs. "My favorite cousin in the whole world was raped."

My heart stops dead in my chest, and I wrap my arms across myself to rub my gooseflesh covered arms.

"I'm so sorry, Ares." I want to reach out to him, to take his hand, or stroke his face but I'm afraid if I show him affection right now, he'll clam up and bring back the showman, the performer.

"The guy got away with it. She'd been drinking..." He waves a hand like it's a tale as old as time. And I unfortunately know what he means. While I haven't been assaulted myself, I've heard plenty of stories, and Mom was a rape victim during her time at college, before she met Dad. And for some reason our justice system seems to favor the criminal, rather than the victims.

"So, I decided to study gender, to become an ally to women. To say fuck the patriarchy, study social justice, to stand up for what's right and to become a champion for victims who can't find their own voice, or who can, and get shouted down by some louder asshole with a dick."

Be still my beating heart.

It turns out that Ares de la Peña is more than parties, sex, and hockey. This is... ooooh this is bad, this is very, very bad. I was fine with shallow Ares, kissing and fingering, and cocky Ares. But this... this is deep Ares.

And he's sharing his hidden depths with me. I... wow. This is huge. I had no idea.

"I..."

"I know. It doesn't quite align with the playboy, bad boy, hockey playing stripper image, right?"

I nod.

"Just because I like having a good time doesn't mean I'm shallow."

Ouch. Yup. I pegged him as being exactly that, didn't I? Guilt trickles down my spine, clogging my pores and making my cheeks heat.

"It's okay. I'd rather you assumed I'm shallow than stupid."

That draws a gasp out of me. I've never made any assumptions about his intelligence. "No. I never thought you were stupid, Ares. Why would you even think that?" Except I have. The joke about him not knowing where the library is scorching my insides.

Another shrug, and now he won't even let me see his sad eyes. My scars are physical, on my face for everyone to see, but his, his scars are inside, and the more he talks to me right now the more I want to reach inside his chest and soothe them somehow.

"I'm not trying to talk you out of your decision. Well, I guess I am, but not in a manipulative way." He pauses. "For a change." He eye rolls, but it seems more at himself than at me.

"I know what everyone thinks about me, what they see when they look at me. And yes, I'm a flashy hotshot who loves to party and have a good time. It's not a facade by any means, but there's more to me than that."

I don't know what to say to that, because it was unkind to judge him by his appearance when he didn't do the same of me. He hasn't ever once let my scars be an issue. He's never pressured me to tell him about my darkness, and he's sitting here in front of me confessing that he's intimidated by my intelligence. Yet he didn't let that stop him from asking me out. That's pretty brave.

I have a lot of thoughts bubbling in my brain, and I'm not really sure I can find my voice to share them, so instead, I stamp down my insecurities. If I'm going to be this man's girl-friend, his partner, I'm going to have to get over my nervous-ness. I can't expect him to be the instigator of everything for the entirety of our relationship.

I cup his face with both my palms, stare into his intense, bottomless brown eyes, and brush my nose against his before sweeping my lips across his. He returns my kiss, his tongue skimming across the seam of my mouth, and I'm only too eager to grant him access.

The kiss is softer than our previous kisses. It's not frantic, horny, lust filled, or demanding. It's slow, deep, and curious. He's exploring my mouth with every stroke of his tongue and his hand rests over my scars. I can't say this is how I expected the day to go. I didn't wake up this morning thinking I'd be Ares's girlfriend, but the more he kisses me, the more time I spend with him, the more I like it.

I have no idea how things are going to work once we step outside the security of his shiny black SUV, but I guess that's future Eloise's problem.

CHAPTER 16
Eloise

"Where have you been?" Dad is waiting in the living room like I was out all night after prom without permission. It's still light outside, but he's glaring at me, his annoyance almost making the air around him vibrate. Each word is gritted out, measured, fueled by irritation.

"I was at school."

"You didn't have classes, Eloise. I have your schedule."

Hugging my binder to my chest, I scowl. What the heck is this? Why is he giving me the third degree? "I was with friends."

His face says he doesn't believe me. *You don't have friends, Eloise.* And that near-true accusation in his eyes slices me deep. "It's that troublemaker again, isn't it?" He holds up a hand. "You don't need to answer me. I can see it written all over your face." His voice is hard as he chastises me.

"I'm not a little girl anymore, Dad."

"Then stop fucking acting like one." He thumps the arm of the recliner as he pushes himself to his feet. "Actions have consequences, Eloise. You're living under my roof. Stop this nonsense with that boy, or we're going to have a problem."

He walks out before my words come back to me, before the pink mist clears enough for my higher brain function to return to something resembling coherence. Did he just threaten me? My house, my rules? His truck starts up in the driveway, and I don't bother to cover my face before I let out a frustrated scream.

He's going to make me choose.

Ares, or my father.

Guilt consumes me, tightening around my chest. It should be an easy decision. Ares is shiny and new, he's temporary, fleeting, there's probably no way we'll last. But yet...

Ugh. Maybe it's stubbornness, outright refusal to let my dad win, but I don't want to give up whatever this is between Ares and me.

I've never been the kid who sneaks out, lies to her parents, and does things they've said they *explicitly* don't want me to. Dad's gone more than he's here, it wouldn't be all that hard to keep Ares a secret from him.

Maybe it's time I became that kid, because I'm not ready to give up either.

CHAPTER 17

Ares

I've made a huge mistake.

I shouldn't have sucked her cum off my fingers in the library. It's all I can fucking think about. One taste, and I want more. I want it all.

I can't let it distract me, though, no matter how badly I want to abandon this game, strip off my pads, throw her down and eat her out until my name is the only one to pass her lips. It's tempting, so fucking tempting, but I can't let pussy, no matter how fucking sweet, come between me and the game.

It's the start of the second period against the Flint Flames. I've already done my stretches and cat-scratched my crease with my skates. I clink my stick off my left post, then my right then my left again, suck in a cleansing breath, breathe out my lingering stresses and distractions, then lean forward, crouching between the pipes.

My life outside this rink might feel like a hot mess express, but in here, in this crease, no matter whose barn we're in, I'm the emperor supreme.

This is my domain.

Some of our outskaters are having a sucktastic game,

though. And if I thought I could find a way to beat the shit out of our captain, Justin Ashe, with his own fucking stick and get away with it, I'd do it.

I dunno where his head is right now, but it's not in this goddamn game. He knows it too, he keeps muttering out loud and cussing himself out every time he passes my net. At least he better be cussing himself out. If he's cussing me out, I'm going to beat him with my stick, Coach be damned.

When the centers slow to a stop in front of the ref, the crowd quiets, tension already rising around the arena. The Flames are strong. We lost to them last night, and we're all going to need to pull together if we're going to walk away from this game with a W. And I really want the fucking win.

Spoiler alert: we don't win. We don't even come close.

My first period shut out is short lived as Talbot from the Flames gets lucky with a rebound. Less than thirty seconds later, he's back peppering me with shots, and while I'm good, great even, if I do say so myself, there's only so much I can do by my fucking self.

I stopped forty-one shots on my goal tonight. Forty-one shots. At some points it felt like I was the only one on the damn ice.

Everything hurts. Everything fucking hurts, right down to the marrow in my bones. I'm exhausted. I'm dehydrated. Sweat is streaming down my face and trickling down my back under my pads. And all I want to do is kick Justin Ashe's ass. He's the captain, the one we all look to, to take charge, to lead, to pick up our spirits when shit gets tough.

His presence was noteworthy on the ice for all the wrong reasons tonight, and we all know it. Dude needs a slap.

The old me—troublemaker me—the guy not afraid to fuck things up because his father would clean up the mess for him, he wouldn't give a shit. He'd be only too willing to throw down with Cap. But this me... this me is on hockey probation for a coach who doesn't give a fuck who my dad is? This me has to play nice. I can't afford to get benched again, or worse, get kicked off the fucking team altogether.

The embarrassment alone would be too great; for me, for the "family"... my brothers would kick my ass, then Papá would start about the money. For a man with so much money he could wipe his ass with hundreds for the rest of his life and have millions left over to play with, he sure is a miser. He never lets me forget that it's his money that's bankrolled and continues to bankroll my entire life.

I'm grateful, of course I am. Parents aren't supposed to keep score, or a fucking tab. I'm convinced he's going to produce a bill on my graduation day and demand I start repayments. *Cabrón*.

So, instead of picking a fight with my captain even though he deserves it, I strip, have an extra quick shower, and take myself out of a situation where my sour mood might result in me getting summoned back into coach's office for another *discussion* about my hockey career and place on this team.

Not least of all because Hayes has gotten pretty good, pretty quickly. And I don't want to be replaced on the starting line-up. The more I watch him, the more we train together, the more I think he might be able to take my place.

Tonight was another game where I gave it my all, and no one even noticed. Hauling my kit bag out to my car, I tug my ball cap down over my face. It's not like the oversized duffle bag won't give me away as a hockey player, or a murderer I guess, but maybe people will leave me the hell alone if I make myself smaller and unapproachable.

I'm about six feet away from my car when Coach calls my name.

"Yeah, Coach?" My stomach is on the ground somewhere as I turn to face him, I might shit myself. Wouldn't that be the icing on the sucky cake today?

"Good game. Tough break." He nods at me and walks off.

I stand staring after him. Hockey coaches aren't exactly known for being warm and fuzzy, or for handing out praise, so for Coach Bales, *good game* is pretty fucking high praise.

I blow out a breath, relief trickling through my muscles, but they're tight. Maybe I'll see if I can pick up a shift and dance off some of this crappy mood, and I'll feel better in the morning.

As I drive past Bitches Brew, I spy Eloise's car. I don't want to get my stink on her with this shitty mood, or worse, say something to upset her, but I haven't left her any hot cocoa in a while. The tingle of mischief makes my nose twitch, and I can't help myself.

She might catch me, but at this point I don't really care if she does. I had this whole elaborate plot concocted around these damn packets of hot chocolate. I was going to plant the idea in her head that she had a secret admirer and convince her that she needed to date me to make whomever it was jealous and show himself.

Then, after a few fake dates with me, she'd hopefully have seen that I'm not a complete asshole, at least not all the time, and she'd agree to a real date like it was all a happy coincidence.

As it happened, I didn't need to do any of that. And looking back, I realize how far I was willing to go to manipulate her into being my girlfriend. That's something I'll need to bring up with my therapist, I'm sure.

Turns out, I needed to be myself and let her take a peek at my brokenness. She didn't run, she didn't pity me, and in fact, she seemed big fucking mad when I called myself stupid. She gets cute nose wrinkles when she's pissed.

I pause on my way to Eloise's car and sneak a glance through the coffee shop window. It's easy to spot her pink hair amid the evening crowd. She's with Tori. Eloise's face is side on to the window I'm looking through, and she looks happy.

She throws her head back and laughs at something Tori says, waving a hand like she's asking her to stop before wrapping an arm across her stomach.

I want to go in. To say hi, to kiss her, and to let the soothing tone of her voice caress my crappy mood until it's all gone. But the way she's laughing, the way she's animatedly chatting to her friend... I don't want to take that from her. I don't want to mar her bright spirit with my bullshit.

She might be glad to see me. She might even invite me to join them, but this is her time with her friend. It's not something I'm going to muscle in on, no matter how badly I might want to. And I *really* fucking want to.

As I'm tucking the packet of chocolate powder under her windshield wiper, Athena's laughter sounds behind me. "What the fuck are you doing, *hermanito*? I can't tell if you're trying to break into that car or dry hump it." She cackles again.

When I lean back and turn to face her, her eyes dance between the windshield and my face. Despite the cool shower I had before leaving the rink, and the cold night air, my face starts to warm.

"Are you blushing? My baby brother is embarrassed? I never thought I'd see the day." Questions flit across her face and amusement lighting up her eyes in the glow of the streetlights. She folds her arms, leveling me with an arched brow over a perfect, piercing stare.

I've always wondered how she mastered it, the inquisition glare, the "give me all the answers I require, or I'll hurt you" face. Was she born that way? Or does she spend hours in front of the mirror glaring and threatening herself.

"Care to explain yourself? Because"—she huffs out a breath—"it appears to me, hermanito, that you're placing a packet of hot chocolate on someone's car window." The disbelief in her voice coupled by the wrinkles on her forehead make me chuckle.

"That's exactly what I'm doing." I resist the urge to fold my arms across my body to protect myself from the force that is my sister. I don't want her to scent weakness and go for the jugular.

I'm acutely aware that my goalie pads are in my trunk if I need them, but she could totally kill me before I got anywhere near them.

"You wanna tell me why?"

I jut my chin out at her. "I do nice things… Sometimes"

At that, she snorts, and in seconds, she's laughing so hard she's doubled over, hand on one knee, and the other holding up an index finger, telling me to hold on for a second while she figures her shit out.

It takes more than a second for her to stand up straight, and when she finally does, she wipes under her eyes with the fleshy part of both thumbs at the same time.

The longer it takes her to recover from her outburst, the more irritation prickles under my skin. I *do* do nice things, dammit.

A beat passes. Two. I can't think of a single nice thing I've done for someone in a long time. Okay, fine, maybe it's been a while.

"*Te amo*, Ares. But the only time you do," she holds up her hands to make air quotes, "nice things, is if something's in it for you."

That stings. Mostly because she's fucking right.

No point in beating around the bush when it comes to my big sister, or giving her any form of my bravado, so I sigh and give into the urge to cross my arms. "It's my girlfriend's car." I realize what I've done the second the words leave my mouth because my sister is now laughing so hard, she might either fall over or piss herself.

Ay, dios mío. I hope she does both. I won't even help. I'll stand here and record it so I can upload it to social media.

"Now I know you're lying." She pants out the words in short breaths between giggles. She wags a finger at me as she presses her knees together. "Good one, but you need to stop before I wet myself."

I guess my silence, or something about my expression clues her in to the fact that I'm not telling a joke. She straightens. "Wait, you're... serious?"

I nod.

Her jaw drops open, she flicks her gaze back to the windshield, lets it linger for a moment before she fixes me with a look I haven't seen before. "You really have a girlfriend, Ares?"

I nod again.

She purses her lips and narrows those fucking know-all eyes. "What? What is it?"

"She's too good for me."

Another snort. "Now *that* I can believe." She shakes her head, understanding dawning on her face. "Wait. That's your girlfriend's car?"

Another nod. She's not normally this slow to follow along with something, so I can only assume she's scheming.

She claps her hands together. "So, she's here? Inside?" She hooks a thumb over her shoulder.

Oh no.

"We should go say hi."

Puta! Hell fucking no. My girl might have a titanium backbone and could handle anything, but she's skittish with me. I'm not sure *two* de la Peñas gatecrashing her girl time is the best idea.

"She does *know* she's your girlfriend, right?" She heaves out a sigh. "Ares, please tell me you're not stalking some poor, unsuspecting college kid. I swear, I'll—"

I hold up a hand to stop her. "She knows. Jesús. You know I'd never..."

Her expression turns serious and she nods. "I know. That was a shitty thing to say, I'm sorry. I'm just... stunned. I can't believe my baby brother is finally in a relationship. This is your first, like, ever, right?"

I rub the back of my neck, praying for an alien invasion to stop this awkward fucking inquisition.

"Point her out to me." Athena slides her arm around my shoulders and turns me toward the window. "Come on. Show me who you're dating. If she's really real, I mean."

"You really don't think I could have a girlfriend?" I don't like this feeling. I'm confident—everything I do in life is something I can thrive at or accomplish. But this, this is new territory, and having my sister laugh out loud in my fucking face when I tell her I'm in a new relationship, well, that's... shit.

"I'm sorry." She jabs at my ribs. "This is going to provide a lot of opportunities for me to make fun of you. Let me have my fun. I know it's a big deal, though."

"It is. And I'm pretty scared of fucking it all up, too. So, if you could dial back the shock and giggles for a hot minute, that'd be great."

She squeezes my shoulders. "You're really into her, aren't you?"

My silence is her answer.

"You have to be. You're leaving her treats on her car after a shitty game, for fuck's sake." She follows my line of sight into the coffee shop. I want to ask her how she knows we had a game. She hates hockey, and as far as I know, she doesn't follow our progress either. But she's already honing in on her target.

"The red head?"

I shake my head. Tori is definitely not my girl. Though, if I fuck up with Eloise, she's going to rip my balls off before my sister can even sharpen her knives. "Pink. The pixie."

She chuckles, her laugh vibrating through my ribs, easing some of my tension. "She's fucking adorable. Does she fit in your pocket?"

That makes me smile. "*Tesoro*."

Athena clutches her chest with both hands and says "aw" really loudly, stretching it out, and now I'm praying for an earthquake to come with the aliens. Athena's stare burns into the side of my face while I keep my eyes forward on Eloise.

"*¿Cuál es su nombre?*"

"Eloise."

"And she agreed to be your girlfriend? She's not a call girl? You're not bribing her or catfishing her?"

Now, I'm pissed off. She's poking fun, but this is a sensitive spot for me and it's really damn uncomfortable. I bite my lip for a beat before I hiss out a slow breath. "She's my girlfriend, Hen. Of her own free will, no monthly fee, no mail order, not a transaction in sight, she said yes." Okay, that even sounds farfetched to me. I can kinda see why she thinks I might have paid Eloise for a date. Not that I'll ever tell her that.

Athena falls silent for a minute as we both watch Eloise walk to the counter to get another round of drinks. "Hot chocolate." She looks at the car. "*¡Ay! Hermanito,* you are a romantic. It's her favorite, *sí*?"

I nod. "I've been leaving them for her on her car and at the gym. She doesn't know they're from me."

"Have you taken her on a date?"

"I'm not a complete dumbass, Hen. I took her for pie. I *was* going to take her for a hot air balloon ride, but she's wary about... y'know."

"The fact our father is one of the richest men in the country?"

"Yeah, that."

The door to Bitches Brew opens and a throng of students comes out onto the street. The door is slow to close. My willpower is faltering. I want to kiss her, to taste her, to hold her. Movement is threatening to burst into my feet and make me charge through the door.

Athena whistles next to me. "You really have got it bad, *hermanito*. I'm very happy for you, though, and I look forward to meeting her." She plants a huge kiss on my cheek.

My brows jolt up. "That's it?"

"That, and if you need me, you know where to find me. You're probably going to fuck up along the way." She holds up both hands. "That's not a reflection of you. We all fuck up, even when it's not our first relationship. Getting to know someone, *really* know them, that takes time, patience, and a desire to put your partner before yourself sometimes."

She pats my chest. "This is so unlike you, Ares. It must be scary as fuck. But from the look in your eyes as you're staring at her, it'll be worth it. This is going to be good for you. Be sure you make it good for her too. And don't let fear freak you out of giving it a fair shot. Just because it's new, doesn't mean it's bad."

"I'm afraid of casting my darkness onto her. She's pure sunshine, Hen."

"Light and dark coexist, Ares. Can't be one without the other."

"I'm afraid this will destroy me." It's like I'm back in confession with Father Feehan, the fears tumble from my lips as easily as my list of sins when I was a child.

She sighs again. It's heavier, charged with something I can't put my finger on, and her eyes turn sad as she places her hands on my shoulders. "It wouldn't be love if it didn't." She hugs me. "Te amo, hermanito."

Then she smacks me. "Get the fuck out of here before

someone calls the cops on the creepy stalker guy humping cars in the parking lot."

Aaaaaand she's back. I flip her off.

"And don't let Abuelita find out about her unless you're the real deal. She'll be buying her wedding outfit before you finish telling her you have a new girlfriend."

I give her a two fingered salute and head back to my car. I can't help sitting at the wheel for a couple minutes, staring at my girl through the window.

Athena's right. Eloise must be something really special for me to hang up my playboy hat. And she is, I feel it in the flicker in my chest when I see her, the sense of calm that settles on me when she's in my space. There's something here. I need to find the cojones to find it and help it grow.

CHAPTER 18
Eloise

"No."

"But Ellie-Bellie..." Tori flutters her eyes at me. "You said we should start doing things together. Fun things. Friend things. Things that aren't..." She taps the books in front of her on my dining room table.

We study together at my house a lot—it's become part of our routine. As much as we love Bitches Brew, it can get a bit distracting, and we end up drinking too much hot chocolate —and although Tori insists there's no such thing, it's not great for the bank balance.

We tried to study at Tori's once, but with the tiny hurricane blasting through the room demanding every ounce of his mama's attention, well, that didn't go so well. Even with her mom helping out, it's like her kid could sense she was there and knew she was doing something boring like furthering her education.

The look on his little face was definitely calling her out. Like, how dare she have the audacity to pay attention to her homework when there were far more important things to be doing, like watching Ryder and the *Paw Patrol* pups getting up to no good.

No amount of snacks could keep him from trying to "help" us study, and no amount of Chickaletta on screen could distract him from the fact that we were there.

"No." I say it firmer, harder, mustering all the resolve I have, adding a scowl for good measure.

"Okay, if you can tell me three reasons why we shouldn't go to the strip club to watch Ares dance, then we won't go." She holds out a thumb to me, clearly ready to count my reasons.

I saw a video of Ares dancing on the internet the night I looked him up. I only clicked one of the links, but there are... let's say a lot. A *lot* of clips of him stripping, pole dancing, partying hard, playing hockey. He has a very strong social media presence that he doesn't seem to contribute much to himself. He doesn't need to.

One of the social media sites even has an Ares de la Peña tribute page, posting stories and pictures about him pretty regularly. I also saw a comment from someone suggesting he should get his own paid subscription service to charge people a monthly fee to watch him dance online from the privacy of their own homes. And to get... other benefits. Like dirty photos.

I'm not quite sure how I feel about that.

"Eloise?" Victoria snaps her fingers in front of my face. She's always Victoria when she's being, well, Victoria. "Are you in there?" She knocks on my forehead. "Or did I lose you to Ares's abs again?"

She's not going to let it go. In fact, she seems to think we should go to Protocol right now on the off chance that Ares is dancing tonight. My stomach flips. I've gone from hungry to nauseous in under a second.

My stomach is gripped in a vise and no amount of rubbing

it under my sweater is making it better.

Victoria holds up three fingers. "Come on. Gimme three."

"Because it's a strip club." I bite out the words under my breath. No one else can hear me, but even saying them out loud at all feels... dirty.

My boyfriend is dirty. And I like it. As much as I'd like to say I only like it behind closed doors, I don't. I guess if I'm being pedantic, I did also like it behind the closed doors of the library. But the alley... watching him with that guy... that was public, very public, too public for me to participate, but I did get a thrill from observing. Maybe I'm a little dirty too?

Just a little.

Maybe.

Cheeks heating, I look her dead in the face.

She shrugs and rolls her eyes at me. "And...?"

I wave my hands. "And it's a strip club. I'm a girl, Victoria. In case you hadn't noticed."

Another eye roll, and I'm starting to feel like I've lived an incredibly sheltered life. Sighing, she leans forward, resting her forearms close to me on the table. "Plenty of girls go to strip clubs. And I don't mean to strip."

They do? "Have you been to one?"

"Not only have I been to strip clubs, I've seen Ares dance in the flesh at Protocol. So, that reason is dumb. And in fact, it serves as a reason you *should* go and see him dance. Then you can tick that off your bucket list. Everyone should go to a strip club at least once in their life."

I'm not sure I believe any of that, but the idea of seeing him on stage, half naked, bending and twisting his body to music might be a little enticing.

"Reason number two?" She leans back in her seat and picks up her drink. It's getting close to dinner time so I'm going to have to think about what to eat before Tori gets hangry. Maybe I'll make some pasta.

I shrug. "I don't even know that he'd want me to go watch him dance." I'm not looking at her, but the weight of her stare on my face makes my cheeks get hotter.

When she doesn't say anything, and I eventually give in and look over at her, she's holding out my phone. "How about you message him and ask?"

The idea makes my stomach swoop. He'd probably think it's a great idea, and that wouldn't help my argument with Victoria one little bit.

"Exactly." She wiggles the phone at me. "Point two is also moot, because you know he'd love for you to go see him. In fact, he'd probably give you a special lap dance. And if you could put in a good word for me, I wouldn't be mad if he gave me one, either." She shrugs, smirk firmly in place on her face.

I'd much rather my boyfriend gave my best friend a lap dance at the strip club. The idea of him grinding against my lap in front of people makes my heart race in the wrong way.

"And number three?"

"My dad would be mad."

"Your dad would be mad about what?" Dad comes into the kitchen, giant pizza box from Zoey's in Marion in hand. It's my favorite pizza place, it was Mom's favorite pizza place, and it's the only pizza place Dad ever gets pizza from anymore. It's endearing really.

My mouth waters as soon as those delicious cheesy smells hit my nose. I can't tell him what Tori wants me to do, what I might be planning. He warned me away from Ares once already, and I really don't want to fight, especially not right here and now in front of Tori. So, I do what I didn't want to do, and lie.

"If I had a party here."

Tori's brows twitch, but like the good best friend she is, she doesn't rat me out to Dad. Instead, she doubles down on my lie.

"Hi, Mr. Downing. My birthday's coming up, and we're spit-balling ideas for where to go." She tosses me a wicked grin. "I was thinking of going to the strip club, for fun."

It's Dad's turn to raise his eyebrows. To his credit, he doesn't say anything off the top of his head. Thankfully. He has this really great skill of speaking before engaging his brain. He learned his lesson, eventually. Mom used to thwap his arm when he'd blurt out something before pausing for a beat to process. He places the pizza box on the table while we move our books out of the way, then grabs himself a beer from the fridge.

I wasn't expecting him home tonight, unless I got my days wrong, or his schedule changed, so I hope everything's okay but don't want to pry in front of Tori in case it isn't.

"I suppose it would be okay to have a party here."

Wait, what?

I stare at him a moment. Who is this man talking to my friend and me? Is it possible he's starting to relax a little? Has he been abducted? Visited by the ghost of Christmas past? Or Mom?

"Depending on who was invited, of course." He pins me with a hard stare that tells me exactly who he's referring to. "And I'd advise you both to stay away from either of the strip clubs in town. They're no place for young girls like yourselves."

Girls. I'll always be a little girl to him. I fight a sigh.

Tori packs up her books and stands to leave. "I'd better get going."

"Stay for dinner, Victoria." Dad doesn't miss a beat as he flips open the pizza box.

We might not be in any way rich, but Tori is a single mom and the daughter of a single mom. I guess Dad feels an affinity with Tori's mom somehow, and he might not think I see it, but he tries to help out every now and then in his own way.

This isn't the first time he's encouraged her to stay and eat with us.

He doesn't need to tell her twice, either. He hands her a paper plate, and she scoops a gooey slice from the box.

She's making all kinds of contented noises as she folds the slice lengthwise, opens her mouth super wide, takes a giant bite, and chews like she's never eaten pizza before in her life.

I'm about to take my first bite when the doorbell rings. I look at Tori, then Dad, then back to Tori. As pathetic as it sounds, almost everyone I hang out with is here. Ares doesn't know where I live, and unless Aunt Maureen decided to spring a visit on us, it has to be the UPS guy.

Curiosity flickers in Tori's eyes as she swallows down a mouthful and wipes her mouth with the back of her hand.

I bounce to my feet. "I'll get it. You eat while it's hot, Dad."

I'm totally down with cold pizza, but Dad is not. I pull open the door expecting to find a delivery service or something, but instead, I come face to face with my boyfriend. My stomach clenches.

He's wearing a dark hoody, backward ball cap, dark jeans, and sneakers that probably cost more than my car. He's not wearing a coat though. Idiot. A handsome idiot, no doubt, but an idiot all the same.

"What... what are you doing here? Wait, better question, how do you know where I live? I... what...?"

He tilts his head and flashes that panty melting smile of his again. Oof, be still my throbbing clit. He leans forward, plants a chaste kiss on my cheek.

"*Buenas noches, tesoro.*"

Dreamy sigh. Why does everything sound so much more adorable in a different language?

"Why don't you invite your *friend* in, Eloise?" Dad's voice jolts me out of my daze. I'm tempted to swing my hands around my head to flap away the love heart bubbles that are probably popping out as I stare at Ares.

Invite him in? To our house? That doesn't sound like a good idea.

"Oh, no, sir. I don't want to intrude. I wanted to bring this." He holds up a bag from GTFO, and I know pie's nestled inside. Delicious, fruity, warm, and buttery crusted, perfect pie.

See? Even Ares knows it's not a good idea for him to come into my childhood home. Drop and run.

"I insist. Come in out of the cold, you're not even wearing a coat."

Ares looks at me, is he seeking permission? Or is he trying to find an out from this now incredibly awkward and cold moment with my dad at the front door. I offer a small smile, my stomach twisting in knots at not only the thought of Ares hanging out in my home when by all accounts he lives in such... opulence. But also the fact Dad's going to be especially mad that I'm hanging out with Ares.

Dad expressly forbade it. Yet, here he is.

"Thank you, Mr. Downing." He tips his head and steps into the house like everything is totally fine.

Back at the dinner table, Tori sucks in a breath and a mouthful of her pizza when Ares enters the room. She said "fuck," but it was mostly hidden by the fact she inhaled a wad of cheese, then started coughing.

"Ares, hey. What's up?" She gives a little wave when she's able to dislodge the wedge of pizza from her throat, then wipes her watering eyes before kicking me under the table.

What does she want me to do? What does she expect me to say? I don't know how he found my house or why he's here. I don't know anything more than she does. I kick her back but miss her leg and kick the chair. That'll teach me for choosing violence.

My pulse is racing. Wiping my palms on my thighs before picking up a paper plate, I hold it out to Ares. "Would you like to join us?"

Dad makes a grunting sound in the back of his throat. I hope he doesn't say a word out of place. I already feel like Cinderella right now, entertaining Prince Charming in my humble abode. I don't need Dad causing any arguments at the dinner table—especially when I don't have any glass slippers at hand to throw at him.

"Zoey's?" Ares points to the pizza.

I nod, attempting to disguise the fact I'm stunned he knows Zoey's. I figured rich people got their food from other places. Rich people places, not regular person places. Doesn't his pizza come diamond crusted and get delivered to him by a scantily clad woman who feeds it to him?

"I'd love a slice." He pulls out a chair at the table, placing the bag of pie on his far side before sitting down, taking his hat off, and accepting my slice. How much pie did he bring? What flavor? And is it still warm? I'm fixating on the pie, so I don't have to think about the fact that the only sound around the table is the ticking of the clock in the next room, and the occasional chewing sound.

It's so uncomfortable. I smile again at Ares, and Dad clears his throat.

Oh, no. No. Nope. Do not. Please Dad, please don't.

"So how did you meet my Eloise, Mr. Peña?"

Ares is somewhere between the guy he was with me in the car and his showman. He's smiling, but not dazzling. He's comfortable, but not cocky. I can't help but wonder if this is the first time he's met a girlfriend's parents. Heck, I'm his first relationship, so that would track.

Ares puts his slice back onto the plate. I'm expecting him to correct Dad on how to say his name, but to my surprise, that's not what he says.

"We met at the coffee shop." It's a version of the truth, but also not quite a lie. He stretches across the table to grab a napkin before dabbing at his mouth.

"Beer?" Dad's expectant stare makes me uncomfortable, but Ares doesn't seem at all fazed by it.

"No thanks." He stands. "I'll get myself some water if that's okay."

Dad grunts. Ares points at the fridge and I nod.

"Does anyone else need a drink?"

Tori raises her hand. "I'll take one, please."

He hands her a bottle of water and takes his seat. I've never seen Dad eat so quickly before. He demolishes three slices, drains his beer, and excuses himself from the table. I'd offer him some pie but, one, he's being rude, and two, I don't want him hanging around the table even longer than necessary.

If there's enough pie for everyone, I'll offer Dad a slice later. It can be my olive branch. Though I don't feel like I did anything wrong, there's a hefty amount of guilt pressing on my shoulders.

Ares brushes my bicep, and I jump. Tori laughs, but it's short lived when I glare at her.

"You really came all the way out here to bring her pie?"

"*Sí*. I did. I missed you, Eloise." He sweeps his fingers across my cheek sending flickers through my body, and it's then I realize that my hair is tied up. I tie it up at home, it's my safe space where I don't have to worry about anyone seeing my face.

My chest tightens.

While Ares has stroked his fingers over my cheek, he's *right there*.

I swallow the lump forming in my throat and squeeze my knee under the table to stop it from shaking. He's my boyfriend and he says he doesn't care, but I can't automatically shut off the angst associated with my scars and my trauma because we're dating now.

"I can leave if you're uncomfortable with me being here."

For a bad boy, he sure can be thoughtful. Did he expect to drive all the way out here to Keystone, find me in an empty house, and do things together? Sexy things?

A flash of Ares eating pie off my stomach comes to mind, and suddenly I want to kick Dad and Tori out in the cold and let Ares eat pie off my body. It's not snowing, but it's November, so it's freakin' cold out.

"No, it's okay. Dad wasn't supposed to be home tonight, so it's a night of unexpected things. I don't mind you being here, Ares."

He looks down at the table. "*Lo siento*. I should have messaged first." His cheeks are pinking up. He's clearly not used to having to be considerate of someone else's life and schedule. He wants something, he buys it. He wants to see someone, he sees them. "I'll do better next time."

I take his hand in mine, slipping my fingers between his, palm to palm. Tori's taking everything in, quietly assessing. She's chewing on another slice of pizza, sipping on her water, but as soon as Ares leaves, she's going to be all up in my business.

Can I get her to stay over so she can be my buffer? Dad's anger radiates through the house. He's not going to let me go to bed until he's told me exactly what he thinks of me seeing Ares—which I already know, and he knows I know.

But since Ares is here, Dad now also knows that I didn't listen. The lecture is going to intensify. It's brewing already.

"Eloise?" Tori nudges me under the table with her foot.

Both Tori and Ares are staring at me, waiting for an answer to a question I didn't hear being asked.

"What?" Looking between the two of them, my Spidey senses tingle. They both have weird looks on their faces.

"I was telling Ares that you wanted to go watch him dance at the club at some point."

If I thought my stomach was swoopy earlier, it ain't got nuthin' on this. It's in freefall. Off the tallest building in the world. I'm going to murder my best friend and bury her body in a corn field. It's not like we're short of those.

"Is that true, *cariño*? Do you want to see me dance?"

I'm caught between a rock and a hard place. I said I would be honest with him, and if I say no, that's a lie. But if I say yes, he'll make it happen.

Yeah, I'm absolutely going to kill her.

He won't judge me for wanting to watch him, in fact, I'm almost sure he'll love it. He's a performer and loves being the center of attention, and I imagine he'd strip and break into something right now if Dad wasn't in the basement.

Actually, part of him probably wants to do it anyway, regardless of who can see.

"You don't need to be embarrassed." He strokes my hand with his thumb, and I lean into it, wanting him to touch me everywhere. "I'd love for you to come and see me dance."

I nod, not sure what to say. Tori is trying—unsuccessfully —not to laugh. "It's a date!" She claps her hands together, glee and triumph oozing from her, and pulls out her phone. "When are you working next?"

Oh. She means business. This isn't one of those "let's do it sometime" things that end up never getting done. My best friend is making sure it's written in stone, sealed with a blood oath, and in her calendar so it doesn't get "accidentally" forgotten about.

I hate my best friend.

Except, a tiny, minuscule, microscopic piece of me is excited at the thought of watching Ares strip and dance to music—but I'll never tell her that. Ever. And I'm still going to kill her for good measure.

Ares tells her when he's next expected at the club, then he tells her when the next home games are for the Raccoons, and she shudders. "Thanks, but hockey isn't my jam." She's turned colder than the tundra in less than a nanosecond.

Either Ares doesn't read the room, or he doesn't care. "It's fun, you should come."

She folds her arms, her lips flatten, and I'm trying to scream telepathically into Ares's brain that he needs to back down. He stares at her for maybe two seconds before he slides back into his chair.

"Did one of my hockey brothers do you dirty?"

That has an almost undetectable reaction from her, but it's there. Her eyes narrow, a muscle in her cheek feathering like she's fighting a wince. We both see it. Ares wags his finger. "Screw whoever he is. Don't let him get in the way of you having fun." Then he holds up his hands, palms facing Tori. "But if hockey really isn't for you, that's cool. It's not for everyone, even if I want it to be. I'll drop it." His gaze flicks to me. My insides start to warm up again after Tori's arctic blast. I'm so glad he's understanding.

I really don't like sports. While I didn't mind the hockey game, and I don't mind going every now and then, I can't see myself becoming a screaming fan every week at the stadium.

They stay for a while, we have delicious strawberry rhubarb pie, we laugh, we hang out and it's all normal, nice, right, even. I was worked up about the fact Tori might be awkward being around Ares and me, but we're not all lovey dovey. I'm not draped over him. We all just kinda exist in the same space. But the time eventually comes for them both to leave and for the inevitable showdown with Dad.

The door is barely closed behind them when Dad's presence lurks behind me. I straighten my spine, close my eyes for the length of a slow breath, and slowly turn to face him.

CHAPTER 19

Ares

Mierda. He sounds pretty mad.

I'm a few feet away from Eloise's front door, box of hot chocolate from Bitches Brew in my hand. I left it in the car by accident and wanted to give it to her before I left. I wanted to tell her the packets of hot chocolate she's been finding are from me.

She hasn't mentioned them, and neither have I, but I want her to know she doesn't have a secret admirer, at least not anymore.

Except, her dad's yelling at her pretty loudly right now. Right there behind the front door. I shouldn't listen. I should drop the box and high-tail it out of there. But I can't unstick my feet from the front path. I want to break down the door, throw my arms around her, and protect her from the words he's saying.

"He's a criminal, Eloise! The only reason he's not behind bars is because of who he is. Actually, not even who *he* is, who his father is. His billionaire dad is keeping him from spending the rest of his days in prison. Is that who you want to be with?"

The rest of my days is a stretch. I'm not a fucking murderer or anything. I've never done anything to warrant a life sentence in the big house. But that's beside the point.

I don't hear a reply from Eloise. I'm not sure if it's because she doesn't say anything, or because he doesn't let her. His booming voice is intimidating, scary even, and my girl is probably trembling inside, and that kills me.

She's not completely mine, not yet anyway. She doesn't trust me, and that's okay; trust is earned not given. But right now, she's mine, and I want to protect her from everything that might hurt her, even her father.

As much as I want to rip his arms off his body and use them to beat the rest of him to death, I can't because at least in part, he's right. His voice is pained, full of worry and fear. He's trying to protect his daughter—he's afraid of losing her like he lost his wife. But he's out of line speaking to her like this. He needs to dial it back.

"He does whatever the hell he wants, Ellie. He doesn't give a shit about you, and he'll drop you when the next pretty girl comes along."

That one stings. Because that's one hundred percent untrue. I'm falling for her. It's fast and it's wild, like everything else in my life, and ironically the exact opposite of damn near everything she is, but it's true. I'm developing feelings for her and that's never happened to me before. It's new, it's scary, but it's real.

He's poking at her insecurities now, and my fist balls at my side. He knows she's self-conscious about her face, her trauma, he can't not know, and he's using that against her. Even if he didn't know, using another "pretty" woman against someone doesn't fly with me.

Society has conditioned women to believe they're not as attractive as the next woman, and that's a deep-rooted belief Eloise holds with her scarred face. I also know that it's utter bullshit. She's as beautiful as any other woman on the planet, with or without her fucking scars.

Flames of anger flare in my chest.

"Who's going to be here to pick up the pieces when he breaks your heart, Eloise? I'm on the road. I can't afford to take time off to comfort you because you were stupid enough to fall in with the wrong boy."

He falls silent long enough to catch a breath. Does he ever stop long enough for her to argue back? Or does he rant at her until he clears his cache of thoughts and moves on?

"I thought you knew better. I thought we raised you better. What would your mother think if she saw you right now? Talk of going to strip clubs, having boys over to the house while I'm not supposed to be here, parties... She'd be disgusted."

My heart pinches, the flames fan higher, the fire burns hotter. Playing the dead mom card is so far from fucking cool.

My girl is crying behind that door right now, and I'm fighting every urge to barge in and rescue her. She'd be embarrassed that I heard, she'd apologize on behalf of her dad for the things he said about me, and she might even be mad at me for interfering.

"I can't even look at you right now."

A few seconds later, a door slams somewhere inside the house. The light goes out behind the door and so does the one in the living room. I drop the box of cocoa on the step and hurry over to my car. Grabbing a coat from the back, I put it on then settle into the driver's seat.

I don't want to leave right away in case she comes outside or needs me close, but I also don't want to sit at the curb with the car running, and heat on, so the neighbors don't call the cops.

I need to message her, but by the time I dig my phone out

of my jeans pocket with cold hands, there's already a message from her on my screen.

Tesoro: I need to talk to you. Can you let me know when you're home, please?

My stomach clenches. I'm not going to let her end this fledgling relationship because her dad's being an *idiota*.

I waste no time calling, twice, but she doesn't answer. My bet is she's crying and doesn't want me to hear her tears.

Ares: *Cariño*, please pick up. I left something for you on your porch. I had it in the car and when I went to bring it back to you... I didn't want to interrupt.

The porch light flicks back on and she crouches to pick it up. I stay where I am in the car but her phone lights up her face as she texts me back.

Tesoro: You're still here.

Ares: I didn't want to leave in case you needed me for something.

She swipes at her cheeks. If I didn't think her dad would lose his shit at her even worse than he just did, I'd cross the street, hold her, and not let go.

Ares: It's taking everything I've got not to get out of this car and wrap you in my arms.

Tesoro: I'm torn on how to answer that. I don't want to make it worse, but I'd love nothing more.

That sparks something inside me. My urge to comfort her met by her desire to be comforted gives me some security I didn't realize I needed. It's nice to know that at least in this instance, when she's upset, she'd like for me to be there with her, for her.

Tesoro: Please don't think he's awful.

Ares: I think he loves you. He wants what's best for you. He's afraid. He said some really out of line shit, but I don't think he's awful.

She reaches behind the door and pulls some boots on her feet and a coat before sitting on the porch step.

Ares: You should go inside. It's cold out.

Tesoro: **I need some fresh air.**

Ares: *Tesoro*, **it's cold.**

Tesoro: **Ares, I have my coat. A couple minutes, then I'll go make cocoa.**

She waves the box my direction, I can barely make it out in the dim light.

Tesoro: **The hot chocolate packets?**

Ares: It was me all along. *Sí.* **I have been mesmerized by you from the first time I saw you in the nail salon. I didn't know how to approach you or get your attention.**

Ares: I had a whole complex scheme concocted in my mind about how to convince you to go on a date with me and everything.

She stands and goes inside, closing the door behind her. For a moment, my breath catches. Has my confession spooked her?

Tesoro: **You're right, it's cold. I'm warming milk.**

Tesoro: **I want to hear all about this wicked plan of yours.**

Ares: It involves making your fake hot-chocolate-leaving admirer jealous while you fake dated me.

Tesoro: **That's funny.**

Ares: Then I was going to use my indelible charm to convince you to forget about the admirer and be my girl for real instead.

Tesoro: **Really?**

Ares: *Es cierto.* **Fool proof, right?**

Tesoro: **How could I resist?**

Ares: Do you need to get out for a while?

Tesoro: **It's bedtime. I should go to sleep. I appreciate** you staying here for me though. And for not beating the door down and kicking my dad's butt.

Ares: I would never.

Tesoro: I've seen the videos. I haven't watched them, but I've seen enough of them labeled 'Goalie fight' right alongside your name to know that you sometimes like talking with your fists.

I can't help but chuckle. She's not wrong.

Ares: What can I say? Your boyfriend is a hot head. It's in my blood. *Soy impulsivo mientras que tú eres tranquila.* **I can't promise your calm will make me less hotheaded...**

Tesoro: I don't want to change you, Ares.

Another tiny piece of my heart clicks into place, another knot unwinding in my chest.

Ares: I figured you'd want to break up with me after... well, after what your father said.

I squirm in my seat, hating that I'm letting this insecurity through the cracks, but I need her to say it, to tell me she's not casting me aside, not even for her dad.

I drop my phone onto my thighs and rub my hands together. I crank the engine, turn the headlights off, and flip the heat up to high. These seat and steering wheel warmers are the best inventions ever made, and within seconds my ass starts to heat.

Tesoro: I don't want to break up with you at all, *cariño*. He'll come around. He's overprotective and scared. Once he sees that you're not converting me to the way of the Devil, he'll relax.

I hope she's right. And I don't miss the term of endearment in her message because my heart literally skips a beat. I don't do affection, I don't do long dreamy gazes, holding hands, or pet names, and yet, with Eloise, I want to. I want it all.

Ares: *Cariño*?
Tesoro: I was trying it on for size. *¿No te gusta?*
Ares: I like it just fine.

I don't want to confess the pathetic truth that no one has ever been so endeared to me that they called me something sweet. Except Mamá, but that's different. Your family has to call you nice things. I'm a give-no-shits kinda guy, and as a result, I kinda get no shits given back. It's never bothered me. It's who I am, but with Eloise... it's different.

It's like vines of ivy are slowly growing through the crevices of my heart and forcing it to beat, to race, to *feel*. It's uncomfortable, but I think that's what growth is supposed to feel like. Maybe? I have no fucking idea.

Tesoro: You know you can't sit outside all night, right?

Ares: I would if I thought it would help.

Ares: Can I see you tomorrow?

Tesoro: Don't you have a game?

Checking the date, I confirm that tomorrow is in fact Friday and our first game of a double header against the Wisconsin Wolves. Not only do I have a game, but I have morning skate, too. Considering our last two games went down in flames—the Flint fucking Flames—I'm going to need to pull my shit together to make sure we don't have a rerun this weekend.

Ares: I do. I have morning skate then I'll lift at the gym, but I don't have class until eleven. Want to meet for breakfast around nine? If you need to study, I can bring some books and it can be a working breakfast.

I know. I sound desperate, needy, like I didn't see her less than an hour ago. But I want to see her tomorrow, to curl my arms around her tiny frame, kiss her forehead, and make sure her dad didn't fuck her up too badly with his verbal assault about her lowlife boyfriend.

Tesoro: **You want to study with me... in public? Aren't you afraid your rep will get dinged by hanging out with me?**

Ares: **I'm going to take a picture of me kissing you senseless and put it on my Instagram for that comment.**

Tesoro: **I might even let you. See you at Bitches Brew, 9am.**

≈

I barely slept. I tossed and turned all night wondering whether Eloise was going to show for breakfast and hang out with me, or whether a night of sleep would somehow make her go back on what she said and leave me. Nervous energy fizzled through me through practice, and I almost knocked myself out at the gym with a weighted bar.

I'd say that it all went fine because I have some supportive teammates who have my back, but as it turns out, that's not all they have.

They have ammunition.

My darling *hermana* mayor, Athena, told my brothers that I'm in a committed relationship with a woman. And every single time I missed a puck or was slow to recover in my crease they cracked a joke about me being distracted by a woman.

The more I denied it, the more they pushed on that fucking button.

Pendejos.

I'm showered, my kit is in my car, and I seem to have lost the chuckle brothers. I wouldn't put it past them to have followed me around campus to catch a glimpse of her. I swear, when any of my siblings land themselves a partner, I am going to roast the shit out of them for all the crap they've given me about Eloise in a few short hours.

I arrive at Bitches Brew about fifteen minutes early, but I figure I'll grab us a table, get our drinks orders in and wait for my girl to arrive. Inside the door, the line is about ten people long, and I dunno about Eloise, but the noise level is a few decibels too high for me to study.

I'm hoping the crowd thins out and people have to get themselves to class, otherwise I'll be taking my girl back to the library. I'm not going to be the reason she flunks out of nursing school. And I refuse to give her dad any additional reasons to hate me.

When I get to the counter the line is as long behind me as it was in front of me. It'll take forever to line up again, so I make an executive decision. I order drinks, and because we've never discussed food choices or allergies before I stare at the menu for a few long seconds before saying fuck it. I'll get a bunch of shit and hopefully she'll like something.

Kelly and Micah are working this morning, and to her credit Kelly doesn't judge me when I ask her for a slice of both flavors of quiches, two of the different scones on offer, a parfait with granola, and two breakfast bagels, one with extra hash browns.

We'll call it a breakfast picnic, and if there happens to be anything leftover that I can't cram into my grumbling stomach, one of us can take it home. Perfect plan.

I wait for our order at the end of the counter, and by the time she arrives, pink cheeked and bundled up in a huge calf-length bright yellow coat, I've found a table.

She looks around, and I throw my hand up in the air, waving to try to catch her attention. She approaches, a shy smile on her face, and as she slides her huge coat off her tiny body and onto the back of her chair I stand up. She stares at me like she's not sure what the etiquette is, and it occurs to me, I don't know either.

This is our first real, in person... thing, and I don't know if we're a PDA kind of couple or not.

¡Por Dios!

I'm tempted to do what I feel like doing. But I don't want to disrespect her boundaries, so instead, I scan her face, looking for signs of discomfort. "Are you okay with hugging?"

She nods.

"Kissing?"

She nods again.

I close the few feet between us and pull her against my chest before tipping her head back and sweeping my nose across hers. Pushing her hair out of her face I take a good, long look into her eyes. *"¿'tá bien?"*

She nods against my face, looping her arms around my waist and squeezing. "I'm better now."

A firework goes off in my chest. Is this normal? I have no idea how people feel like this all the time and don't end up lifting off into the atmosphere.

I kiss her. It's light, it's brief, and it's familiar. It's not enough, not by a long shot, but I'm conscious that we're in public, she's probably hungry, and no one likes cold breakfast bagels.

I step back, brushing my fingers across her cheek before I gesture for her to take a seat. Wait, is that a Zamboni on her shirt?

I point at her torso. "*Tesoro?*"

Her head snaps up from the plates of food lined up on our small table for two.

"Are you wearing a hockey sweater?"

Her face turns the color of tomatoes as she nods and stretches her shirt out with both hands for me to read.

It's a Nashville Devils hoodie and it says, *Hockey gives me a zamboner.* I can't help the laughter that bursts from me. My girl, who hates sports and is clueless about hockey, is wearing the weirdest fucking hockey shirt I've ever seen.

"I have questions."

She shrugs, tipping her head at the food. "I have questions too."

"Ah. *Sí*. Well, I didn't know what you liked, how hungry you were, or if you had any allergies, so I kind of... got a bit of everything."

She shakes her head. "You could have texted."

"Where's the fun in that?"

Relief courses through me as she picks up half of her sliced breakfast bagel. "No allergies." She takes a giant bite. Her eyes roll back in her head as she makes yummy food noises and takes another.

"I don't like pickles, mushrooms, or coffee."

"That's it?" I pick up half of my own bagel and take an equally giant bite.

She nods. "There are a few other things that aren't my favorite, but for the most part, I'll try anything once."

My brow quirks at that, and she giggles. "I seriously can't believe the amount of food you got for the two of us."

"*Cariño*, you're dating a hockey player. We can eat."

Her eyes widen again at the plates. "This much?"

I shrug. I had a protein shake already this morning, but I could definitely make a good faith effort at clearing this table.

"Your turn." I wave my bagel at her. "What's with the shirt?"

"Victoria ordered it for me online. She says she saw an ad on social media and thought of me. She also insisted I wear it out today. I was going to take it off in the car, but it's cold."

That sounds like something any one of my teammates might do, though I have an overwhelming urge to attack her shirt with a Sharpie and write #32 instead of hockey, then scrawl UCR Raccoons where the Devils logo is.

I'm not thrilled at another team being anywhere near my girl's tits, though that's the least of my problems right now since my twin brothers and my fucking sister are walking towards our table.

Eloise is currently oblivious to the fact she's about to get accosted by a whole lot of fucking de la Peña in one go. I try to shake my head at my siblings, silently pleading with them to reconsider what they're about to do.

"Why are you shaking your head? Is the bagel bad? It tasted delicious to me."

I lean forward, dropping my food onto my plate and cupping her chin with my palm. "I am so fucking sorry."

The pulse in her neck skips faster as the color drains from her face. "For what?"

"My brothers and sister are making a beeline for this table, and there's no door behind us to escape out of."

"You told your family about me?"

"My sister. She saw me at your car putting hot chocolate under the wiper. She thought I was stalking you. Then she told my brothers." I take her hands in mine, though I can't rest them on the table because of all the fucking plates. "They think it's adorable I finally have a girlfriend, and by adorable, I mean they think it's fun to make an endless number of jokes at my expense. I never told them we were coming here. I'm sorry."

She shakes her head, and her freshly dyed pink hair falls forward. "If you're okay with me meeting your family, I am, too."

I scan her face looking for a sign that she's uncomfortable or lying to me. I don't care who the fuck wants to meet her, if my girl isn't feeling it, I'm not above throwing her over my shoulder and leaving an Ares and Eloise shaped hole in the wall if I have to.

"You're sure? I can tell them to fuck off if you aren't ready."

She nods, her lip caught between her teeth. "I'm ready."

I ease back into my chair, waiting for my family to descend, and while Eloise thinks she's ready, I'm not sure I am.

CHAPTER 20
Eloise

If I'm going to meet Ares's siblings, it's better to do it all at once, right? Instead of spreading the pain out over a longer period of time? I really don't know. All I know is I might poop my pants right now from the way he's looking at me.

Are they going to grill me? Probe me for all my deep, dark secrets? Does he think they won't like me? I don't think he's embarrassed by me. I mean, the way he looked at me when I arrived makes me feel like I'm lucky to have my clothes on right now. He didn't seem to mind a public display of affection, in fact, it seems like he craved it.

But I don't get why he's gone so pale, and his usual mask of cockiness and bravado seems to be slipping juuuuuust a bit.

"*¿Qué lo qué, hermanito?*"

Three of the most beautiful human beings I've ever seen surround our table. One of the twins pulls two chairs over and plops down like he's here for the day. Okay then.

Offering his hand to me, he flashes a megawatt smile. "Apollo."

I risk a side-eyed glance in Ares's direction. His eyes are

fixed on me, burning with intensity. He gives the most imperceptible nod before he slides his foot between mine under the table and rubs his calf against my leg.

My heart wants to burst from the silent support he's giving me, the consideration that I might not be ready for all of this to descend on me, and I admit, I fall a little harder.

"It's nice to meet you Apollo, I'm Eloise." I shake his hand, making sure to make eye contact. I'm not afraid, a little anxious maybe, but that's every day ending with Y. I don't know what they want, whether it's to suss me out or embarrass their youngest brother, but I do want to make a good impression.

The other twin stands over his shoulder. "Artemis." He offers his hand and I shake it, giving him a smile.

Athena has a paper cup in her hand. She puts it on the table and sits on the other chair Apollo brought over, which puts her closest to me, our knees touching. She's the one I'm most intimidated by, the one I'm most worried about. If not *liking* me, then at least not hating me.

If rumors are to be believed—and there are many, many rumors around UCR at any given time, especially about Ares's family—she might be the thorn in her brothers' sides, but she also protects them with the ferocity of a mother dragon. I'd rather not get singed.

She offers me her hand and a warm smile. "Athena."

My chest loosens a little, and it's only now that I realize how constricted it's been for the past few minutes.

"So *you're* the girl who has managed to convince my brother to give monogamy a try."

It doesn't sound like an accusation, more like she's shocked, amused, and trying to figure out what my magic is.

Apollo has already picked up one of the scones from our table and is slathering a thick smear of butter onto it. I roll my lips. Ares was right, they are some hungry boys those athletes, and I guess mi casa es su casa when it comes to siblings sharing food.

"It's so nice to meet you." Athena picks up her drink and takes a sip. She leans toward me. "Blink twice if you're being held against your will and need to be rescued from my asshole little brother."

Her accent is warm and rich, her tone light and playful, and I'm finding it hard not to crush on my boyfriend's sister right now. She's... wow. She's a real life goddess.

Ares grunts. I laugh and shake my head. He reaches across the table and tucks the hair on my good side behind my ear. He really doesn't like when I hide, and right now his signals are all telling me that I don't have to. He wants them to see me, which injects a little more courage into my next words.

"I'm here of my own free will. Though," I gesture at the table. "He bribed me with hot cocoa and snacks." I shrug. "I'm a sucker for snacks."

She nods. "I understand. I, too, answer the snack sirens' call regularly."

That makes me laugh. I like her already. She's not at all as cold and standoffish as the internet has led me to believe she is. She falls silent as she regards me, then turns her attention to Ares, who is rod stiff in his seat as though he's preparing for an onslaught of ribbing from his big sister.

He's still stroking my leg with his foot under the table, and I start stacking the plates so I can make space to hold his hand without smashing something if he needs me. I've never seen him off kilter like this. He's always poised, composed, confident. Right now, however, he's almost like a little boy.

Apollo points the corner of his scone at me. "So, how'd you two meet?" He swings it to Ares before taking a bite.

My face heats, and Ares grins at me, a sparkle in his eye. I didn't really see him at the salon the first time he saw me, and the first time we really met, I tripped over my tongue, then he was buried inside another guy.

His grin stretches wider. He must know I'm reliving the moment in my head. "I saw her when I was getting my nails done, but she didn't give me the time of day."

I eye roll. "You mean I didn't even notice you were there." I turn to Apollo. "He gets prickly when people don't take notice of him."

Artemis snorts but doesn't say anything. Athena's smirk says she's enjoying the exchange.

Ares's smile is still on his face, and it's genuine, so I know he doesn't mind me poking fun at him. "Then I saw her again at the restaurant."

He arches a brow, tipping his head. It's as though he's challenging me to spill the beans. Do I tell them the truth, or do I nod and smile?

"The night we made the wager with the Snow Pirates."

Apollo's eyebrows twitch. He meets my eye over the last bite of his scone and smirks. "Wasn't that the night you...?"

Ares licks his bottom lip, catching it between his teeth and nods. I don't know if I'm mortified, or hot as heck under the hood, but either way, I shift in my seat. A movement not lost on Athena, who regards me with a curious, probing stare.

"I bumped into him outside the restaurant."

Apollo's body starts shaking with quiet laughter. "*¡Ay, dios mío!*"

Athena bumps me with her elbow. "What am I missing?" Her stern glare flits between her brothers.

"Ares was..." I clear my throat, my skin sizzling from the gaze of four siblings. "Somewhat preoccupied outside the restaurant."

Athena shakes her head before covering her face with her palm. "Of course, he was."

The twins are laughing out loud at this point, and Ares is

picking at a slice of quiche looking awfully proud of himself. "I invited her to join me and Séb, but she didn't want anything to do with me."

"I don't blame her." Athena leans over the table and flicks his forehead. "*Sucio*."

"He wooed me, though. Won me over."

"Eventually," Ares offers, eating the last of his quiche.

Athena picks up the other slice and pulls off a corner. "There's a fine line between wooing and stalking."

I'm so glad the noise level in this place is pretty loud, so the chances of the people sitting around us hearing the details of my relationship is low.

Okay, lower.

Artemis must take pity on me because mercifully, he changes the subject. Or maybe my cheeks are making the entire coffee shop too warm, and he needed a break. "Do you like hockey, Eloise?" He gestures to my sweater. I groan.

Ares cracks up laughing. "She hates sports. Her friend gave it to her as a joke. Isn't it the best fucking thing ever?"

I take a drink of my hot chocolate. "I've been to a hockey game with my dad. Uh. Since we're on the subject, I was thinking of going to one of your games this weekend."

I'm not lying, I have been. I wanted to mention it to him this morning. I was fascinated watching him play, the focus and concentration behind his mask, diving and moving so fluidly, so gracefully. I wouldn't mind seeing him again.

I don't miss Ares's brows shooting up his forehead as he chokes on a mouthful of coffee.

"I just... I don't really want to go alone."

Athena's stare is hot on the side of my face before she speaks, I move in my chair again.

"None of your friends like hockey?" She's not criticizing me, in fact, she sounds pretty impressed. Hockey's *the* sport here at UCR. Most schools are all up in their football or other sportsball things, but UCR is the place to be for hockey, so it's unusual to find someone who doesn't at least have a finger on the hockey pulse. I guess the commonly held belief that Athena doesn't like hockey is true, too.

I grip my palms together in my lap, fighting the urge to twist them, tug on my shirt, or pull my hair out from behind my ear. I don't cower, though. I meet her eyes and shake my head. "So far I've only made one friend here at college, and she'd rather set herself on fire than step into the stadium."

Apollo chokes on the parfait he's now eating. "Arena," he coughs out. "It's not a stadium. It's a rink or an arena. Or simply the Trash Can if you'd like."

I giggle. Raccoons playing in the trash can—it's cute. I shrug. "I know nothing about sports. In fact, my first game with Dad, I thought it was a ball you were chasing across the ice."

Everyone laughs, even Athena, and we draw some bemused looks from those around us.

"Anyway," I try again, once they've managed to stop guffawing at my ignorance. "My high school friends all fell away after my accident." I swallow, but no one says anything. "And my boyfriend plays on the team, so it's just me."

I survey the serious faces around the group. Ares's face shows no pity—to be honest he looks thrilled I called him my boyfriend to his siblings. The others are hard to read. They might feel sorry for me, but it's not obvious.

"Is it okay to go alone to a hockey game?" I deliberately avoid looking at Ares when I ask. He's protective, and I already know from the way his leg tensed under the table that he doesn't like the idea of me being out by myself at night. "I'd like to support him, even if I don't understand any of what's going on down on the ice."

Athena's face softens, and a smile teases the edges of her mouth. "You know you're adorable, right?"

And now I want the ground to open up and swallow me whole.

"It's very sweet of you to want to support your boyfriend. Even if he is my *pendejo* brother. And for that reason, I'll come to a game with you this weekend. I'll bring my friend Savannah, introduce you to her, and you'll have made three friends in college."

Artemis nods. "She dates a player on the team, too. So, I'm sure she'll be happy to sit with you at games. And if you're interested in learning, she can help too."

Apollo pauses his spoon on the way to his mouth. "And if you're *really* interested in learning... Well, the three of us play, and while Hen does a great job at pretending she hates the sport, she's actually pretty savvy. We've got you." He jerks his chin at me before eating a heaped spoon of parfait sprinkled with granola.

I look at Ares, wondering what he was so concerned about me meeting his siblings for, and smile. Is this what it feels like to be adopted by a family? They talked to me for a matter of seconds, and now I'm suddenly part of their group. Maybe it's skin deep and they'd be like this with anyone Ares brought home, but maybe it's the start of connecting with people on a level I've craved for a while.

Ares's mouth moves, silently asking if I'm okay, and I nod. What would he do if I said I wasn't? It's hard not to be okay right now. Despite their intimidating presence, the de la Peñas seem like pretty nice people. They spend the next hour with us, hanging out, asking questions, about me, my life, the things I like to do.

I'm sure they want to ask about my face, my accident, my family. Everyone does. Curiosity is completely normal, but I can't say I'm not grateful that they don't bring it up, not even once. In fairness, they spend most of their time mocking their brother. Turns out, him having a partner he sees more than once is a pretty big deal, and they're not letting him forget it.

He mouths *sorry* at me for the three hundredth time, and I shake my head. "I know you had a life before me. It's okay."

No one says out loud that they don't believe he can stay committed to one person for any length of time, but there are undertones of accusation, jibes about his revolving door sex life. I expect each veiled barb to bother me, to make me jealous, or insecure, but they don't.

I believe him when he says things are different with me. I'm not sure what that says about me, or him, or us, but I do.

When they all stand up to leave, a pang of sadness strikes in my chest. Being an only child, having a small circle of friends, this... this feels nice. As though she senses my sadness, Athena curls her arms around me, pulling me awkwardly against her and squeezing.

She picks my phone up from the table and offers it to me. "I'll give you my number and we can talk about going to a game. Does tonight work better for you or tomorrow?"

"Either." I shrug, trying to contain my joy that she wants to hang out with me again as I unlock my phone.

"I'll check with Vannah to see what works for her and get back to you. It's truly been a pleasure, Eloise. When Ares told me he'd found someone to settle down with I thought wonders would never cease." She pauses and shakes her head. "In fact, I thought he'd mail ordered you from some far-off land. Or bought himself a blow-up doll from the sex shop on 66th. But I'm very glad to have been wrong. You're an absolute delight, and I'm thrilled you gave him a chance."

She turns to Ares, thumps his shoulder. "Don't fuck it up."

I roll my lips to smother a laugh, but it comes out as a squeak.

Ares rubs where she struck him. "You're really coming to

watch us play?" Hope and incredulity are layered through his words. I guess coming to a game really is a big deal for her. It makes me warm and fuzzy that it's me that's getting her in the door, but what's the personal cost to her? She doesn't go for a reason, right?

"Yeah. Don't fuck that up either."

I can't help but laugh out loud. It feels good, too. The twins say their goodbyes and the three of them leave. Just when I think I might have my boyfriend to myself for a hot minute, a chair squeaks across the floor from the table next to ours.

A blond guy with boy-next-door vibes and broad shoulders nudges Ares. "Does this mean you're joining my romance book club, Casanova?"

He turns to me and winks. "Hi, Eloise. I'm Justin. I play on the team with Ares. It's a pleasure to meet you."

I shake his hand, and the warmth the de la Peñas made bloom in my chest flares again. It seems as though dating Ares has opened a door to something I wasn't expecting, cementing another piece of my heart.

Ares hitches a brow to me, tipping his head to Justin, silently asking me if I want him to make him leave. An unspoken conversation with only a look.

I shake my head, taking the last, cold sip of my drink. It's all good. It's better than good. And despite the fact I have to sit, clueless, through a hockey game this weekend, I'm looking forward to meeting the rest of his friends, and maybe even making some more of my own.

CHAPTER 21
Ares

The music vibrates through my veins, booming around the rink as I wait to take the ice for warmups. My girl is in the stands, not for the first time ever, but she's there for me and only me. I have to admit, that feels fucking incredible.

Athena and Savannah picked her up earlier and the three of them went out for dinner. As concerned as I am that Hen may have told her all my childhood secrets and produced embarrassing baby pictures, Eloise's texts before I got to the arena seemed happy.

She was a little anxious about hanging out with my sister again, especially without me as a buffer. I get it—Athena is a fucking force of nature, but under that armor of hers, she's a pretty cool chick. I even think there might be a heart in her chest somewhere—though I'd never tell her that out loud.

I saw the way my *tesoro* laughed when my brothers and sister invaded our space at the coffee house. She seemed so joyous to be surrounded by people who accepted her on the spot, no questions asked. My siblings and I might bicker and fight sometimes, but underneath it all, we're solid. They've stood by me through so much, and at this point they're probably relieved I've found someone to tame my wild ways.

I snort. Like that'll ever happen.

But we rally hard around each other. Athena and Apollo are both single at the moment. Athena chooses to stay single, but Apollo seems to be having a drought. It's self-imposed, since his last fling took pictures of them naked in bed and shared them all over the internet. And we all despise Artemis's prissy, entitled mouthpiece of a girlfriend so we hardly ever see her. But I have a good feeling about bringing Eloise into the family fold, even if when and how it happened wasn't what I planned.

The Raccoons skate out onto the ice and my brothers follow me to my net. Warmups follow the same pattern every time, and if my brothers don't put me through my paces before every game, well, I'm not sure what would happen, but it wouldn't be good.

Before I can even scratch up the ice in my crease with the blades of my skates, Apollo points to something behind the plexi. I follow his line of sight and my gaze lands on my girl. She's grinning at me as she waves then does a slow spin, arms out by her sides. She has UCR colors painted on both cheeks, she's wearing my high school jersey with my name across her shoulders and my number on her back and biceps, and she has UCR colored ribbons holding back part of her hair from her face.

Up from her face. Her hair isn't all down around her cheeks. I don't even know what to do with that.

So many things hit me at once. Her huge smile, the sparkle in her eyes, the fact that Athena, or my brothers, went to the trouble of digging out my old high school shirt. I don't even know where they'd have gotten it from. My girl is showing off her scars. Okay, so face paint covers most of them, but this is the most exposed I've ever seen her before, and it shoots a thrill of something through my body. I've never felt such a surge of emotions before and it's making me a little unsteady on my skates.

My sister and my girl in the stands to cheer me on in a game? I feel like I've won the Stanley fucking Cup.

Tesoro blows me a kiss, and before I know what I'm doing I'm catching it in my glove and pretending to tuck it into my pants.

Fuck. I'm never living this down.

I spin to face my brothers who, surprisingly, aren't doubled over laughing. Instead, they are looking at me as though they've never seen me before. I don't blame them. I've never seen these pieces of myself before, either. It's new for all of us.

We warm up as usual: stretches, my brothers putting me through my paces shooting a few dozen pucks at my face. Hayes and I are the last two to leave the ice.

When the lights dim and we take to the ice twenty minutes later, I'm focused and ready. I'm ready to impress my girl and my sister, I'm ready to remind Coach Bales that he didn't make a mistake when he signed me to the team, and I'm ready to absolutely destroy the fucking Wolves.

Shut. Out.

It's not even a close game. We annihilate them 4-0.

"You fucking *owned* them!" Hayes yells over the riotous applause around the rink as he comes my way. Our chests collide as he launches himself at me, and our goalie hug tonight is so fucking extra that even I can't stand it. But fuck it, we deserve to celebrate that win and the crowd adores nothing more than a little goalie love.

My shut out earns me the first star of the game and my

high soars even more. In a sea of black and green in the stands, I search for my pink-haired girl, the only person I give a shit about.

This rush is intoxicating, addictive, and if I'm not careful I'm going to need to go to rehab again, only this time it'll be for an obsession with a tiny pixie.

Hugs and head pats continue in the locker room. The electricity from our win thrums through the air, and the guys are on top of the world. I shower as quickly as I can, and when I get back to my bag, Athena has texted to say the girls will meet us in the bar.

I'm half a foot out the door when Coach's voice yelling my name stops me in my tracks, my equipment bag catching on the door frame.

"Yes, Coach?"

He approaches me with his lips flat, his eyes hard, and his expression unreadable. When he finally blinks, his lips twitch. "Good game tonight, rookie. We should have scouts in the Trash Can for every game if you're going to play like that."

"Scouts?" My eyes widen. I wasn't playing for scouts, I was playing for my girl. No way in fucking hell I'm going to tell that to Bales. Does this mean I'm not on probation? Am I out of his crosshairs?

"Yeah. Scouts." He claps a hand over my shoulder. "And a little bird in a fancy-ass dress suit tells me that Iowa is interested in my starting goaltender."

Iowa. Our home state NHL team is interested in me.

Only one person I want to share this news with, and she's waiting for me in the bar. I thank Coach, tell him I intend to stand on my head again tomorrow, and he tells me to be in his office at nine tomorrow morning.

This time there's no crushing anxiety on my chest because I've done nothing wrong, and it's to discuss my future in the big leagues.

It's time to go kiss my girl.

Her back is to me when I enter the bar, but there's no sneaking up on her when the crowd goes wild at my entrance. Most of the guys are already in line for a drink, and Justin catches my eye over the crowd, pointing to our usual section at the back of the bar for nights like this.

I'm not interested in Justin, though I'm relieved he finally pulled his head out of his ass and played a solid game. I'm not interested in the line for beer, though when Apollo asks what I'm drinking, I ask for a Coke.

The only thing I'm interested in is the pink-haired sprite running at me from ten feet away. She launches herself at me, and I catch her with ease, her legs looping around my waist. She plants both palms on my cheeks and squeals. "I have no idea what most of that was, but you did so good!"

Her praise lights me up inside.

I skim the length of her thighs with both hands under her knee-length jersey with my name stitched into the fabric and cup her ass. The first thing I'm doing tomorrow is ordering her a Raccoons shirt with my name and number on it. Once it gets here, I'm going to fuck her senseless in it, so that every single time she comes to a game, we'll both be reminded that I banged her in the shirt she's wearing.

Searching her face for permission to kiss her senseless in front of all these people isn't necessary, because she lays one on me, for all to see.

It starts off a chaste brush of our lips and noses but quickly turns hungry, feral, she nips at my bottom lip and her body shakes in my arms as she giggles. My teammates are whooping and cheering around us, and when she pulls back her chest is rising and falling pretty heavily.

¡Por Dios! What a fucking kiss.

What. A. Fucking. Kiss!

I want her to kiss me like that after every single game I play from now on.

I have a raging boner that I'm not even going to try to hide. One drink. One fucking glass of Coke and then I'm hauling my girl out of this bar and fucking her until she can't walk straight, the first chance I get.

CHAPTER 22
Eloise

I can't believe I did that.

I can't believe I vaulted off the ground into his waiting arms and then kissed him until his lips started to swell.

My stomach swirls with nervous energy, but the smile on his face and the warmth in those chocolate depths of his assure me that it wasn't an unwelcome advance. And if that wasn't enough, as he slides me down his front to plant me on the ground, the hard-on poking a tent in his dress pants is a pretty good indication of how he's feeling about it.

I've never been applauded for kissing someone before, but I didn't dislike that, either. For a hot minute I forgot we weren't the only people in the room, and the fierceness that he gripped me with, well... I'm glad that girl boners aren't as noticeable as guys'.

Part of me wants to link my hand with his and drag him out of the bar, but the comradery, the energy surrounding us, makes me want to stay a while and let it wash over me.

I've never been a huge fan of crowds, especially crowds of

strangers, but Ares grips my hand and snakes me through the crowd until we get to a quieter part of the bar in the back. Tori has decided to make an appearance for a drink, she's sitting next to Athena on one side. On Athena's other side, Savannah has planted herself firmly in Justin's lap, and it's as though the rest of us aren't even there.

She's stroking the side of his face as she sweeps her nose across his and grinning at him like he hung the moon. Maybe he did. I don't know him.

I like this smaller group. It's a welcoming crowd. I don't know any of the players without their names and numbers pasted on their bodies, but even when they were stamped with their surnames, they all moved way too fast for me to keep up anyway.

Apollo catches me staring over the heads of some of his friends and lifts his glass to me. I give an awkward wave. Artemis either sees or senses his twin has spotted someone because a second later, he's waving at me too.

Here I am, surrounded by a lot of incredibly attractive men in suits. My fingers drift to my face. I can't touch my scars because I'll smear the face paint, but the temptation to take my hair back down to hide my imperfections burns like a red-hot poker in my cheek.

Before it can consume me, a hand slides into mine, a chair pulls closer, and a nose is in my hair. "Are you okay, *tesoro*?"

My stomach is tight, a dull throb grows behind my eyes. I'm only drinking water, so I'm hoping that'll wash away the brewing headache. I don't want him to know that I might not be okay, that I'm uncomfortable, because he'll make me leave, and we just got here, so I nod.

"You're a terrible liar. *Dime, tesoro, ¿qué pasa?*"

The intensity of his stare on me is most certainly a distraction from the fact I feel like the ugly duckling sitting here among all of this beauty. When I look at his face, his eyes are only on me, no one else.

To him, it doesn't matter that his sister is a supermodel, or that Tori has curves for days, or that Savannah's skin is so flawless she probably doesn't even need to moisturize. To him, it doesn't matter that half a dozen girls are wearing skirts barely covering their butt cheeks waiting at the edge of the space for the team. Their shirts are low cut, and they keep waving over at whatever players' attention they can catch.

To him, right now, I am the only person that matters, and he means it, so I owe him the truth.

"I feel self-conscious being here." I twitch my eyes to my right to indicate the beautiful people. "There are a lot of really hot people here."

His deep chuckle distracts me from my embarrassment about my gnarly face, and my tingling girl parts remind me that she's ready to play.

"*You* are a really hot person, *tesoro*." He plants a kiss on my cheek, sliding a little closer to me. Our thighs are touching, like some form of silent support, reinforcement. "If you want me to swoop you into my arms like Justin did with Savannah, I can. But I can't promise I won't finger you until you come, screaming my name right here in front of all our friends."

That makes my breath hitch. My cheeks are constantly flushed and on fire when I'm around him. I'm glad it's loud in here, because the little squeak that escapes me is embarrassing. A part of me wants to test whether he's serious or not, even though I know he is.

"Say the word, and I'll get us both out of here, okay?"

I nod, tension unfurling from my neck and shoulders. It's nice to know that he won't make me feel guilty if I need to leave. He's had a big night, and he probably wants to hang with his teammates, but he's thinking of me.

How is this sweet and considerate guy the same guy who I read about online?

A player has moved to sit next to Tori. I don't think she's noticed his presence yet because she and Athena are watching Ares and me with a mixture of caution and intrigue. It's as though Athena expects him to mess up somehow. She looks ready to either jump in and stand in front of me, or she's ready to kill him. I'm not sure which.

I offer her a small smile, which she returns. I'm surprised her protectiveness is directed toward me and not her brother. I wouldn't be surprised if a lot of people threw themselves at the boys in her family in a bid to get rich, quickly. Maybe that's why she's staring at me. Maybe she's waiting for me to make a move on his wallet.

I gulp and meet his eyes again. In the light, they look black. He never looks at me like I might not be enough for him. In fact, he looks at me the way Savannah looks at Justin. Does he think I hung the moon too? Because he should totally know better—I'm way too short to hang anything.

A nervous laugh bubbles up inside me as I lean forward to plant a kiss on the tip of his nose. "I thought you'd celebrate your win with a drink." I gesture to his soda on the table.

"Recovering addict and alcoholic." He picks up his soda and takes a drink. "Choosing my sobriety is a celebration in itself."

I don't really know what to say to that. Like all things Ares, he came right out and said it, leaving it hanging between us like some awkward third wheel on a date. I'm a rule follower, and it didn't even occur to me that he couldn't and shouldn't drink. Never mind the trouble he could get into if he did and was caught. Now I feel like an idiot.

"Don't worry, *tesoro*." He strokes my face, and that *might* have been a purr that escaped me at his touch but the music's too loud, so there's no evidence to prove it. "I have no secrets from you. I can talk to you about anything. Don't feel bad for bringing things up. If you have questions, I don't mind."

I nod and kiss him again. It's a teasing sweep of our lips together and at the contact, I'm starved for more, wanting to sink into his lap like Savannah did with Justin.

A glass smashes to my right, and I turn my head in time to see Victoria pushing to her feet. The guy who had moved closer to her is soaking, liquid dripping from his nose and chin and seeping into the pale blue dress shirt that has two buttons opened at his neck. I'm guessing that's her glass smashed on the floor. Was it deliberate?

It could go either way with her.

She's already gone, weaving through the game night crowd toward the door, but she's left her coat and her purse. Ares is already on his feet, offering me his hand.

"You stay. I'll take her purse and coat and come back," I assure him.

He doesn't look convinced, but he sits down again. Without a backward glance, I snatch Tori's things and follow her out the door. A million questions burn in my mind, but I can't assault her with them as soon as I find her.

I burst out into the cold night air and look both ways, but she's gone. I hurry down the steps of the bar, toward the end of the path leading to the parking lot, but there's no sign of her anywhere.

"I'm over here." A sniff follows her words. When I turn, she's sitting on a wall to the left of the door to the bar, and she's crying. I haven't known her for years or anything, but Tori doesn't strike me as the crying type, which serves only to add another question to my growing list: why is she crying over some hockey player in a bar?

"I don't want to talk about it." She holds out her hand for her coat. When she slides it on, I hand her the purse.

I'm trying to respect her boundaries, but I'm worried.

Something clearly triggered her enough to dump a drink on the guy. Did he touch her?

"Okay. We don't have to talk, at least not right now. But I need to know if he hurt you."

The bitter laugh that follows makes something ache in my chest. "He was a perfect gentleman. Didn't lay a finger on me. And I didn't mean for the glass to smash, it missed the edge of the table." She shrugs like that's all the answer I need.

It's not. But pushing her won't make her any more forthcoming with what in the name of all things holy pushed her to dump a glass of liquor over the head of someone who she's said wasn't being a butthead.

"Did he say something?"

She levels me with a glare. "Please leave it, Eloise. Please?"

"I'm trying, but Ares is going to want to know what his friend did to upset you so much you threw a drink over him. Oh!" I clap my hands together. "Do you want Ares to kick his butt for you? I could get him to do that." I'm joking, but something flickers in her eyes that says she wouldn't mind if the hockey player got beaten up. She doesn't laugh at my joke, either.

"Tell him it's a case of mistaken identity. I thought he was someone else." She pulls me in for a quick hug. "My Lyft is here." Pointing to a car that has pulled up to the curb, she takes a step. "I'll let you know when I get home, okay?"

I'm reluctant to let her go, but she clearly needs her space. I tuck my lip between my teeth to stop any of my words from falling out, and instead nod. Something isn't making sense for me in this situation with my best friend, but I don't have time to mull on it because as soon as I turn to face the door of the bar, my boyfriend comes out.

His suit jacket hangs over his bare arm. His shirt sleeves are unbuttoned and pushed up his forearms, but I don't have time to linger on his really hot arms because blood is dripping from his face onto his button-down shirt.

"What on earth?"

He's scowling, clutching a Kleenex to his face, but he seems to have the wrong spot because more blood falls on his shirt instead of seeping into the tissue. He's alone, and he's muttering to himself in Spanish under his breath.

"Did you pick a fight with the guy Tori dumped a drink over?" I don't know that other guy, but he's *definitely* having a bad evening. I feel sorry for him.

"Raffi? No, *tesoro*. I didn't hit Raffi." He pauses to slip his jacket on, holding his tissue between his teeth. He starts toward where his car is parked, but I press a palm onto his chest to stop him.

"What happened, Ares?"

He relaxes against my palm. "Some of the Wolves seem to have escaped their curfew and came to the bar for a drink."

So, he beat up on the opposition for no reason? Discomfort is claiming my body in waves. I stay silent, waiting for him to clarify what happened inside the bar before I make any rash decisions, but I'd be lying if I said I wasn't concerned about his brash behavior.

"They came over and started trash talking." He rolls his eyes. "They made fun of us. When you blew me a kiss before the game."

Oh, no.

"I guess there's a video in circulation."

"You punched him because he made fun of you?"

His eyebrows twitch, but he shakes his head. "No, *tesoro*. I didn't start this one. I'm on my best behavior these days." He winks at me, and I swear my panties dissolve between my legs. "I'm trying to turn over a new leaf."

I take the tissue from him and dab at the blood trickling down his face. It's coming from his nose, which is reassuring.

He won't need stitches. I pinch the bridge of his nose, and he winces.

"Lo siento, cariño." We need to get the bleeding to stop. I have wipes in my purse, but we aren't there yet. And I think his fancy shirt is ruined.

"I'm not saying I was innocent. I may have verbally provoked him."

I nail him with a stare but stay quiet as I hold his nose firmly and push his head forward a little to get better grip.

"He threw the first punch."

"So why are you out here alone, and he's inside?"

"The Wolves got kicked out the back door. I came to find you." He holds out my purse. "We can go back inside if you want, but I wasn't sure if you needed to go with your friend."

I have so many words swirling inside me right now that none come out. I stare at him. His hard-cut jaw with a few days growth, his high cheekbones, his perfectly styled, thick dark hair. Who is this man in front of me?

"I'm sorry for embarrassing you, *tesoro*."

Shaking my head, I let go of his nose and take a look at the damage. "You defended yourself, Ares. That's nothing to apologize for." The bleeding has stopped, so I hunt out a wipe from my purse.

His breath tickles my face while I clean him, and he's quietly staring at me.

"What?"

He shakes his head. "You're not angry at me?"

"For defending yourself? No. I'm not angry at you, Ares." Wanting his warmth, I lean into him. I'm drawn into his orbit, and I don't want to be let go.

From the way he's looking at me, he was expecting something different in my reply. "I'd rather you didn't mess up this beautiful face of yours, but I'm not angry at you. I'm worried about Tori, curious about what drove her to dump a drink on your friend."

He grunts. "That was hilarious. He really has no idea what he said to make her lose it on him."

That surprises me. "Really?" I figured that level of hate had to be for someone she knew, especially since she said he didn't step out of line.

Ares wraps his arms around me, pulling me against his firm body. "I want you, *tesoro*." His words are simple, but they make every nerve ending in my body flare to life. "And I'm not sure I'm going to make it home." He jerks his chin downward like his rock-hard length isn't pressing against me.

I shiver, and he seems to think it's from the cold because he reaches to take his jacket off, but I stop him. "Let's go."

His mouth curves in a knowing smile, but this time I'm not embarrassed. I want him too, and I don't care that he knows it. As he guides me to his car, his hand on my lower back, he leans into me.

"If it was warmer out, and it wasn't our first time, I'd fuck you against the side of The Den."

My head turns to face him, and he's grinning. He isn't kidding.

"Or I'd bend you over the hood of my car and fuck you." He reaches across my front to open the passenger door. "Or if I had an ounce of self-restraint, I'd wait till I got you into the back seat of my car, and I'd fuck you there instead."

I've never had sex in any of those places, and now I want sex everywhere. An ache pulses between my thighs, and I'm not sure *I'm* going to make it home.

Ares guides his SUV out of the parking lot and sets off for his apartment, his hand resting on my thigh. It's not far and the roads are pretty empty. I try to stare out the window, to press my legs together, to count from one to one hundred to distract myself from the fact I want him to pull the car over and make me come again.

My phone vibrates. It's a message from Tori telling me she's home safely and she hopes I have a good night with twelve winking emojis.

When Ares's hand slides between my thighs and pulls my knees apart, I whimper. When it slides under my jersey and into my pants, pausing for a beat to stroke the hair at my apex, I moan.

"Please, Ares. No teasing."

He pauses, and I bite into my bottom lip as he maneuvers the car around a corner. He's toying with me, driving both the car and my need higher and higher, and dammit, I want to come.

He trails a finger through my slit, murmuring in Spanish about how wet I am. It's possible his filthy mouth is even more of a turn on in his native tongue. I lift my hips, trying to get some friction between his finger and my clit, but instead of giving me what I want, he pulls his finger out and sucks on it.

"We're here." He's already halfway out of the car. The parking garage is full, but it's dimly lit, and I'm considering taking my clothes off and letting him ravage me against the vehicle. Or the wall.

He pulls my door open, an animalistic look in his eyes, and when I reach for him, he's already there. He lifts me out of the car, closing the door behind me and pushes me back against it. His fingers tangle in my hair as he presses into me, kissing me hard, and fast, and desperate.

I'm already pushing my pants down my thighs as his mouth plants wet kisses down the side of my neck. He's going to mark me again, and this time I don't care.

"Cameras," he pants, skimming his hands up my bare thighs.

I've kicked off one of my shoes and one leg of my pants

and panties. I'm shielded by the car behind me and Ares in front of me. But in truth, I wouldn't care if someone caught it all on tape. I'd re-watch it every day for the rest of my life because when he picks me up and wraps my legs around him with that glint in his eye, it's the hottest moment of my life.

"Can't wait." I huff the words out between frantic kisses. My nails scratch his scalp as he drags his teeth across my jaw, the sensations on my skin talking straight to my core. Somehow, he holds me in place and opens his pants.

"You're sure?"

I nod. He's been with a *lot* of people and the risk of STI flashes in my brain like a mosquito that won't leave me alone. "Protection?"

He doesn't raise an eyebrow or say a word. Instead, he nods, pulls out his wallet, and he's sheathed and teasing my entrance before I know it.

He kisses me like his life depends on it. "Are you sure?" His need for my consent is so freakin' hot.

"I'm sure, Ares. Please, just... please take me."

He brushes against the lips of my pussy and sinks inside me, but I don't have time to dwell on it because he's gripping my hips and thrusting into me like a man overcome. He's not particularly big. For some reason I expected him to be, well, frankly, hung like a stallion, but there's no stretch or sting between my legs. It's long, but not particularly girthy. I can definitely handle this.

His hips piston his cock deep inside me. He's not only pierced, he's *very* pierced. Multiple hard ridges rub against my inner walls with every movement he makes, and it's driving me closer to the edge with each thrust.

His face is buried in the crook of my neck while my head tips back against the car window. He's taking me hard, deep, and when our mouths meet again it's a frantic collision of need and lust. His fingers find my clit, and it takes only seconds for me to ignite around him, which seems to only drive him harder.

He doesn't stop. Not when I bump my head off the glass when I tip it back to scream his name, not when my orgasm finishes raking its way through my body, not even when his car alarm starts going off behind me.

He's wild, consumed, and muttering how "fucking glorious" and how beautiful I am in a mixture of languages between bites and kisses and thrusts inside me.

The car alarm falls silent. The echoes of our skin slapping together, our heavy breathing, and the squelching of my arousal as he pounds my pussy smack off the walls of the building around us.

It's not long before he swells inside me, a string of curse words bursting from his mouth against the hot and sweaty skin of my neck. He thrusts two more times and stills everywhere but his mouth. It keeps kissing me, burning a trail up my neck, along my jaw and chin until he reaches my mouth.

Now that I've had him once, I need him again. I wiggle in his arms and pull my face back from his enough to speak. "Let's get inside." The lights of the car are flashing. We're on borrowed time before the wailing starts over. He ties off the condom and shoves it into his pocket. Pulling out his keys, he silences the car alarm.

Crouching low, he seems to be moving to help me get dressed, but instead, he's looping my panties through my pants, tugging at them until they're free, then tucks those into his pocket too.

When I tip my head in question, he flashes me a wicked grin before helping me get my pants back on. I'm glad for his help because with these wobbly legs, I'm not sure I could do it by myself.

His hand slips into mine, and I follow him into the building. He's grinning like the cat who got the cream, and I know he's not done with me any more than I'm done with him. Anticipation sparks in the air around us as we wait for the penthouse elevator.

The walls are cream, and the floor tiles are shiny and black. A picture of some rural setting hangs on the wall, but I don't have time to investigate. The doors to the elevators slide open with a ding.

Ares murmurs, "Round two."

CHAPTER 23
Ares

I have her against the wall of the elevator before she can say a word. She huffs out a breath. Under the fluorescent lights, I can see her properly. Her face is smeared with face paint, the black and green of my team colors mixing together in thick streaks on her skin. Her eyes are bright, spots of my blood are dotted on face paint that's gotten onto the front of her jersey.

My jersey.

My woman.

Mine.

I'd never have called myself a possessive man before I met her, but I'm powerless to fight this need to claim her building inside me.

I hoist her up into the corner, my cock painfully hard again, and grind against her.

"Ares." Her voice is as coated with arousal as the panties in my pocket. "People might get on the elevator."

Gripping her against me, I spin around to face the key pad so I can unlock the elevator. "Private elevator for the penthouse." I grab my wallet and smack it off the pad on the wall behind her back, hoping the damn thing connects and I don't have to put her down to find the specific card. "It's just us."

She looks over my shoulder. "Camera."

I don't turn to look at where she's inclining her chin at the red blinking light in the corner. I know where every camera in the building is. And they aren't for show. "I can have security pull the tape in the morning." I cup her pussy, grinding the heel of my hand against her.

She moans, tipping her head back to reveal a new line of bruises I've bitten and sucked along her neck. With each floor the elevator car passes, I work her into a new wave of frenzy. My fingers are slick between her folds, and the more I caress her clit the louder she gets.

She bends forward, clamping my arm against her like she might fall over, wavering on her feet.

"I've got you, *tesoro*." But I don't stop fingering her, slow and measured strokes juxtaposed against her sharp and quick breaths.

When the elevator car eventually comes to a stop, I half carry, half drag her into my foyer. I was going to wait until we got to the bed, but I can't. I'm agonizingly hard again, pressure building throughout my whole being. I need to get inside her, to hear her moan and writhe under me as I bring her to the edge and we both fall over together.

The motion sensor lights in my living area buzz to life, and she gasps. "It's so... bright." Something flickers in her eyes—an insecurity I haven't seen before, and it gives me pause.

We're momentarily interrupted as Bacon shuffles out to investigate. He sniffs us both, snorts, and goes back the same direction he came from. I bet Puck sent him to scope out whether or not we had food.

"What is it, *cariño*?"

Eloise shakes her head. "Are we going to the bedroom? I'm sure the lights aren't as bright." She squints, holding her hand up to protect her eyes, but it's an exaggeration. She's spooked about something, the bright lights, but why?

Her purse has somehow made it onto her torso on the journey up to my apartment, looped over her head and dangling next to her stomach. I open it, grab a wipe from the packet, and start the process of cleaning the smudged paint from her face, delaying our progress to the bedroom. I need to know what demons she's fighting so I know how to help her slay them.

Her hand touches mine. "I can do that." She smiles, but it's not a light-up-her-eyes kind of smile that I'm used to from my sparkly-eyed beauty. "Definitely don't want to get paint on your sheets." Nervous energy pours from her body, anxious and scared. I'm about thirty seconds from having my girl bolt back down the elevator shaft and out into the street.

"Fuck the sheets." I grunt and keep wiping at the paint, long slow strokes slowly revealing her skin underneath. "I want to see your pretty face."

Flinching at my words, she gasps again, though this time it sounds strangled, like it got caught somewhere in her throat on the way out.

"Tell me what's wrong, Eloise."

Her anxiety is heavy in the air, thick and unyielding. It emanates from her in rolling waves, and I don't know what I've said or done to make her uncomfortable.

Her eyes well with tears, and her jaw is trembling so hard I'm not sure she'll be able to keep it attached to her face. I wrap her into a tight hug, holding her against me, unsure of how we went from fucking in the parking garage to tears, but I'm holding onto a tiny thread of hope this isn't something I've done. Except it usually fucking is. Does she already regret sleeping with me?

"Can we keep the lights turned off?" Her muffled voice is so quiet against my body it barely registers.

I don't know where this is going, but I have a feeling I'm not going to like it. "Are they hurting your head?"

She pauses, then shakes her head. I pull back from her and crouch down. Dotting kisses on both tear-stained cheeks before licking her salty tears off my lips.

"Please talk to me, Eloise. Whatever it is, we can figure it out together."

I pull out my phone and push a button, dimming the harsh lights around us to a warm glow, but I don't make it dark. I need my girl to know that the light isn't her enemy, it's not something to fear or shy away from and that while she might feel comfortable hiding in the shadows, we can't live in the dark forever.

"I haven't been..." She sniffs, buries her head deeper into my shoulder, and I'm not sure if it's down to embarrassment or sadness. "My ex..." Her body quivers, and mine freezes. If her ex so much as accidentally caught her hair in his fucking zipper, he's a dead man.

"He never... we never..." She sucks in a breath and straightens before looking me in the eye. She pulls herself together right in front of me and it hurts that she thinks she has to. She has no idea how fucking brave she is, how strong and capable. "We never did it face to face. He didn't want to look at my scars."

Something in my chest snaps. Fury zips through my body like someone lit a fuse and flames are racing to the fuel, ready to blow. But as much as I want to go and find that fucker ex of hers and make him beg for me not to tear him into tiny pieces and feed him to my fucking pig, I draw in a slow breath through my nose.

This isn't about me, this is about my beautiful, sweet, self-conscious girl, and there are things I need to do for her.

I cover her mouth with my finger before crouching a little and throwing her over my shoulder. She squeals, wiggles her legs, giggling and smacking at my ass while demanding I let her walk, but I don't stop until I reach my room.

I drop her onto her back, right in the middle of my bed, then tear my shirt from my body. It's ruined and covered in blood, but even if it wasn't, I need her to see how I can't fucking wait to bury myself inside her again. How I need my naked skin pressed up against hers.

Buttons clink as they land on the hardwood floors and the noise that started as a giggle from Eloise turns into a pained groan as she trails her hungry stare over my body.

We haven't seen each other naked yet but she's looked me up online. There are pictures. Lots of pictures. The only piece of me not on the internet is my cock, though if she looked hard enough, she probably saw that too. She licks her lips, scrambling to tuck her thumbs into the band of her pants.

"¡*Tranquila!*"

She stills on the bed, watching me with curiosity.

"I need you to listen very closely to me, okay, *tesoro*?"

She nods.

"Your ex was a *pendejo*, and we're done talking about him." I toe off my shoes and kick them to the side before stepping on the edge of my socks to release my feet. "Here's what's going to happen, and I need for you to tell me if you're not okay with any of it. ¿*Bien?*"

Another nod.

"I'm going to rip those pants off you." I unbuckle my belt, sliding it out through the loops, and drop it to the floor unceremoniously. "I'm going to curl my hand around your throat so the only place you can look is into my eyes."

The rise and fall of her chest quickens.

"And I'm going to fuck you in my jersey until you forget all about your ex and how shitty he made you feel. ¿*Bien?*"

She nods again.

I push my pants and boxers onto the floor. Stepping out of

them, I flash her a smile. "You are a strong and beautiful woman. And while I will undoubtedly want to fuck you from behind sometimes, it'll be in front of a mirror so I can watch your pretty face turn pink and your eyes roll back in your head while I drill my hard cock into you."

Her hand starts to travel down her stomach, but I hop on the bed and pin both arms above her head with one hand. "Don't move."

She interlinks her fingers, already writhing against my black satin sheets. I waste no time tearing her pants from her body, and after a quick argument with her bra, we manage to get it out from under both her shirts without her taking off my jersey.

I roll back onto my knees, fisting my cock slowly so she can see how hard and needy I am for her, how ready, how precum slides down my head. She closes her eyes, turning her head away from me.

Gripping her chin, I turn her back. "No, *tesoro*. There's no place for embarrassment in our bedroom. Watch what you do to me, how much I want you."

Her eyes spring open wide, and I let go of her face, moving my hand back to my shaft. Her fingers twitch toward me, and I cover her hand with mine, placing it on the hardware studded along my dick.

"It's a Jacob's ladder." My cock isn't chunky, but it's long and has seven rungs of a Jacob's ladder lining it. Fucking hurt like a motherfucker and took three people to get it done, but it was worth every second of pain. Ribbed for both our pleasure.

Her thumb skims the metal balls on one side of each rung, and she hums. "It's so pretty."

Not all cocks are created equal. There are some really ugly as fuck dicks out in the world. With my shiny hardware, she's right, mine is pretty. But it's nowhere near as pretty as my girl. And while it's not as thick as some of the dicks she might have been with, I have a PhD in how to use this, and I'm not going to stop until she comes apart on it.

"Are you wet for me, *tesoro*?"

She spreads her legs, showing me that the curls covering her pussy are matted with arousal. It shatters the last strand of my self-control. Seating myself between her legs, I reach across her into my bedside drawer for a condom.

As much as I want to ride her bare, it's something we'll need to work up to. I've fucked a lot of people. A fact I'm sure is on her mind as much as it is mine.

When I'm sheathed, I waste no time in sliding through her pussy, enjoying the little moans she lets free. "You're beautiful, Eloise."

She shakes her head, it's slight, but I catch it and it makes the animal inside me rattle against his cage.

"*Sí, tesoro. Hermosa. Preciosa. Eres mía.*"

Her eyes flex wide, and she nods at the last one. I leave my cock at her entrance, dangling, grazing, waiting, despite the raging rapids in my veins demanding I sink in deep.

"Tell me you're beautiful, *cariño*."

Rolling her lips between her teeth, she shakes her head.

I sit patiently, my cock twitching against her pussy. This is more torturous for me than her, but I hate how she feels about herself, I hate how she sees herself, and I wish more than anything that she could see herself the way I do.

"*Dime, tesoro.* Tell me how gorgeous my girl is."

She shakes her head again, but it's less convincing this time. Her back arches, her hips thrust toward me like she's chasing my tip, but I won't give in. I won't back down. I won't give either of us what we need until she tells me what I need to hear.

I lean forward and kiss her forehead, not missing her grunt of frustration. "Tell me."

Her voice barely a whisper, she mumbles *something* but it's too soft.

"Louder, tesoro. I can't hear you."

Her scowl is adorable and might have me convinced she was truly pissed if her eyes didn't betray her. "I said I'm beautiful."

"You are, cariño, you are. And I'm going to fuck you all night long until you believe it."

I sink balls deep into her with one stroke. She's hot, tight, and wetter than she was outside at the car. I hook my hands behind her knees and draw myself into her as far as I can go, before I do exactly what I told her I would.

I collect both her hands and pin them above her head, holding them down and bracing them into the mattress for purchase.

My other hand holds her face toward mine, cupping her throat and sweeping my thumb over her cheek. "No closing your eyes." I slant my mouth over hers, and she opens on an exhale. Our tongues tangle together lazily but the impatience inside me spikes out of control as I thrust harder and harder into her.

I piston quicker, deeper, my balls slapping against her with every thrust, but it's not enough. Skimming one hand down her body, I stop to grope her tits over my shirt. I haven't gotten my hands on them yet, but right now isn't the time. I need to fuck her, really fuck her. I need to fuck her with so much conviction that she'll never again wonder if I find her beautiful, or if I want to fuck her with the lights off or her back to me.

"Tell me you're beautiful, Eloise."

I pinch the skin of her hip as I grip her, relentlessly pounding my dick inside her with rhythmic jerks.

"I'm—" She moans as my hardware rakes down her wall

with each stroke, sending a shiver through her entire body. "Beautiful." My hand constricts around her throat.

The closer I charge to my release the jerkier my thrusts become, but I am not coming before my girl. I release her hands, but she holds them in place above her head while my fingers slip between us, finding her slick clit.

"You're beautiful, Eloise."

"I'm b-b-beautifuuuuuu—" She falls over the edge on a scream that pushes me harder.

Not giving her a second to recover, I keep slamming into her, driving myself into her darkest places, claiming her as my own. My balls tighten. My ass muscles clench.

I throw my head back, coming on a primal roar that rips from my chest as I spill inside her. I make a mental note to go see the doctor for an STI/STD test because I need to fuck my girl bare and explode inside of her for real. I need to claim her in every way I can.

She clenches around me, holding me in a grip. It doesn't feel intentional until she pulses around my dick. When I meet her eyes with mine, she's smiling at me. "So are you, Ares."

"So am I, what?"

"You're beautiful too."

Another piece of my heart clicks into place as I stare at this beautiful woman with tears welling in my fucking eyes. "I'm falling for you, Eloise."

CHAPTER 24
Ares

My room smells of sex. Delicious, hot, all-night-fucking-long sex.

The low sun out the window streams through the blinds, warming my skin. In my haste to get Eloise into bed last night, I forgot to draw the blackout curtains. I forgot a lot of things, like putting the quilt back on the bed, or eating something other than her sweet and juicy pussy.

My hands are tucked behind my head and her face is pressed onto my chest, her pink hair fanning across me.

Despite the infamous man whore my reputation says I am, I've never woken up with someone before. Not ever, not once. In fact, I've never brought anyone back to my place before. I always fucked at my partner's place, or somewhere outside, or in a car and then left.

Fucked and fled.

That was my MO. And sure, I fucked a lot of people. Why the hell not? If God didn't want us to fuck around and find out, he wouldn't have attached such fun toys to us to play with.

But with Eloise, everything feels like my first time. My *last* first time. I already know, with everything I am and everything I have that she is it for me.

I can't resist reaching out and stroking the delicate skin of her shoulder. I don't want to wake her, we barely got any sleep after a long night of sexual discovery, but my fingers are drawn to her skin. I dust a kiss on her forehead as she huffs out a quiet snore.

I've always wondered what the benefits of having a long-term partner are, of being locked down by the same person. For me, I like to keep things fresh, guys, girls, sometimes both at the same time... The concept of being with one person for the rest of my life was always laughable.

As I stare down at the beautiful woman in my arms, I wonder if I could make that shift for her. Or if she could meet me somewhere in the middle.

The image of me eating her out while someone fucks me in the ass makes my dick spring to life. Is she open to the idea? Or could she be open to the idea? Maybe that's a hard limit for her. If it's a hard limit for her, would that be a hard limit for me, too? Do I need to have all sides of my sexuality to be fulfilled to be happy?

I think I do.

So many questions. And despite her limited sexual experience, Eloise might have some give. Maybe I'm naively hoping we can find some space for us both to be happy and sated. And more than that, I want to find that space.

Therein lies the key. You've got to want it. And I want my pixie with every breath I fucking take.

I missed her waking up, because she's dotting kisses on my chest and making adorable early morning noises. We have another game today, and as much as I want to spend hours tracing her every line and learning her body's reactions to my every move, I don't have time.

She clamps her hand over my hard cock and pumps a few times. "Aren't you spent after last night?"

"Goalies have a lot of stamina, *tesoro*." I groan as her hand tightens.

We did a lot of things last night. She rode my face until she drenched me with her cum, then returned the favor by sucking me like a fucking champion until I blew my load all over her face.

I grow harder at the memory of dragging my fingers through my cum on her scars, like I was somehow permanently mixing us together. When she sucked my cum off my fingers, I almost lost it all over again.

Another groan ripples through me as she pumps harder, faster, but I don't want to start my day with anything less than her pussy holding me in a vise when I come. I turn her onto her back before dragging my fingers across her perky tits.

They're not quite a handful and are so fucking responsive that I barely have to touch them to pull a moan from her.

"Are you sore?"

I don't know if she's clenching or how girls can test if they're aching without getting up and walking around, but she shrugs. "Not enough to stop."

It's all the invitation I need before I roll on top of her, reaching for protection from my bedside table. Guiding my sheathed dick inside her already slick pussy, I'm two thrusts in when a familiar meow meets my ears.

Oh fuck. I didn't close the door.

Eloise's eyes flex wide.

"Ignore him—he can wait a few minutes." As soon as the words are out of my mouth, I know they're dumb as rocks. Leaving the door open was a rookie fucking mistake. I'm lucky Puck didn't invite himself into my bed during the night while pixie and I were having many, many orgasms. I can only conclude we were making too much noise for his majesty, and he stayed the fuck away.

Except, now he's hungry.

I go back to kissing her, sliding myself in and out of her, slowly, casually, lazily. Last night I was in a rush to have her, this morning I'm in a rush to keep her. I intend to worship her like the queen she has no idea she is.

After a minute or two of increasingly loud meowing, a weight lands on the bed, and I know I'm fucked. Puck is hungry, and he doesn't care that I'm balls deep in my girlfriend coursing toward my blissful release. In fact, that's a hindrance to him getting food.

He hops onto my calf and saunters toward my ass. The quilt is on the floor, the sheet is somewhere tangled at my feet, and my cat is making a beeline toward my naked balls.

"Ares?"

"Don't move." My whisper comes out pained. I can't see the fucking cat, but I can feel him, his tiny death claws moving toward my ass. "The cat's on top of me."

Her giggles might be cute, but she's not the one about to get her butt cheeks sliced open by an impatient, hungry cat.

He didn't make an appearance all fucking night, but now, *now* he shows up. Asshole. Cock blocking asshole. Ha. He might end up being a cock destroying asshole if I'm not careful.

A cold, wet cat nose hits my butt cheek, and I jump with a whimper, making Eloise hit her head on my headboard. This isn't going well, but I can't deny it's funny as fuck.

She's laughing so hard, tears are streaming from her eyes and dripping onto the pillow as she rubs the side of her head. We're both laughing, it's impossible not to. If I don't laugh, I'll cry, or worse, I'll give in to the temptation to buck the cat off me like I'm a fucking mechanical bull. That wouldn't end well, for any of us. Puck would double down and sink those talons into me, and while I generally like a bite of pain in my sex life, I don't have an animal play kink, and I have no desire to kill my cat by flinging him full force at the wall.

How the fuck do I get out of this with my junk intact?

Eloise is laughing so hard she's started to hiccup.

Puck sweeps his cold as fuck nose against my ass cheek, again, and bats me with his paw. Twice. I'm so fucking tempted to fart on him, but I don't know that I'm at the farting in front of my girlfriend phase yet. I dunno what cats dig and don't dig either, for all I know it could be some kind of mating call to this weird-ass cat, and I'm in enough trouble as it is. So, I hold it.

He escalates the butt-batting to head-butting my ass, and for such a tiny little thing, he's got some strength. I groan, dropping my head onto Eloise's shoulder. This is *not* at all how I had planned our morning to go.

"Okay, Puck." I sweep my arm behind me trying to shoo him, but the sneaky bastard is tucked out of reach. "I'll get you food."

He doesn't move. It's like he knows as soon as he gives up threatening my balls with his claws, I'm going to go back to fucking my girl.

Because I am.

I push up onto my palms, hoping the movement doesn't cause him to overreact and dig in, because I have no real clue right now where he'll fucking dig.

Eloise's body is still shaking with laughter as she tries to gulp down air. "We're being held hostage by your cat. We'll get ours, when he gets his." She snorts, tears streaming down her face, and the warmth in my chest can't be anything else but love.

"Come to Thanksgiving with my family."

Her eyebrows shoot up her forehead, then smush down over her eyes before she cracks up again.

"What?"

"Your dick is buried inside me, your cat is holding your man bits hostage, and you pick now to ask me to your family's Thanksgiving?"

"Seemed like a good idea at the time?" I shrug, a chuckle rolling through me. She's right. My timing could probably have been better, but I've always been an impulsive kinda guy. "You said your dad is going to be on the road right? Or he's usually on the road for holidays? Well, come to my house. You've already met my asshole siblings, so the hard part is done."

"Can we make sure you're going to survive this incident with your cat before we start talking about the future?"

"I know you have a point, but you're stalling."

She dissolves into giggles again. "I can see it, having to tell your sister that you're in the hospital for a severed penis and her thinking I'm savage and punishing you for something."

She has a point. Athena would probably offer to chop something else off too.

"And for once I haven't done anything wrong." I kiss her. "Think about it though. I'd love for you to come with me." And I mean it. I've never taken a girl home before. Or a guy. I've never had any long-term relationships worth bringing home. Even Athena has brought someone home. Once. And it didn't last long.

I carefully shift my weight, removing my dick from the most perfectly snug pussy on the planet, and rotating enough so Puck doesn't feel like he's falling and latch on, but also enough that I can see where the fuck he is. Thank fuck I'm a goalie with great mobility because getting him off me requires a certain amount of pretzel twisting, and from the hungry look in my *tesoro*'s eyes, she wants me to do all manner of fun pretzel bending with her next.

When I stand up, cock dangling in the wind, there's a

snort from the door. The pig has joined the party. Puck now stands next to Bacon, both of them staring at me like *I'm* the fucking problem.

Pendejos.

I'm getting a pet sitter. Someone to distract them and take Bacon for some exercise while I'm busy doing... things, like Eloise. I'm also buying a pig pen for him to sleep in. Clearly it was a mistake giving them free reign of my space, and it has come back to almost literally bite me in the ass.

I shower and get ready for practice while my girlfriend strokes my pussy and pets my pig. Unfortunately for me, neither of those things are euphemisms for my dick. Or even her own fucking pussy. I shouldn't be jealous of her giving attention to my pets, yet here we are.

When I head out to go to the Trash Can with my girl's panties tucked into my pocket, I'm lighter, happier, like I'm somehow both walking on air, yet more grounded than I've ever been in my life.

Yeah. This girl might be The One. And I'm not even a little bit scared.

Trashcan Tattle with Tabitha

Tittle Tattle 'round the Trashcan tells me that our wild child netminder, the one and only #32, Casanova himself, has finally settled down into a relationship.

Someone needs to check that hell hasn't frozen over, Tattlers, or make sure the definition of monogamy hasn't changed in the dictionary for that matter, either. As the youngest of the de la Peña brood, Ares is not at all known for his commitment to anything other than the game.

He's been seen cozying up with a pink-haired delight—nope, not as you might have guessed, our beloved barista from Bitches Brew—rather a fellow freshman local whose name this humble reporter has not yet been able to procure. It's only a matter of time, though.

I find myself hoping that our resident bad boy has finally found the person to bring calm and stability to our goaltender. Further rumors suggest scouts have been sniffing around the Trash Can, with prospective offers from NHL teams not only here in Iowa and in Minnesota, but also Calgary, and Nevada on the table.

Will our King of the Crease stick around in his home state?

Or will he opt to play for a team farther afield? And what will that mean for his cotton candy-haired girl?

Heard a rumor? Spied one of the delicious de la Peña brothers or any of the Raccoons out in the wild? Click here to contact Trash Can Tattle with Tabitha.

CHAPTER 25

Eloise

How is this my life?

I left Ares to come home and shower. He offered to let me join him for his "quick rinse," but if I'd gone with him, I'd definitely be walking funny, and he'd have been late to practice.

Later.

In fact, I might already be walking funny.

My hair is twisted on top of my head in a towel. I'm clean, I'm dressed, and I'm making a hot chocolate—because you only live once, and the night I had constitutes as the most exercise I've had in a while, so I need to balance that out with an influx of chocolatey calories. Or something.

I'm really not sure whether Ares was in sound mind when he invited me to his family's Thanksgiving, and I'm not sure whether or not he'd have told anyone else in his family. He strikes me as the impulsive guy who turns up to dinner with friends without having told anyone he was bringing any.

Only one thing for it. I need to settle my anxiety and double check with someone in his family that it's okay for me to go in the first place. I would literally die of mortification if I showed up and no one expected me. Die. Like, dead.

I lean against the edge of the kitchen counter and pull my phone off charge.

Eloise: Hey Athena, it's Eloise. Ares's girlfriend.

I feel like an idiot, but the three dots telling me that she's typing appear pretty quickly.

Athena: You're the only Eloise I know, Pixie. Talk to me, Goose.

Athena: It occurs to me that you might not have seen Top Gun, so I'll follow that up with a "What's up?" To make doubly sure you catch my meaning.

I smile, enjoying the fact she's already calling me a nickname. Is that a Dominican thing? The de la Peñas all seem to call each other a variety of names and now they're giving me nicknames too. Now isn't the right time to admit that I haven't seen *Top Gun* or the new one, *Maverick* or whatever.

Eloise: Ares invited me to Thanksgiving.

Athena: My brother Ares?

My smile has developed into laughter. I knew something was hinky about him asking me.

Eloise: The one and only.

Athena: Invited you to Thanksgiving?

Eloise: Yup.

Athena: At my parents' house?

Eloise: Affirmative.

Athena: You're sure he didn't invite you to Friends-giving? The guys do that sometimes. I mean, I dunno if they're doing it this year or not, but it's come up a few times.

Athena: I mean... I got off the phone with my mom, and she didn't mention anyone was bringing a plus one.

My stomach tightens. I don't want to be an imposition, or a spectacle for that matter either.

Eloise: LOL! He definitely said Thanksgiving, not Friendsgiving, with you guys. I figured it was an impulse invitation. I don't have to go. I needed to know whether he'd cleared it with anyone first.

Athena: Oh, girl. Ares never clears shit with anyone. You absolutely DO have to come! It's no big deal. I'll talk to mamá and make sure she's expecting you.

Eloise: Are you sure? I don't want to be any trouble.

Athena: You're literally the opposite of trouble, *amiga*. Unfortunately (for you) you're one of us now. You're always welcome.

Tears snake down my cheeks, dripping onto my clean shirt. I don't know how to describe this feeling, this... acceptance? These people barely know me and already Athena's going to bat for me, or whatever the hockey equivalent of going to bat is, for a holiday meal with her family.

Mom would like them, too. The de la Peñas, I mean. They're fun, vibrant, and enthusiastic like she was. I bet she'd try to reform Ares of his playboy ways, but she always saw the good in people, their kindness, their spirit, and she never let something like an addiction or a rough upbringing cloud her judgment of someone's soul.

I clutch a hand to my chest, the unexpected punch of grief hitting so hard my chest physically aches with her loss.

Would she really like Ares? Would she be proud of me? Would she like my pink hair?

She wouldn't ever have gotten upset with me for it—she always encouraged my self-expression. We talked about me cutting my hair and both of us getting matching tattoos together in the car right before she died.

I doubt she'd have approved of my reasoning, though. She'd have told me to own my scars and not hide my light from the world. She always said that in a world as dark as this one, bright lights need to shine brighter, not dull their shine.

But she'd have supported the shift to shorter, brighter hair more easily than Dad did. For. Sure.

Eloise: Can I bring anything?

Athena: I doubt it, Mamá always goes overboard for family dinners. But if there's something you really like to have at Thanksgiving, you might want to bring it.

Eloise: My mom made a great potato salad.

Athena: I fucking L-O-V-E potatoes. They're my favorite food group. Now if you don't bring it, I might cry.

I can't imagine Athena ever crying, but I'm totally here for her potato enthusiasm and now I'm resolved to make it next week to bring with me. I'll make a double batch because I've seen those brothers "snacking" on second breakfast, and there's no way they will be able to leave Mom's potato salad alone.

Oh my God. What if they live in a mansion? What if they have a dress code for Thanksgiving dinner that amounts to more than "stretchy pants to enable adequate carb consumption"? What if they eat fancy food like snails and caviar for Thanksgiving dinner? Oh. No. Nope. This isn't good. What if they have three forks and no manual on which to use?

Another embarrassing nightmare plays out inside my brain. My mind races. If I don't stop it, I'm going to talk myself out of going before I've even fully talked myself into it.

Eloise: What do I wear?

Athena: Whatever the heck you want to wear.

Athena: Calm your tits, skippy. We're people too. I get that it's intimidating.

Athena: Okay, fine. I don't get that it's intimidating, but I'm guessing that's why you're asking. We live in a big house, with flashy cars, but underneath all the expensive, shiny crap, we're human too.

Very, very, very, very rich humans, sure. What if I use the wrong freaking fork and they all laugh at me? Ohhhhh, boy. I need to get off this spiral before I crash into something.

Athena: This is a regular meet the parents kinda deal.

Athena: Except my dad can be an asshole to the boys sometimes. So, I should probably apologize before we even get started.

I open the fridge and pull out the pack of grapes. I'm tempted to shovel even more chocolate in my face, but grapes will have to do.

Athena: You've already met the majority of us. Abuelita is going to LOVE you. But I warn you, she's going to threaten to hit at least one of us with her shoe a minimum of twice. And she will have your wedding to Ares planned before dessert.

I can't help but laugh at that. She sounds like a hoot.

Athena: She might also tell you that you need more meat on your bones and offer to make you *pasteles en hoja*.

Eloise: Is now the right time to mention I've never had those?

Athena: *¡Ay, no!* She would 100% get up and go make them right then and there. Fake it. Save us all from the *pasteles en hoja* production line.

I like their grandma already.

Athena: Look, if you'd like to make an impression, that's one thing. But Ares is already head over heels for you, and like I said, you're one of us now. The rest is window dressing. I know you're nervous, that's normal, but my parents' opinions don't matter, and even if they did, they're going to love you.

Athena: If you need tips: Abuelita likes Junior

Mints. Mamá likes Gerber daisies. Dad hates everything so don't even try.

But those are both so... normal. I draw in a deep inhale, forcing myself to release it slowly before doing it again, and again, and once more for good measure. Maybe they aren't the hoity toity family I expect them to be. Maybe Athena is right and they're like me, except, rich, famous, powerful, beautiful and perfect.

Athena: If you need cover, I can come pick you up and we can arrive together with Ares. I don't know what his plans are. I'm not sure he knows what his plans are. But we'll figure it out. And we'll come up with a safe word you can use if you need some air, and a different one for if you need to all out escape. Okay?

Eloise: This isn't your first rodeo, is it?

Athena: My family is... a lot. My brothers and I have had safe words since we were six, and we aren't afraid to use them.

Eloise: This isn't comforting.

Athena: Don't panic, Pixie. We've got you.

And it feels like they do.

Thirty minutes later, I've given up on trying to study, a ball of nervous energy. I'm not going to tonight's game, but before he left for the rink Ares asked if he could see me after. And by *see* me, he totally meant fuck me. He said he meant to see me, too. But I'm starting to think he has some post-game excess vigor he needs to work off, and I'll be interested to see if this is a pattern. I'm also more than interested in helping him take care of any extra energy he might have.

He blew my mind twelve ways to Sunday last night, and I have the bruises to prove it. I touch my fingers to my neck. I'm going to have to wear a turtleneck for the next few days, and I can only hope these hickeys are gone by Thursday. It's not quite the impression I want to make on my boyfriend's parents.

I smile to myself, reliving the way he looked at me, the hunger, the animalistic need to be inside me, to claim me. The pain in his eyes when I broke down in his living space and told him that I was uncomfortable having sex with the light on.

From his internet profile, he seemed like such a carefree person. Lively, fun loving, obnoxious, and okay, an asshole. But the more I get to know him, the more I realize he has a lot of deep feelings.

I'm not sure Mom would approve of his methods of making me face myself and my self-loathing, but she'd appreciate his intentions all the same. She might even have encouraged him.

Yeah. I can't study. Not with images of Ares's head between my legs making them shake so hard I accidentally kneed him in the face floating around in my mind. I'm getting all worked up and hot and bothered when I should be reading boring statistics and figuring out how to be a nurse and do, you know, nurse-y things.

The radio is playing, and I'm tackling the pile of dishes in the sink when the front door slams, sending my heart galloping like a prized racehorse.

"Eloise?" Dad's voice booms throughout the house.

Blood chills in my veins. I know that tone. I'm in for an ear-bending, and it's going to be a long one. "In the kitchen."

He storms into the kitchen, drops his backpack on the dining room chair and turns to me, accusation in his eyes. "What do you think you're doing?"

I resist the urge to say cleaning, and I drop the sponge into the sink of soapy water. It's on the tip of my tongue to tell him to spit out what I've done wrong this time, but I don't. I stare at him, brows raised in silent question.

"I told you to stay away from that fucking boy." He points his finger at me and takes a step in my direction.

I'm not sure I've ever seen him this angry. We never cussed in the house when Mom was alive, but since she died, he's grown to play fast and loose with the F-word. It makes me cringe every time he says it. Not because I mind profanity. If I did, I couldn't date the god of war himself. But because it marks how big the change in him has been since she left us.

"Don't try to deny it."

I'm not. Okay, fine. I considered it for a fraction of a second, but I decided I wasn't going to deny it.

"I saw the stupid newsletter thing on the internet."

Stupid newsletter thing?

"The hockey gossip column thing? Tabitha what's her name? One of my buddies gets her newsletter. She said you're dating that rich boy. Eloise, what do you think you're doing?"

He points at me again. "And what the fuck did you do to your neck? Are those...? Hell no. Eloise." He pinches the bridge of his nose. "Are those hickeys on your neck?"

I don't need to answer that one, the bruises speak for themselves. There's literally no other explanation for the trail of marks down my neck and throat.

"What do you have to say for yourself?" He plants his hands on his hips, puffing out his chest.

I expect him to continue, but he tips his head like he's waiting for me to answer. I'm not sure what to say. Any answer I give him is going to piss him off. So, I stick with the truth.

"I'm a grown woman, Dad. I'm not a little girl anymore."

He snorts.

"I can make my own decisions on who to spend time with."

He snorts again. "Decisions. Ha. Mistakes you mean."

"If it's a mistake, it's mine to make." I cross my arms.

"I don't like this, Eloise. What would your mother say?"

I hate that he's using my dead mother as a weapon against me, that he casually throws her into conversation like the weight of her death doesn't crush my chest every day. He uses her name as though I don't torment myself enough with questions of "What if?" and "Would she?" and drown in guilt every single day I wake up and she doesn't.

"Mom would say to follow my heart, Dad."

He chuckles, but it's unkind. "She would send you to your room to think about your behavior and how you're embarrassing yourself."

My blood fizzes under my skin. I can't remember the last time I felt so calm and centered, so like myself, and he's trying to ruin it for me. I was finally in a better place; I've found people who don't make me feel like a freak and he's trying to take it from me. I refuse to let him.

"Just because you're embarrassed by my behavior, doesn't mean it's embarrassing."

"I don't even recognize you anymore, Eloise."

"Well, maybe if you stuck around long enough to spend time with me, you might have a better idea of who I am these days."

He jerks back, as though I physically smacked his face, and while I spoke in anger, I don't regret what I said. He's been on the road a *lot* since Mom died. It's as though he can't bear to be anywhere near me.

Even if I didn't look like her, the scars on my face are a constant reminder to him of what happened. That I lived, and she died. I get it. But what he doesn't seem to realize is that while he can walk away and not look at me, I don't get that option. And I've got to find my way through the tall grass by myself.

Despite legally being an adult, some days I need my dad.

"I leave again in the morning."

Surprise, surprise.

"But I'll stop by over the holiday next week."

"I have plans." The words are out of my mouth before I have a chance to filter. His eyes narrow, hurt and anger flaring in them.

"With whom?"

I can't help but catch the edge in his voice. He knows with whom, but he wants me to say it. Like I should have preempted the fact he's going to be present for the holiday for a change. I'm not a mind reader. Again, maybe if he stuck around to have a conversation...

Heaving out a sigh, I force my shoulders away from my ears. "With Ares and his family, Dad. He knew I'd be alone for the holiday, so he asked if I wanted to join him for dinner with his parents."

"Well, cancel. You won't be alone."

"I won't cancel." I clear my throat but don't look away.

"Excuse me?"

"I said I won't cancel my plans with Ares for Thanksgiving, Dad."

His face falls. "You're serious?"

I nod. My innards have crumbled to ash, but something deep inside me is resolute, determined not to back down on this point. He can't pick me up and put me down when it suits him, when he wants to scold me, punish me for behaving in ways he doesn't approve of.

"What have you become, Eloise?" He shakes his head and turns to leave.

"What have you become, Dad?"

An hour later I'm curled up on Tori's couch with Wyatt eating Goldfish crackers and string cheese while watching *Home*. The guy from the *Big Bang Theory* is hilarious as the little alien dude, but not even Sheldon Cooper can make me laugh right now.

"Aunty Ellie?" Wyatt pulls my attention to the empty snack bowl.

He doesn't need to say anything. I'm slacking in my duties as snack wench. A few minutes later, I'm back on the sofa with a refill. I'm not sure how many Goldfish crackers counts as too many Goldfish crackers, but my little snuggle buddy doesn't seem to think we're there yet, so we clink our plastic bowls together like we're clinking glasses of Champagne and dive into round two. He's not telling me the whole truth when he says his Mom won't mind if I give him more.

I'm probably being played right now, but I also don't have the energy to argue, and I'm digging the cuddles. I'm quite happy to buy them with cheesy crackers.

Tori's taking a shower, her mom is working, and Ares is currently on the ice. The live updates on my phone tell me he's having another excellent game. Or at least, I think he is. He hasn't let any in yet, and they're in the second period.

I have at least another hour before I see him, maybe more if he chooses to go to the bar. Tori knows something's wrong with me, but she hasn't pressed the issue. It won't last.

I'm using her child as a human shield. Like maybe if we keep watching kid's movies, she won't find the time to push me. At the rate I'm chowing down on these snacks, I'm going to need to stop by Target and refill her pantry.

I'm sure there'll come a point of maximum snack consumption. When the sour taste in my mouth and the queasy feeling in my stomach will abate, and the warm fuzzies will kick in.

At least I'm not crying. Well, not anymore. I sat outside Victoria's house for an hour crying in my car, and I didn't feel any better. Hence the snacks and the movies on her couch. But I'm on borrowed time. It's past his bedtime.

I protest more than Wyatt when she turns the TV off. She puts him to bed in record speed, and with him gone I lose my buffer. I have to face up to the fact my best friend is going to peel back the bandages from today's emotional wounds and make me talk to her.

"Here." She thrusts a glass of what I hope is wine and not straight up liquor in my face. "This will help."

"I'm not sure anything will help." I tell her everything. My anxiety about Thanksgiving at Ares's parents' house, the argument with Dad, and how much I miss my Mom.

When I'm done, my throat is raw, my voice hoarse, and I've gone through half a box of tissues. My phone chimes, and I know before I even pick it up that it's from Ares.

Ares: I'm done with the game, *tesoro*. Do you want me to pick you up? I can meet you somewhere if that's easier.

His subtext is pretty clear: If your dad is around and you don't want the headache, we can meet somewhere else.

"Tell him where you are, and he can come get you here."

I raise my brows at her, unsure of what her plan is, but she holds up her hands. "I don't want you driving like this."

She has a point. I'm pretty raw and frazzled. There's every chance I'll end up in another car crash, but I'm not sure I want him to see me like this either.

"Invite him over, E. Relationships aren't only about the good times. Let him in." She taps at her chest and speaks with such conviction I can't really argue.

"You know you owe me an explanation about what happened at the bar, right?"

She nods. "I know. I'm not ready yet though. When I am, you'll be my first port of call." She's tired, dark circles underline her eyes, and an air of sadness has hung around her since the bar that I can't penetrate.

"Anything I can do for you?"

She pats my thigh. "You're already doing it." Jerking her

chin at the phone in my hand she smiles. "Bring your boy over. I'll go make popcorn."

She's way more chill about Ares coming to her house than I was when he showed up at mine. I stare at the screen for a long moment, thinking about what Victoria said to me about letting him in. I guess it's time to show him my demons and hope he doesn't run away.

CHAPTER 26
Ares

I knew something was wrong before I even stepped off the ice and into the locker room after the final buzzer. I can't say how, and I had no clue what, but something felt not quite right.

A congratulations message was on my screen from my *tesoro* by the time I had my shower and got dressed, but when she asked if I could go to Tori's to see her, the heavy feeling in my stomach grew.

I'm waiting at a red light on Edgewood. I needed to get gas, then someone had broken down closing off a lane, and traffic was surprisingly dense. It's as though the universe has conspired against me to keep me away from my girl for as long as possible.

It makes my nerves all the more frayed. I don't know what's wrong, but something's tugging in my chest. I need to see her, to look at her face and know she's okay.

When the light changes, I gun the gas. There are no parking spaces outside Tori's house, so I circle the block a few times growling and grunting under my breath until I find one. It's not a particularly *legal* parking space, but right now, I don't care if the neighbors call the cops. I'll pay the damn fines. Or buy a new fucking car. Whatever.

Tori opens the door as I walk up the path. The dim light from the house illuminates her like some angry celestial being surrounded by a warm glow. She folds her arms, puffs out a breath I can see in front of her face, and holds up her hand like a stop sign.

"If this is a bit of fun for you, it's time to turn around and walk away, hotshot."

My feet stutter to a halt. "It's never been 'a bit of fun' for me," I say with finger quotes. "I care about her." From the look on my girl's best friend's face, she doesn't believe me.

"I'm falling for her, Tori. I'm in with both feet." I stupidly point down to my toes like they add some extra weight to my statement.

Tori's mouth twists like she's trying to fight a smile, but it's short lived before the concern from a few moments ago shadows her face again. "It's not pretty in there. She had a fight with her dad."

Tori doesn't need to elaborate. Eloise's father has issues with me. I hoped I'd have more time to convince him that I'm not the guy he thinks I am. At least not anymore.

Okay, so I'm kind of still that guy, but I'm trying to be better. Every single day I choose my sobriety and the game, and now I choose Eloise, too. Trying has to count for something, right?

None of that matters right now as the acid in my stomach threatens to creep up and into my mouth. She's going to choose her father. There is no other alternative. Family first, that's what Papá has drilled into our heads since we were little.

Family first.

Siempre.

Which means when I walk into that house, the only girlfriend I've ever had, the only woman I've ever had real feelings for, is going to break up with me.

As much as that sucks, the idea that she's on the other side of that door, struggling with her own emotions, that she's sad and needs a hug, that her dad might have yelled at her again... that transcends everything else.

I give Tori a nod and walk straight past her into her own house. In the living room, Eloise sits on the sofa, leaning forward, her elbows on her knees, her hands covering her face and her pink hair hanging over her fingers like curtains.

Her shoulders shake as she sniffles, and my heart collapses in my chest. I hop over the back of the sofa, startling her when I land on the cushion next to her. Barely giving her time to react, I scoop her into my arms and drag her onto my lap.

She burrows her head into my shoulder and lets go. As she cries, I stroke her back and whisper all the good things I can think of, it'll all be okay, just let it all out, I'm here, and I've got you. But none of it feels like enough.

Because it isn't.

I did this to her. I made her feel this bone-deep pain making her cry uncontrollably on my shoulder. The thought alone makes me want to join her in her tears. But I don't. I hold her until it passes. Because this situation isn't about me, not really, it's about her, and she needs comfort right now.

"I'm sorry." Her mumbled words against the damp skin of my neck makes my heart crack even more.

I shake my head, not sure I can trust myself to say anything.

"I'm sure this isn't what you had in mind for after your game."

It's not. When I stepped off the ice, I wanted to fuck her until she saw stars, but now, now I want to hold her until she's okay. "No need for sorry. It should be me apologizing, *tesoro*. I don't like coming between you and your dad."

She stares at me, the pain in her eyes making it hard to breathe, and the urge to kiss her until it goes away is strong. "Honestly, I think he'd be like this about any boyfriend I brought home."

The growl is in the back of my throat before I can stop it. There is no other boyfriend, and there won't be. But the idea that there might have been, well, I don't like that so much.

She pats my chest, soothing me, as she curls smaller on my lap. She's already tiny, so I'm not sure how she makes herself smaller.

Swallowing down the bitter taste in my mouth, I steel myself. "Do you want to end things?" I need to know off the bat what she's thinking, where her head is, whether I'm going to leave this house with my heart shredded into tiny pieces by my pixie.

Her head snaps back so quickly it brushes the edge of my jaw. That could have been a disaster. She's shaking her head, the sadness in her wide eyes replaced with fear.

"No, Ares." She caresses my face with her palm. What does she see on my face while I'm staring into her sadness and fear? Is that what she's looking at in me, too?

I nod, but the tightness in my chest doesn't dissipate. She turns my head back to hers, sweeping her nose against mine the way I love, before touching her lips to mine.

"I'm not leaving you, Ares. I feel more like myself than I have in a long time, and that's because of you, because of us."

I had planned on taking her back to my place, but she stays planted in my arms for hours, until long after Tori goes to bed. Eloise tells me all about her mom, the accident, the months that followed, and how badly she misses both of her parents.

She tells me about her injury rehab, her physical therapy, and how for a little while she wasn't sure if she'd regain the use of her arm. I can't imagine how terrifying it must have been for her to be dangling upside down in the car, with blood dripping from her body, while watching her mom die right before her eyes.

And yet, she's a ball of bright light and strength. I almost feel guilty for not being there for her at that time, which is stupid because we didn't even know each other. But that's a lot for anyone so young to go through, especially when the remaining parent checked out as well.

She tells me about her therapist, and how without her, she'd probably not be here. I want to send her a gift, but nothing feels like it's enough for a "Thank you for saving my girlfriend's life" present.

I could send her a new car, but the last time I did that for someone, my sister kicked my ass. Apparently, a car is overkill for a thank you gift. My therapist at the rehab center didn't know what to do with herself when she saw it. I'm pretty sure she pissed herself.

Eloise's favorite serial killer documentary runs on the TV until she falls asleep in my arms, beyond exhausted. Tori doesn't have a spare bedroom, so I have no choice but to wake up my girl and take her back to my apartment. After the day she's had, sleeping on a couch isn't going to be good for her at all.

I leave a note for Tori, thanking her and telling her I've got Eloise with me at my place, and I hold her hand on the drive home as she dozes, her head against the cool car window.

"I still want to come to Thanksgiving with your family if that's okay."

I swear, when she tells me things like this, it's like flares detonate in my chest. I don't think she has any idea, either. "It's more than okay."

I help her get into one of my old shirts before tucking her into bed beside me. She's out cold within seconds, but no amount of watching her chest rise and fall with even breaths can drag me under. I don't know how we're going to get through this if her dad isn't on our side, but I need to try. I need to think of something, somehow, for us to be together that won't destroy us both in the process.

~

The sound of my phone ringing drags me from a fractured sleep. The bed beside me is cold, and if it wasn't for the faint smell of strawberries on the pillow case, I'd wonder if last night was a dream.

Papá's name flashes on the screen in front of me, and I groan. I have enough going on in my life without him giving me shit for whatever it is I've done to tarnish the family name this week.

Family. Fuck. With everything going on I'd all but forgotten about Thiago. Sourness bubbles in the back of my throat. I bet that's how he feels about Papá, too. Asshole probably never looked back.

Should I hire a PI to look for him? Am I ready for what he might find if he does?

My phone screen flashes again and my stomach dips. I get it though. This thing with Eloise's father has made me realize how much my behavior has the potential to impact others. Sure, for a lot of my history, I was young and foolish, drunk and high. For a lot of it I didn't give a flying fuck... But even as I'm starting to grow up, to outgrow... that past follows me, and I can't shake it.

It's a harsher lesson to learn than any of my family, or therapists at rehab have tried to teach me until this moment. And while not all of my past is worthy of front page news or embarrassment, enough of it is that my *tesoro*'s dad doesn't want me to be with his daughter.

I pick up the phone, and before I can even say hello to Papá, he's yelling at me in streams of Spanish. Apparently,

Athena told Mamá that I'm bringing a plus one to dinner in a couple of days, and that's disrespectful to my mother. Not the bringing someone part, no, the fact I didn't tell her myself or give her enough advanced warning.

I try hard not to snort. This guy has some nerve. I'm pretty sure Thiago is my half-brother and Papá is lecturing me about being an inconvenience and disrespecting my mother. I'm also pretty fucking sure that fucking another woman and knocking her up is disrespectful to Mamá, and it's on the tip of my damn tongue to say as much.

I love my mother, and throughout everything I've tried my very best to protect her from the worst of my behavior and not to disrespect her. She has a way with Papá that is likely the only reason I haven't been cut off from the family fortune or murdered and never heard from again after all my shit. But more than that, she's my world.

I suspect I'm her favorite child, but she'd never admit it out loud. I have no idea how, but she has a soft spot for me. Maybe it's because I was her last? I don't know. But I'm getting the impression that dear old Dad wants something to complain about for complaining's sake. I let him flame out. When he's done, or at least done for now, I ask him if it's okay for me to bring Eloise to dinner. He scoffs and says of course it is, as though it was never a question.

I know Mamá, she always makes so much food that we need to share with our neighbors. She's a social butterfly who loves people, and she wants to marry all four of her children off to good partnerships as quickly as possible, so I knew that even if I turned up unannounced on the steps of my childhood home with a date, Mamá would be fine.

I dunno what bug is up Papá's ass today, but it's not me, and for once it's not my drama. Certainly not at 8am on a Sunday morning after little sleep and what feels like a hangover, even though I wasn't drinking.

The only way to stop the lecturing in my ear and go find my girl is to be apologetic and mean it, to pander to him and tell him everything he wants to hear. So, I tell him I'm sorry, I'll apologize to Mamá, and after another few minutes ranting, calling me a selfish, petulant little shit, he finally relents. I can breathe again.

When I turn around, my girl stands in the bedroom doorway holding a tray. She's made omelets and toast, and she's smiling at me. It's soft, it's warm, and I feel it all over.

"You hungry?" She shuffles toward me, handing me the tray so she can climb back into bed beside me, and it's as though everything in the world makes sense in that one moment.

I'm absurdly in love with this girl, and I don't know what to do with myself.

CHAPTER 27

Eloise

Despite having seen Ares every day this week, I'm standing smoothing the front of my perfectly pressed dress for the millionth time while I wait for him and Athena to come pick me up.

It's Turkey Day.

I've made more potato salad than I had any business making, and my stomach is in knots. Dad didn't come home like he said he would. I checked in with him, and he told me he's fine, he's working. If he could have told me that on Tuesday instead of when I texted him this morning to see where he was, it would have saved me hours of cooking a turkey dinner for him to have when he got back that will now likely go to waste.

I don't know why I thought turkey was a good peace offering, but it kept me busy yesterday and out of my own head.

A car honks out front. As I'm locking the front door, he whistles out the window. *"Te ves muy sexy con ese vestido."*

My cheeks flame hot. It's a constant state of being these days. I wasn't going for sexy with this dress. I was going for pretty, conservative, sensible, parent friendly. But when I spin to face him, his tongue dragging across his teeth, I can almost hear his dirty thoughts.

I shiver. We haven't had sex in days, and I'm starting to wonder if I should have worn pants because he's already—as Tori says—eye-fucking me. I perhaps should have given more thought to covering myself up because he's looking at me like he can see through my dress.

Athena leaves the passenger door open as she climbs into the back seat.

"I could sit in the back—"

She cuts me off with a look. *"Siéntate."*

Leaning over the center console, I plant a quick kiss on Ares's cheek. When I reach back to tug my seatbelt on, he grabs me, cupping my face briefly as his hand skims my jaw, and his fingers tangle in my hair. He kisses the breath from my body. I let out a dreamy sigh when he pulls back and clicks the belt in for me.

I chance a glance back to his sister, but she has her nose buried in her phone. Still, she totally knows what her brother did to me, and that clawing at my chest is level ten embarrassment.

He clucks his tongue before putting the car in drive and pulling away from the house. "She doesn't care."

"He's right. I don't care." She meets my eyes in the side mirror and gives me a small quirk of her lips.

I stay silent the entire ride to their house, the butterflies in my stomach warring with bees, and making a flapping buzzy sensation that I really don't like, and no amount of swallowing will get rid of.

The driveway up to their house is longer than my street. And as we round the final bend and their mansion comes into view, Ares takes the hand resting on my thigh and squeezes. *"Tranquila, amor.* Breathe. It's going to be fine."

Easy for him to say—he's grown up with this life, this

wealth, these people. This is all new for me, and I'm intimidated as heck.

And let's not even get started on the "What if his parents don't like me?" thought process.

The huge door to the house swings open and an older version of Athena steps out. She's wearing a red dress that pinches a little at the waist before dropping to below her knee. Her dark hair is swept into a chignon at the nape of her neck, and her makeup—including perfectly matching red lipstick— is flawless.

She grabs Ares in the biggest hug and plants a series of kisses on his cheek before standing back at arm's length and cupping his face with both palms. "You look good, *mijo pequeño*."

He's anything but a little boy, and the color of his face is approaching the color of her dress. "Mamá, this is Eloise." He pauses, searching her face. "My girlfriend."

A high pitched shriek penetrates the air as she hurls herself at me, awkwardly hugging around the Tupperware box of potato salad in my arms. Ares shrugs, grinning at me like he warned me this would happen, like he told me everything would be fine.

"Eloise, it's so good to meet you at last. I've heard a lot about you." She slaps Ares's arm. "Not from Ares."

He has the decency to look embarrassed, which makes her pinch his cheek and grin harder. Athena rolls her lips between her teeth. It's clearly killing her not to laugh out loud at her younger brother's expense.

A smaller, older woman stands in the doorway at the top of the steps taking everything in. Ares leans toward me and whispers in my ear that it's his paternal grandmother. I recognize her from the restaurant, but she looks different, more polished, younger, and she's wearing shoes as expensive as my entire college education.

Didn't Ares tell me she occasionally threatened violence with her shoe? I figured he'd mean a flip flop, or a tennis shoe, not a pointed toed, pointy heeled, super expensive shoe. I feel like being on the receiving end of that would result in puncture wounds.

Their mom ushers up the steps where Abuelita cups both my cheeks and gives me a silent once over. She smells of cinnamon, and I'm hoping that's because she's made some of her delicious baked treats that I've tried at the restaurant. Ares said she's the master behind Guac n' Roll's success.

He also said he suspects she's over a hundred years old, but standing in front of me right now, she can't be more than eighty. Maybe even younger.

"Welcome to the family." She gives me a squeeze, and I'm not sure she spoke loud enough for anyone else to hear but me. I'd say it's a leap to welcome me to their family, but from the minute I met his siblings I've felt like I belong here.

The younger of the Mrs. de la Peñas ushers us all inside. Apollo and Artemis are already milling around the table grazing. They both hug me, while Ares's hand stays firmly on my lower back.

A banquet's laid out on the table. Mrs. De la Peña takes my box of potato salad and sets it beside a dish that looks like potato salad too. Only hers has eggs and apple pieces in it.

A huge ham rests in the center of the table adorned with pineapples, and I sneak a glance at Ares. Will he be able to eat ham now that he has his own porcine companion?

Bacon is the sweetest pet, and I don't know that he'd be happy to learn that Ares went to town on one of his cousins. Can pigs smell guilt on people like dogs and cats can? They always know when you've been hanging out with another animal. Will his pet piggy give him shit for eating pork?

Ares hands me a plate and guides me around the banquet.

There is no other word for it, it's a spectacle. There is so much food I imagine they'll be eating this for days, maybe a week.

"That's *moro*, rice cooked in black beans." He points to another dish. "Sweet potato casserole, but ours has pineapples and marshmallows on top. Salad." He drops his voice. "But who wants greenery when you can have carbs?"

He winks at me, his boyish charm oozing from every pore. He's doing his level best to make me comfortable in their overwhelmingly ornate home. I'm afraid to sneeze in case it damages something or leaves a mark on the white... everything.

High ceilings, wide circumference pillars, and what I'm one hundred percent sure are genuine crystal chandeliers surround me in an open space that I'd guess is supposed to be some form of dining room.

I'm trying not to think about how much the plate in my hand cost, or how much it would cost to replace if my trembling hands were to drop it.

He points to another dish. "*Pastellitos*, these have meat, but Mamá and Abuelita usually make dessert ones too." He gestures toward a second table. "Guava and cream cheese *pastellitos, dulce de leche pastellitos,* pumpkin pie, *flan*, and bread pudding."

My mouth is watering, and I'm fighting a strong urge to head straight for the sweets. "It all looks so amazing, Mrs. de la Peña. Thank you so much for letting me join you for Thanksgiving." There is barely a quiver to my voice, and Ares's presence so close to me has settled my trembling fingers for now.

Abuelita waves a spoon my direction. *"Lo hice todo."* She winks as she tells me she made it all. "We'd need the fire department on standby if Gabi was left unsupervised."

One of the boys snort, and Ares's mother, Gabriella's face heats but she doesn't say anything. Ares points a fork back at his Abuelita. "Mamá is a pretty damn good cook, Abuelita." He waits until his mom turns her back before planting a kiss on his grandmother's cheek and whispering, "But you're better."

She nods, puffing out her chest and taps his bicep with a spoon. "Why didn't you bring her home sooner?"

I'm almost embarrassed for him, but he's taking the good-natured ribbing from his family in stride, so I sink into the positive attention our relationship is getting.

He bumps his grandmother with his elbow as he takes a heaped pile of rice from the dish to his plate. "She needed to be ready for all this."

With a huge sigh, Abuelita pats his cheek. "You're not wrong." She looks at my plate with derision and shakes her head. "You haven't taught her how to eat right yet?" She clicks her tongue rather loudly before doubling the portions on my plate, grumbling to herself in Spanish about how I have no meat on my bones, and I need to fatten up.

After making small talk while filling our plates, we move into a dining room where Mr. de la Peña is already sitting, reading a document. Gabriella hands him a plate of food, and he grunts what I hope is gratitude at being delivered his meal.

Abuelita mutters something loud enough for the rest of us to hear about him being a grown-ass man and being able to fetch his own meal. Mr. de la Peña at least tips his head to his wife who nods back. It's like they're speaking a weird, silent language that isn't sign language. Is this how rich people communicate? There are no words anymore? Looks and head tips?

I expect awkward silence as we eat, but the chatter is lively and engaged. I find myself glad that Abuelita loaded up my plate because it's so delicious that I keep shoveling forkfuls of food into my mouth. I'm definitely going to need a doggy bag. I've never tasted anything like this, and Guac n'Roll is my favorite place to eat. Abuelita has been holding out on Cedar Rapids.

I'm eating the most delicious flan that was probably ever created when Mr. de la Peña points his spoon at me. What is it with these people pointing things at each other? "What happened to your face?"

The air flees my lungs, and I suck in a mouthful of dessert, causing me to cough, but I don't miss Gabriella's gasp, Athena's *"¡Papá!"* or Ares's "What the fuck?" as I take what have to be my final breaths.

At least if I'm going to die, it's a delicious way to go. Death by flan.

Abuelita leans across the table and smacks the back of his head. From the noise, it wasn't a soft smack, either. *"Mira, muchacho del carajo, ¿acaso yo no te enseñe mejor que eso?"*

I'm not sure whether I want to laugh at the fact Abuelita smacked him like a child and called him the son of an asshole, or cry at the fact he called me out at all.

One thing's for certain though, I'm glad she didn't slip off her Louis Vuitton stiletto and turn it into the infamous chancla Ares has told me so much about. Or a shank for that matter. I imagine there'd be plenty of people with a lot to say about a little old grandmother shanking her billionaire son with what would have to be a $14,000 shoe. The woman is all class and sass.

Not to mention getting blood everywhere. Everything is so... white. And expensive. Maybe they have staff to clean that up for them.

Mr. de la Peña holds his hands up and bursts into a tirade in Spanish about how he never meant any harm by asking the question. From the fire in Ares's eyes, I'm not sure he believes him.

Ares takes my hand on his lap, stroking the back of my fingers with rhythmic sweeps while my other hand flutters to my face. I've traced my ugly scars every day since the bandages came off and their ridges and twisted skin disgust me every single time but they're part of who I am.

Clearing my throat, I shift in my seat. "I was in a car crash, *Señor de la Peña*. I had extensive facial injuries and a badly damaged arm."

Abuelita's lips are in a thin line. "You owe him nothing."

Ares mutters in agreement.

Sr. de la Peña grunts, nodding, though I'm not sure if it's at my answer or grandma's acknowledgement that I don't owe him anything. "We have connections. We could get someone to fix it for you."

This time Abuelita reaches for her shoe.

I don't know if I'm more embarrassed or affronted. I guess this is how people with money behave, like throwing a few dollar bills at an issue would make it go away.

Ares and Athena are both raising their voices to their father, and it's my turn to stroke my boyfriend's hand. I'm sure Mr. de la Peña meant no malice with what he said, but his bluntness and lack of empathy have definitely riled his family. And me.

"It's okay, Ares." I try to soothe him, even though it's not okay at all. But he's furious. He's telling his father that while he might think it's an innocent question, that it's rude. He's also using a few words I don't understand, and I'm not sure I want to.

After a couple of minutes arguing back and forth with his family members in heated Spanish, Mr. de la Peña throws his hands up.

"I'm sorry, Eloise. Forgive me. Sometimes I have access to people that others might not and if you would ever like a consultation with some of the best plastic surgeons in the world, I could arrange that for you. That's it. That is all I was trying to say. I meant no harm or offense with my question." He glares at Ares, as though it pained him to apologize to me.

"I appreciate the very gracious offer, *Señor*. But I can't afford to miss that much class at this point in my life." I need to change the subject from my face before Ares explodes beside me or before I start digging a hole in the floor to swallow me up.

Gabriella uses that piece of information as a seed to a topic change as she asks what I'm studying in school.

"Nursing. When I was younger, I wanted to be a doctor like my mom, but I think nursing is a better fit for me."

As we eat, my fingers caress the side of my face. My scars run from above my cheekbone to below my jaw line, and span from where my ear meets my neck to close to my nose. In parts. the skin is twisted like vines, and in others it has been stretched thin and almost but not quite smooth.

These scars remind me that I'm alive and my mother is not. No matter how many times he offered me the chance to visit with high flying doctors, I would decline. Erasing the scars would erase one more bit of her.

Ares drops his spoon to the table, pushes back his seat, and walks away. One of his brothers stands, I'm not sure which since one of them got a haircut, and now they both look identical, but I shake my head. It needs to be me who goes after him.

Not knowing what I'm going to face when I catch up with him, I drop my napkin onto the table, excuse myself, and follow in the direction of my angry man.

CHAPTER 28
Eloise

Ares disappears up the grand staircase in the middle of the foyer, and part of me regrets not sending one of his siblings after him. I'm going to get lost and die in the belly of this ginormous building. They're never going to find my body.

I tiptoe to the top of the stairs and follow the corridor to the left. An empty hallway stretches before me, identical white doors on each side, and no indication of where my stewing boyfriend has gone.

Thankfully, one door is open a crack, and I hope with everything I have that it's the right door as I push it. He's shirtless, pacing back and forth like a caged lion. The ink on his chest says *Family* in black and red ink script that's hard to read unless you get up close and personal with it.

Family.

His family is clearly complex, and he loves them all dearly. Is he tangled in knots about my dad? Or about his dad? Or is he rethinking our relationship?

"I'm fine, *tesoro*."

I wave a hand at him. "You're clearly not fine, *cariño*." I take two steps toward him, and he takes a step back.

"He has no manners! *Cabrón*." The words burst out of him with a flail of his arms. "He thinks because he's rich he can say what he wants, to whomever he wants, without consequence." He spins on his toes and takes a few steps in the other direction.

I move into his space, placing a hand over his racing heart. "Stop pacing, Ares."

He won't look at me, his eyes cast down to the floor. "You should leave, *tesoro*. I don't like you seeing me unable to control my temper like this."

I'm not afraid of him. I don't fear for my safety. He's not lashing out or destroying the Tiffany lamp on the bedside cabinet. He's mad. And it's comforting.

I skim my fingers over the ink on his chest, then the lion curled around his bicep. His shoulders sag as he hisses out a slow breath between his teeth. "You're playing with fire, Eloise."

"Then I'll get burned. Talk to me. Tell me what's really got you so twisted up like this." It's a guess. Maybe he is this bent out of shape because his father asked a question about my face, but if that's the case, he's in for a rude awakening.

Before I changed my hair, people pointed and stared all the time. Kids would come right out and ask what was wrong with my face. Sometimes they'd cry when they saw me in the mall. I never got used to it, so I changed my appearance to reduce the number of small children I made cry while out shopping.

"I think he's having an affair. Had an affair. Maybe having." He blows out air and slips his fingers into his hair, tugging it at the roots. "I don't fucking know."

I don't know what about his father being a butt to me has triggered this line of thinking. It's fractured and disjointed, but I don't want to press him. I want to hold him.

"Do you want to talk about it?"

He shakes his head. "Not here, not now. But... Agh." He swings his arms down by his sides and starts up his pacing again. "Family first. Family always." He's muttering under his breath, switching between Spanish and English, and I only catch every other word.

An affair is an awful thing, but I don't get why it's made him retreat upstairs, strip off his shirt, and wear out the carpet as he walks back and forth over the same six feet.

"I think I have a half-brother. He came to see me on campus."

My stomach free falls. Oh, wow. This is clearly more than a sordid one-night thing with his secretary. I don't know what to say. My mouth has gone dry.

"I needed to get away from him before I confronted him. I was suffocating in his ego and lies at the table." He turns to me, anguish paling his face. "Family first, my fucking ass. I called the kid a liar and sent him away, *tesoro*. I saw the family resemblance, I denied it, and I rejected him."

The pain painted across his face fractures my heart. "It's okay, Ares." I reach for him, but he puts both hands up and steps back.

"It's not unusual, you know. Rich Dominican men taking a mistress." His tone turns bitter. "Having a secret child with their bit on the side." He scrapes his hand over his face before interlinking his fingers against the back of his neck and walking a few more steps. "This kid... he wasn't a kid, Eloise. He was our age, or close to it. How—?" His voice breaks.

He clears his throat and tries again. "How long has he been cheating on Mamá? Are there more? Affairs *and* kids? Do we have a full family that we know nothing about? More than one? The kid was so desperate, Eloise. He wanted my time, and I sent him away."

His jaw trembles. I'm not sure I can keep it together if he loses it.

I rush forward to him, but he doesn't let me wrap him in my arms. "It's okay, you had a shock. It's all well and good having the benefit of hindsight but you were caught off guard, Ares. It's a natural response."

"It's not okay." His voice gets louder. He holds up a palm, shaking his head. "I'm sorry. I don't want to yell at you. This isn't your fault. I'm sorry for making my problems your problems."

"I'm your girlfriend, Ares. Your problems *are* my problems."

Tears glisten in his eyes. Seeing him so vulnerable and cut up like this makes me warm inside. Gone is the hotshot, the playboy, the stripper, the brash trouble maker making headline news, and in front of me is a passionate, beautiful man with a big heart and a raging river of emotions. And he's showing me. Only me.

I fight the urge to rub at my chest. "It's going to be okay, Ares. We can find him again."

He sniffs and faces the window. "That's just it, I don't want to." He laughs, but it's hollow. "I have the means and the money to pay someone to do it. But then, I'd have to face the fact it's all true. That my father is no better than any of the other men he does business with. That he's not above reproach. That he's maybe been an asshole to Mamá." His fists flex at his sides.

The deep wine-colored drapes are still open. The sunset out the window is one of the prettiest I've seen, and at some point, I want to take a stroll in the beautiful gardens below. But for now, I need to find a way to reach Ares, to comfort him.

I step up to him and curl my arms around his middle. I turn my face so my cheek rests against his muscular back. His chest heaves with the effort of sucking in and pushing out every shaky, ragged breath.

After a long beat, I tighten my grip, refusing to give up. I need to try to help soothe him when he's in this much pain. I can't take it away. I can't make his father not be a cheating butthead. But I can hold him. I brush my nose against his back, dotting kisses on his skin. I don't know why he's naked to his waist, but it doesn't matter. I'm glad for the opportunity to have my skin touch his.

"Eloise." My name is a pained plea. His body is tense, unyielding against mine, and I'm not sure what to do other than be here and keep kissing his skin.

I'm too little to reach the tops of his shoulders with my lips, but no matter how many kisses I sweep across his back, he's not relaxing, and his chest just keeps heaving. He's so mad, so hurt, so full of guilt.

"I'm so sorry he made you feel uncomfortable, *tesoro*. I should have warned them. I should have—"

"Shhhh. It's okay. We aren't responsible for the actions of our parents, right?"

He grunts like he wishes that were true.

My thumbs stroke his stomach. It's as muscular and firm as the rest of him, though I can't say I've thought about how defined his stomach is until right now. And it's pretty defined.

"What can I do?"

He shakes his head.

"Do you want your siblings? I can go get Athena." When I loosen my arms a little, his hand clamps down over both of them. He jerks me against his back.

"No. I don't need them."

Does this hotel-esque building have a gym? A punching bag? Does he need to go skating on the ice to clear his head? Or dancing? I'm sure that would help work out some of the knots in his tight muscles. I'm desperate to help him. Every single fiber of my being is screaming to do something to take his agony away, but I don't know what.

"Tell me what you need, *cariño*. I want to help."

He turns to face me, cupping my face with both his hands. The small action was something that brought me great anxiety at first and now the gesture brings such affection and tenderness that I can't imagine him ever not doing it.

"You are helping." He kisses me. It's soft and gentle and over as quickly as it started, but I'm not done. I'm greedy. I need him to kiss me until the sadness in his eyes fades away, until the cheeky grin reappears on his face.

Wrapping my arms around his body, I brace him against me and kiss him again. He pulls back, drops his head to mine and heaves out a sigh.

"Eloise, you're killing me."

I ignore his protest and kiss him again. He's growing hard against my stomach, but I'm nearly sure the tension in the rest of his body is less than it was. If kissing him senseless is what it takes to make him relax a little, then I'm absolutely going to do it. It's the only thing I have left to try.

He's murmuring against my neck, telling me how much he loves me, how much he needs me, and how I'm his anchor, grounding him amid the choppy seas. Spanish may be a romantic language at the best of times, but it's downright swoon-worthy when the man you're head over heels about is whispering sweet nothings to you.

I pull my head back, forcing him to look into my eyes. "Te amo, Ares."

The words are barely out of my mouth when he covers my lips with his. My hands caress his face, growing damp as his tears hit my skin. I plant my hands on his shoulders and jump, hoping he'll catch me, and I won't end up clinging to him like a spider monkey. He folds my legs behind him with a groan.

Peppering kisses down my neck, he turns us so my back is

facing the window, then walks us toward it until the cold glass meets the fabric of my dress. He doesn't make a move, doesn't try to feel me up or do anything, but I need him to. My body is burning, yearning for him to touch me, yet all he's doing is dragging his lips lazily across my skin.

I drop an arm from resting on his shoulder and move his hand from my waist. I need it between my legs. My dress gives him easy access, and when he pushes my panties aside, skimming his fingers over my pussy, I can't help but moan.

"Yes. Please." I nip at his ear, trying to provoke a reaction, trying to unleash whatever anger and passion he needs to let go of right now. "Ares, please."

I barely hear his zipper opening, and I'm trying not to think about how he's so skilled at holding me up for so long and getting himself into position to take me the way we both need him to.

"No protection." His voice is a pained growl.

"I'm on birth control."

He searches my eyes for permission. I nod. No words, no hesitation, he thrusts inside me in one smooth motion. I don't have time to think, or breathe, or adjust, because he pistons his hips against mine. The metal of his piercings grinds along my walls, and I'm not sure that I can keep quiet when he's railing me this hard against the window.

He's relentless as he grips my hips. Rage, passion, and need are driving him into me over and over but when his eyes hold mine captive, a bottomless pool of love reflects back. The sex is frantic and primal, but the emotion held in his eyes is enough to destroy me.

I'll let him. In fact, I need him to.

He grunts with each thrust, and I know he's getting close. I let my eyes roll back before fluttering closed. "Let go, Ares."

As he shakes his head, a bead of sweat trickles down his temple. "Not before you."

This isn't about me. I don't need the release he's chasing so desperately as he drills into me against the glass. I open my eyes. "Please? I need you to let go."

He searches my face with his probing gaze, his eyes flitting between mine, once, a second time, and whatever he sees must satisfy something inside him because it spurs him on. Harder, faster, deeper... sweet mother of—holy guacamole!

I didn't think he could get any further inside me but the faster he thrusts, the deeper inside me his piercings hit. I shove my face into the crease of his neck and hope that my noises don't carry downstairs to his family.

He comes on a long, low moan that sounds almost painful before stilling. His breaths are sharp and rapid as he comes back to me. He showers me with kisses, and I never want him to stop.

"Ares? Where are you?"

I can't tell which one of the twins is hollering for Ares, but we probably don't have a lot of time left. Ares grins at me before sliding his dick out of me and back into his pants. When he sets me back on the floor, he gets onto his knees.

"No, Ares," I hiss. "Get up. You don't have time. Later. Please."

He shakes his head, his forehead braced against my stomach as he walks his fingers up my thighs under the fabric of my dress. "Shhhhh."

Grabbing the elastic of my panties, he drags them down my legs. When they're on the floor, he jerks his head so I step out of them. He nudges my legs apart and uses the panties to clean me up before folding them up and tucking them in his pocket.

I don't have time to decide how I feel about it, or ask why he's collecting my panties, but he clearly has a thing for my underwear, so I start planning a way to use that to my advantage in the future.

Maybe I'll mail him a pair of my panties. Or perhaps I'll hide a pair in his hockey bag for when he goes away on trips.

"You go back down first, I'll come down in a few. I need to gather my thoughts."

His face doesn't suggest he's upset anymore, and I don't want him to feel crowded either, so I nod and head toward the door.

When I step out into the hall, I tug my dress down and hope the wind doesn't pick up when I leave his house. The last thing I need is to flash his family on the way down to the car.

I shudder at the thought. How embarrassing for his family to think I didn't wear any underwear to a family gathering.

I turn the corner, ready to face the rest of the de la Peñas, and almost walk into Athena. The relaxed, post-sex euphoria is short lived as my body seizes up on the spot.

She knows. There's literally no way she doesn't know. Her lips are pressed into a line and her perfectly sculpted brow is arched over her perfect eye as she jerks her chin to point behind me. "Is he feeling better now?"

I bite my lip, not wanting the self-conscious, hysterical laughter rattling in my chest to burst out of me. Managing a nod, I let out a little of the breath I'm holding.

"Good. I need to talk to him. Thanks for softening him up for me." She sticks her tongue out and winks at me. "I can't talk to him when he's a bloodthirsty ball of anger."

I don't know whether to laugh or cry. But I nod again and hurry past her, taking the stairs with caution so I don't end up bare ass over head on the way down. At the bottom, I take one last look back up at Athena. She gestures for me to keep going, and as I return to the dining room, sans panties, I can only hope Ares won't be mad at me for letting her go to him when he's feeling like this.

CHAPTER 29
Ares

"Why is your shirt still off?" Athena's voice echoes around the sparsely decorated guest room. When I turn to face her, she nails me with a look that says she knows what I did in here with my girl. I don't give a shit.

I'd bet she passed her on the stairs, too. "On second thought, why's your shirt off at all?"

I raise a brow at her and she grunts. "I know what you did, *hermanito*. I figure you're a pro at quickies, and there wasn't much time for stripping down."

I may be a pro at quickies, but that one was the best quickie of my entire life. I shrug. "I couldn't breathe right with that thing on. I needed space."

"From... your clothes?"

I fix her with a glare, and she puts both hands up. "Sorry, no judgment here."

"You wouldn't understand."

"Try me." She plants her hands on her hips, and she's not going anywhere any time soon. But I'm not ready to talk to her. I'm not ready to tell her what I know. And yet, that's why my shirt is off, because this secret is in the darkest recesses of my chest, eating me from the inside out.

Maybe a problem shared is a problem halved. They wouldn't say it so often if it wasn't true, right? Fuck if I know.

What I *do* know is that Hen doesn't need this in her life. This constant gnawing at her insides by a shitty secret of the *cabrón* downstairs that we shouldn't be forced to keep

Athena's face pinches with concern. Few people in this world can make her features look like that. She's the walking embodiment of family first. Blood family and found family. When Hen brings you in, you're in.

Eloise, for example. Now that Athena has accepted her into our ranks, that's it. Even if the worst should happen between my *tesoro* and me, Athena will always and forever have a place for Eloise in her life. It's who she is.

Her circle is small by design, but those in it have the protection of a mother dragon. She also idolizes Papá. I really don't want to bring this shit to her door. It was bad enough when we had to tell her Santa Claus isn't real.

"I can't help you if I don't know what you're facing." There is no censure in her eyes, no accusation lacing her voice. My parents generally assume I'm up to no good. I get it— there were a few years where I absolutely was a shit, but they *always* believe I've done something, or am doing something, or need bailing out from something.

Athena gives me the benefit of the doubt, and I appreciate that. She doesn't assume it's me who has fucked up. Because for once, it isn't.

"Come on, *hermanito*." She plonks herself on the edge of the perfectly made bed and pats the space beside her. "Tell me what has your panties in a bunch."

I grin, pausing to stroke the soft fabric in my pocket before I sit beside her. Even that helps me feel somewhat better. "I don't think I can, Hen." I avoid looking at her. "I don't want to hurt you."

She loops her arm through mine and rests her head on my shoulder. "What are big sisters for if not to help you when you need it?" She snorts. "And to kick your ass when you're being *un culo*."

I don't fight the smile that breaks out on my face, but it's short lived. "It's about Papá."

She stiffens beside me. I can't look at her, but she stays quiet.

"I think we have a half-brother, Athena." As soon as the words are out, a knot that's been sitting heavily on my chest for weeks untangles a little bit.

She doesn't gasp, doesn't rear back, she doesn't react at all. My heart trips inside my body, pulse racing too fast. Is she in shock?

I give her a beat to process, but her face doesn't change. Wait... She knew? She knew about Thiago, and she didn't tell us?

I know. Rationally, I can't be upset with her because I've known for a while too. And her MO is to run interference and protect us, usually from ourselves, sometimes our parents. But this... She's protecting Papá. And I'm less okay with that.

She sighs against me. "I was wondering if Mathias would reach out to you since he's not too much younger than you are."

Mathias? Who the fuck is Mathias?

My stomach sinks. This... this can't be. Surely Papá wasn't stupid enough to wet his dick in *two* women who weren't Mamá and get them *both* pregnant.

What the fuck? Maybe he didn't care about Mamá and whether she found out about his dalliances or not.

No amount of deep breathing could calm me down in this

moment. "Hen, it wasn't someone called Mathias. It was a boy called Thiago."

That makes her rear back as a kaleidoscope of emotion rolls across her face: confusion, betrayal, soul-deep pain, anger; the gang's all there.

"No. H-he said that was the only one. He said Mathias was the only one, Ares." Her world literally falls apart in front of my face. Turning to my sister about this was supposed to make me feel better, but instead, I've destroyed everything for her. I should have stayed the fuck quiet.

Her face falls, her jaw trembles, and her eyes well with tears she doesn't seem to fight as they course down her cheeks. I can count on one hand the times I've seen Athena cry. She's the *Goddess of War* for fuck's sake. But right here, right now, as I snake my arms around her, pulling her close, I'm not sure if she's ever going to stop.

After a few long and heart aching moments, she lengthens her spine and meets my eyes. I'm still shirtless, so her cold tears are trickling off her face and down my chest. She wipes her cheeks with the heels of both hands and sniffs. Shaking her head, she sniffs again.

The transformation back to cool, calm, and collected Athena happens right in front of me, which makes me wonder how often this happens. I've never seen anyone recover from crying like that so quickly.

"You confronted him?"

She nods. "Damn straight I did. I might idolize the man, but I won't have him tell me to keep my knees together and not embarrass the family since I was thirteen fucking years old, while he's out whoring around knocking people up." Her voice has a hard, bitter edge to it.

I can't really blame her. That's pretty fucked up.

"We need to find them, Ares. We need to figure out the extent of his... conquests. We need to protect Mamá."

I'm surprised the last one makes it onto her list. Athena has always been a daddy's girl, and her relationship with Mamá is probably best described as tumultuous. Mamá is always criticizing and picking on the smallest of things when it comes to Hen, and Athena almost always takes Papá's side.

"We should tell the twins."

She shakes her head and hisses out a breath between her teeth. "We can't. Apollo is working with him on some deal for the business. They're expecting to close over Christmas."

"But that's a month away. You want me to keep this from them for another month?"

She nods. "We have to. If Apollo knows, he'll lose his shit. And he's petty enough that he'll fuck up this deal on purpose then regret it the next day. You know how committed to the family business he is. We can't let him detonate his dream in a moment of anger."

I don't like it, but what she's saying makes sense. All four of us have the capacity to be hotheaded and lash out at any given time. If he blows up whatever the fuck he's working on for Papá, for whatever wing of the business he's been entrusted with now, it won't end well. Then, he'll resent us for having told him and fucking him up in the first place. She's right that we have to wait.

"Do you talk to him, this Mathias guy?"

Her cheeks pink as she nods. "Sometimes. Not very often. He has other siblings, I have other siblings, and neither of us were really in a position to go any further than the occasional check in over text."

"I get it. When Thiago approached me at school, I called him a liar and chased him away. I feel so guilty, Hen. He was so fucking excited to have found me, to be talking to me, and I threw him away. Just like Papá did." The words jam in my throat like an ice ax in the side of a cliff.

Athena takes my hand and squeezes. "We'll figure this out, okay? Together."

Her confidence in our ability to take on our family issues and win is admirable, but we're outgunned. "Do you think there are more?"

Her mouth pulls into a thin line. "Until today I thought Mathias was the only one. Now..." She whistles. "I dunno, Ares. If there are two, there is a real chance there could be more."

I don't know what to do with that. How do we find them all? Do we even want to? What would we do when we found them? Do I want to meet them?

Too many questions. I want to rip my skin off, climb out of my body, and leave. Everything's too hot, too tight, and I can't keep up with the questions whirring around inside my brain.

Why would he do this to us? To Mamá?

"I hate him." The words are out before I can stop them. To her credit, Athena doesn't flinch. She barely bats an eye.

"I'm not his biggest fan right now, either. But he's our father, and once we've calmed down we can figure out what we want from our relationships going forward. Right now, we need to protect Apollo from this for another month until the ink is dry. Then the four of us will figure out what to do next."

She walks to the window and stares out over the backyard.

We have a plan, a direction. I might not like the situation we're in, but it's better setting a deadline to tell the boys. Hell, it really does feel lighter having shared it with Athena, even if it crushed a piece of her spirit. There might be something to that old saying after all.

"Athena?"

She turns back to look at me.

"Do you think Mamá knows?"

When her face turns sad, it's like a blade to my chest. "The wife always knows."

She takes my hand and leads me back downstairs. Eloise is chatting to Abuelita on the sofa, cradling a mug of something between both hands. Artemis sits close by, quiet, listening, watching, chiming in once or twice.

I don't know what they're discussing, but my girl looks tired. Maybe she needs to be rescued, taken home, and put to bed with a nice cup of tea. Tea is good for sleep, right?

"She's darling." Mamá's voice is quiet and next to my ear.

My throat is clogged with emotion so I can't answer, only nod. I don't think I ever expected to be this guy. The relationship guy. The guy whose girl laughs and hangs with his family. And yet, this feels so right I can't ever imagine how I was able to survive so long without it.

"Will you be needing the ring soon, Ares?"

I smile at how well she knows me, how she can see that Eloise is different, how she's my end game, how in such a short time, she's already become my whole world. Mamá has three rings, one for each of Papá's male offspring. The rings are kept in a safe until we need them to propose to our future husbands or wives.

I almost choke on my saliva. Because there are now at least five male heirs to Alonso de la Peña's fortune.

Because of some time-honored sexist bullshit, Hen doesn't get a ring. But my brothers and I vowed a long time ago that if we liked the guy we'd all pitch in to help him buy a ring worthy of our ethereal sister.

Shaking my head, I answer Mamá's question. "I don't want to spook her."

She touches my shoulder and kisses my temple. "It's so good to see you happy, *mijo*. So grounded. She's good for you."

She has no idea how right that statement is. I haven't touched a drop of alcohol since she became my girlfriend. I haven't been to a party or fucked a single person in the street —or anywhere else for that matter. I've danced because the music, the movement, it's in my soul, but everything else has just... stopped.

At first I thought it was out of fear, that if I did any of those things, I'd lose my pink-haired pixie, but in fact, I don't feel the same way I used to. And while in the beginning that felt uncomfortable, I'm letting it happen now, and it's not bad at all.

"She's it for me, Mamá."

"I know, *mijo*. So does Abuelita. She likes her. There was talk of *pasteles en hoja* making while you were upstairs with Athena. We both approve."

I groan. "She's tired, Mamá. No *pasteles* tonight. I should get her home." I guess something in my tone conveys how unhappy I am at the prospect.

"What is it, Ares?"

Eloise is now playing chess with Apollo while Abuelita threatens him with her fancy shoe. "Give her a fighting chance," she says as she taps her pump in the palm of her hand.

I tear my gaze from them and turn to face Mamá. "Her dad hates me." I don't need to qualify my statement or explain in any way. She knows. She's lived it.

Her sigh is weighty, telling, tired. She traces her fingers along my hairline, pushing my dark hair from my face. "It's time to step up, Ares. Be the man she needs you to be, make it so that no matter what her father thinks of you, you're beyond reproach from the moment you met her. It's time to invest in yourself, your future, and that means thinking of someone else."

The words "for a change" hang between us, unsaid.

"Being in love with someone means you have to protect their heart before your own. If you're not ready to do that..."

She shrugs and glances at the scene over my shoulder. "Nothing else matters, *mijo*." Regarding me for a beat, she pats my face with her palm. "Are you scared?"

Terrified. But I'm loath to admit it. I don't need to because a small smile appears on her face as she nods.

"Good, you should be. Being afraid to lose the person you love most means you will do everything in your power not to mess up." She looks back at Eloise. "Go talk to her father, Ares. Tell him you love her, and you want to look after her forever. And when he doesn't believe you, show him, and show him over and over until he trusts you to care for his daughter the way she deserves to be cared for."

This whole conversation feels like it's laden with meaning on multiple levels, mangling the racing organ in my chest. It's on the tip of my tongue to say something to her, to come right out and tell her that Papá is a cheating *pendejo*, but I can't. She looks so happy right now, so proud, I don't want to ruin the moment by bringing her life down around her ears.

"Can I ask you something?" Her voice is quiet, hesitant.

"Sí, Mamá. Cualquier cosa."

"Would you like to have children some day? I know it's a deeply personal question, and I have no business asking. I always assumed you wouldn't be interested." Her face is red, and she nibbles on her lip.

I can't blame her for thinking that my selfish ass wouldn't ever want to settle down and have a family. I admit, it's not something that I've grown up wanting or dreaming about.

I turn back to the chess game, where everyone is highly focused as Abuelita coaches Eloise. She has no chance of beating Apollo at chess, no matter how smart she is. He's a master of the game, and he plays it daily. But my girl is resolute, her face set in a firm line, and her little button nose turned up with determination blazing in her eyes.

"Sí. I definitely think I'm interested."

CHAPTER 30
Ares

It takes another hour before I can extract my girl from the clutches of my adoring family. She's being sent home with enough food to feed her entire street, a pair of shoes from Mamá's closet. One minute I was going to the bathroom, the next, Mamá was presenting her with a still-in-their-box-with-stickers-on-the-soles pair of hot pink shoes to match Eloise's hair.

I think my family loves her more than they love me.

In fact, I'm sure of it.

And while I don't *need* her father on my side, I really would like it if he was.

When we're finally allowed to leave, it's with the promise that we won't be strangers, that we'll come and visit more often. I'd like that, and I find myself hoping that my girl would, too.

We're pulling out of my parent's driveway when she yawns. "Ares?"

Sliding my fingers into her palm, I squeeze. *"Sí, mi amor?"*

"Would you mind if we made a stop before you take me home?"

"Where do you need to go, *tesoro*?"

"Mt. Calvary Cemetery. I'd like to introduce you to my mom."

I'm not sure if her words press the fragments of my heart closer together or make the temperamental organ shatter into more pieces, but that damned lump is back in my throat, making it impossible to answer. I hold her hand for the entire drive. By the time we arrive, I'm shaking. Somehow this feels even more important than meeting her dad.

"I can wait here if you'd like." Offering her an out tastes bitter on my tongue, but if she needs time with her mom without me, I can wait.

She shakes her head. "Do you have cups in this fancy schmancy car of yours? Your mom said she was putting a bottle of non-alcoholic wine in the cooler she sent me home with."

Turning her head away from me, she shrugs. "I haven't been here in a while. I was thinking I could catch her up, you know? Celebrate some things with her." She still won't turn to look at me. "It's stupid."

It's not, not at all. I know how much she misses her mom, how much her loss impacts her on a cellular level every single day. I cup her cheek, turning her head back toward me. "It's not stupid, and I'd really love to join you. Let me grab the bottle. If it comes to it, we'll drink straight from the bottle." I lean across the center console to kiss her forehead before getting out of the car.

I expected the bottle Mamá sent Eloise home with to be a six-thousand-dollar bottle of Armand de Brignac Gold Champagne. It's her favorite, and she's excited, already planning weddings and babies for the two of us. It's adorable as fuck.

I don't even know whether or not Eloise likes Champagne or would be able to tell from tasting it that it's not cheap, but I had made a mental note to get rid of the bottle before she has a chance to Google it.

Except it's not Armand de Brignac. It's still a two hundred buck bottle of alcohol-free Champagne, though. Mamá wasn't being intentionally flashy, that's not who she is. But I also didn't get a chance to tell her that our wealth and lifestyle is incredibly overwhelming for my girl. I don't want her to feel weird about drinking an expensive bottle of Champagne at her mother's grave when she already feels foolish for the whole thing to begin with.

I don't have Champagne flutes. But I do have red Solo cups and a can of ginger ale. I grab two cups, one for her and her mom, and in case the Champagne tastes like shit, tuck the can into my pants pocket before grabbing two coats, closing the trunk, and helping my girl out of the car.

It wouldn't have been somewhere I'd have picked for us to spend time, but wandering through the cemetery in the cool night air is oddly soothing. Her hand snug in mine, she walks next to me in silence, her breath sending little puffs of steam into the air. There's a peace here that I often struggle to find outside the gates of the cemetery.

When we get to her mom's plot, fresh flowers already adorn her grave, and some dead ones that Eloise collects together and sets in a pile to the side. "Dad comes pretty often." She crosses her legs and sits straight down on the grass. Her mom is in an edge plot, and a grassy path leads all the way along the perimeter.

I place the two plastic cups on the edge of the grave, giving Eloise a cautious glance. I don't want to disrespect her mom, or her, or the sanctity of the cemetery, but at the same time, I want to include her mom as though she's right here with us.

With a concerted effort, I pop the cork on the Champagne and pour some into the two cups before taking out my can of pop. Even though it's alcohol free, it still tastes like shit.

"You're not having any?" The surprise in her voice is obvious, but she quickly recovers. "Sorry. I just... If it bothers you, we don't have to... I don't have to."

I cover her lips with my finger. "It's okay, *tesoro*. It doesn't bother me. I just don't like it. Some days it might, though, and I might need your help to be strong, but here, now, with you..." I don't know how to finish that sentence. It wouldn't matter if it was a bottle of tequila. I feel invincible, powerful, in control. She makes me feel like I can battle even my darkest demons and win.

"So, the second cup is for my mom?" There are lights around the cemetery, and the moon is pretty full in the clear sky overhead so I can see the emotion clouding her pretty green eyes.

"Of course. It'd be rude to sit here chatting to her without offering her a drink." I boop her nose like she's silly for even asking.

"I don't even know where to start." She sips from her plastic cup.

"When was the last time you were here?"

She shrugs. "It's been a while."

"Start with tonight, with Thanksgiving dinner, and work backwards until you feel like she's caught up?"

She smiles, takes another drink, and gets started. Hearing her talk about Thanksgiving with my family makes my heart expand. She talks like she's known them her whole life, laughing about Abuelita and her chancla, recalling the kindness of Mamá gifting her shoes, and grumbling about how smart Apollo is.

I'm not sure whether or not she realizes it, but they all loved her right back. Even Papá engaged her more than I'd have expected. Granted he was a bit of a prick about it, but still. If he disliked her, he'd have ignored her. I'm more than familiar with his practices.

I don't know how long we sit, but at some point Eloise moves to sit with her back against my chest, and my arms wrapped around her. She's on her second cup of Champagne, and she's laughing, telling her mom all about Bacon the pig and Puck the psychopathic black cat.

A twig snaps, leaves rustle, and when I focus, a figure stands in the shadows. From this position, I can't protect her, so I untangle myself from her and spring to my feet. Her dad steps into the light.

"Mr. Downing." I don't know what else to say. I was curled up on the ground of the cemetery with his daughter, an open bottle of Champagne next to us while we chat to his dead wife. I admit, it might look pretty weird. He won't know that there's no booze in the bottle. Shit. Shit. Brushing the back of my neck, I struggle to come up with a way to diffuse the situation.

He clears his throat. "When I saw your car in the parking lot, I admit I was ready to storm up here and kick your ass all the way into that empty grave down the hill."

I swallow. I don't think he's joking, and he's more than capable.

"But when I got up here, and saw Eloise laughing, talking to her mom." He pauses, his Adam's apple bobbing. He addresses my *tesoro* directly. "I haven't seen you so happy in so long."

Eloise remains quiet, seated on the ground, while her dad jabs a finger in my direction. "I swear if you hurt her, I will hurt you."

"If I hurt her, I'll hurt myself." The words are out of my mouth before I can think on them, but I mean every one. The idea of letting her down in any way makes my stomach hurt.

He nods before sitting down next to Eloise on the grass. I don't know whether to stay or go. I don't want to be around for something so private, but I also don't want to be gone if he yells at her again. I won't let that fly.

He seems pretty calm, so I take a few steps back.

"I thought about what you said."

Eloise grimaces at her father's words. I've seen that face. I've lived that face. Regret over saying something in the heat of the moment.

"No, it's okay." He takes her hand between both of his. "You were right. I have changed. You can't live through a trauma the way we did without changing. I know I pushed you away, I know I fucked up, and I'm sorry."

My girl is crying, tears streaming down her face. This is most definitely a family moment, one I'm not going to ruin by inserting myself into. She and her dad need to heal and maybe this conversation, together with her mom, can bring around some much needed mending to their relationship. I head back to the car as quietly as I can. I'm not leaving her, in case she needs me, but also expecting her to go home with her dad.

CHAPTER 31
Eloise

My palms are sweating, my heart racing. I've never brought anyone to Mom's grave before and Dad looks pretty furious, even in the dim light. No matter which way I cut it, this is going to be an uncomfortable conversation, and the bubbling liquid in my stomach is making its presence known as I suck in shuddering breaths.

"I'm sorry, Dad."

He gestures for me to sit on the blanket before joining me. "What are you sorry for, Eloise?"

"Disobeying you. I know you don't like the idea of me spending time with Ares."

He scoffs. "The boy is a reprobate, Ellie."

Discontent bubbles under my skin. I'd usually bite down my anger at my father, squashing it until it fits in the small box in my chest. But I'm not sure I can this time.

"I've seen stories about him."

"Not everything you read on the internet is true!" My hands burst away from my body in frustration. I want to shake him. "Okay, fine." Twisting my hands together in my lap, I lock them down. Talking with my hands is one thing, but when I get big mad, my hand gestures get big to match.

"Sure, most of the things you've read on the internet about him are true. But that's not the whole picture. He's different, Dad. I really wish you'd just give him a chance.

"Like I gave that last piece of shit you were with, a chance?"

My gasp echoes around the concrete headstones surrounding us. "Daddy!" My stomach falls.

"No, Eloise. That's what he was. A no-good piece of shit. And this one seems worse. I don't quite know how that's possible, but it looks to be the case. I won't let you go down that road again. I saw what he did to you, how he treated you. It wasn't okay. And until you know that it wasn't okay, and you're strong enough not to let the same thing happen again, I have no choice but to protect you from yourself."

"I'm not a child anymore, Dad. You can't just decide you don't like my decisions and make them for me. And no offense, but since Mom died, your choices haven't been much better."

He flinches like my words smacked his face. "You're right, and we'll talk about that in a minute, but right now we're talking about you, and your choices, and these boys you keep getting tangled up with."

"Boys? Dad, you make it sound like I have a long line of suitors. I've had two men in my life. Yes, I'll admit, the first one wasn't good for me. He was... I..." My cheeks heat as the desire to swear flares in my chest. "He wasn't a good person. He didn't treat me right. But Ares... he's... misunderstood. He's kind, and funny, and yes he's wild and carefree, and yes he's a recovering addict, but those things are just pieces of who he is. If you could look past what you read on the internet, I swear you'll see the things I see."

I'm pleading with him now. The thought Dad might

make me choose between my father and my boyfriend is corroding through my body like acid. "Please, Dad. Please just give him a chance. He's not the monster you think he is. He sees me. He loves me. He cherishes me." I wipe the tears dripping off the tip of my nose. "And like it or not, he is my choice." I straighten my spine to make my point.

He stays quiet for a long, painfully outstretched moment, before heaving out a sigh. "I just want to keep you safe, Ellie." The agony in his voice is palpable, making my tears fall harder. "I know I've checked out a bit since Mom..." Grief stops him from finishing his sentence, but he glances at her headstone, raw agony painted across his aging features.

"She's not here to help me make the right calls every time, kiddo. I was so angry after she... she... passed away. I felt like I should keep my anger, my grief, at a distance from you. Once I'd processed it, I didn't know how to come back." He's crying now, too. "I failed you. I know you needed a father when you lost your mother, but I didn't know how. I didn't know how to be what you need when I lost everything."

He reaches for me, and I don't fight his embrace. "I couldn't stop what that asshole did to you Ellie, and I'm so afraid you're going to let boys keep breaking your heart." He sweeps my hair back from my face. "You deserve the world. You are beautiful, and worthy, and you are the strongest person I've ever known."

His words wash over me like aloe on sunburn, taking the sting out of the past few years of grief. "I'm sorry I've been tough on you. I'm sorry I've been invasive. But you're right. You're a grown up now, and you can make your own decisions. If that boy is your decision, well, I'll support it and do my best to get to know him."

A fresh wave of tears crashes into me. "Thank you, Daddy."

"But if he hurts you, I don't care who his big shot, rich guy father is. I'll fucking kill him."

CHAPTER 32
Ares

A persistent knocking on the passenger window snaps me out of a deep sleep. A blurry glance at my watch tells me that over an hour has passed since I left them at the graveside. Out the window, my girl looks exhausted huddled against her dad's side.

I unlock the car, and he pulls open the door, standing back so she can hop inside.

"Are you still okay to take me home?"

I'm surprised, but I'd never say no to her. "Of course, *tesoro*." I risk a glance at her father, who nods.

"See you at home." He gets into his truck but waits for me to move before starting the engine. He follows me at a safe distance, and I can't help but feel like my driving is under scrutiny right now. On one particular stretch of road, Eloise inhales a sharp breath, her nails squeezing into my hand.

"*Tesoro?*"

"I'm fine. Don't stop."

She doesn't look fine. In fact, she looks like she might throw up in the footwell of my SUV.

"Should I pull over?"

"No!" Her shriek is pained. She leans forward, head in her hands, and rocks back and forth.

Screw her dad. I gun the gas and get us the hell away from whatever the fuck that was. After a mile or two, I touch her back. *"Tesoro?"*

Her tear-stained face turns to me. "That's why I rarely go to the cemetery. That road. That's where... w-w-where..." Tears stream down her face all over again, and I want to pull the car over, haul her into my lap and hold her.

"Oh, Eloise." I stroke her face with one hand as I control the car with the other. "I'm so sorry. I didn't know exactly where the accident was."

I feel like an inconsiderate asshole. It didn't even occur to me when she screamed that she was reliving her trauma. She shakes her head at me, but it does nothing to uncurl the tightness stabbing my chest.

"I need to get better about traveling on that road. I know I do, I just... It's so hard." She swallows loudly. "My therapist said it'll take time. But every single time I'm on that road I can hear the car smashing. I can smell the leaking gasoline, the blood. And I can *feel* the pain."

Her hand drifts to her face and she falls silent, staring out the window lost in her thoughts and tears and grief. When we get back to her house, her dad pulls into the driveway right behind us.

"You staying?" he asks as we walk toward the front door.

I hadn't planned to, but now that he mentions it, it's pretty late, even for me. "I don't want to impose."

Mr. Downing snorts, opening the door. "You'll sleep in separate rooms. I'm not ready to face the fact my baby girl is canoodling." He grunts. "With a stripper."

Clearly, I have some work to do to gain the man's respect, but this is a huge step forward. Abuelita always tells me not to look a gift llama in the mouth. That's not how the original saying goes, but she likes to be authentic. Using llama means she can claim she invented the phrase. I'm not going to be the one that tells her that's not how things work.

I wait for an exhausted Eloise to follow her dad into the house before I bring up the rear, mostly in case she collapses from all the exertion of the evening. Tonight hasn't gone quite how I planned, but I guess I'm having a sleepover at my girlfriend's house.

CHAPTER 33
Eloise

"Eloise?" Ares shakes me awake. He's standing next to my bed. My bed, in my home.

I don't have time to dwell on the fact Dad and I made up some ground between us last night. Or that he and Ares did as well because his sad face makes me think someone died. I bolt upright in bed, panic seizing my entire body in a chilling instant.

He curls his arms around me, squeezing me against his chest, not letting me move even an inch. "It's okay, *tesoro*. Easy. I'm sorry for startling you. I need to go."

"Oh my goodness, it's game day!" My words are muffled against his shoulder as he chuckles.

"Back to back games in Minnesota. I'll be back Sunday afternoon, okay?" He pecks my nose, a scowl creasing his forehead. "I don't want to leave you."

That makes me giggle. My guy is falling for me as much as I'm falling for him, but nothing will ever take the top spot from hockey in his affections. It's something I knew before we even started talking. The moment I looked him up online was the exact point where I discovered I'd forever be the mistress in his life.

Oof. I flex internally at my poor choice of words.

Part of me wants to grab him and make him say goodbye properly, and the other is acutely aware that Dad is on the other side of the wall, probably listening.

"I'll see you Sunday, okay?"

He nods, clearly as unhappy about the situation as I am, not least of all because his penis is standing at attention in his pants.

He kisses me in a promise of things to come, on Sunday, after a weekend of being apart. I groan as he leaves, rolling over in bed, pulling the quilt over my head. Maybe I can lie here and sleep the weekend away and my aching girl parts will forgive me for not jumping his bones.

About fifteen minutes after he's gone I bolt upright in bed once more. The Raccoons have lost most of their away games so far this season. They've had a few injuries and bad luck, but the unspoken belief from Ares, and okay, me a little too, is that it's because I'm not there after the games for him to... blow off steam. What can I say? His goaltender superstitions are rubbing off on me.

Ha. Rubbing off. I should have rubbed him off this morning before he left. Maybe I can take one for the team and help him out this weekend somehow. A grin stretches my face as I spring out of bed to grab my case from the bottom of my closet and disconnect my phone from the charger.

Unlocking it, I open my underwear drawer. I didn't even get to hide a pair of undies in his kit bag. I push a button on the screen, her name is the first contact in my phone, and I hit call.

Jamming the phone between my ear and my shoulder, I start tossing clothes into the bag. I'm sure I won't need many, but I'm a girl, which means I pack thirty-five pairs of underwear for a two-day trip. It's perfectly logical, even though there's every likelihood that bringing thirty-five pairs of underwear will mean that Ares steals another pair, or twelve, from me.

"Hola, amiga. ¿Qué lo qué?"

"Athena!" A sudden wave of panic engulfs me as I realize what the h-e-double-hockey-sticks I'm actually doing.

"Sí. Did you call the wrong number?"

I stand totally dumbstruck.

"Eloise?" Her voice sharpens. "What's wrong?"

"N-nothing. It's fine. I'm fine. I just..." I just what? Wanted you to help me get to Minnesota today so I could do dirty things with your brother after his game as a good luck charm for the team?

"Eloise? Eloiiiiise. Talk to me, Goose."

"It's a stupid idea."

She snorts. "All ideas are stupid. What makes them not stupid is whether or not they work out."

That makes a weird kind of sense that I don't have time to dwell on. "I need to get to Minnesota. Today."

Silence stretches on the other end of the phone. I'm starting to think the call has dropped, but when I clear my throat, she starts laughing.

"You want company?"

"Y-you want to come with me?"

She crunches on something. "Sure. I have nothing planned this weekend. Why wouldn't I want to travel to another state to deliver my brother's girlfriend so he doesn't lose back to back games against the Snow Pirates?"

I can't help the gasp that escapes me. "I... I..."

"I might hate the game, amiga, but I love my brothers. I know all their stats. And Ares..." She whistles. "He sucks when he's not around you. You're in his head."

I'm not sure it's that I'm in his head rather than that he

has nothing to put his... never mind. We're exclusive, and B.E. (before Eloise), he would probably have hooked up with someone after the game.

I don't know whether to puff out my chest or climb inside my suitcase. "I'd love some company." My voice is small, but she heard me. Keys click on the other side of the line as she hums to herself.

"Do you need to be picked up?"

"No, I can make my way to the airport."

"I'll pick you up."

"But—"

A door slams, she locks it behind her, then the click of her heels on the tiles as she drags a bag behind her. Was she sitting around with a packed bag waiting for me to call?

"I'll be there soon." The call drops. I'm staring at my screen not sure what the heck just happened, but excitement fizzes in my stomach. I don't know if Ares likes surprises or not, but this one's going to be great.

He's told me about his sister's driving. I *should* have thirty minutes before she arrives at the door, but I'm guessing it'll be closer to twenty. I better get my ass in the shower.

Eighteen minutes later a growly engine revs outside the house, then a horn blasts. Athena is nothing if not subtle. I kiss a disgruntled Dad on the cheek, plead with him not to worry, reassure him I'll call to check in and hurry outside. Both Athena and Savannah are in the car already, so I hop in the back seat, pulling my suitcase in with me.

"Okay." I buckle up, because if I don't, I'm going to quickly wish I had. "Can one of you please explain how you were ready to go and at my house in less than thirty minutes."

Neither of these girls are low maintenance. Perfect hair, perfect makeup, perfect nails. There's no way they threw stuff in a bag and drove here.

Athena meets my eyes in the rearview. "I always have a go-bag ready. It's got a few days' clothes, toiletries, some emergency cash. Everything I need at a moment's notice."

I shouldn't be surprised that she's literally ready for anything. But I am. It's genius, except that doesn't explain why Savannah is here, and I assume she has a bag too, unless she borrows Athena's emergency things.

As if reading my mind, Savannah turns in the passenger seat. "I've been friends with her for long enough to expect the unexpected. I got caught short once, without underwear. Hers don't fit me." She jerks a thumb at Athena. "And I *hate* going commando. Never again. I have a bag packed next to hers at the door at all times. Just in case." She claps her hands together and yelps.

"It's been ages since I've needed it though. This girls' trip is going to be so much fun! I'm so glad you called Hen. It's fucking impossible to get her to go to games, but between us we can tag team her so she has no choice."

"It's not really a girls' trip. I'll find something else to do while the two of *you* go cheer on your hockey Neanderthals." She barely takes a breath before she pulls a hand from the steering wheel and holds it up to Savannah's face. "And *yes,* I know Eloise's Neanderthal is my brother, but that doesn't change the fact he's a dumb jock."

She winces, catching my eye in the mirror. "He's not dumb. I take that back."

That makes me smile. He's sensitive about his intelligence, or rather, feeling like he's lacking and knowing that Athena recognizes that in him shows me that no matter what she thinks of his chosen profession, she's truly in tune with his emotions.

By the time we get to Minnesota, I'm full of nervous energy. I almost didn't board the plane. Not because of the anxiety, but because Athena hadn't told me it was a chartered flight. A tiny, *very* private plane that carried the three of us.

Every time I think about how expensive that ride was, I feel sick. The only answer I got from Athena was an eye roll. "It's Cedar Rapids, it's not like there are planes to Minnesota every twenty minutes," she'd said when my feet refused to move toward the small plane.

I knew this. I guess in my haste to do something nice for my boyfriend I didn't think the logistics through. And we didn't have time for the road trip. The flight was so nice though—we had snacks and drinks. But as we walk into the arena, the Champagne in my stomach threatens to come back up.

We get a few looks from the Snow Pirates fans, but on the way here, Savannah said their arena is reported to be one of the friendliest. We are wearing Raccoons colors, but since Ares doesn't know to look for me, I won't need to hide.

I decided, since Athena spent a crap-ton of cash to get us here, I would wait until post-game to surprise him. Speaking of Athena, she takes her seat to my right. She says she couldn't find anything to do for the night, but I think she wanted to hang out, even if that means sitting through a hockey game.

Part of me thinks she secretly loves the game and the fact her brothers all play, but she's a puzzle with some of the pieces missing. I can't figure her out at all.

By the time warm up is over, I'm vibrating with glee, and I'm not even sure why. I'm not a huge fan of surprises, but I guess I love giving them to people. To my left, Savannah practically bounces in her seat, either my energy is contagious, or she's as excited as I am. I sent Ares my typical "Good luck," pre-game selfie with Bacon. I recycled an old one because I was on my way to the airport, but he doesn't seem to have noticed.

He *did* say that a couple of the guys were making fun of him over it. Like he cares. He just thinks it's cute, and he gets a little buzz from the guys winding him up.

Athena spits a loud curse in Spanish. I turn to see what's

wrong. She holds up her phone so I can see. A *Trash Can Tattle with Tabitha* is on her screen telling us that Ares's backup netminder has signed a contract with the NHL team in Iowa City.

His backup got Ares's dream gig. My brain freezes. Despite his blasé attitude about everything in the entire universe, I'm sure he wanted that placement more than he wants to breathe. He wants to play pro hockey, and he wants to play it in Iowa. The team now has a full goalie roster and no room for Ares. He's going to be so upset when he finds out.

Athena shows me all the major sports outlet websites and my stomach lurches, it's everywhere. As the puck drops, I can only hope he hasn't seen it yet.

The home team scores within the first thirty seconds, and around thirty seconds after that, they score again. It doesn't take long for them to rack up four goals, and I can tell from the glumness on either side of me, that this is a high scoring first period. I'm going to guess he saw the article.

It's not my fault, but perhaps if I'd left a pair of worn underwear in his hockey bag, this could be less of a... a... disaster? I dunno, there doesn't seem to be an adequate enough word for what's unfolding in front of me on the ice. Is there a technical term in hockey for cosmic catastrophe?

Apollo and Artemis flank Ares at his goal. He's clearly pissed. From where I'm sitting it looks like he's been muttering to himself for the whole game. He'll have been tearing himself down. I don't know much more about the game than I did a few months ago, but to me it looks like it wasn't all his fault.

I wince. I don't think that matters in any sport where there is a goalie. They're an easy scapegoat, and it seems they're the first person that gets blamed when things go south.

Oh boy. Things off the ice aren't shaping up to be much better either. Athena is going to kill someone. Not metaphorically. Like, literally. Maybe even with a straw fashioned into a shiv. A guy in the row in front of her is vaping. *Vaping*! Indoors. Not only that, he's pounding beers and growing more and more obnoxious with each drink.

The Raccoons pull back a goal, but it's a short lived celebration when the Snow Pirates sail another one past Ares. I can hear his yell of frustration from up here, and when he takes a swing of his stick at his goalpost, I can't say I'm surprised.

The "twig," as he calls it, snaps clean in two, but he makes a point of picking up the other half before skating to the bench. He's being pulled. At least he's tidying up after his own tantrum.

I shake my head as his backup skates into his goal. This has to hurt. I gasp and turn to Athena. "I need you to get me backstage."

She snorts. "We need to educate you more on the game." She shakes her head but holds her hand out to me. "But let's get you *backstage*."

I don't know how she does it, or who she's slipped cash to, but a few minutes later I'm waiting around the corner from the players dressing room for my guy. Bouncing on the balls of my feet, I have no idea how this is going to go, but when he growls, "Leave me the fuck alone, Apollo." I know I might be next in the firing line.

When he rounds the corner, his eyebrows jump up. "E-Eloise?"

The pain on his sweaty face breaks my heart. "Eloise," he repeats it with more conviction but doesn't say anything else before charging at me, picking me up and spinning me around. For a long moment we stand, me with my feet dangling and his face buried against my shoulder.

He could probably do with letting off some of his aggression, but there is no way I'm doing anything sexual right here in the corridor. All I have is words. And somehow, they have to be enough to save him from self-destruction.

When he eventually puts me down I'm kinda soggy, not in a hot way, in a sticky goalie, smelly boy sweat way, but I have a job to do, and I'm not going to let this sweaty man stop me. Cupping both his hands, I stare straight into his eyes.

"This is not your career defining moment, Ares de la Peña."

He opens his mouth to say something, but I'm not done.

"Ah, ah. No. It isn't. This is not you. This is fear, this is frustration and anger, and dare I say it, jealousy. But this is not you."

He visibly sags in front of my eyes.

"Are you done right now? Have you given all you can give to this game?"

He shakes his head, his intense eyes holding mine as much as mine hold his.

"Then you gotta dust it off, champ."

That makes him smile, and I realize I have no idea what to tell him to do out there.

"Go back in there and tell that coach man to put you back on the field. Treat the next period like the first one, and if that one sucks, treat the last one like the first one. Clean slate, each time and do your best."

"Coach man?" A new voice joins the conversation. Apollo stands over Ares's shoulder, grinning.

"Field?" Artemis cracks what I'm learning is a rare smile. If I wasn't with his brother and *very* happy, my panties would have combusted at the bright flash of his teeth.

"Shhh." I silence them over his shoulder. "I'm doing my best, okay? We all know I am undereducated when it comes to hockey, fine, sports, and that's not the point of this anyway."

"What is your point, *tesoro*?" His voice is by my ear, his lips find my cheek, and he brushes my skin with a soft kiss.

"My point is that this isn't you. You need to get your stupid jock head out of your butt and get back out on the ice. I do, too, before your brothers need to bail out two of their siblings this evening."

Ares's jaw drops. "Hen is here too?"

"You think I could figure out getting here on time for the game and using my awkward charm to get down here to see you all by myself? Well, thanks for the vote of confidence. But, no. She's up there watching with Savannah." The last bit is a whisper. "If you tell Justin and ruin her surprise, I'll set Athena on the three of you."

Apollo elbows Artemis. "She's learning quickly."

I squeeze Ares's cheeks, plant as big a kiss on his lips as I'm comfortable doing with his sweaty twin brothers watching every move, and I turn to leave.

A hand grabs my wrist, and when I turn back to face Ares, his eyes ignite. He walks me back to the cold, concrete wall, and he *kisses* me.

I sag against the wall and into the sweaty man kissing me and sigh into his mouth. When he finally comes up for air, his forehead meets mine, our noses touch, and his breath tickles my face.

"I love you, Ares."

He plants another quick kiss on my lips. "I love you, *tesoro*. And thank you." With that he turns to face his brothers, as I walk away from them, Apollo asks if Ares feels better, and it's Artemis who replies for him.

"His anchor is here. He's fine."

I stumble into the wall, palm outstretched, the other one pressed to my chest as I take a few deep breaths. I always thought I'd need an anchor; I never thought I'd be one.

When I take my seat in the stands, Savannah hands me a drink. "I wasn't sure what you'd like, so I played it safe with water."

"Thanks."

She's shoveling popcorn into her mouth like it's her last meal. "Want some?"

"I'm good." Actually, I'm starving, but the idea of eating without knowing what the next period will bring, makes me queasy.

"How was he?" Athena doesn't take her eyes off the freshly surfaced ice pad.

"Mad. Like, really mad. Short of having him take me against the wall, I did my best."

She grunts. "I'm sure you did." She dissolves into laughter.

"What?"

Savannah crunches on a mouthful of popcorn before either answer me. "I bet she's imagining Ares trying to figure out how to fuck you with all his goalie gear on." She joins Athena in her laughter.

"I hadn't thought of the logistics, okay? There were way

too many people around for me to consider that. The most he got was a kiss, a reminder he's got this, and I told him to pull his head out of his backside." I keep to myself that I'm sure his penis would have found a way through those pads if he wanted it badly enough.

Athena holds out her fist, and I bump it with mine. "He better not fuck this up."

"Athena, I think wanting a win when they're down by four goals is a big ask."

"I meant you, amiga." She pats my thigh. "He better not fuck things up with *you*."

I'm all warm and fuzzy inside as the second period starts. The idiot in front continues to get louder with each passing second on the game clock, but our boys look stronger, more focused down on the ice.

Any time a Snow Pirate gets the puck, the Raccoons swarm around him. They've clearly tightened their defense because the Snow Pirates barely get near Ares, but when they do, he's ready.

Apollo scores the next goal, and while it's five to two, it makes me feel better. The next time play starts, two of the Snow Pirates shoot up the ice toward my boy. I scoot to the end of my seat, breath caught somewhere between hope and a prayer.

Ares pulls out a big save followed by two rebounds as he struggles to cover the puck to stop play. When the whistle blows, I spring to my feet, cheering, loud and proud. I'm the only one in the entire arena screaming for Ares, but I don't care. My guy is back. I hope.

Some of the other Raccoons skate past Ares, tapping his pads or patting his shoulder. The message is crystal clear, even to me: we've got you.

I never thought I'd be choked up at a game, but this

display of brotherhood unfolding in front of me is a sucker punch to the feelings.

Loud guy drops another F bomb and Athena mutters, "That's it." She stands up and steps over the empty seat in front of Savannah, giving the loud guy and his two friends a great view of her butt in those jeans.

I think one of them swallowed his tongue, and the other two want to swallow hers.

"May I?" She points to loud guy's lap, and he nods, his tongue literally hanging out of his open mouth.

She drops into his lap and curls a palm over his jaw as she leans in and whispers something in his ear. She looks uncomfortably balanced, and I can't figure out where her other hand is.

I don't know what she's saying, but the guy flinches, grimaces, and nods frantically. She stands up after no longer than a minute, pats down the front of her shirt, and climbs back over the chair. This time none of them ogle her booty.

Savannah is barely containing herself. I'm mostly stunned at how she managed to get the loudest man in Minnesota to stop talking. I lean toward Athena. "What did you say to him?"

"I threatened to burst his balls if he dropped another F-bomb during this game or took another hit from that fucking vape of his."

"And he believed you?" I believe her, but I know her. She'd most *definitely* bust his dangly bits without so much as breaking a nail or a sweat.

"Of course he did, since I had them in my hand."

There isn't a single peep from loud guy for the rest of the game, and despite our best efforts, UCR fall short, losing five to four. It was almost the greatest comeback ever. I'm glad that Ares didn't let another goal in. I don't know how secure those net things are, but if he'd let another one in, I imagine he'd have tried to throw the net like it was somehow to blame.

I'm anxious when the whistle blows. After every game, win or lose, Ares and his backup practically jump on each other for a goalie hug. Considering the news that was announced pre-game, I'm wondering if that dynamic will change now.

My worrying is for nothing. Ares and Hayes bounce into each other for an epic hug. They pat each other on the back, before parting. Hayes says something to Ares, who ruffles Hayes's hair. They're going to be just fine.

Ares is the first Raccoon to emerge from the arena, and as his team filters out of the building behind him, he launches himself at me again, picking me up, and spinning me around so fast that his ball cap comes off.

I'm laughing by the time he puts me down and kisses me, hard. *"Gracias, tesoro."* He kisses me again. *"Gracias."*

"You dropped something." Scott—I'm trying to learn everyone's first names, and Ares tells me he's the twin's best friend—holds out Ares's ball cap with a wry grin. When I look down at the hat, I see why.

A pair of lace panties is stitched to the inside. *My* lace panties to be exact. The first pair Ares stole from me. The man in question meets my questioning gaze with a boyish grin, sweeps his hair back and replaces the hat, shrugging like it's no big deal that he has my freaking *underwear* on his head.

With a groan, I drop my forehead to his chest, before snapping it back with a gasp. "Ares, please tell me you at least washed them first."

He pulls me back to his chest, placing his mouth beside my ear. "I could, *tesoro*. But that would be a lie."

I can't help the giggle that bursts from me. "Ares, you are incorrigible."

Scott doesn't seem at all fazed at the events unfolding.

Maybe it's not as weird as I think it is, when your boyfriend steals your worn underwear and sews it into his baseball cap.

"We're ordering pizza for the hotel. Are you girls staying locally?" Scott addresses me directly. A couple of months ago this might have intimidated me, or made me self-conscious, yet right now, I'm part of the group, and it does things inside my chest I can't explain.

"Athena booked us in the same hotel." I have no idea how she figured it out, but I'm learning that with Athena, fewer questions is probably best.

"Pizza?" Scott points his finger at me, and I nod. Enthusiastically. I'm famished.

"Allergies? Dislikes?"

"No Hawaiian for me, otherwise it's all fair game." The unloved stepchild of pizza, but it was Mom's favorite. I still can't figure out how.

"No deliciously juicy pineapple on your pie, got it." He grabs Ares's shoulder and leans in to speak quietly. "Great recovery out there."

Ares doesn't say anything, but he nods. I guess there's nothing really to say. Ares blames himself for the loss and nothing anyone says, and no recovery, no matter how great, will convince him otherwise.

"See you at the hotel." Scott follows the rest of the Raccoons to the bus.

"Aren't you going with him?"

Athena rented an SUV, but it's not big enough for her three hockey brothers and the three of us. "I had a car brought over during the period break."

As though waiting to be summoned, a guy appears and hands him keys.

"You just... had a car brought over?"

He nods. "You coming?"

I shake my head, the wonders of rich people and the

convenience their money can buy a tad overwhelming. "I need to tell your sister I'm with you."

"I already told her." He holds out his hand and leads me to his rental, we drive to the hotel as though Godzilla is chasing us through the streets of Minneapolis. He screeches to a halt outside a hotel that's close to, but much fancier than the one Athena, Savannah, and I checked into earlier.

"Ares, this isn't..." I trail off when he holds his palm up.

"Change of plan."

"What about pizza? We are supposed to have dinner with your team."

He gives me a smirk, charged with lust and promise. "I don't feel like eating pizza tonight, *tesoro*."

I follow him like a puppy through the lobby, stay quiet when he gets in line to check in, and my stomach flips when we enter the elevator.

The inside of the elevator is all mirrors, even on the ceiling. It's weird seeing myself on all sides. The doors barely close before he backs me into the corner and kisses me hard, deep, and with furious passion. I can barely keep up, trying to steal breaths between kisses. He jerks my pants down under the near calf-length jersey before spinning me to face the wall. "Hold on."

"Ares... someone could stop the elevator." I meet his eyes in the mirror.

He's already got his hard dick in his hand, pumping it slowly, the tip glistening under the bright light. "Then I better fuck you fast, *sì*?"

I'm so turned on right now I don't know which way is up. I spread my legs as far apart as I can, curl my fingers around the rail, and push my bare butt back to him.

Sliding his fingers into my hair, he wraps the short, pink strands around his fist, holding my face in place. "Watch me, *tesoro*. No closing your eyes, no turning your head, eyes on me, *sì?*"

I nod, nibbling on my lip. I glance at the keypad—thirty-three floors in the building, and it's a Friday night. No way we aren't getting caught. My mind flashes back to the first time I saw Ares with the guy outside the restaurant, and how turned on I was in the car, but do I really want to risk getting caught having sex in public?

In the end, it doesn't matter. Ares slams his dick into my soaking wet pussy in one thrust, making me moan. His grip on my hair tightens as he bucks his hips against my ass, slowly at first, setting a rhythm. The harder he fucks me the harder he grabs my hair and the more the sting prickles across my scalp.

I'm going to come. My eyes drift closed, rolling back in my head, and my hair gets a sharp tug.

"Open, *tesoro*."

I open my eyes, meeting his intense stare in the mirrored pane of glass in front of me. The elevator dings as it passes another level, I resist the urge to look at the keypad. With every slam against me, Ares grunts, his balls smack off my body. He's riding me harder and harder with each thrust.

I'm so close. My orgasm is brewing deep inside when something touches my ass. He's moving his hand from my waist to between my cheeks, exerting a little pressure on my tight hole, and my eyes widen in the mirror.

I've never had anything there before, and I'm not sure I want to, either. He tilts his head, a silent question as he keeps pounding his dick deep inside me, the metal rails on his cock scraping my inner walls with each movement.

Sucking in a deep breath, I nod. I trust him. If I hate it, he'll stop in an instant. Something penetrates my ass. I don't think it's his thumb, maybe his pinky? It's a strange sensation, and I want to scream at him for trying something new here, now, when we could be interrupted by anyone. His finger slides in a little deeper, and I moan again, even more loudly.

He's fucking me in earnest now, but the finger in my ass goes slow, in and out, in and out, inching in a little more with each thrust. I have no idea how he has the coordination for multiple speeds at the same time when my soul is leaving my body in this elevator, but he's playing me like a perfectly tuned piano.

He comes on a roar, removes his finger from my ass and tucks himself back into his pants. I reach to get mine, but he stops me. My own climax was out of reach, but he'll finish me off later. He always does.

He sweeps the hand that was in my hair between my thighs, and I swear he's pushing the cum trickling out of me back inside with his thumb. He licks his thumb before bending to pull up my pants.

Snapping the elastic of my pants against my skin, he meets my eyes in the mirror. "I'm going to want those panties, *tesoro*."

The door dings and an elderly couple step onto the elevator. Ares wastes no time spinning me around, lifting me over his shoulder, and smacking my backside. If there was any doubt about what we'd been doing in the moments before the door opened, there isn't now.

Throwing them a salute, he grins. "Have a great evening, folks."

I can't see their faces because I'm dangling like a ragdoll staring at Ares's bubble butt, but the woman giggles. "Make sure you take good care of that girl, young man."

"You'll hear how much I take care of her from your room later tonight, ma'am."

"Oh my!" The woman's voice replies. "We should go back to our room, Bill." She giggles.

"You know we never last without a good meal in our stomachs, Delores. Let's eat first."

"Listen to the man, Delores. Enjoy your dinner!" Ares is already halfway down the hall, and I'm guessing Delores stuck her foot in the door so she could enjoy watching me being manhandled down the corridor.

As he carries me toward our room, he rubs my clit through my leggings. Though in truth, I can't tell if he's trying to get my panties even wetter for his own enjoyment later, or if he's determined to make me climax out here in the hall.

The wail that escapes me isn't quiet or at all ladylike, and I'm sure Delores and Mr. Delores can hear me from down the elevator shaft.

"You came all this way for me, *tesoro*." He swipes the key at the pad on the door and lets us inside. "Now it's my turn to show you how much I appreciate it." He drops me to my feet and drags my jersey over my head.

"I'm going to eat that pretty little pussy of yours all fucking night long, and then I'm going to eat it all over again in the morning."

My mouth hangs open as I stare at his dirty mouth. He rubs his hands together and stalks toward me like a predator claiming its prey. I step back, but I'm already tugging my shirt over my head.

When I unhook my bra and drop it on the floor, pacing backward toward the bed, Ares licks his lips, his eyes devouring me before he feasts on me.

The backs of my knees meet the side of the bed, and I flop back, starfishing on the mattress. He tugs my pants down my legs, stops at my ankles to yank my shoes off, and then I'm naked.

This man is hungry, and I am totally here for it. I tuck my feet close to my butt, bending my knees, and putting myself on display for him. The way he looks at me makes me feel powerful, desired, and as though he would burn down the world for me if I only asked. Once he's finished tongue-banging me, at least.

He drags his fingers through my slippery folds, making me purr. "So wet, *tesoro*. And so full of my creamy cum." When the pad of his thumb meets my clit, I squeal. It's not going to take long. Everything is swollen from the banging in the elevator. He brought me to the edge and pulled back at the last second so my body is eager, desperate, in sore need of release.

Chanting his name as he circles my clit, I raise my hips. He slides one of his fingers inside me, pressing so hard on my g-spot I see stars, and the pinky from his other hand finds its way back into my ass again. I arch my back.

"You liked my finger in your ass, *tesoro*?"

I'm mumbling, I'm not sure whether it's to myself or to him, but my nerves are on fire, and I need to come. It's a matter of seconds before I detonate on his hand. He doesn't let me orgasm down from my high though, he buries his face between my legs and doesn't stop for hours. Wave after wave of undulating pleasure crashes into me as I soak his face and the bed.

Every time I come, I think it has to be the last time, but he licks my clit with renewed energy and my body obeys every sweep and swish of his tongue and flex of his fingers against my walls.

By the time the morning comes, we've barely had any sleep, and my legs are wobbly. When I open the door to head down for breakfast, a bag sits on the floor.

I pick it up, take a peek, and turn back to Ares.

"What's that?"

I pull out the note sitting on top of the things inside the bag.

Dear Ares and Eloise,

It was a pleasure meeting you on the elevator, and it sure sounds like you both had a very enjoyable evening. For the record, so did I.

I saw this and thought it might come in useful.

Kind regards, Delores

P.S. If you see Bill at breakfast could you tell him how you did that thing with your pee pee that made her scream like she was having an exorcism? I'd owe you one.

I don't know if I'm traumatized or mortified, but I can't help but laugh. There's a heating pad, a cool pack, and some sore throat candy. She also threw in some chocolate bars, chips, some muscle rub, and a pregnancy test.

I can't control my laughter, but Ares's eyes spark with fire once again. "She sent snacks. We can go downstairs after I get another taste of that delicious pussy of yours."

He's insatiable, passionate, and the most beautiful man I've ever laid eyes on, and he's all mine.

CHAPTER 35

Eloise

"You ready?" Ares holds out his hand to help me down from his SUV. Scooping up the canvas tote bag on my lap with one arm, I accept his help with the other.

Dad is waiting for us at the gates to the cemetery. He nods at Ares in greeting, and Ares tightens his hand around mine.

"Mr. Downing." Ares has accepted the olive branch between them with both hands but errs on the side of formal politeness when they're in each other's presence. It's kind of cute. I'm more than confident that will change in the future, but all progress is good progress.

We make our way to Mom's grave together in silence. Listening to the rustle of the leaves and the wind whispering among the gravestones, my heart squeezes. I miss her so much the pain is as tangible as the breeze on my face every single second of every day.

When we reach her headstone, Dad unfolds the picnic blanket while Ares helps me unpack the bag in my hand.

"What's the cake?" Dad jerks at the cardboard box in Ares's hand.

"It's *tres leches* from Ares's family restaurant in town." My mouth is already watering. It's one of my favorite cakes in all the world. Abuelita de la Peña insisted on giving us the whole sheet cake when she heard where we were going to be this afternoon. Baked fresh this morning.

As excited as I am to have a slice now, I'm even more looking forward to the slice I'm going to have for breakfast tomorrow once the flavors have all had time to marinate.

By the time Ares slices up the cake, I'm drooling. Dad has poured plastic cups full of non-alcoholic apple cider, I've handed out napkins and party hats for the four of us.

When I get comfortable on the blanket, cross-legged, Ares pats my hand in quiet reassurance. The last time I was here was a difficult moment for me, but after that long conversation with Dad about our relationship, we've both made a concerted effort to improve things.

Dad lifts his cup, a tremble in his hand barely visible. "Another birthday beyond the grave, darling."

My throat clogs at the affection in his voice and the tears welling in his eyes. My heart hurts, for his loss and my own.

"It has been a busy one for our Ellie-Rae. She has quite the update for you this year."

I give him a watery smile. So far, we have had more birthdays together when Mom was alive than we have had since she's been gone. But each year since her death, we come here with cake and party hats, no matter how busy Dad gets, and tell her all about our year. It's a celebration of achievements, of life, of love, and this year, Dad suggested Ares come along with us, which just about burst my heart in my chest.

"I know you've met Ares, but I don't think he properly introduced himself to you the last time he was here." Dad's eyebrow raises, and Ares flushes pink.

He clears his throat. "Hi, Mrs. Downing, my name is Ares, and I'm in love with your daughter." His eyes never leave mine, even with Dad's hard stare piercing him side-on. "What else do I say?" He half-whispers at me.

Grinning at him, it's my turn to pat his hand. "Tell her what you've accomplished in the last year, or what you want to accomplish in the next one."

He takes a long drink of his apple cider before he rubs the back of his neck, his face still red. "I've been thinking that I'd like to start a charity, a foundation of some kind. For recovering addicts and alcoholic athletes. I think it's an underserved space, and considering my own experiences with addiction and playing hockey... well..." He clears his throat again. "I think I could really do some good there. Even if I'm only a college rookie."

Dad tips his cup to Ares. "That's a noble goal, Ares. And with your resources I think you could make a real difference in the industry."

Ares tries to hide his embarrassment behind another sip of his drink, but I see him. I always see him. My god of war with a heart of gold, my happily ever after, my strength, my love, and the man I'm going to change the world with. I can't wait.

Epilogue

ELOISE

(One month later)

My heart is racing so hard it might burst out of my chest and run away. I don't blame it—about fifty three percent of me wants to run away too. I don't know what I was thinking when I came here, and now the house lights are dimming, music's playing. And I know that any minute now, my boyfriend is going to come out onto that stage and take his clothes off.

I've watched *Magic Mike*. I know how this goes. They often pick volunteers from the audience, and if he sees me, I'm screwed. It's ladies night, and the place is full, packed to the rafters with excited women, hands full of ones, ready to throw them at the men set to come out and entertain us with their bodies.

When the music starts, my heart stops.

Five men take the stage, holding long, black umbrellas and wearing trench coats. Oh, sweet mother of all that's holy, they're going to *do* the *Magic Mike* dance. As if she can hear my thoughts, Tori squeals at the top of her lungs beside me, clapping her hands as they start to dance.

By the time Ares is wearing only a tie hanging down the middle of his chest and black pants, he's not only spotted me, but he's dancing *only* for me. I felt the shift in him the moment his eyes locked onto mine, and my breath left my body.

The man really is a god, standing with his pecs shining under the spotlights, women screaming at him, throwing money on the stage at his feet. But the only person in the room he's giving any of his attention to is me.

For his solo dance, he comes out in a plain, fitted white t-shirt, dark jeans, and his signature, backward ball cap. I don't know how he makes such plain clothes look so out-of-this-world sexy.

The girl on my other side elbows me. "You are such a lucky fucking woman." Her bright orange drink sloshes over the edge of her plastic cup. He's not hiding the fact that I'm his. In fact, he's making it obvious on purpose.

Nelly's *Hot in Here* starts and the crowd goes wild. I don't know why he's singing about it *getting* hot in here. It's been hot in here from the second I walked in the door. Which is really saying something since it's December in Iowa.

I try to avoid his gaze as he pulls a chair onto the middle of the stage. It's for him, right? Surely he wouldn't... Oh... no. No, no, no, nooooo, he's coming over.

Tori is screaming at the top of her lungs. She's a traitorous best friend, and I'm firing her from the position as soon as I get out of this situation. He reaches his hand out to me, and the asshat has the nerve to wink at me. Wink!

He pulls me onto the stage with ease, urging me to sit on the chair in the middle of the stage. I'm only mildly concerned about people staring at my face, about them thinking I'm punching above my weight. I know how bitchy women can be.

What does a Greek God like Ares de la Peña see in a mangled faced woman like her?

It would have bothered me more a few months ago. But every single day that we've been together, Ares makes me feel like a goddess. And it doesn't matter what anyone thinks about me—he loves me for who I am and that's all that matters.

The bass vibrates the floor under my feet as Ares eyes me like he's not surrounded by a few hundred women who all want him to do nasty things to them. He eyes me like I'm the only woman left in the world after some form of apocalyptic disaster. Like I'm the only woman who has what he needs.

How I manage to keep myself from publicly reaching climax, I have no idea. But when he back flips into my lap and grinds himself against my thighs, his perfect bubble butt bobbing up and down right in front of my face, all sense leaves my body.

And I spank him.

The screaming of the crowd can't distract me from the fact he's growing hard against my legs. Since he had the nerve to pull me up on stage during my first time seeing him dance, it's fair game. I spank him again.

He's still wearing his pants, but I'm sure if I pulled at them hard enough they'd come apart and his little undies would *definitely* display his excitement. It's tempting, but I don't want him to lose out on his tips for the night. Brian the pie guy needs them.

Spinning to face me, he disarms me with a bright smile. I know that smile. That smile says I'm not going to be able to walk tomorrow. And my pussy tingles. I'm already wet. He could take me right here, right now, and I'm not sure I'd care. I've never been more turned on.

My breathing is rapid, my nipples are struggling to stay within the confines of my bra, and I'm so freakin' wet.

He yanks off his pants, revealing Calvin Klein tighty whities, and somehow the volume of the room rises even further. He gyrates his hips, his erect penis, right... there... and I can't help but lick my lips.

Leaning forward, he rolls his body up against mine, placing his head so close to me that a shiver travels down my spine. "Come backstage, *tesoro*. I need you to take care of this before my next dance."

Ares

I still can't believe Eloise came to my show last night. I grin. I knew she'd come around eventually—she's been curious as hell. But when they brought the lights up and that familiar pink bob caught my attention, everything changed.

My dick gets hard thinking back to our fuck in the dressing room after the show. Quick, dirty, and right in the middle of the dressing room for any of the other performers to walk in and find us. My girl likes the occasional thrill.

Climbing into my car parked outside The Den, I fire up the engine. When my hand touches the gear stick, it meets unexpected fabric. Flicking on the interior light, I inspect the fine lace draped over the shifter.

I'm starting to think that someone blabbed to the girls that our games against *The Phantoms* are an excuse for the team to get together at the bar and shoot the shit. They're an imaginary team our predecessors came up with in a bid to hang out more with their brothers. It's the Raccoons worst kept not-a-secret.

Obviously, my pink pixie heard where I'd be and left me a gift.

I'm holding them, gliding them through my fingers when Scott opens the door. "Okay to give me a ride?"

I quickly sniff the panties, warmth spreading through my chest that she's worn them before leaving them in the car, and my cock hardening again at the idea that she's now waiting for me in my apartment with no panties on. I shove them in my pocket, also glad I picked up some new panties for her on the way to the bar. I feel bad taking them and not replacing them.

If I keep taking them and she runs out...will she go commando for the rest of our lives? I wouldn't be mad about that.

"Dude. You are obsessed."

I wag a finger at him. "It'll happen to you at some point. Watch how much shit you give me. I'll return it tenfold when it's your turn."

I don't know where the twins are, but Scott's like a third brother to all of us. He's cool, so it's not an imposition to take him back to the hockey house on my way to my girl.

When he doesn't answer, I sneak a look at him before pulling out of the parking lot. "Unless you've already got someone and you're not admitting to it."

He doesn't rise to the bait, but the faraway look in his eyes as he stares out the window makes me wonder.

If I'm honest, I always thought he and Athena would get together. They've known each other since we were all kids, but the older we all got, the less likely it seemed. Not that they don't get along, they do. But it seems that she's focused on her career, and while not a player, he doesn't seem to be the relationship guy.

If anyone can handle Athena, I think it could be him. I'm not sure the twins would be quite so down with the idea, but fuck them, it's not their lives. At least that's my opinion. Not that anyone ever listens to it.

It's on the tip of my tongue to suggest he ask her out when

he points at something up ahead. "The road's closed up ahead. You'll want to turn here."

He's right, flashing lights and a police blockade mean we have to take a diversion. It's a couple of days after Christmas. I shudder, catching a glimpse of a mangled vehicle as we take the detour. Poor fuckers. There's no good time of year to get into a wreck, but over the holidays... I dunno, there's something even shittier about that.

We both get lost in our own heads for the last few minutes of the drive. I drop him off, make my way home, and from the minute I open the door, my girl's shrieks and giggles echo from the bathroom.

I open the door to chaos. Bubbles are everywhere. Eloise is fully clothed and in the tub washing Bacon and telling him what a good boy he is, and Puck is nowhere to be seen. He hates water so I'm sure he's as far away from this nightmare as he can be.

Also, I'm jealous she's stroking my pig and telling him he's pretty.

"You know you're still wearing your clothes, right?"

She snickers. "I've had a night, Ares de la Peña. Don't start with me." She brandishes a giant yellow sponge, pointing it my direction. "Your stupid cat thought... I dunno what the heck he thought, but he decided to investigate what I was doing with Bacon. For the record"—she goes back to cleaning the pig—"I was filling the bath and getting him ready for a wash. Well, Puck climbed up on the bath as it was filling and leaned over a bit too far."

Oh no.

She points the sponge at me again. "Yeah. Exactly what you think happened, happened. He went crashing into the bath, water and bubbles flying everywhere, squealing like he was being murdered. And when I went to help him..."

"*¡Ay, dios mío!*"

She sticks her arm out. Under the bubbles are red welts all over her forearm. "I should have let the little scamp drown."

Bacon's head turns to her like he knows what she's saying, and she scratches behind his ear. "I wouldn't ever have let him drown, baby boy. By that point, the bathroom was soaking, Bacon was terrified and refused to get in the dang bath, so I had no choice."

I pop the plug from the bath, and lift Bacon out as the water drains. When he's dry, I shoo him away to find Puck to check on him and offer my hand to my girl. Even sopping wet with suds in her hair and cat scratches over her arms, neck and cheek, she's a vision. How the fuck did I get so lucky?

"How was the game?" She arches her brows, and I'm busted, but I play along. If I don't admit to it out loud, then it won't have been me who let the cat out of the bag about playing the *Phantoms*.

"Oh, you know." I plant a kiss on her sudsy forehead. "The boys played hard."

She nods slowly. "I bet they did."

I tug her panties from my pocket, dangling them in front of her. "Does this mean you aren't wearing any? Or are these yesterdays?"

Shrugging, she sighs, dramatically. "Are you getting complacent with me, hockey god? You used to check these things for yourself and now... now you come right out and ask." She folds her arms, a wicked gleam in her eye. "You wanna know if I'm wearing panties"—another shrug—"find out for yourself."

After I've stripped her down and taken her hard and fast over the bathroom sink, we leave the wet bathroom to be cleaned up later. I carry her into the bedroom with legs wrapped around my waist.

"Brought you back some new panties today."

"You did?"

I nod at her, brushing my nose against hers before lying her on her back on the bed. "They have the days of the week on them."

She purses her lips. "Smart. Then I'll know when you steal one and which ones you steal."

Mierda. I hadn't thought about that.

"Actually, I bought you new boxers today too. They're right there."

I lean up on my elbows and on the bedside table is a pair of boxers printed like a poke-ball, the red and white ball thing that captures Pokémon.

"Try them on," she urges with a giggle.

Reluctantly, I give her what she wants and stand up. She's shaking with quiet laughter as I slide the underwear up my legs and as soon as they're on she points at my cock. "Dickachu, I choose you!" She snorts before bursting into hysterical laughter. "I've been waiting all day to say that."

Her laughter, her energy, her whole vibe is contagious. Mamá already gave me the ring. I told Dad and Abuelita that I'm going to marry her, and as soon as I'm sure I've gained her father's trust that I'm not going to ruin her, I'm making this woman my wife.

She scrunches up her face as I drop back over her on the bed.

"What is it?" I ask.

"Something's been on my mind for a while now."

"Okay, spill."

She worries her lip between her teeth, and it's nothing small. *Por dios.* This woman better not break my fucking heart when I have a shiny ring in a box under my bed ready to make her mine forever.

"You're bi."

"This isn't news." It's also not where I expected the conversation to go.

"I..." She searches my face. Over the past few weeks her anxiety, her hesitation, her walls have all started to come down, and she's gotten better about opening up to me. Her confidence has bloomed, and it has been beautiful to watch. But there are some things she's not quite there on.

"Come on, *tesoro*. You can tell me."

"I'm scared I won't be enough. For you." She casts her eyes away from me, but I cup her cheek and turn her back in my direction. "In the future."

"Never going to happen."

"But you like guys too. What if... what if you have needs I can't fulfill? I don't think I want to share you, Ares. Maybe someday, but maybe not."

I stop her frantic thought process with a deep and slow kiss. "*Tesoro*, I love you. I'm with *you*. If there ever comes a time when I need more from you sexually, I'll sit you down and talk to you about it."

She nods, but she doesn't seem convinced. I need to give her more. She's a rational thinker, so if I approach this from my feelings, I don't think I'll get through. That leaves logic-ing her out of her anxiety.

"Would you be willing to finger my ass?"

Her eyes flex wide before she tilts her head. I can almost see the cogs turning. She nods.

"Would you be willing to try a strap on? Fuck me in the ass with it sometimes?"

Her cheeks turn pink, but she runs through her thought process again before another nod.

"Then please, amor, tell me what I could possibly need from you that you aren't prepared to try, at least once?"

Kissing her again, I skim my hand along her arm, down the side of her thigh, and hook my fingers behind her knee, bringing it up so her leg locks around me. Not once have I ever thought she wouldn't be enough for me, and I hope to fuck I never gave her that impression either. She's my world.

Sure, I like both men and women, I like having things in my ass, toys and cocks alike, but since she came along, I'm happy, happier than I've ever been, or could have ever hoped to be. "You're enough, Eloise. You're all I need." I pull back a little. "Though if you ever want me to eat you out while someone fucks me in the ass..." I shrug. "I wouldn't be mad about it."

Something flickers in her eyes. I kiss her neck. "Or if you want me to fuck you while someone else fucks me... that could be arranged."

Her breathing quickens. She's into dirty talk, and she's not ready to talk about sharing me with someone else, maybe she never will, but the fantasy is enough to make my rock-hard cock press against these ridiculous boxers.

I kiss her again, getting lost in the scent of strawberries. Every piece of me wants to propose right here, right now, but she'd smack me, call me irrational, and say not yet. I need to wait until graduation, when she's a full-fledged nurse and ready. I might ask her every now and then in the meantime, though, just to make sure she's aware of my intent.

Our front door crashes open. I jump, and Eloise covers her chest.

"Ares?" Artemis screams at the other side of my apartment.

Something's wrong. Very wrong.

"Get dressed, *tesoro*." I grab a pair of pants from the drawer, hopping into them as I move into the living space.

"Ares?" Artemis cries again.

My insides are like goo, but from the anguish in his voice, I'm going to need to be strong right now, for him if nothing else.

"What's wrong, Art?"

He has my go bag in one hand. He's crying, pale, and his whole body shakes like he's freezing. "Y-you need to come."

I nod, already sliding my shoes on. I'll grab socks from the bag en route to wherever we're going. "I need to grab a shirt and jacket, then I'll come. What happened?"

A couple of shirts hang over the back of my dining room chair. Too dirty to go back in the drawer, but not dirty enough to wash yet. I slide one of those over my head. Artemis isn't looking at me, his eyes are focused somewhere past me.

"Artemis." My voice is sharp, commanding, and enough to snap him out of whatever he's caught up in inside his head. At least for a second.

"It's Apollo."

My breathing quickens as I struggle to keep my inhales slow. I can't succumb to panic. Whatever has happened to Apollo means one of us needs to stay calm.

I've never, in my entire life, seen Artemis lose his shit like this. That alone is enough to make cold dread curl its tendrils around my body, but that also means he needs me.

I grab a hoody from behind the door. Eloise appears and rushes to Artemis. She sees the same thing I do. Panic. Her reaction is instinctive, and I hope that for both their sakes Artemis doesn't push her away.

He curls his arms around her and sobs. "He's been in an accident. We need to go to the hospital."

Outside the building, a town car waits. Smart. No use risking another one of us ending up in hospital. The driver closes the doors behind us. Eloise clings to Artemis in the back seat. At this point I think she might be the only thing holding him together.

His whole body trembles. He leans forward, head in his hands, his hair falling forward.

"Was he alone in the car?"

"I don't know."

"Is he critical?"

"I don't know."

"Are our parents at the hospital?"

"I don't fucking know anything. Can you back the fuck off, please, Ares? Just... not right now."

He flexes his fists and starts mumbling under his breath. I'm pretty sure he's praying in Spanish. It's been a while since I've spoken to the big guy upstairs, but I join him.

It takes a lifetime to get to St. Luke's though the clock only registers thirteen minutes. When I get out of the car, take Eloise's hand, and head for the double doors, I hope with everything I got that my brother will be alive inside this building.

Pre-order book 3: Crashing the Net, now!

If you're not ready to say goodbye to Ares and Eloise, you can sign up to my newsletter and pick up their Bonus Epilogue here.

Also by Lasairiona McMaster

Two for Interference - Minnesota Snow Pirates book 1

Minnesota Snow Pirates books 1-3 Boxset

Freezing the Puck - Cedar Rapids Raccoons book 1

Two for Tacos - A Snow Pirates Novella

www.Lasairiona.com

Author Note

What's with the Greek Gods in this series, Lasairiona?

Good question, dear readers. I saw a movie during lock-down #127 in 2021 where there were a trio of brothers called Apollo, Artemis, and Ares. It wasn't in English, but it was a love story. It's called *Through My Window* and it's about a girl called Raquel who has a longtime crush on her neighbor, Ares, who she has never spoken to. This movie triggered the inspo for this whole new series and within a couple days I had titles, characters, tropes, the lot. Just like my Snow Pirates series, it was like a lightning bolt, so I knew I couldn't ignore it.

I struggle naming characters—in case you haven't noticed with my early work (that I've recently pulled down to make better) where I have a Jeremy and Johnny in the same book. And then I added a Justin.

I have a whiteboard in my bedroom/office where I jot down names that I like as I encounter them, and Ares, Apollo, and Artemis called to me. I felt like they needed some adult supervision though, and there was nothing else to be done but give them a badass big sister, and I couldn't call her something like Carol, so Athena was born.

I have so much planned for this family, you guys. I really do. I can't wait for you to get into the lives and hearts of the de la Peñas and love them even a fraction as much as I do.

Ares being the youngest and the most outrageous, he demanded to go first. And sweet baby J in the manger, this book was a freakin' ride, y'all. For those of you who don't know my process, I used to be a pantster (writing by the seat of one's pants) but as the books stacked up, I realized that discovery writing, as it's also known, isn't necessarily how I work. So, I turned to plotting.

I outline each series at a high level before I start. I break it down into books, character pairings, tropes, even things like their ages and what they study in college are all details that I know before I sit down to write.

Ares and Eloise were *supposed* to be a fake relationship trope. I had a fully fleshed out outline ready to rock, and after writing about ten thousand words they went, nope, fuck this.

I know, you guys will all think that I'm the author, I should have full control of my characters, right? If only. In a perfect world, that's how it would be. But the reality is that we are just a vessel, telling other people's stories, and if it's not right, they won't let it go.

My characters never let me cram them into a box they don't belong in. And you know what? For a few scenes, I tried. I wanted them to follow my plan, I didn't want to write into the dark, I was scared, intimidated, and I felt like I knew better.

After reading some posts online from an author coach, I decided that I needed to trust my intuition, I needed to let the characters loose to tell their story the way they say it needs to be told, and I'd go from there.

I set the outline aside, and let the words come.

I write damn near every day. Every morning I sprint from 6-7.30am with the best sprint partner in the world, Tracie

Delaney. And my daily word count ranges from 2k-3k words. It's generally 3k a day, that's my goal.

Ares and Eloise had me churning out 5-7k word days. Now, I'm not saying I can't have a 5k word day, but usually when I do, I need a day or two to recover because I'm exhausted, and the word count will drop the following day.

Not with this book. These characters possessed me, I was their minion. They dragged me through the pages. Two days ago I wrote 6300 words, and yesterday, Saturday (a day I was supposed to not work at all) I hit 7,000. I was up again at the ass crack of dawn this morning writing again.

I think part of it was that I started plotting Apollo's book, and Ares got pissed at me for entertaining his brother before he was done with me. His punishment was relentless writing. I've never been so absorbed.

It's also longer than I had anticipated it being. I had 80k on my wall of sticky notes, and it's going to be closer to 100k when all's said and done (bonus epilogue and all my bloviating in the back matter.)

I dunno, y'all. I really don't. For the most part, this book poured straight from my soul. It flowed like it was the most natural thing I've ever written. Every now and then the god of war dug his heels in and gave me shit.

It's been quite the experience, quite the learning curve, and the finished product is a book that might end up being my favorite book I've ever written (Don't tell the others, at least until I'm finished writing these freakin' gods!)

I have a minor-league hockey playing friend who is a recovering drug addict, and I know of some NHL players who have been in a similar position over the years. One such player that long-time hockey fans will recognize is Theo Fleury. He played for my home team, the Belfast Giants, for a season and took Belfast by storm.

Fleury was convinced by a friend to move to the United

Kingdom to play with the Belfast Giants of the Elite Ice Hockey League (EIHL) for the 2005–06 season. He scored three goals and added four assists and a fight in his first game, against the Edinburgh Capitals. He scored 22 goals and 52 assists in 34 games, as Belfast won the regular season league title. Described as the "most talented" player ever to play in the United Kingdom, Fleury was named the EIHL's Player of the Year and voted a first team All-Star by the British Ice Hockey Writers Association. Fleury argued with visiting fans, as well as officials, which led him not to return to Belfast in 2006–07. (Wikipedia)

The fans of some away teams were not at all kind to Fleury while he skated on their ice. They threw some horrible, unforgivable shade at him for being a drug user. Not just the fans, but the announcer at one rink in particular, too. In truth, I can't really blame him for losing his shit at people. I would have as well.

And while I don't necessarily agree with everything he wrote in his book about his time with the Belfast Giants, watching him skate on the ice and meeting him has always been one of my fondest memories of hockey night in Belfast.

My friend, Shaun, suggested I read Theo's book to get a little more insight into playing hockey with an addiction. Why am I mentioning this? Because I know lots of readers have a tendency to say 'that'd never happen,' or 'it doesn't work like that' and this is me letting y'all know that I know of at least one person where it *did* work like that. And sharing snippets and glimpses of his story, his journey, as well as reading Theo Fleury's journey (among others) is my way of broaching the discussion of addiction, recovery, and male mental health in hockey—which those of you who have been with me from the start know is my jam.

Acknowledgments

Lewis - As with every book, my number one acknowledgement is to my little boy, Lewis. He's eight right now, and he's the most supportive person in the entire universe.

Just yesterday he turned to me in the car, completely unprompted and without context, and said, "Mama, if Grandad was still alive he'd be so proud of you."

I forced past the lump in my throat to say thank you, and we talked about how my dad loved to talk about money. In my family, we didn't have any, so in our house the measure of success was often how much money someone was making.

I told Lewis that we know that to be untrue because he thinks I'm hugely successful (and by many of my measurements, I feel like I am too), but I'm not yet making a lot of money. I told him that I hope for that to change this year and he said, "It absolutely will change this year mama. You're going to reach your goals."

When I tell you that his words punched straight through my misbelief, my impostor syndrome, and right into the center of my being, I'm not exaggerating. I told him that I want him to hold on to that faith, that belief, that unwavering confidence in my abilities, and apply it to himself too. That believing in yourself is one of the hardest, and most important things to do during life. To that, he said. "I'll help you believe in yourself, mama."

You guys, this kid. This. Kid.

I wanted to write that story here, today, so when he's older and he's struggling to dig real deep and find his self-belief, I'll remind him of this moment, and tell him that I've always, and will always believe in him as much as he believes in me.

Tracie – For those of you who remember earlier today, or yesterday, or last week when you started Ares and Eloise's story, this book is dedicated to her. I slid into her DMs a couple of years ago when she submitted a story about a pink vibrator at the airport to an anthology I was putting together, and the rest is history.

I talk to her every single day. I'm not exaggerating. If, for some reason, we aren't at the computer sprinting at 6am, we'll at least have sent each other a message to check in. When she went away for three weeks last year, I felt like I'd lost my arm— my left one, not the useless right one that doesn't do much of anything for me.

She's everything from my sprint partner, to my career coach, to the voice-of-reason big sister when I'm having a meltdown. I don't know what I'd do without her, and I hope to never find out.

Irene – For helping me not offend the entire Dominican Republic and Spanish speaking parts of the world. I don't know what I'd do without you pushing me forward on the days I struggle hardest, but I'm sure as shit glad I adopted you as my bestie in Madrid.

Fancy – Thank you for not letting me set this one on fire. Edits hurt. And I don't mean the 2k filler words I cut from the manuscript. The actual edits, the layering, the depth, adding context, all the things that for about a week I thought I couldn't do. You were right, this story needed to be told, even if it hurt.

Lassalle – Without you coaching me through my not-a-tantrum, I'm not sure I'd have let Ares see the light of day. I would have kept him in the basement and electrocuted him from time to time. Thank you. Your logic and rational thinking might have frustrated me, but you helped me see that this book couldn't be erased and that I needed to follow through. I love you.

Theo Fleury – Thanks to you and Jenn for coming to Belfast to play and bringing a very important discussion into so many lives. And for entertaining the crowd. Belfast might have been 'bush' but you held your own and many of us enjoyed it immensely. Thanks also for sharing your story in your book. It was a hard read in places, but I appreciated the honesty and felt a kinship in my desire to write openly about abuse and mental health.

Jake Stack – my favorite goalie! He never bats an eyelid when I message him with hockey questions, goalie questions, or when I want to share some of his lyrics in my books.

Brian Marshall – my favorite radio DJ from Rock 108 in Eastern Iowa. Y'all, I met this dude at a tailgate at an Iowa Hawkeyes football game – my FIRST football game – and we became fast friends. When he told me he wanted to interview me on his radio show I thought he was full of shit. He's a great guy, with a great show, and he's been one of my biggest cheerleader's in the greater CR area in Iowa. I didn't put a puck demon in this one, Brian, maybe next time.

My Alpha readers—Amy R, Katie 'Violence' Wilks, Savannah. **My Beta**—Erika and my proofreader Corinne. Every book has new challenges, and y'all help me through them with minimal impatience, exasperation, and maximum enthusiasm. I appreciate you.

My editor - The biggest thanks, as always, goes to my editor Jessica Snyder. It's during the pre-editing stages when I'm writing this, so God only knows what she's going to think of this one. But that's a future Lasairiona's problem. And a future Jessica's problem too. I'm cackling as I write this because she has NO IDEA.

My cover designer - Kate Farlow over at Y'all That Graphic for bringing my boys to life on the covers.

And finally, to my ARC readers, my Facebook reader group *Margaritas, Men, and Mischief with Lasairiona*, and to each and every one of you who pick up this book: a bazillion thank yous. I truly hope you loved it enough to pick up the next one. Tell your friends! And if you're not in my group —come join us, we don't bite (unless you ask us to!)

About the Author

Lasairiona McMaster writes sassy, classy and badassy women and strong, yet vulnerable men. She challenges reader's expectations by openly dealing with mental health issues, often exploring tough-to-handle topics and 'taboos' and books with a whole lotta heart.

She can either be found enjoying a gin and lemonade by the Irish sea, or baking sweet treats in her kitchen while singing at the top of her lungs. When she's 'home' in Texas, and isn't eating fresh-popped popcorn while buying things she has absolutely no need for in Target, she can be found at Chuys eating her body weight in chips and queso and washing it down with a margarita swirl. She loves to make friends out of strangers.

 facebook.com/QueenofFireLas
instagram.com/queenoffirelas

Made in the USA
Middletown, DE
10 October 2024